THE RETURN OF LANNY BUDD II.

TIMELINE

Each book is published in two parts: I and II.

THE RETURN OF LANNY BUDD II.

Upton Sinclair

Simon Publications

2001

LCCN: 53005202

ISBN: 1-931313-30-X

Distributed by Ingram Book Com pany

Printed by Light ning Source Inc., LaVergne, TN

Pub lished by Si mon Pub li ca tions, P.O. Box 321 Safety Har bor, FL

An Author's Program

From a 1943 article by Upton Sinclair.

When I say "historian," I have a meaning of my own. I portray world events in story form, because that form is the one I have been trained in. I have supported myself by writing fiction since the age of sixteen, which means for forty-nine years.

… Now I realize that this one was the one job for which I had been born: to put the period of world wars and revolutions into a great long novel. …

I can not say when it will end, because I don't know exactly what the characters will do. They lead a semi-independent life, being more real to me than any of the people I know, with the single exception of my wife. … Some of my characters are people who lived, and whom I had opportunity to know and watch. Others are imaginary—or rather, they are complexes of many people whom I have known and watched. Lanny Budd and his mother and father and their various relatives and friends have come in the course of the past four years to be my daily and nightly companions. I have come to know them so intimately that I need only to ask them what they would do in a given set of circumstances and they start to enact their roles. … I chose what seems to me the most revealing of them and of their world.

How long will this go on? I can not tell. It depends in great part upon two public figures, Hitler and Mussolini. What are they going to do to mankind and what is mankind will do to them? It seems to me hardly likely that either will die a peaceful death. I am hoping to outlive them; and whatever happens Lanny Budd will be somewhere in the neighborhood, he will be "in at the death," according to the fox-hunting phrase.

These two foxes are my quarry, and I hope to hang their brushes over my mantel.

Author's Notes

In the course of this novel a number of well-known persons make their appearance, some of them living, some dead; they appear under their own names, and what is said about them is factually correct.

There are other characters which are fictitious, and in these cases the author has gone out of his way to avoid seeming to point at real persons. He has given them unlikely names, and hopes that no person bearing such names exist. But it is impossible to make sure; therefore the writer states that, if any such coincidence occurs, it is accidental. This is not the customary "hedge clause" which the author of a *roman à clef* publishes for legal protection; it means what it says and it is intended to be so taken.

Various European concerns engaged in the manufacture of munitions have been named in the story, and what has been said about them is also according to the records. There is one American firm, and that, with all its affairs, is imaginary. The writer has done his best to avoid seeming to indicate any actual American firm or family.

...Of course there will be slips, as I know from experience; but *World's End* is meant to be a history as well as fiction, and I am sure there are no mistakes of importance. I have my own point of view, but I have tried to play fair in this book. There is a varied cast of characters and they say as they think. ...

The Peace Conference of Paris [*for example*], which is the scene of the last third of *World's End*, is of course one of the greatest events of all time. A friend on mine asked an authority on modern fiction a question: "Has anybody ever used the Peace Conference in a novel?" And the reply was: "Could anybody?" Well, I thought somebody could, and now I think somebody has. The reader will ask, and I state explicitly that so far as concerns historic characters and events my picture is correct in all details. This part of the manuscript, 374 pages, was read and checked by eight or ten gentlemen who were on the American staff at the Conference. Several of these hold important positions in the world of troubled international affairs; others are college presidents and professors, and I promised them all that their letters will be confidential. Suffice it to say that the errors they pointed out were corrected, and where they disagreed, both sides have a word in the book.

Contents:

BOOK TEN: THY FRIENDS ARE EXULTATIONS

BOOK SIX

They That Sow in Tears

16

Best Draw My Sword

I

LANNY and Laurel had a special and particular reason for listening to the radio and for looking at headlines whenever they walked past a newsstand. But they couldn't do these things all the time—especially not when they had waited for many weeks and might have to wait for more. They had to go to the office and read their mail and dictate answers; when they were at home they had to put their minds on editing a manuscript or reading a book.

And so it came about that somebody else got the news ahead of them. Lanny was in his little office, busy dictating letters to his secretary, when there came a tap on the door. It was a girl, one of those who opened the mail; she was half breathless with excitement. "Oh, Mr. Budd—excuse me for interrupting—something terrible has happened."

"What is it?" Lanny asked. He could pretty nearly guess and had prepared himself for a first-class job of play acting.

"Oh, Mr. Budd, my sister lives in New York and works on the *Daily Mirror*, and she just telephoned me they have a headline coming out—"

"Yes, yes," said Lanny. "What?"

"A big headline on the front page that says, 'Hansi Robin Jugged.'"

"Good heavens!" exclaimed Lanny. "What does that mean?"

"It means arrested, sir. And—and—"

"And what?"

"And Mrs. Robin!" Presumably the girl had been trying to say "and your sister," but she hadn't been able to get out the awful words.

Lanny did his first-class job. "But what for?" he asked.

"It says they are Communist spies!"

So Lanny did no more dictating that morning. He jumped up and went into the radio room and turned on the receiving set. He knew by heart where to look for news at any particular period. The girl had followed him, and his secretary and others in the office came streaming in. He might have closed the door and kept the radio low, but that would have been cruel. They were all bound to know it before long, and they might as well get it here as anywhere. He turned it up, and the whole office came to listen. They heard:

". . . arrests continuing. The FBI refused any further comment on the matter. They would not state the location of the photographic studio, but rumor has it located on Delancey Street. A pickup truck was loaded with photographic material and papers at the place. Several of the alleged conspirators were arrested there and others at their homes. It is said that one of the Russians involved enjoys diplomatic immunity, but this is uncertain, and the FBI refused to discuss the question. They have been watching the spy ring for months and have obtained a great deal of evidence, both at the spy center and at the homes of those spies who are employed in the factory.

"It is not known whether or not the home of Mr. and Mrs. Robin has been searched. Both he and his wife have been active in the Communist party and have made no secret of their beliefs. The arrest will cause a sensation in the musical world, as Hansi Robin is considered one of the greatest living violinists, and his wife has been his accompanist for most of their married years. They have made extensive tours in Europe. They lived for nearly two years in Russia and have expressed their satisfaction with what they found there.

"Bessie Budd Robin comes from one of the oldest and wealthiest families in Connecticut. Her father is Robert Budd, president of Budd-Erling Aircraft in Newcastle, Connecticut, and her mother is Mrs. Esther Remsen Budd, daughter of the president of the First National Bank of Newcastle. Hansi Robin's father is Johannes Robin, who was reputed one of the wealthiest capitalists of Germany and was jailed by the Nazis and lost his fortune there. He is now head of the sales department of Budd-Erling Aircraft in New York.

"More news in just a moment, but first here is an important word from our sponsor. If you use Babyskin Soap you can be sure of having a complexion as beautiful and fair as any baby's. Babyskin Soap is made from the purest olive oil from Italy and coconut oil from the glamorous isles of the South Seas. We guarantee if you will use Babyskin Soap for just one week you will discover"—and so on for sixty seconds, and after that the scores of a golf tournament in Florida, and then intercollegiate basketball matches that might or might not have been "fixed."

II

It was permissible for Lanny to be disturbed by that news and to jump into his car to drive to the house to tell his wife. That left the members of the staff in their different rooms to chatter excitedly. There wouldn't be much work done for an hour or two; that too was excusable.

At home Lanny discovered that Laurel had just been told the news by a neighbor and friend of the program who had called up. Alone by themselves, husband and wife didn't have to do any play-acting. They could shut their door and discuss quietly the course of events. Lanny said, "Evidently the FBI means for Hansi to go on. If they hadn't arrested him it would have been a giveaway."

"How long do you suppose they will hold him?" Laurel asked.

"I don't know what the federal procedure is. No doubt they will be admitted to bail."

"Poor Hansi! It will give him a dreadful black eye."

"Yes, but on the other hand it may take him into the very heart of the Communist underground. That, I am guessing, is what the government is figuring on."

The telephone began ringing. It would ring all day. One friend after another called up to commiserate, and some, of course, out of curiosity, in order to be able to tell *their* friends how the couple were taking the dreadful news.

Presently there was a call from New York, a woman's voice. "Mr. Budd? This is Mercy Colfax. I don't know if you will remember me; you had tea in my studio in Greenwich Village many, many years ago."

"Oh yes," Lanny said politely. "I remember you very well, Miss Colfax."

"I am the secretary of the Liberal Defense League. I would like very much to see you, Mr. Budd—as soon as possible."

"Could you come out to Edgemere?"

"With pleasure, Mr. Budd."

"Very well then. Come to my house, please. I expect to be at home the rest of the day."

"I will come by the first train."

Lanny hung up. "Mercy Colfax," he said to Laurel, who was in the room. "She is Bryn Mawr and Boston Back Bay. I met her several times in the old days when I was knocking about in Greenwich Village.

She's been in all the radical groups. Someone said she was Communist, but I didn't worry about that in those days. We were all practicing what we called the 'united front.' We found the Communists useful because they were hard workers; we called them 'good radicals.' "

"What do you suppose she wants?"

"She announced herself as secretary of the Liberal Defense League; that will be a Commie front, no doubt. They have taken up all the good words and poisoned them. You can't say 'liberal,' you can't say 'democratic,' you can't say 'people's,' you can't say 'worker's' any more. She is coming to ask me to put up bail for Bess and to help pay her lawyers."

"What will you say to her?"

"I'll say plenty. It will be a show you won't want to miss, but I want her to think we're alone, so you can listen at a crack in the door. She might become confidential, or she might get angry and say more than she means."

"Mercy?" said Laurel. "What an unusual name for a Red."

"She's old Puritan, of course," he answered. "Probably some of her forefathers came on the Mayflower. In her bones she is still proud of them, you can wager."

III

It took Miss Mercy Colfax a couple of hours to make connections and reach Lanny's home; she arrived in a taxi and may have come all the way in it. He remembered her as a sturdily built, round-faced woman with flaxen hair cut short, in the fashion of the flappers. Now her hair was longer and snow white, but her face was still unlined, and she held herself with dignity. Seated in the living room of the Budd home she stopped for no preliminaries. "I suppose, Mr. Budd, you have heard the terrible news."

"I have heard it three times over the radio and about a dozen times over the telephone, Miss Colfax. It is a blow to me, and a worse blow to the family. We all knew that Hansi and Bess were Communists, but we had no idea they were engaged in underground activities."

"I am shocked to hear you say such a thing, Mr. Budd. Surely you will not prejudge this case! I assure you most earnestly that Hansi and Bess are perfectly innocent, the victims of a wretched conspiracy inspired by the redbaiters."

"I hope you are correct, Miss Colfax," said Lanny mildly. "Before we go any further, let me ask you one question. Are you a Communist?"

The lady's tone became precise and puritanical. "I am, as I told you, Mr. Budd, the secretary of the Liberal Defense League, and I have come to see you in that capacity."

"Yes, but I do not know about the League, Miss Colfax, and I can only judge it by its secretary. Are you a Communist?"

"What my personal beliefs are surely have nothing to do with the question, Mr. Budd."

"From my point of view they have everything to do with it, so I hope you will answer my question."

"Please let me tell you what I have come for—"

"You understand of course that if you refuse to answer the question I have to assume that you are a Communist."

"I cannot help what conclusions you draw, Mr. Budd. I beg you to hear what I have to say."

"Certainly I will hear you, Miss Colfax, but I wish you to know in advance that I know I'm listening to a Communist."

"I assure you, Mr. Budd, that this series of arrests is an act of provocation on the part of the reactionary forces in our government. It is an effort to intimidate those few intellectuals who have had the courage to speak on behalf of peace and against the frenzy of red-baiting that has seized our public."

Lanny's tone was no less precise. "You have refused to admit that you are a Communist, Miss Colfax. I will tell you that I have known many Communists, and I know all their phrases, and when a Communist talks about peace and freedom I am not fooled for a single instant. I am not going to argue with you; I am just telling you that your generalized words are meaningless to me."

"It can't be meaningless to you, Mr. Budd, that your sister and your brother-in-law have been thrown into jail—Hansi Robin, one of the great musical artists of our time!"

"Yes, Miss Colfax; but I did my suffering a long time ago, when I saw that they were becoming Communists. I warned them what would happen, and now I have a clear conscience in the matter."

"And you mean that you would let your own sister rot in jail?"

"I mean that I know perfectly well my own sister will not be in jail more than a few hours. I know that my own sister belongs to an organization which has immense resources, collected in part from our enemies abroad and in part from wealthy dupes at home. Let them put up the bail and pay the Red lawyers. I certainly will not."

"I have never been more shocked, Mr. Budd—"

"I'm truly sorry to shock you, Miss Colfax, and I am not speaking sarcastically. From your first name alone I would know who your forefathers were and what your heritage is. Bess has the same heritage, and so have I. I say to you what I said to her years ago: I know that you joined the Communist party from the noblest of motives, a real sense of mercy, of pity for the poor and oppressed. It is terrible indeed to see such idealism betrayed. I beg you to open your eyes to the facts and realize that your cause has been taken over by gangsters. It has become a counterfeit revolution. It has broken all its promises and forsaken all its dreams and blasted all the hopes of its followers. It has become history's horror. You and I who were good radicals back in the old Greenwich Village days have no place in the program of such men. They use us so long as we still have power and can be of use to them; but the moment they have the power and need us no longer, we become a mockery to them. We become nuisances and pests, and they throw us into jail, they subject us to hideous tortures, they send us to slave-labor camps where we exist on eight hundred calories a day and fade away in two or three years of the diseases of malnutrition; or more mercifully they take us into a dark cellar and shoot us in the back of the neck and then carry us out and dump us into a crematory."

This granddaughter of the Puritans was sitting rigidly, her fists tightly clenched and the blood mounting into her well-rounded cheeks. "I see, Mr. Budd, that you have fallen a hopeless victim to the red-baiters!"

"Redbaiting, Miss Colfax? Redbaiting is the crime of telling the historical facts about the Communist party, that it has taken up lock, stock, and barrel the program of Tsarist imperialism. It has taken the tactics also and has multiplied them in horror. Don't you know how Engels promised that the state would wither away and how Lenin endorsed this? How much withering have you seen? Don't you know that all the old Bolsheviks, the old idealists who were Lenin's comrades and friends, have every one of them been foully murdered?

"I have been in the Soviet Union, Miss Colfax; and before that I knew some of those men in Europe. My own uncle Jesse Blackless was one of them; he was a painter and a fairly good one, and he gave his whole life to the cause. When I was at the Yalta Conference I met him secretly and found him a wretched, disillusioned, heartbroken old man. I knew Lincoln Steffens, who died in the same state of mind. Don't you know the list of old Bolsheviks whom Stalin and his minions of the Gaypayoo have had shot or poisoned? I will call the roll to you"—and Lanny began, like a drill sergeant calling off the names of his squad: "Zinoviev, Rykov, Rakovsky, Kamenev, Bukharin, Krylenko, Smirnov, Tukashevsky, Piatakov, Karakhan—"

The list was too long for the woman's patience. "That will do, Mr. Budd," she said. "I was told that you were a liberal man, but I see I have wasted my time."

"I hope that *I* have not wasted *my* time, Miss Colfax," he said very gently. "I have planted a seed; and sometimes a seed may lie dormant for years before it begins to sprout and take root. I have told you the truth, and it will lie in your mind, and someday you may begin to relate your observations to it, and your mind will change. If ever the time comes that you really believe in democracy and understand freedom as your forefathers and mine understood it, you may come to me with a cause that is honest, and I will not refuse help."

That was the last affront to her New England conscience. She got up and stalked out without another word, and Laurel, who had been standing behind the door, came forward, wreathed in smiles. "I am relieved," she said. "I was afraid she might consider it her duty to shoot you."

Lanny replied, "The combination of perfect Boston and Bolshevik is horribly strange. I am sure that in her heart she looks down upon the 'kumrads' from a great height."

IV

Lanny called up his father to see how he was taking it, and more especially how Esther was taking it. Robbie said, "I was worried because I couldn't prepare her, but I found that she had prepared herself."

Lanny wasn't surprised, for he knew that Esther Remsen Budd, another daughter of the Puritans, had intelligence enough to look at the world about her and observe where it was going. "She had it out with Bess a long time ago," said her husband, "and she guessed what Bess was up to. What she insists now is that I must go to the jail and put it up to Bess once and for all. If she will promise to quit the Communists for good we will put up the bail and get the right man to defend her."

"Of course she won't do that," Lanny said.

"I know," replied the father. "But we must give her the chance, and then our consciences will be clear. Esther says if I don't go she will. I just talked with Johannes about it, and he says he will do the same thing for Hansi. It won't do any good, of course, but we will go together."

"How is Mama Robin taking it?"

"He's terribly worried about her. The poor old creature—he says she hasn't stopped crying for a moment since she heard the news. He's afraid it will kill her. You had better call her up and say something kind."

Lanny made a sudden resolution. "I'll do more than that," he said. "I'll go see her and let her weep on my shoulder."

That would be no new thing, for Lanny Budd had met Leah Robin in Berlin when she was in the utmost despair and terror. Her husband was in the hands of the Nazis, who were forcing him to part with everything he owned in the world. Her youngest son, Freddi, had disappeared, and she was a fugitive, hiding like a terrified rabbit. Lanny had been able to get the husband, wife, and the older son out of Germany. He had tried to help Freddi, but in vain; Freddi, her baby, her gentle and kind one, who had played the clarinet so charmingly and had never done harm to any living soul! After the Nazis had brought him close to death with their tortures—because he was a Socialist as well as a Jew—they had turned him over to Lanny at the border. He had died in France and been buried according to Jewish ritual on the Riviera near Lanny's home. Some thirteen years had passed since then, and Leah had found a safe home in America; she was no longer rich, but then she had never wanted to be rich, so she had insisted to Lanny. All she wanted was enough so that they could live in peace.

V

Lanny got into his car; there was nothing more important that he could think of at the moment. He took the familiar drive across the great bridge over the Hudson, and in due course came to the comfortable home on the shore of the Sound. A Jewish maid opened the door and told him that Mr. Robin had left for the city. She called Rahel, who was living in this home, along with her new husband and new family. Rahel said that Mama was upstairs in her bedroom; she wouldn't eat, she wouldn't see a doctor, wouldn't do anything but sob her heart out.

"Maybe she will see you," Rahel said, and Lanny replied, "I'll go up and see her. Don't say anything about it."

He was an old friend of that family and went upstairs and didn't even knock on the door, just opened it softly. He saw the old woman lying on the bed with her face down, making the sounds of an animal that has been stricken to death. She really wasn't an old woman, not yet sixty, but she felt old and acted old, because she was a Jewish woman and was afraid of the Lord her God, whose name she would not pronounce; she knew He had stricken her, and it could only be because of her sins. She had dressed in black ever since Freddi's death and had no thought of or interest in this world except to take care of the people she loved and save them from the afflictions that had cursed her own life.

She had known pogroms as a child and had fled first from Russia and then from Germany, and now—*Oi! Oi!*—her afflictions had followed her here! "Terrors are turned upon me: they pursue my soul as the wind: and my welfare passeth away as a cloud. And now my soul is poured out upon me; the days of affliction have taken hold upon me. My bones are pierced in me in the night season: and my sinews take no rest."

Lanny closed the door and came quietly to the bedside; she had not heard him. He said in a low voice, "Mama."

The old woman raised her head and stared at him. He had never seen such a face of misery, of utter despair. He came at once to the point. "Mama, I came to see you as soon as I heard the news. I'm going to tell you a secret. It is a most important secret, and you must promise me, you must give me your solemn word, you will not speak a word about it to anybody on this earth."

She went on staring, as if her thoughts were confused and she was not quite sure that he was there. "Yes, Lanny," she managed to whisper.

"Not to Johannes, not to Rahel, not to anybody—*any*body! You will make me that promise?"

"Yes, Lanny."

He sat on the bed beside her and lowered his voice, almost to a whisper. "Hansi is not a Communist."

"*Aber*—what? He is in jail!"

"Hansi is working for the government, for the FBI. He is pretending to be a Communist and getting their secrets."

The old woman's eyes widened and her jaw fell; her voice was a faint murmur. "*Ach, Gott der Gerechte! Aber*—why is he in jail?"

"They had to put him there with the others. If they had left him free it would have let the others know that he is against them."

"*Um Gottes Willen*, Lanny! You are *gewiss?*"

"I know all about it. He has been pretending to agree with Bess, but he does not agree with her."

"*Ach*, that woman! She is your sister, Lanny—I must not say anything bad about her!"

"You must be sorry for her, Mama, as we are for all blundering human souls. She became a Communist because she believed they meant justice and freedom for the poor. She has been betrayed; the movement has fallen into the hands of evil men, but she cannot see it. She will suffer terribly for her blunders; but you have no cause to worry about Hansi."

"How long will they keep him, Lanny?"

"I have no doubt that the Communists will raise the bail and get them out in a day or two. Then they will make a hero out of Hansi; they will trust him with their secrets. It is very important work that he is doing."

"Oh, Lanny, he is such a *good* man!"

"None better, Mama. I was forbidden to tell you this, but I could not bear to see you suffer; and now you must keep the secret."

"Oh, I will keep it! *Gott sei Lob!*"

"You will have to be a bit of an actress. You must not look happy. You do not have to weep so much, but you must look sad and worried. You must cry a little."

"Oh, I could cry for joy, Lanny—if you are sure, really sure!"

"You can take my word for it, I am sure. Laurel knows it, but nobody else, not even my father. You must not tell Johannes."

"*Oi*, the poor man!"

"He is a man, and he will be able to stand it. Hansi will not let him put up bail. He will not make any promises, he will have to play the game according to orders, and you must play your game. Just tell the family that I have assured you that it will be all right, that Hansi will be bailed out, and that they do not beat prisoners in jail in New York— at least not if they behave themselves and do what they are told. You can say that I have assured you, that I don't believe Hansi has done any harm to anybody and has merely spoken what he believes. He is a good man and you are going to stand by him."

VI

So the old Jewish grandmother got up and wiped the tears from her eyes and straightened her hair a little, and they went downstairs. Rahel and the servants were not too much surprised, for they knew that Lanny Budd was a magician and his power over Mama was great. He could not quite call spirits from the vasty deep, but he had been able to go into Nazi Germany and buy the father of the family out of prison, and no doubt he would do the same thing for one of the world's top violin virtuosos.

So Lanny turned on the radio and got a station that was giving news. No war had broken out that day, no airplane had hit a mountain, no streamliner had gone off the track, so the newscasters had plenty of time for the uncovering of a spy plot and the arrest of half-a-dozen Red conspirators, including a famous musician and the daughter of a millionaire industrialist. And now—*Ach, Gott der Gerechte!* what was this? The man was telling how the federal agents had been to the suburban residence of the notorious couple and had ransacked their home and carried off boxes full of papers; they had dug in the garden underneath a seckel pear tree and had come upon a large family wash-boiler, a metal cylinder three feet wide and almost as high, covered with a top and carefully sealed with tar. It had been there no one knew how long, and it was packed solid with papers and documents; the load was so heavy that it took three men to lift it into a truck. What was in those papers the FBI wouldn't tell, but they had carted it off and no doubt were studying all the secrets of the Communist party.

"*Oh, mein lieber Hansi!*" exclaimed Mama and wiped her eyes with her handkerchief. Lanny didn't see any tears, but it was a proper gesture. It was such a serious matter he couldn't think that a pious grandmother was exactly enjoying herself; but, he reflected, there must be a certain amount of actress in every woman. Such had been the testimony of that long-suffering ancient called Job: "They conceive mischief, and bring forth vanity, and their belly prepareth deceit!"

VII

Lanny drove back to New York in a more cheerful frame of mind. He was as excited as a boy over this spy story, the mystery of which had been building up in his mind for a long time. He drove through the city on purpose to pick up the afternoon papers, and when he had got an assortment of them he found a vacant space by a curb and parked his car and glanced through them.

The story made the front page in every case; it had everything the public wanted: crime and detection, high life and low life, glamour and wealth. Bessie Remsen Budd undoubtedly belonged in what the newspapers call "the highest social circles." If she wasn't beautiful any longer, she certainly had been, and the newspapers had her early pictures. Hansi Robin undoubtedly belonged high in the world of music, both in America and in countries abroad. The Jones Electrical Works had a most commonplace name, but it had undoubtedly manufactured great quantities of proximity fuses for the Armed Forces and had made improvements in the device which were the very ultimate in secrecy.

All newspapers have what they call "the morgue," a huge file of envelopes containing everything they or other papers have published about any individual. The larger and more well-to-do have the person's story all written up to the moment, so that when he dies, marries, or gets arrested, all they have to do is to put the new developments at the top of the story and they are ready to go to press. So in these newspapers Lanny could read all about Hansi Robin's career and the career of Bessie Remsen Budd. Nobody was quite sure whether her name was really Bess or Bessie; her friends called her whichever happened to be easier in the sentence.

The papers told who her father was and who her half-brother was and gave something about the careers of both. They told how she had accompanied Hansi at his concerts, and now he was accompanying her as secret Red agent. They told about the obscure accountant in the office of a fuse factory who had managed to get access to confidential papers, correspondence, orders, blueprints, and technical specifications. He had taken them on Saturday night and turned them over to Bessie Budd, who had taken them to New York, where a photographic studio disguised as a stationery store had photographed them, and then they had been taken back to the accountant on Sunday. The FBI had gathered in both the Robins, the accountant, the two operatives of the photographic studio, and the two Russians who had been delivering the material to ships in the harbor. It was a clean sweep and a perfect job, and the FBI was sure it had the goods on all the parties who had been caught.

Lanny read these accounts, and by that time there were new editions on the stands, with new headlines. He bought those and learned about the family washboiler which had been dug up from under the seckel pear tree in the garden of a sumptuous villa in a fashionable Connecticut shore town. Such are the adjectives upon which newspapers thrive; and it was inevitable that some bright lad in the office of a tabloid, seeking for the alliteration which makes for picturesqueness, should dub the find the "boilerplate papers."

"Boilerplate" to a newspaper means the material which is sent out from some syndicate or central agency to hundreds of newspapers all over the country. It is put into type and papier-mâché "mats" made

of it. For the fast rotary presses on which big newspapers are printed
this material is curved exactly in the shape of boilerplate—and when
in the newspaper office the metal stereotype is made it looks still more
like its name. So inevitably a mass of documents buried in a family
washboiler became "boilerplate papers"—and the name would stick.
The Federal Bureau of Investigation would say no more than this:
they had come into possession of highly secret papers of the Communist underground, and these might be the means of landing some
conspicuous persons in a federal penitentiary.

VIII

Lanny drove home and told Laurel what he had done. She was
startled to hear that he had revealed the secret, and he told her, "If Post
had given me the secret I would have felt bound; but I got it myself,
and so I felt free to use my own judgment. I am sure Mama will
keep it."

The telephone had been ringing all day. It had become a nuisance,
but they had to answer, because there might be something important.
Robbie called to report on his visit. He and Johannes had obtained
permission from the U. S. Marshal to interview the prisoners, who
were in the Federal Detention Headquarters. Bess was alone, with
a matron in charge. At first she hadn't wanted to see her father but had
consented when he insisted.

She was quiet and apparently serene; she was sorry to hurt him and
especially sorry to hurt her mother, but there was nothing she could
do about it. She had her convictions and was standing by them. She
was not interested in being bailed out; of course if the comrades
arranged it she would be pleased, but she certainly didn't want to be
bailed out with Budd-Erling money or on Budd-Erling terms. She was
a Red and meant to live and die a Red.

"So that's that," said Robbie. "When someone is bent on martyrdom
there is nothing you can do but oblige them."

Lanny asked, "How is Esther taking it?" and the answer was,
"Esther is the quiet sort. She sheds her tears inside. We can't change
that either."

Robbie went on to add that Johannes had had no better success than
he. Hansi wouldn't listen to any compromise and didn't want to talk
about it.

A little while later the elderly Jew was on the telephone, asking,
"Lanny, what on earth have you done to my wife?"

"No harm, I hope."

"You have made her all over. What magic pills do you carry?" It was the Johannes of old, a shrewd, experienced man of affairs, hard-driving but generous outside business hours, and always with a touch of humor. Nothing was ever going to get him down—not old age, not the Communist movement.

Lanny answered, "I told her that Hansi loved her and he was doing what he thought was right. Also, that the U. S. Marshal doesn't torture his prisoners and that Hansi would soon be out on bail."

"I told her all that, but it did no good."

Lanny was about to add, "I told her that I had been arrested several times, and it wasn't fatal." But he realized that Johannes had been arrested too, so that was no argument. He said, "How did you find Hansi?" And the reply was, "Stubborn as a mule. He says he knows what he's doing, and we are not to worry about him."

"How are they treating him?"

"He has no complaint. They've put him in the room with that accountant, the fellow who stole the documents, so they say. Hansi says he is a good comrade and they are friends, so it's all right."

"Maybe they will let Hansi play the violin for him," suggested Lanny, and they chuckled.

When Lanny told his wife about this he said, "You see, the government people have put Hansi in with that other fellow, and in the night they will whisper secrets."

"Too bad they can't find a woman friend for Bess!" remarked Laurel. She had a bit more of acid in her make-up than her husband.

IX

Next morning the telephone began to ring early; Lanny was shaving and hurriedly wiped his chin. A voice asked, "Is this Mr. Lanning Prescott Budd?" When he answered that it was, "I wonder," said the voice, "if the name Virgil Smathers means anything to you?"

"The name sounds familiar, but you must excuse me—"

"It was more than thirty years ago. Don't you remember when you were a student at St. Thomas's Academy you met a young Methodist minister who told you about how badly Budd Gunmakers had treated their strikers?"

"Oh yes!" Lanny exclaimed. "I remember well. You were the first one who opened my eyes to what was going on in America."

"I hope your eyes are still open, Mr. Budd. I am now the minister of the Wesley Methodist Church of Brooklyn. I called up because I want very much to come to see you."

"A good many people are asking to see me just now, Mr. Smathers, and I don't want to be disobliging but I must ask one question. Are you going to ask me to put up any bail?"

The voice smiled audibly. "No, Mr. Budd, I promise; and I won't take but a few minutes of your time. If you cut me off and tell me you're not interested I'll not have my feelings hurt."

"All right," Lanny said. "I'll be in Edgemere all day. Come to the office of the Peace Program."

Toward noon the visitor showed up and presented his card. Lanny had recalled a slender blond young man of ascetic appearance, wearing spectacles. He still had the spectacles but the hair had turned gray. Evidently his salary had not been large enough to permit him to accumulate that comfortable rotundity which comes with middle age in America. He was still the earnest ascetic, the professional man of good will.

"It is a pleasure to meet you after all these years," said Lanny. "What can I do for you?"

The visitor came to the point at once, as he had promised. "Mr. Budd, I wish to tell you first that I am not a Communist; I am a servant of Jesus Christ and Him crucified. But I am one who is sometimes called a fellow traveler because I really believe in peace and good will and try to practice what I preach."

"I appreciate the distinction, Mr. Smathers. What is it you want to tell me?"

"Last night I was called to a conference of half-a-dozen persons to discuss the situation which has arisen involving your sister and brother-in-law. I never met Mrs. Robin in Newcastle, she was only a child when I was there, but I have met her more recently. I have never met Mr. Robin, but I have heard him play, of course. At the conference last night it was agreed that Mrs. Robin is a class-conscious and thoroughly disciplined Communist and will know how to take what comes; there is no need to worry about her. But so far as Mr. Robin is concerned there was general agreement that he is not really a Communist; he came into the movement because of his love for his wife and his inability to live without her. He is a great artist, and therefore an especially sensitive man. We are quite sure that he knows nothing about espionage and has no idea that such activities are possible. He is an idealist and an entirely nonpolitical person; he surely does not belong in the arena of political strife. I hope you agree with that."

"Assuming that I do, Mr. Smathers, what is your idea?"

"Our idea is that this should be pointed out to the government authorities. A man is not legally responsible for what his wife does; it cannot be legally assumed that he knows what she is doing. It is our idea that an arrangement be worked out whereby charges against Mr. Robin would be dropped upon the agreement that he will give up every form of Communist activity. You surely know that he is a man who would keep his word."

"I know that. But I have no idea that he would give such a word."

"Neither have we, Mr. Budd, but the inquiry could be made."

"Would that mean that he would go on giving concerts under the auspices of Communist-front organizations and raising funds which support Communist activities?"

"Of course it would not, Mr. Budd. The idea is that Hansi Robin would make his appearance only under the auspices of established musical agencies. It may be no one would come to hear him."

"Who are the persons offering this proposal, Mr. Smathers? Are they Communists?"

"Two of them are ministers like myself; two others, I believe, are Communist sympathizers; and two are important and active Communist party people. There would be no use making the proposal unless it had some authority behind it. Mr. Robin would be told to make the agreement and keep it."

"Unfortunately, Mr. Smathers, Communists do not have a very good reputation for keeping their agreements. To whom do you expect to make this proposal?"

"It is the FBI which has made the arrests. Presumably they are the ones who would make the decision. It cannot be that they have any real evidence against him. I am told that by people who know."

"But I don't know those people, Mr. Smathers, and I don't know the FBI. Why should you come to me about it?"

"Because it seems to us that you are the logical person to make the approach. The FBI knows your program and will not suspect you of having any improper interest in the matter."

"I am not afraid of being suspected, Mr. Smathers. What I am afraid of is putting myself at the service of men who have no respect for their pledged word and are laughing at me behind my back while they make a fool of me."

"I assure you, Mr. Budd—"

"You are wasting your time assuring me of anything, Mr. Smathers, except that you yourself are a Christian gentleman. You cannot assure me about anything regarding Communists because I know them and their doctrines. Surely you must be aware that Lenin advised his followers to lie, to use every subterfuge to overcome their enemies; and I do not believe that any truth can be got by lying or that any love can come out of a gospel of hate."

"I can only assure you, Mr. Budd, that this proposition is a sincere one."

"Will you tell me who the party leaders are who make this proposition?"

"I am sorry, Mr. Budd, I am not authorized to do that."

"You see, they are playing with you, and they are trying to play with me. They are enemies of the government which serves us and in which we believe."

"Even enemies have to parley, Mr. Budd. If there is going to be peace there has to be a truce."

"Peace, Mr. Smathers? The Communists can have peace any day, but they cannot have it while they are followers of Stalin."

"Then you're not willing to approach the FBI, Mr. Budd?"

"I will approach them on one condition, and that is, that you will give me the names of the Communist party leaders who are making the proposition and undertaking to see that Hansi Robin will keep it. You are not a Communist, and you cannot speak for the Communists, so I would just be inviting the FBI on a hunt for a mare's nest."

X

They parted, and Lanny went and told Laurel of the proposition, but not until they were driving home, where there could be no chance of being overheard. "What are you going to do?" she asked, and he told her, "I'll go and tell Post about it anyhow, but I'll not let the Communists know that I'm telling him."

He telephoned at once to Wilbur Post, saying, "I have something to tell you, but I don't think I ought to come to your office, because I imagine there will be reporters hanging around."

"A safe guess," was the reply, and the busy man made an appointment to meet Lanny on a certain corner at a certain hour. Lanny drove there and picked him up and told him about the visit from the Brooklyn preacher.

"Smathers," said Post. "Oh yes, we know him." There was significance in the special way he said it. He added, "It is our practice to be cautious in what we say about individuals, but I suppose I may quote what I read about him in a newspaper: 'He has a soft heart and a still softer head. He is a sob-sister who wears pants.'"

Lanny assented to that description and told what Smathers had proposed. The other had a good laugh over the odd situation; then, becoming serious, he said, "I don't believe the real top Communists would endorse such a proposition. Hansi Robin is too valuable to them, both as moneymaker and headline-maker; of course they don't care a damn about his art."

Lanny inquired, "I take it that your having Hansi arrested means that you expect to go on using him?"

"Yes, surely."

"Well, suppose that Smathers were permitted to see Hansi and make that proposition to him. You could post Hansi in advance, and he could turn down the proposition flatly. He could make a speech declaring his undying loyalty to the party, his willingness to make any sacrifices, his determination to stick. That should make him solid with them and incline them to give him information. It would have that effect with Bess, I know."

Post thought that over. "Mightn't be a bad idea," he said. "They are all to be taken before the U. S. Commissioner and bail will be set. No doubt the Commies will be on hand with the cash, so we'll have to work quickly on your proposition."

"I've been thinking about it," Lanny said. "We mustn't do anything to suggest that you know me or that I know you. Perhaps the quickest way would be for you to call Smathers up and ask if he knows a man named Lanny Budd. When he says yes, you say, 'He telephoned saying you had a proposition for me. Why don't you come in and make it direct?'"

"All right, I'll do that," replied Post. "It can't do any harm, and it might do some good. There are one or two strands missing in the net we have woven around those people. They will all be as busy as bees getting things hidden and establishing new lines of communication."

"That finding of the boilerplate papers sounds like something big," said Lanny, who was not above human curiosity.

"I don't mind telling you it's a stroke of luck. We are working day and night on the papers, sorting them out and indexing them. It may be weeks before we know everything we've got. It may surprise you to know that Hansi Robin had nothing to do with that discovery."

Lanny dropped the official a block or two from his office and drove

on about the affairs of the Peace Program. Every now and then his
mind would come back to that fascinating mystery: who could be the
other spy in Bessie Budd's life? Somebody had written two anonymous
letters, and it was likely that this same person might be the one who
had betrayed the secret of the buried boiler. There were two women
servants in the Robin household, and Lanny and Laurel had discussed
them both; there was a gardener, and he was a likely prospect. He was
a Finn and seemed a stupid fellow—but then he might be a government
agent pretending to be a stupid fellow.

The burying of a boiler three feet in diameter requires a lot of
digging; it could have been done at night, of course, or on a Sunday;
but could the signs of such digging be hidden from a gardener? If
there had been a grass sod, that could have been replaced with care;
and if the gardener had been got out of the way on some pretext, the
job might have been done in daylight without attracting any other
person's attention. If Hansi didn't know about it the job must have
been done while he was away on one of his many trips. Lanny had
planned such schemes himself and knew that Bess was no less capable
and certainly no less determined. But she had two opponents working
against her and apparently suspected neither of them. She must now
be suspecting at least one of them. What a lot she had had to think
about, shut up in durance vile with nobody but a marshal's matron
for company!

XI

It was a trying situation for the newspaper reporters. The whole
country was on tiptoe with curiosity about this case, but what could
the reporters get? The prisoners were kept incommunicado, except
for their lawyers, and the FBI had no more information to give out.
The Communist party, of course, was willing to talk without limit,
but all they had to say was propaganda. They were shocked by this
persecution of innocent persons; it was a shameless violation of fundamental civil rights.

It was known that the president of Budd-Erling Aircraft and the
head of its foreign sales department had been to interview the two
prisoners in whom they were interested, but neither would say a word
about what had occurred. The director of the Peace Program would
say only that he disagreed with his sister's ideas but was sure that she
held them sincerely. Photographs of the various parties were, of course,
available; and the newspapers could send photographers to take pic-

tures of the hole in the ground under the seckel pear tree and of the stationery shop on Delancey Street. One of the papers even published a photograph of a Soviet ship at one of the docks in Brooklyn; and that was all.

So it was both figuratively and literally a godsend when a gentleman known to his flock as the Reverend Smathers came forward with the information that he had been permitted to interview Hansi Robin. Certain of the New York Communists, moved by the love of art and respect for a great artist, had volunteered the assertion that whatever Bessie Budd Robin had been doing, very certainly her husband had known nothing about it, and he had been arrested only because he lived in the same house with a well-known and active party member. This statement had been made to the FBI, and the suggestion had been offered to Hansi Robin that he might agree to remain what he had always been, a strictly nonpolitical person, and to confine his future appearances to strictly nonpolitical assemblages.

But, said the Reverend Mr. Smathers, Hansi Robin had firmly turned down this offer. He had insisted that his motive was loyalty not merely to his wife but to the cause of freedom of opinion and expression. He refused to make any compromise with the frenzy of redbaiting which had seized the country. He was innocent, and his wife also was innocent, and he believed that the others were innocent.

The "sob-sister in pants" took occasion to add that he believed it also. When the reporters asked him about the boilerplate papers he said the Communist party was a legal organization, a part of the American political system, and they had a perfect right to take care of their records. When they knew that their motives were being misrepresented and their financial accounts and membership lists used for purposes of persecution, it was natural that they should take precautions to conceal these. This was a free country, wasn't it? And a minister of the Gospel was supposed to preach peace and good will toward men, wasn't he? "If that be fellow traveling, come and join me!" said the Reverend Mr. Smathers.

17

The Evil That Men Do

I

SIX of the seven accused persons were brought before the U.S. Commissioner. The seventh, a Soviet official, claimed diplomatic immunity, and all that could be done in his case was for the State Department to request his recall to his own country. The other six were Oskar Johanssen, the accountant; Bessie Budd Robin and Hansi Robin; Carl and Lucille Sedin, alias Carpenter, the photographers; and J. Dumbrowsky, the Russian messenger.

The Commissioner said this was a very serious case, and inasmuch as accused Communists had sometimes been known to turn up missing he felt it his duty to set the bail high. He set it at twenty thousand dollars for five of the defendants and thirty thousand for the Russian, for he, not being an American citizen, might be assumed more likely to disappear. The bail was promptly put up by a surety company. Undoubtedly that company had required guarantees; but that was a private transaction and did not appear in the court records or the newspapers.

In the case of the Russian this meant charging the Soviet government thirty thousand dollars for its spy. That government didn't mind, having plenty of gold mines in Siberia, to say nothing of those it had in the penthouses on Manhattan Island. To that government it was, of course, not desirable that one of its agents should be convicted in an American court. Whatever the price, they would pay it. The man would disappear from sight the moment he left the courtroom and would never again be seen.

What would happen to him when he reached his own country was a matter for guesswork. The known facts were, first, he had failed, which is something absolutely forbidden by his government; and, second, he had lived in America and learned what clothes Americans wore, what food they ate, and in general how many more privileges

315

they enjoyed than any Russian except a commissar. He might be tempted to mention what he had seen to some other Russians, and therefore the only safe thing was to ship him off to one of the gold mines. What he said there wouldn't matter, because he wouldn't live more than a year or two, and neither would the persons to whom he said it.

After that matters settled down again; if it hadn't been for jokes about boilerplate papers the public would have dismissed the subject from its mind altogether. Lanny and Laurel were left to speculate about the Hansibesses. They would go back to their home; and what would they be doing? Hansi had shown himself a hero, a brave and determined friend of a great cause. Bess would love him—and how would Hansi like it? Laurel said he would stand it; men didn't feel about sex as women did. Lanny answered that there was a good deal of the woman in Hansi.

And what would Bess be doing? Lanny ventured the guess that she was through as an underground operative. Her lawyers would forbid it, and the party bosses would agree. They had a strict rule that the party and the underground were to be kept entirely separate—so much so that many party members didn't even know there was an underground and would ridicule the idea, calling it redbaiting.

And, of course, when any underground worker got arrested and got his pictures in the newspapers, that person could no longer be in the underground. He would repudiate it, and it would repudiate him. So now the daughter of Budd-Erling would become a "name character." She would cash in on her publicity and become a champion of her cause, one of its martyrs. Quite possibly she might take up again her role as Hansi's piano accompanist. But perhaps only Communists would want to hear them now.

II

Such was Lanny's guess, deduced from Communist principles as Hansi had explained them; and the guess proved to be correct.

A week or so after the hearing Lanny was called to the telephone early in the morning. A deep bass voice enunciated, "Same place, ten o'clock this morning." Lanny thought for a moment and then growled back, in a voice that might have come out of the lion's cage in the zoo, "O-o-o-oh-kaay." He hung up, laughing, and told Laurel about it. Then he called his secretary and told her to postpone a couple of appointments.

He got in his car and took the roundabout drive to Central Park. He met Hansi in the usual way. The first words the violinist spoke were, "I want to thank you for what you did for Mama."

"You have seen her?" Lanny asked.

"I went to her first of all. She caught me in her arms and began to cry, and I thought it was going to be one more painful scene. But she took me upstairs and shut the door and whispered in my ear, 'Lanny told me! Lanny told me!' She cried some more, but these were tears of joy, and I was glad you had done it." Then Hansi added, with joy of his own, "I'm to have a vacation. Post says I don't have to do any more Communist work."

"You mean you won't have to testify?"

"Post says my testimony may be needed; but I don't have to go around playing music and raising money for Communist-front organizations. I'm going to write a concerto."

"That sounds fine, Hansi. And Bess?"

"She is through with the underground. She will not recognize one of her old associates if she meets one on the street. She is to take a lecture trip and tell the comrades all over the country that the red-baiters set a trap for her; that those papers dug up on our place had been stolen from some of the offices of the party; that others were forged and planted with the rest. It is a typical Wall Street plot."

Hansi went on to tell how he had sat in at meetings with the party bosses. As one of the prisoners he had a right to be there. He had helped to plan the defense and had reported to the FBI the details of the program adopted. Then he had asked Post to let him off from further work. The party wanted him to tour the country with Bess; he would draw the crowds and she would pump Communist doctrine into them and raise money for the defense. He didn't want to do it and Post had agreed that it would be poor tactics.

So Hansi had told his wife that he had had all the excitement he could stand; he was on the verge of a nervous breakdown and must have a rest. He was just as devoted to the cause as ever, but he wanted to make his contribution in music and not in the field of politics. Bess had been disappointed, but he had brought her to agreement.

"Do you think she suspects you?" Lanny asked.

"I don't think so; but it may be that she wouldn't let me know. She has become very cautious. She is terribly humiliated by her failure and spends a lot of time brooding over it, trying to figure out who can have betrayed her. She put me through a grilling as to what I could possibly have said to you."

"I tried to have something to do with it," Lanny remarked, "but you got ahead of me." He said it with a smile, trying to keep down his heartache over this case.

III

Hansi told about the arrest, which had been made in the morning while he and Bess were having breakfast. Half-a-dozen men had come, three of them in a limousine and the others in a station wagon. Some had taken posts at the exits of the house, and others had rung the doorbell and pushed their way in past the servant.

"Apparently none of them knew that I was in on the plot," said Hansi. "Anyhow, they made it realistic. They told us we could finish our breakfast, but we didn't have much appetite. Then they took us into the living room and put us in two chairs, and a man sat in front of us and never took his eyes off us. He forbade us to talk. They had warrants and insisted that we should inspect them. I had told Post the servants were Reds, so they were put out of the house with their belongings; I didn't see it, but no doubt they made sure the people didn't take anything else. They took us upstairs and let us get together a few odds and ends in two handbags—a toothbrush, a comb, and so on. Then they took us out to the car, three of the men. They didn't put handcuffs on us, but they watched us every moment, as if they thought we might try to swallow poison. The other three men stayed behind with the station wagon. They had a warrant to search the house—they made me look at that. They did a thorough job of it and took away all the papers that might reveal our doings."

The prisoners were taken to the Tombs. "I don't know about the others," Hansi said, "but they fixed us up comfortably, Johanssen, the accountant, and me—I suppose you read about him in the paper. He is a Dane, a blond fellow, very quiet and determined, bitter when he talks frankly. It was my business to make friends with him, so I told him about my trips to the Soviet Union and all the wonders I had seen there and how I loved the Russian people I had known—which is true enough. He had every reason to trust me, and he did. He told me the story of his hard life. He got his head cracked in a strike, and that made him into a Communist. He dropped out of party work several years ago, took a new name, and joined the underground. He studied to be an accountant on purpose and then got a job in the Jones plant. He stole the combination to the safe where the classified papers were kept. He was introduced to Bess—he didn't know who she was. He just knew her as Mary, and she knew him as Jim."

"He told you all that in the cell?" demanded Lanny.

"They had caught him with the safe open, so he figured the jig was up; but he talked in a low tone. They told him they had got me nailed down too, so we were comrades in misery. He wasn't worried over the prospect of several years in jail—he said he could keep busy educating some of the men in there, and they would make as good workers as anyone else once they became class-conscious."

Lanny brought up the subject he had discussed with Laurel. "Tell me, Hansi, are you going to live alone in that house?"

"I'll get along all right, Lanny. I will lose myself in my work."

"Shall we be able to see something of you?"

"After Bess goes on her trip next week. She is terribly afraid of you, and I mustn't have any quarrel with her—surely not until the trial comes off. If the Communists got the faintest idea of what I'm going to do they would come down on me like a ton of bricks. They might shoot me."

"If you want to hide we will hide you," Lanny said. "You can tell Bess the newspaper reporters are hounding you."

"I wouldn't have to lie about that; they've been trying to bribe the servants."

IV

Lanny went home and told his wife about Hansi's idea of living alone, but she didn't think much of it. "Who's going to see to getting out his laundry every week?" she demanded. "Who's going to manage the servants? And those two boys at vacation times? Above all, who's going to keep the other women away from him?"

"It is not good that the man should be alone"—so Hansi's Yahweh had declared, and Laurel agreed with Him. If Hansi were left alone he would be surrounded and besieged by adoring females. It was absolutely necessary that he should get the right wife, otherwise the wrong one would get him, and a second failure would ruin his life.

"For heaven's sake, don't let him know you're thinking about it!" said Lanny. "He'd run away to China."

"He doesn't have to know," was the reply. "Men never know. The women attend to it."

Laurel set aside her stack of letters and manuscripts, and made Lanny do the same, and they canvassed the field: the ladies who worked in the office, those who came as volunteer helpers, those who wrote letters, those who had been met socially in New York and

Baltimore and Hollywood, in London and Paris and Berlin. It wasn't
going to be an easy problem; some were too old and some too young;
some were talkative and some not good-looking enough. When Lanny
suggested that this last might not matter so much to Hansi, Laurel
replied, "Hansi is a man!"

It ought to be somebody who was musical, not necessarily a per-
former, but somebody who loved music, else how could she stand
the racket? It would have to be somebody who was clever, else how
could Hansi stand her? It would have to be somebody who was honest and dependable, and Laurel feared that these were growing more
scarce. They canvassed possible advisers, and Laurel said they must
not leave it to Mama Robin; kind good soul, she was orthodox and
would pick out some submissive girl who would be horrified if Hansi
ate a pork chop, would never consent to have butter on the table when
meat was served. And suppose she took to wearing a wig! Lanny's
mother knew great numbers of women, young and old, but they were
worldly women, otherwise Beauty would have no interest in them.
So she was out!

Lanny, taking the matter lightly, pointed out that Europe would
be a favorable hunting ground; Europe was full of women who would
like nothing better than to marry an American and be brought to his
utopia. But Laurel said that the women of Europe were neurotic; they
were at loose ends and would require a lot of sorting out. He assured
her that, unfortunately, he had met very few of late. His acquaint-
ances had been mostly middle-aged or elderly men who had been
battered by the war and were staggering to their feet again; or middle-
aged Americans who were trying to help them and being blamed for
all their troubles.

Then the facetious one remarked, "We may have to put an adver-
tisement in the newspapers." To which Laurel answered, "All you'd
have to do would be to throw a net over Hansi after one of his concerts; you'd catch a score of candidates; but how would you pick
one? Women don't follow him home because they know he's married
and they've heard that his wife watches him; but when the fact is
published that he is unattached he'll have to get double locks on his
doors."

All this might seem a trifle premature, since Hansi was living in supposed connubial bliss with his lawful wedded wife, and both of them
were under indictment for a felony and liable to ten or twenty years
in a federal penitentiary. But women have their ways of doing things
that men say cannot be done. Laurel was going to keep her eyes open

for a likely candidate, and when she met one she would invite her to lunch and probe her character. If Laurel, in her role of gentile *shadchen*, or marriage broker, should decide that the woman was right, she would arrange a dinner party. Later on Lanny would say to Hansi, "What do you think of Miss Smith?" and Laurel would say to Miss Smith, "What do you think of Hansi Robin? Too bad he is under indictment, isn't it?" If it should turn out that the two parties thought well of each other, Laurel would remark to the lady, "You know, Hansi isn't as much of a Communist as he thinks. It was Bess who got him into this, and there's quite a possibility that they might break up over the situation. But you mustn't say a word about it to anybody, not even to him!"

That's the way people who know the world get what they want in it; and if what they want is something good it's not so bad.

V

It was the month of March, which is fabled to come in like a lion and go out like a lamb. It was in its roaring stage; there was snow at night and then in the morning the weather turned warm and there was slush on the ground. Lanny had had a touch of flu, so he didn't go to the office. When he saw that the sun was shining on the front porch he went out in his dressing gown and sat for a while; at that undependable season every ray of sunlight was precious. He was there when Laurel came home with the mail, and she handed him a bundle of unopened letters.

There were always some addressed to him personally, and he had become expert in picking out those that were important. Business letters had the imprint of the firm in the corner, whereas fan letters were usually handwritten and many of them crude in appearance. Airmail letters took precedence, and especially any with German postage stamps. One was in Monck's familiar script and started off with the sentence, "The deaf girl cannot be found; we sent a man to look for her, but no luck."

That was all on that subject, and Lanny was left to speculate. Had Ferdinand betrayed Anna Surden, or was it she who had betrayed him? Of course there was a possibility that she had found herself a man and had gone off with him; but that was unlikely, she being in a land with many more women than men. It was far more likely that she had been caught; and if so, how much had she told? There was no reason to believe that she would protect either Monck or Lanny; certainly no reason to think that she would stand torture for either of them. It was no crime to be trying to catch counterfeiters, but in this case it seemed likely that the counterfeiters were in league with some government authorities, whether German or Russian. Betrayal would make further efforts more difficult, if not impossible.

Lanny could reflect upon the near impossibility of achieving anything against a police state. He had just witnessed the arrest of a Soviet spy in New York, one who had been caught redhanded, together with his American abettors. The law had required that he be arraigned in court immediately—a public procedure. The law required that he should be admitted to bail and that the bail should not be "excessive." Now the man had disappeared, and the newspapers were reporting that he had been put on board a Soviet steamer in Baltimore and was gone. The Soviet government had been able to get back its spy and all his secrets by the payment of thirty thousand dollars, which figured out less than one-thirtieth of a kopeck per capita of the Russian population—certainly a moderate charge.

On the other hand, when an American spy was caught in Sovietland, the silence of the grave followed. You couldn't find anybody who had ever heard of the person; if you inquired of the authorities they would say they had never heard of the person and what business was it of yours anyway? Instead of making an appearance in open court the person was buried in a dungeon and subjected to elaborate processes of torture until he told everything he knew, or everything that the police state wanted him to say that he knew.

Yes, that was one of the many differences between a free society and a dictatorship over the proletariat. Lanny had been for all his thinking life a strong civil-liberties man; but now his mind was troubled by the question whether civil liberties should be extended to the enemies of civil liberties; to persons who were cynically and implacably determined to destroy the civil liberties of everybody in the world but the members of the Politburo.

VI

Monck's letter went on to discuss the situation in Berlin, concerning which he was as pessimistic as always. He reported that the cold war was growing warmer, and he was sure the Soviets intended some drastic action. Their propaganda was incessant, and very effective with the Germans, especially in the East. The American efforts were pitiful in comparison. The RIAS people meant well, but they had almost no funds and hadn't yet been able to get a promised building entirely repaired. "Can't you do something with the authorities in Washington?" Monck pleaded.

He concluded, "Your old friend is living in the mountains with his family. We have been able to make his acquaintance." Lanny knew that meant Kurt Meissner and that Monck was again in contact with the Völkischerbund. Lanny had had no idea that Kurt would keep his promise to abstain from anti-American activities, and he had been afraid that Monck would have a hard time penetrating the difficult shell of that conspiracy. Here was another group of men who didn't believe in civil liberties and who were not troubled with any moral scruples whatsoever.

Thinking these troublesome thoughts, Lanny went into the house and turned on the radio and heard a horrifying story—the death of Jan Masaryk. He had jumped, or fallen, or been thrown from the third-story window of his official residence and smashed upon the pavement of the courtyard below. The news came, of course, from the Communist government, which had seized power in Czechoslovakia, and naturally they said it was a suicide; but Lanny never believed it for an instant. He knew Masaryk too well to think that he would run away from the fight; he hated the Communists too much to be willing to oblige them. It was no surprise when later the story came out that he had been attacked in his bedroom and beaten to death with a piece of furniture and then thrown from the window. "When you hear of my death you will know it is the end," so he had said—meaning, of course, the end of his country.

There were civil liberties for you! There were the Reds who in America were praising civil liberties and claiming the privileges of them! Lanny paced the room, cursing them in his heart—and the fools in America who swallowed their poisonous propaganda. Lanny had had many qualms over the idea of helping to send his own sister to prison and of advising Hansi Robin to divorce her; but the last trace of doubt faded from his mind as he stood in imagination by the broken body of that genial gentleman who had gone back deliberately to his homeland, offering himself as a sacrifice, a protest, an appeal to the free world. To Lanny's mind came the lines which Byron had written on the prisoner of Chillon:

> Chillon, thy prison is a holy place
> And thy sad floor an altar, for 'twas trod. . . .
> By Bonnivard! May none those marks efface!
> For they appeal from tyranny to God.

VII

A few days later came another letter from Monck. He had promised to keep Lanny in touch with developments, and now he stated, "Ferdinand's father is as active as ever. I enclose a sample, so you may see that the old fires are still smoldering." He added, "I am reading a story called *Treasure Island* by Stevenson and finding it extremely interesting. You should read it."

Lanny pondered that last. He was sure it was code; Monck didn't have any time to be reading adventure stories generally taken as suitable for boys. Always cautious, he would seldom put things in plain words and trust them to the mails. There were too many spies where he worked, and it was too easy to steam open a letter. The word "treasure" told Lanny that Monck was on the trail of some of the jewels and gold the Nazi fanatics had buried. Lanny didn't know whether there was an island in the Tegernsee, but he knew there were islands in some of those mountain lakes, and it might well be that the Völkischerbund knew of treasure hidden on one of these.

There was a bit of paper enclosed, and Lanny opened it. Like the letter, it was in German, and done on the same typewriter. Obviously Monck had typed the copy:

"We have a right to salvation, the right of the believers. Our salvation must be won by ourselves. We hold our heads high. Our way was straight and without blame. We ask no man to give us back our honor; we possess it! We have made no terms with the enemy; we are ourselves."

There was the voice of the unregenerate Nazi! There was *das Wort* —"the Word"! Guzman had told Lanny that Kurt's prophetic utterances consisted of only one sentence at a time. But apparently Kurt's daimon was becoming importunate; or had Monck put several of "the Words" together?

Anyhow, it meant that Kurt, who had made Lanny a pledge of honor, was not keeping it. He had taken the Nazi will-to-rule and made it into a *Mystik*, a thing superior to manmade laws and to merely human rights. It was the old notion that the end justified the means. In German it was even more fanatical: *Der Zweck heiligt die Mittel.* The verb means more than justifies, it means hallows, sanctifies. The German determination to take the mastery of the world became a holy thing; moved by this divinely inspired impulse, they had made three attempts in a period of less than seventy years, and now Kurt was telling them to cherish the impulse in their hearts and get ready for a fourth try.

But meantime had come the Stalin Communists, repudiating the old gods and setting up a new one. Oddly enough he too was of Jewish origin; he was the Diamat, the Marxian dialectic! In the realm of this new divinity everything was automatic and inevitable; it was materialistic determinism. His followers were fated to seize the world and rule it whether they wanted to or not—or perhaps it would be more accurate to say that they were fated to want to. They were fated to hate capitalism, and to hate it so bitterly that they would rise up and abolish it and set up a dictatorship of the proletariat. Presumably those individuals who seized the power and became the rulers were fated to believe that they were the ones who were worthy to do so. The end was that they got the power, and this sanctified whatever hideous means were required to keep it.

So there were the Reds, facing their conquered Nazi foes, both sides with fanatical hatred blazing in their hearts. And in between them stood a third set of men with a wholly different set of notions in their heads, men from thousands of miles overseas, wedged in between the old antagonisms, separated from them by no more than an imaginary line drawn down the middle of a city's streets. What whim of an ancient malicious god or of a dialectical synthesis had brought it about that Americans should be in *that* situation?

Certainly the Power, whatever it was, had not brought it about that the Americans *wanted* to be there. Lanny Budd had met hundreds of "Amis" on the scene, all the way from the lowliest GI to the five-star general at the top, and he had not met a single man who was not yearning in his heart to be back in Abilene, Kansas, or Dead Man's Gulch, Montana. But here they were, bound by some notion of duty; by an idea, inherited from their forefathers, that men should be free and that no nation should be permitted to conquer and enslave another. They didn't know how to dress it up in metaphysical language, they just said in their stubborn, matter-of-fact way that they believed in the free world and were saving it; so they stayed. And Lanny, reading this letter from his friend in Berlin, thought that if there had ever been a more explosive situation in history it was recorded in some book he had not read.

VIII

A few days after the death of Jan Masaryk, Lanny attended a session of the United Nations at Lake Success. He heard the discussion of a resolution that the UN should investigate the situation in Czechoslovakia. He heard a speech by the Soviet delegate, denouncing this motion as an insult to and an outrage upon the Democratic Peoples' Republic of Czechoslovakia. This Soviet representative was still Gromyko. He was young, and so had never known anything but the Soviet system; he was one of those robots which the system was now turning out by the million. He had a perfectly expressionless face and spoke with a perfectly expressionless voice. Every evening he telephoned Moscow, reported the situation, and got his instructions; the next day he rose up and said what he had been told to say. He knew, of course, that very few people in the audience understood what he was saying; it all had to be translated. He voted against the resolution, and when it was carried he walked out; that too was automatic.

A few days later Lanny listened over the radio and heard General Marshall, the American Secretary of State, announce that we would stay in Berlin regardless of all protests and at all hazards. Also Lanny heard that the United Nations Commission on Atomic Energy had announced that it had reached an impasse in its efforts to arrange for atomic control. The Soviets would never agree to inspection of the atomic plants in their country, and they persisted in their demand that the UN must first forbid the use of atomic weapons and require their destruction before there could be any steps toward general disarmament. It was obvious to all the world that the only thing which had so far kept the Soviet Union from taking possession of Western Europe was that supply of atomic bombs which the United States kept dangling over the Kremlin; the Soviet demand was equivalent to a statement that they would not give up the intention to march.

IX

Under State Department auspices there had been set up in New York a radio organization known as the Voice of America, whose purpose was to make known the country's ideas and ideals to the rest of the world. A Congress dominated by isolationists wouldn't give it much money, and the great news associations wouldn't sell it any of their product. To Lanny this was an illustration of the incredible length to which the profit system would go in the effort to protect itself against government competition; but so matters stood, and the Voice didn't go to law about it. It was free to use the news once it had been published, and to people listening in Siam, Tasmania, and Chile a few hours' delay didn't make much difference.

The Voice was forbidden to broadcast in America; it used short wave only, and as time passed it would be able to get more money and set up short-wave stations at strategic points surrounding the great Communist empire. This, of course, would be taken as a hostile action by the rulers of that empire. The Voice gave the facts, and there was nothing the rulers feared more. They would expend a large part of their radio funds to make clattering noises that would drown out the sounds of VOA. They would spend more of their radio energy in denouncing those statements which their own people were not supposed to have heard.

This was a new form of the cold war, and, like all the other forms, it would grow less cold as time passed. Thomas Jefferson had written that truth had nothing to fear from error where reason was left free to combat it; but reason was not left free inside the Communist empire, so the only way for reason to have a chance was for the news of the day to be translated into forty or fifty different languages and beamed in the direction of the lands where those languages were spoken. Many of those lands were poor and not many persons in them had short-wave radio sets; but the hope was that a few persons would get it and would be moved to go out and spread it by other means and at whatever risk, even of life. That had always happened so far in history, and the assumption was that it would continue to happen. A long time before Thomas Jefferson one of the old Hebrew prophets had stated that "truth is mighty, and it prevails."

VOA hadn't the money to hire the top men away from private industry. It had to find men who were willing to take small salaries in return for the privilege of saying what they believed. There were many of these, and some were competent; others made mistakes. Always they worked under a sniping fire from both sides, the left and the right. The Communists, who had penetrated everywhere into newspapers, magazines, and radio, were quick to find fault with anything that was done in the name of the free world; and they could count upon the support of reactionary congressmen, isolationists who wanted nothing to do with foreign nations except to sell them a bill of goods. VOA had to have a large staff of translators, people who could read and write and speak the most unlikely languages; and it wasn't always possible to be sure that their translations were correct. The most elementary ideas had to be explained; and sometimes it would be discovered that the American brand of humor was different from that of the Singhalese or the Egyptians.

People working under such pressure were glad to have the help of a volunteer group such as the Peace Program. The little Peace paper was full of quotable extracts, and tape recordings were made of the programs and supplied to both VOA and RIAS, thus increasing many-fold the effectiveness of the effort. It was casting bread upon the waters, and it came back in the form of a constant stream of letters from all over the world. Great numbers of people were listening and getting the facts; and in his own way each was laboring to spread knowledge and understanding. The outcome of all that effort lay upon the lap of the gods.

18

Love Gilds the Scene

I

LANNY was worried about his wife. He was certain that she was overworking. She was so conscientious that she considered it her duty to see every visitor and to answer every letter personally. She was keeping two secretaries busy; she would lie in bed with a stack of letters, reading them and marking them with instructions. She hadn't had a vacation in a long time, and Lanny set himself to lure her away. Let the well-trained subordinates take over the work, under the supervision of Rick and Nina, and then by and by this pair too could have a rest and a change.

There was Hansi, left alone in that big house, except for the servants. The boys had gone back to school after their Easter vacation, and Bess had gone off on a speaking tour. She had quarreled with him before she left, accusing him of cowardice, or at any rate of moral slackness, because he was dropping his Communist activities. What was the good of saying you believed in a cause if you didn't work for it? And what was the value of a concerto compared with saving the proletarian state?

The trial was nearly two months off, and Lanny said, "Why not kidnap Hansi and give him a little fun?" He called up Wilbur Post of the FBI and asked about it. With Bess away, there was no possibility of Hansi getting any more information from the Reds. He was brooding over the dreadful publicity that was coming, the problem of what his friends would think about his conduct in spying upon his wife— an awful thing. Why not take him away and keep him cheerful? Post arranged the matter with the United States Commissioner, and Hansi agreed to keep in touch with that official.

Lanny had another meeting with his friend and put the proposition to him. They wouldn't let Bess know where he had gone or whom he had gone with. He would just write her a note, saying that he was taking a trip to get away from his troubles. If she guessed that her ideological enemies had something to do with it, that could do no great harm. The three of them would take things easy and see the sights on the way. They would stop in auto courts, and Hansi would take along his fiddle and some music paper and could write when he felt like it. He could ride in the back seat and think his own thoughts —provided only that they were cheerful.

The violinist was agreeable, and they arranged a completely secret getaway. Hansi went back and gave his instructions to the servants, wrote his letter to Bess, and packed up his belongings. Next morning he called a taxi and had himself driven to a nearby town, and in front of the post office he piled his belongings on the curb. He paid off the taxi driver and saw him depart, and stood there until Lanny's car showed up. Nobody had noticed him, and his belongings were safely stowed, and they set out for New Jersey and the South.

II

By late afternoon they were just above Washington, and they stopped at one of those comfortable motels which by now had spread all over the country. They hired two little cabins, with a shelter in between for the car. Then they drove and found a café and had dinner and came back to the cabins. They had a radio in the car, and another set they could take inside, so they could always get the news, and afterward they would sit and solve all the problems of the world. They were three old friends who understood one another's minds;

they could disagree without displeasure, and it was pleasure enough just to be near one another.

In the morning they drove into the city and rolled around like all the other tourists. It was amazing the way the place grew; there were always new buildings and new projects. Lanny didn't go to the Treasury Building, or to the Pentagon, or to the State Department; this was a pleasure trip, and they went to the National Gallery and spent the day looking at great art. The basis of this display had been the Mellon collection, and Lanny, an ardent young radical, had greatly disliked that shrewd banker named Andy, who had dominated the financial affairs of the nation and helped to bring on the great panic of 1929. Less than nineteen years had passed since that time, but what a lot of history had happened, and how the world had changed! Hitler had changed it, then Roosevelt, and now Stalin was having his try.

One of those who bore the praise or blame for the collection had been the English art dealer Duveen, a fabulous personage whose art had been the hypnotizing of multimillionaires and persuading them that he was the world's supreme authority on "old masters." He had understood that the way to make art works valuable was to put high prices on them, and he had put prices in the hundreds of thousands, and the multimillionaires had been enraptured. He had made so much money that he had become an English lord. Hansi said that someday there might be a Lord Lanny, and they had a laugh over that.

Anyhow, there were the paintings, and many of them were really grand. To look at them one after another was to be transported through the ages; to have the pageant of history made real to you, the continuity of human life and of civilizations in their endless variety. It was to have the imagination stimulated and the understanding extended. It was to be taken out of your narrow self, to be freed from your petty cares, to visit past ages and strange climes, and to be impressed with the infinite mystery of being.

Lanny, who for a quarter of a century had been earning his living as an art expert, knew these painters and their life stories and the ages in which they had lived. He knew the costumes they had worn and the homes in which they had been housed and the rulers or prelates who had patronized them and supplied them with their subjects. He could point out how the painter had balanced his design, how he had harmonized his colors, and the technique of his brush strokes—also where modern work had been done on his masterpiece. They found all this so fascinating that they decided to spend another night in the auto court and another day in the National Gallery.

III

Then the great bridge across the Potomac, and they were on their way southward through Virginia, past some of the battlefields of the Civil War. The effects of that war were still felt. It was still "the Wilderness"; the fields were barren and the cabins unpainted. But they went past speedily, and the warm sunshine was a delight.

U. S. 1, the thousand-mile highway was called, and that at least showed no signs of dilapidation. You could make good time, and Lanny was a fast but careful driver. He watched the cars in front, and those behind in his little mirror. When one of those "bumper chasers" settled on behind him he would move a foot or two over to the right and slow up and let the lunatic go on by himself. He had a precious cargo—including Hansi's violin—and he took the best care of it.

They spent a night in Savannah and drove about admiring magnolias and live oaks bedecked like Christmas trees with Spanish moss. They went on to Florida and drove about in old St. Augustine, the most ancient of American towns, with horse-drawn hacks which might have come down from the time of the Negro slaves who had driven them.

Here in Florida American millionaires had sought for profitable and sometimes agreeable things to do with their money. One had built a railroad all the way down the East Coast, with a chain of luxury hotels. Now the motor highway paralleled the railway and the broad white-sand beaches. Along the way was the world's most elaborate aquarium, with all the creatures of the subtropical seas. You could look below the surface through plate-glass windows and imagine yourself swimming there; you could look from above and watch the huge dolphins jump out of the water to take fish from their keeper's hands.

They drove all the way down to Miami with its gambling palaces, which they did not patronize. They crossed by a highway to the west and went up Florida's west coast with its sponge and tarpon fisheries. It is a tremendous state and has become all America's playground, to say nothing of its winter-vegetable garden. In the flat interior lands it was raising great herds of cattle about which the tourists knew nothing. If you drove through its boundless pine forests at twilight you would see deer crossing the road and would have to watch out for them. The highway was hot, but they dressed accordingly, and the motion of the car provided a breeze; they found it delightful.

No one knew them or paid any attention to them, except to render the services for which they paid, and that was always done with courtesy. For Hansi it was wonderful; he had never been here before and could look at new scenes and discuss them with his friends and really forget the problems and horrors and griefs of his life. He was traveling incog, and since his name had to be entered in the registers of motels they had an amusing time discussing a suitable name. It had to be Jewish, of course, and they wanted it to sound as much so as possible. So he had become Mr. Moishe Zinsenheimer.

In the evenings he would shut himself up in his little cabin and play for dear life, for never must his fingers be allowed to lose their flexibility. The effect upon the neighborhood was electric. Americans were used to hearing such performances over the radio, but few of them had ever heard it "live," and somehow they had not actually realized that human fingers could perform such miracles of agility. They would come out of their cabins and stand near Hansi's cabin, listening. Sometimes they would stand through the whole performance and never make a sound and speak in whispers when it stopped.

They were people from all over the land, and invariably they were polite and respectful. They would ask Lanny and Laurel who this was, and always the answer would be that Mr. Moishe Zinsenheimer was a refugee from the Nazis in Rumania. "Is he famous?" they would ask, and the answer would be that he had been famous in Europe. These little fictions did not harm anybody; and of course it would have done no good to say that he was the notorious Red who was under indictment for espionage and stood to get ten or twenty years in a federal prison.

IV

St. Petersburg, Florida, was the city which boasted that the sun shone every day of the year, or almost; it was the place to which the old people of America who had saved up a little money came to die. In the meantime they went fishing, pitched horseshoes, and on Saturday nights had square dances. Hansi Robin had never caught a fish in his life, and he never did anything with his hands that he could possibly avoid doing; but it amused him greatly to let an old lady from Iowa teach him to dance the Virginia reel, and he went through the capers with spirit. He learned the meaning of "dosy-doe" and "sashay your partner." French words underwent a strange transmogrification when they traveled to Florida by way of Ioway.

Yes, it was fun. Hansi had played the peasant dances of all the countries of Europe, but this was the first time he had ever been on the receiving end. When the dance was over he went up to the country fiddler, who played with the instrument held to his chest, and said politely, "May I borrow your violin for a moment?" The man looked perplexed but handed over the violin and the bow. Hansi took his stance, struck three loud chords, and plunged into the playing of one of those frenzied Hungarian gypsy dances which he had made one of his specialties. The audience stood amazed; no one moved from the spot. Their eyes opened wide, and their mouths too, the better to take in the sounds, perhaps. And when the music ended with a wild flourish they broke into a storm of applause.

This was an American audience and no one shouted, "Bravo"; they shouted, "More" and, "Give us another." Hansi might have stopped the dancing and turned it into a concert, but he bowed once or twice politely, handed back the fiddle and the bow with a word of thanks, and literally fled from the place. Let them remember it the rest of their lives, and let it be a mystery to them! He had taken a chance, for somebody might have heard him play at a concert, and the story might get around and reach a newspaper.

V

They continued northward, trending toward the west, and came to a steel bridge with a sign on it reading "Suwannee River." They stopped the car and got out and walked on the bridge. So this was the stream made famous the world over by a song! The poet had misspelled the name, leaving out the *u*, and people looked it up in the gazetteers and encyclopedias and couldn't find it and drew the conclusion that the river was fictitious. But it was very real. It didn't in any way suggest "the old plantation"; on the contrary it suggested the jungles of the Congo. The water was dark, the river narrow and deep and overshadowed with thick, almost black trees. It had come two hundred miles from a swamp in Georgia, and they would have liked to get out and hire a power boat and be taken as far up it as they could go. But they remembered that it was the mosquito season, and they got into the car and went on, singing the song while Lanny drove.

The coast swung to the west, and the highway followed. They came to Pensacola but did not ask to inspect the great naval airbase— having with them a notorious Communist under indictment in New York. They came to Mobile, an old Southern city on a great bay, and they drove through streets lined by old houses with tall white pillars and double balconies, enclosed in gardens with walls covered by honeysuckle and trumpet vines. And presently it was the Mississippi Sound, a long shell road lined with stately old homes. They stopped in Biloxi, and in a Creole café they ate what was called a gumbo, a kind of fish chowder much like what Lanny had eaten in Marseille and known as bouillabaisse; it contained a variety of the edible creatures that swam in that sea, in addition to tomatoes, rice, okra, and peppers, and when you had eaten a large bowl of it you were through for the day.

They did not go on to New Orleans but westward to Baton Rouge. This was Louisiana, the stamping ground of Huey Long, who had promised to make every man a king and had made himself their emperor. He had built a political machine not so different from that of Hitler, but he had not gone to war. He had left himself an elaborate set of monuments in the shape of beautiful highways and steel bridges, everyone of them with his name on it. The tourists spent the night in a motor court outside the capital, and in the morning crossed the broad Mississippi on a ferry loaded with cars. They drove slowly up the Red River, full of mist, following its planless windings and turnings until they came to Texas.

Then they would drive four or five hundred miles straight westward with hardly a turn. First there were farms and then there were oilfields, black with derricks and crowded with traffic. After that were the endless grazing plains, hundreds of miles of them, with mesquite trees so big and so regular you could hardly persuade yourself it was not an orchard. But the only fruit was mistletoe—enough of it to have served for all the Christmas kissing of the ages.

It was monotonous driving, but Lanny never got tired of it. Hansi could sit in the back seat and compose his musical themes in his mind, and Laurel could read the stack of mail which she had got in Dallas. She telephoned every single day to make sure the precious little ones were getting all they needed; also to the office to make sure the speakers were keeping their engagements and everything going on schedule.

VI

So they came to El Paso, the Pass. They would have liked to have a glimpse of Mexico, but Wilbur Post had specified that Hansi was forbidden to leave United States territory. They crossed the Rio Grande where its course turned northward; the highway wound up through the pass, between mountains strangely white—not snow but rocks. From then it was all mountains, one range after another, with rocks piled in endless strange forms—towers, temples, fortresses, monuments; it was hard to believe that nature had made them. They were of every color you could name—red, yellow, black, green, gray, and blue or purple in the distance. It was desert country; the streams ran madly in the spring and dried up in summer. There was agriculture only where dams had been built and the water was tamed.

First New Mexico, then Arizona. The days were hot and the nights were cold, but the cabins in the motels were air-conditioned and every comfort had been provided for the tourists. A century ago the emigrant trains of covered wagons had toiled through these passes, hauled by horses and oxen, and many of the venturesome had perished of thirst or had been killed by the fiercest of Indians. Now there was an endless ribbon of smooth concrete, and every few miles a filling station where you could get not merely gasoline but cold soft drinks and candy bars. You could not drive for half an hour without coming upon a café with a quaint name or a hamburger stand labeled "Eats." It was migration made easy, and people had found out about it; there were thousands of cars that went westward and didn't come back. The population of California was growing at something like a quarter of a million a year.

Somewhere to the north in that wide state of New Mexico Budd-Erling had an airfield where it tested jet engines and planes; Lanny and Laurel had visited it twice during the war. Immediately after the war it had been closed down, but now it was starting up again. But the trio didn't visit it; you just couldn't take an indicted Red into such a place, and you couldn't explain that he wasn't what he was supposed to be. Not even to the president of the company could you explain it!

They went on across Arizona and down the valley of the dry Gila River to Yuma, the hottest place in the United States. They crossed the Colorado River and into a city where the temperature was something like a hundred and ten degrees. They got themselves an air-conditioned cabin and stayed in it until the sun went down, and then the steering wheel of the car was so hot that it burned Lanny's hands and he held a newspaper in between.

They made the trip through the California desert at night. Thousands of tons of dates were ripening in the great orchards, and there were miles and miles of melon vines which they could not see in the dark. It was the wonderful Coachella Valley. The highway ran almost straight for forty miles and then climbed up through a straight pass between mountains two miles high. Alongside the highway moved a line of freight cars that seemed to be half a mile long; two or three Diesel engines pulled it, and two more pushed it from behind, and up it went and up. Lanny could go faster, and they passed the whole line and came over the ridge, first into the cherry country and then down into the orange groves—a hundred miles or so of these.

VII

So they came to Hollywood, land of all the world's dreams, with almost as many stars as the Milky Way. Lanny and Laurel wanted to stay here for a while and meet some friends. But Hansi had friends here too and certainly couldn't go about without being recognized and getting into the newspapers. He said not to worry about him, he was perfectly comfortable in a little cabin and had some musical ideas that he wanted to get down on paper. He had been impressed by the landscape of America and by the people of the highway who had been so genial and courteous. He might someday shock the musical world by introducing a composition based on the folk tunes he had heard in Florida. Also, he had a couple of books to read, and he would get the news with the radio set; when he was hungry he would go to an obscure little grocery and buy what he needed.

The last time Lanny and Laurel had been here they had been seeing the world in a trailer and had parked it on the estate of their wealthy and fashionable friends, the De Lyle Armbrusters. These socially ambitious persons maintained a combination of salon and swimming pool for the Hollywood great, and so they were the front door to paradise. Lanny telephoned, and they exclaimed with delight and said to come right away. Lanny explained that they were taking a motor trip and had "no clothes"; but De Lyle said that didn't matter a bit, his affairs were never formal, and besides there was a new style known as "California casual." Men wore flannels and light blouses with huge tropical flowers on them, and no hats; presently they took off everything and put on trunks and lounged by the swimming pool and got tanned. "Come to lunch, come to dinner, come any time." Then De Lyle added, "Genie is calling, she says come right now. Rose Pippin is here, and you will be crazy about her."

Lanny said, "Okay," and of his wife he asked, "Who is Rose Pippin?" Since they had been busy saving the world from war they hadn't paid much attention to Hollywood doings. Lanny knew of pippin as a kind of apple and wondered if any parents who had that name could be so unkind as to name a child Rose. But Laurel said it was probably a stage name. Hollywood characters who came from Brooklyn chose for themselves names that were supposed to be glamorous. Maybe Rose Pippin thought she would be called "a pippin," and maybe she was.

The last time they had visited the Armbrusters, Laurel had been actively collecting material for stories and had made a bit of money out of her visit. She always hugged the idea that when she had completed the ending of wars she would go back to the writing game; and now the old impulse stirred in her blood. "Let's go," she said.

So they put on their most completely "casual" costumes—really expensive, of course—and went up Benedict Canyon Drive until they came to an Italian Renaissance villa of twenty or so rooms built on the side of a mountain. It was in just such villas on the hills above Cannes and in a place called Californie above Nice that Lanny had first met the Armbrusters, who were spending their money and acquiring culture by entertaining all the celebrities they could get hold of. Later they had realized that most of the celebrities were assembling in Hollywood, many of them driven there by the war. This was the only place left where genius could make "real" money, so the couple had brought their millions to Beverly Hills.

Genie, short for Eugenia, came out with both hands extended. "Oh, how perfectly ducky! Where in the world have you dropped from?" She kissed Laurel on both cheeks and hugged Lanny—she had known him since they were children, dancing together at parties.

She called them both "Darling"—she called everybody that, and so did everybody else. She bubbled over with delight and said they must come and stay at the villa and they would have such a lovely time "chewing the fat." Then she asked quickly, "Have you read *The Rabbit Race?*" When they looked blank she exclaimed, "Good heavens, haven't you even *heard* of it? Where have you been keeping yourselves?" She informed them that *The Rabbit Race* was the best-selling novel of the day. It had been selected by a book club, and besides that it had sold a quarter of a million copies. Hollywood had bought it for a hundred and fifty thousand dollars and was making it into the funniest movie ever heard of.

Genie, lowering her voice as if to conceal the fact of their ignorance, told them that Rose Pippin—that was her real name—had been born and raised on a ranch in a little place called La Mesa down near San Diego, and the family had lived, or almost failed to live, by raising rabbits. "You know how rabbits multiply," she said. "She has made the most hilarious fun out of the habits of rabbits, and, of course, all the neighbors and their habits too. Everyone has been laughing their heads off over it."

"Will her feelings be hurt because we haven't read it?" asked Laurel.

"Heavens, no! She will make jokes about you. She's the gayest thing you ever met, and the fact that she has made several fortunes hasn't spoiled her a bit."

VIII

So they went into Genie's large and sumptuous drawing room—the first time Lanny had been in it he had counted fifty Hollywood "personalities," or so he averred. At present there were only two persons in the room, one being De Lyle and the other a woman of thirty or so, rather tall, solidly built, obviously an outdoor person. When she gave you her hand you perceived that it was a hand of honest toil, and her feet were firmly planted on De Lyle's enormous Khotan rug with its "five blossoms" pattern. When you looked into her eyes you discovered their sparkle; the fun bubbled up in her like the water in the mudpots of the Coachella Valley. When she laughed at her own fun she shook like the little earthquakes of that same region.

She had grown up on a ranch on the outskirts of La Mesa and had never been anywhere else. A ranch in the Far West, as she explained in the book, could be anything from a couple of town lots to a couple of million acres. This had been a small family ranch and had been planted to alfalfa, which had to be cut by hand and fed to rabbits. When you had a thousand rabbits in pens it was absolutely incredible how much green stuff they would eat and how heavy it was for a small child to carry.

The phrase Genie had used, "the habits of rabbits," was one of the chapter titles of the book. The habits of rabbits, Rose explained, were three: first they nibbled, second they cohabited, and third they produced litters. After the multiplication of rabbits came the subtraction, when the buyer carried away the mature males. There was never any addition, and no division, said Rose, because when all the children of the family had been fed there was nothing left. "We were so poor," she said, "we lived on cornmeal and the milk from one cow, and we worried for months where the money was coming from for the taxes."

"Genie has been telling me about the wonderful life you two have been having," she said. "Me, I have never been outside of Southern California. So you see what an ignoramus I am. I had never even heard of your Peace Program."

"We hadn't heard of your book," said Laurel, "so we can be honest with each other."

"What a relief!" said Rose. "I am so tired of people who tell me they have read it, and I find out they haven't; or if they have read it they say the same things I've heard and heard."

"And," put in De Lyle, "she doesn't like Hollywood!" De Lyle himself adored the place and thrived in it; he had added a couple of inches to his waistline since Lanny and Laurel had last seen him. His round, rosy cheeks beamed satisfaction with the social success he was having. He possessed the private telephone number of practically everybody of importance in "the industry," and when he invited them to a party they came. The reason was they knew they would meet everybody else who was important. He was the steward of a country club that had no dues or charges of any sort.

"Why don't you like Hollywood, Miss Pippin?" inquired Laurel, pursuing her literary purpose.

"At home on the ranch I had the wild idea of writing a book. I wrote it with a stubby pencil on any old scraps of paper I could find. I wrote it exactly the way I wanted it, and I thought it was fun. Then, to my surprise, other people thought it was fun too. Now Hollywood has bought it and brought me up here and is paying me five thousand dollars a week to pretend to be a script writer. There are three other writers, all of them anxious to get something into the picture so as to justify their salaries. There is a director, a producer, a supervisor, a head of the production department—a whole hierarchy. They all sit in conferences and discuss every scene and every line of dialogue. Their test of whether a thing will go over is whether it has gone over before, and whether that was long enough ago for the public to have forgotten it. My book has only one virtue, that it is different; and the picture is going to have only one virtue, that it isn't different from anything."

"And aren't you enjoying Hollywood society?" It was still Laurel, hot on a trail.

"Enjoying it, Mrs. Budd? Enjoyment is for those who see the pictures, not for those who make them. What I'm going to do is to go home and write another book, this time about the habits of Hollywood, and it won't be so funny. Hollywood is a lot of people clinging to a raft in a storm, all trying to avoid being pulled off by somebody else; a lot of people worrying themselves sick about prestige and measuring it in money. I could tell you funny stories about Hollywood, but you are a writer too, and I have to save them for my book."

"And what are you going to do with all your money, Miss Pippin?"

"I'm tucking it away in my stocking, and I'm going back home and buy me a woman-size ranch, a tractor to drive, and a horse to ride, and maybe a couple of hired men that I'll manage."

"And a husband?"

"No, indeed. I've watched the rabbits too long!"

IX

They chatted for a while about Hollywood pictures and their costs and Hollywood personalities and their salaries. Rose told funny stories —it didn't mean a thing that she had said she wouldn't; the impulse to share them was compelling. Laurel must have liked her, for presently she asked, "Do you care for music, Miss Pippin?"

The answer was that the family had got a radio set, but the little brothers and sisters made too much noise. (There had been multiplication of Pippins as well as of rabbits, it appeared.) Then she added, "The first thing I did when I sold a story to a magazine was to go to San Diego to hear several concerts—the first really good music I ever heard."

Laurel said, "The reason I ask is that we have a friend with us, a very extraordinary violinist. He is a refugee from Rumania and hasn't yet been introduced in America, so you probably never heard his name— Moishe Zinsenheimer."

Rose said she hadn't heard it and was pleased when Laurel suggested that she might like to meet this man of genius. Laurel said, "To sit in the room and hear him play is quite an overwhelming experience," and the reply was, "Oh, don't let me miss it!" She gave Laurel her telephone number—a secret celebrities quickly learn to guard.

Driving home, Lanny said, "Well, what do you think of her?"

"She's a sensible woman and very good company, but I'm afraid she wouldn't appeal to Hansi."

"Why not?"

"She's not very feminine, and she's too positive."

"Bess was positive."

"Yes, indeed—and their marriage is breaking up."

"Hansi gets his head up into the clouds," Lanny said. "He needs a woman whose feet are firmly planted on the earth."

"Well, she can qualify in that respect. Did you notice the size of her feet?"

"I noticed she had on sensible shoes, the kind you advocate, so you oughtn't be too mean to her. A husband and wife ought to be different, otherwise the marriage adds nothing to either of them."

"Yes, but not too different," was the answer. "Anyhow, we'll let them meet and see."

They were taking a copy of *The Rabbit Race* along with them. It had been presented by De Lyle and autographed by the author. Most persons when they know they are to receive a visit from a celebrity are satisfied to get one copy of the new book and place it on the center table in the drawing room. But De Lyle's middle name was sumptuous, and his idea was to order a dozen copies from his bookseller and have them autographed and then distribute them to his friends; in that way the whole world would know that he had snared another lioness.

They read some of the book aloud that evening. Mr. Zinsenheimer—who was staying in another motel for security reasons—came over and listened. They had a good time, for it was really a humorous book. The habits of rabbits served merely as a theme song, a pretext for a study of the habits of humans. The determination of rabbits to perpetuate their race was entirely shared by humans and was equally alarming in both, for neither would have left any standing room upon the earth if they had had their way. Likewise the humans would eat all day if they could, and many of them did, with disastrous consequences. The book was a study of the misadventures of a large ranch family and its neighbors, their morals or the lack of them, their quirks, their delusions, their comical misadventures. The humor was earthy and explicit; that was perhaps why it had delighted Hollywood—and also why the picture would have to be different.

"I'll be glad to play for her," Hansi said. "But what a funny name. It's hard to believe that it's real."

"It would be funnier yet if you should marry her," said Lanny. "Mrs. Rose Pippin Robin—you would have to go and live in an orchard."

"Oh dear!" said Hansi. "Let me get rid of my old wife before you get me a new one. I'm trying so hard to get over my heartaches about Bess."

They phoned to the potential Mrs. Rose Pippin Robin and said they were not sure how long they would stay in Hollywood, so could she come in the morning? She said she had an engagement at the studio, but they didn't really need her, and anyhow they never got started until eleven. Could she come early in the morning? They settled upon nine o'clock.

X

It was an odd encounter, as odd as anything in *The Rabbit Race*.
Hansi had brought his fiddle and played for Lanny and Laurel a new
theme he had been elaborating. They were talking about it when
there came a tap on the door; they opened it, and there was Rose,
with her feet firmly planted upon the one concrete step before the
cabin. She came in, and Lanny, the host, said, "This is our friend, Mr.
Moishe Zinsenheimer."

Rose suddenly stopped and stared. "Oh, but—" she said, and hesi-
tated—"but I heard you play. I heard you in San Diego."

What could Hansi reply? He didn't know and just stood there.

"But," persisted the woman, "you are Hansi Robin!"

It was a truly embarrassing moment. Lanny, who had faced many
emergencies in his life, had the quickest wit. "Hansi Robin is his professional name," he said.

"Oh, I see!" was the reply, and then, "But—but I thought—I read
in the papers—"

"He has been released on bail," said the ever-ready Lanny. "We
have taken him away from it all."

"But"—she seemed to have a hard time thinking of any other word—
"why didn't you tell me, Mr. Budd?"

"I didn't suppose that that would have any special interest, Miss
Pippin."

"It just happens that it does, Mr. Budd. I have rather positive convictions on the subject of Communist spies. I have convictions on the
subject of all Communists and what they are doing to our country. I
don't tolerate them if I know it."

"I ought not have to tell you, Miss Pippin, that under our law a man
is not assumed to be guilty until he has been proved guilty."

"Am I to understand then that you think the FBI has had a man
arrested without having the evidence?"

"I don't want to prejudge the case, Miss Pippin, but I can assure
you that Mr. Zinsenheimer is an idealist and a man of high principles—"

"I know all those fine words, Mr. Budd. We hear them all the time
here. This place is full of Communists and Communist agents, and when
you find it out and say so you are called a redbaiter. I made up my
mind that I was going to speak out, and speak out clearly, whenever
the occasion arose. Let me make it plain, I'm not any sort of reactionary. I know poverty, I was brought up in it, and I've known all the

bitterness of defeat. I believe that social changes were needed and that many are still needed, and I am willing to work for them and help; but I want it done in the American way, by educating the people and by using the political remedies we have in our hands. I tell that to the world, and I'm telling it to you and Mr. Zinsenheimer."

It was a very good speech and was delivered not without eloquence. To Lanny it was one of the funniest situations he had encountered in a long time, and it was hard to keep himself from chuckling. He said, "Miss Pippin, do me the favor to sit down and let me tell you a little story. We spent a good part of last evening reading your book, so we know a lot about your life. I would like to tell you just one anecdote out of mine. Do please hear me."

She complied; but she sat on the edge of the chair, very stiff and straight, as if she were saying that she might get up at any moment and go.

Said Lanny, "When I was young I too objected to poverty, and I made speeches that shocked the wealthy friends of my mother and father. Then later I made the discovery that Adolf Hitler was preparing to seize Europe and that he stood a good chance of success. It happened that through a German friend I had met him, and I decided I would cultivate his acquaintance and learn all I could about his movement. I did so, and for years I was working as what you call a spy on Hitler and the other top Nazis—Göring, Goebbels, Hess, and so on. In order to carry on that dangerous task I had to make everybody in the world think that I had become a Nazi sympathizer; I didn't tell even my own mother or father the truth about myself. And one day in the home of one of our old friends, a baroness who lived near the Cap d'Antibes, I was expressing some of my sentiments to the effect that Hitler was the wave of the future, Europe's best guarantee of security, and so on. Among the company in that room was a woman writer of short stories, a rather small person, but she had a hot fire inside. She spoke up and told me what she thought of me; as the saying is, she took the top of my head off. I went away chuckling over it. Sometime later it happened that the lady found out the truth about me, and then we were married, and here she is. Don't you find that a suggestive story, Miss Pippin?"

She was staring at him hard. "Mr. Budd, if I understand you correctly, you are hinting that Mr. Robin—Mr. Zinsenheimer—is secretly helping our government."

Lanny said very gravely, "Miss Pippin, if by any possibility such a thing were true, it would be a breach of security for me even to hint at it. I am sure that if such a bit of information were to come to your knowledge you would understand that you might be doing grave harm to the government by mentioning it to anyone else."

"Yes, Mr. Budd, but—"

"Furthermore, you will understand that a man who possessed information damaging to the Reds and was prepared to appear in court and give testimony—such a man might be in real danger of his life. I could give you a list of persons who were working against the Reds and have been murdered, and not in any remote, half-civilized land but right here in the United States. They have been shot, or beaten to death, or thrown out of windows, or have just never been heard from again. So you can see that a man in that position might be advised to disappear and not show up until the time of the trial. I am sure that if you, as a loyal American, were to meet such a man and recognize him, you would not be so indiscreet as to go off and speak his name; especially not in a place like Hollywood, where there are so many newshounds hunting their prey. How does that seem to you, Miss Pippin?"

"The first thing I would say, Mr. Budd, is that such a man ought not to come to a place like Hollywood."

"It might happen that he was hiding in a place outside, but was tempted into Hollywood in order to meet a young lady whose book had interested him very much. It might be that the young lady had expressed a desire to hear him play the violin, and his impulses of kindness had got the better of his discretion."

"Mr. Budd," said the young lady, "I don't know you very well—"

"If you really want to know me, Miss Pippin, you might go somewhere to a short-wave radio set and hear our Peace Program tonight. My wife and I started that, and we have been directing it from the beginning. You would discover that we have not been taken in by the Communist or fellow-traveler idea of peace, which consists in sitting still while a boa constrictor prepares to swallow you. What we are calling for is a world order, with a court to which all nations will submit themselves. It will be a free world for all those nations who are willing to let other nations alone; and if there is any nation that sets out upon a course of aggression we will be ready to meet force with force. The way you spoke, I imagine that is according to your ideas."

"Yes, Mr. Budd; but I don't know Mr. Robin either—"

"That is even easier. The way to know Hansi Robin is to listen to his music. Since the age of five he has been working day and night to learn to express himself with a violin, and millions of people have learned to know him that way—people all over the world, in Russia, in Australia, in the Argentine. Now here he is, willing to play just for us three. Don't you think it would be nice to hear him?"

XI

So Hansi played. He had guessed that this ranch girl's taste would be simple and that the old favorites would be new to her. He played Raff's "Cavatina," which has a lovely melody on the G string, enabling Hansi to produce his most heart-warming tone. You can take it as a love song, or you can take it as a prayer; in the middle is a gentle disturbance, a clamor not unknown to either of these varieties of experience; and then the melody climbs to the top of the E string with piercing harmonic notes that are like the opening up of heaven:

> Sweet, sweet, sweet, O Pan!
> Piercing sweet by the river!
> The sun on the hills forgot to die,
> The lilies revived, and the dragon-fly
> Came back to dream on the river.

Hansi Robin did not indulge in any histrionics when he played music. He did not sway and swing to it or make himself into any sort of actor. He stood straight and stiff, closed his eyes, and hoped that you would close yours and have no sense except that of hearing.

When he finished nobody spoke a word. He waited a bit before playing the "Londonderry Air" in Albert Spalding's transcription. It is gentle and charming and consonant with country life; he was speaking directly to a country girl. And then Lanny said, "Now show us some of your tricks"; so Hansi launched into the finale of a Vieux-temps concerto. There was a composer who had set himself to exhaust the possibilities of the violin, everything that men had learned to do with it in the course of centuries of diligent experimenting. The music came faster and faster, madder and madder. It went leaping up a scale through half a dozen octaves and down again; there were double stoppings, triple stoppings, arpeggios and pizzicatos. It was like mounting on a wild horse and galloping over the prairie or over the mountaintops. The crazy creature bucked and kicked—it was a rodeo conducted on four strips of a cat's intestines. To be in a small room and watch it as well as hear it was a breath-taking experience.

And when Hansi finished, in a hailstorm of notes, you were breathless and expected that he would be breathless also. But he wasn't—only a little warm. He had been learning to do this since childhood, and it was second nature to him. His mind was a storehouse of millions of musical notes, and he never had the slightest trouble sorting them out; he never had a doubt which note came next or what precise movements of the fingers would produce it.

"Marvelous, marvelous!" exclaimed Rose Pippin, and Hansi replied, "The eye of one of your rabbits is more so."

The ranch girl was in no hurry to leave. She said that the studio didn't care a thing about her; they would have paid her to stay away and not bother them with her suggestions. She said that meeting new friends was far more important. Real friends were scarce, and every new one was an extension of your life. You learned new things and you shared new experiences. It was evident that that was the way she looked on Hansi Robin; she was completely fascinated by him. He was the whole of the old world to her; he was not merely music but all culture; he was dignity, and at the same time he was fame; he was not merely Paris and Berlin and New York, he was Palestine and the Old Testament. She plied him with questions and listened closely to his answers. Lanny wondered, Is she falling in love with him, or is she planning to put him into a book?

He could have found out by asking, because she was the frankest of creatures; she hadn't a particle of guile that he could discover. She said, "Look, you people are wonderful to me. I've met a lot of phonies here in Hollywood, people who are acting culture, acting elegance and glamour, and at the same time trying to cut one another's throats. Can you stand a critter just off the ranch with the soil still behind her ears?"

"Indeed we can," said Laurel promptly and added, "Rose."

"Oh, I know I'm a character, and I might be picturesque in a book; I've never been anywhere but La Mesa and San Diego, and I don't know anybody that's anybody. When I meet people like you I feel like I was being introduced to Beethoven."

"You'll get over that soon," said Laurel. "Remember, kind hearts are more than coronets—or even Hollywood Oscars."

"Couldn't we go and have lunch somewhere? I mean, as my guests. We could drive away off where nobody would recognize Mr. Robin."

"You must get used to calling him Zinsenheimer," said Laurel with a laugh. "It would have to be some very obscure place."

"Some dump if you like," said Rose. "Believe me, I've eaten in a lot of them and was glad to get a hamburger sandwich or a malted milk."

XII

Put that way the invitation was hard to refuse; so she took them in her car and drove them right fast out through Cahuenga Pass. Presently they took a side road leading toward the Mojave Desert, and on the way they found a little "dump" where they were sure that none of the Hollywood glamour people would condescend to stop. There was a table for four in the back corner, and they put Hansi in a seat with his back turned to the rest of the world. There they had ham and eggs and hot cakes with syrup. They were careful not to call one another by name, and when they talked about the evil state of the world none of the three world travelers said anything about possessing inside knowledge. Rose couldn't take her eyes off Hansi and didn't try.

Then they drove some more, and there was Hansi on the front seat with Rose, and Lanny and Laurel in the back seat, very much amused but keeping quiet and listening. Hansi never was much of a talker, but he had to talk now because Rose plied him with questions about everything that had ever happened to him and all the wonderful people he had ever known in the world. She wanted to hear about Rotterdam where he had been brought up, and about his music teachers and what they were like, and about his mother and his father and his dead brother Freddi; and then about Berlin, and the yacht trips to the Mediterranean; and about the Nazis and their cruelties, and how Johannes had lost his fortune and was making another small one in New York; about Paris and the Riviera, and London, and Moscow, and Sydney, and Buenos Aires, and other places where Hansi had made concert tours. One curious thing they noticed—not once did she ask about Bess, and not once did Hansi mention her. Rose must have known, for she had read the stories of the arrest and they had gone into detail about the wife.

All motor rides have to come to an end, and when this end was near Rose said, "I don't want to be a nuisance, but I hope we can see more of each other."

Laurel hastened to say, "Of course we can." Then with tact and kindness she asked, "May we give your telephone number to Hansi?"

"Oh, indeed you may!" was the reply. "And if you'll call up, Mr. Zinsenheimer, I'll be delighted to take you for a ride, anywhere you want to go. I promise not to take you where you might be recognized, and I won't breathe a word about you."

Hansi said, "I don't want to impose upon you—"

"Please don't look at it that way," she interrupted. "I'm just so sick of the motion-picture business I don't know what to do. I was making up my mind to run away to New York and see if the book business could be any better."

So that was the way they parted. She delivered Hansi to the motel where he was staying, and then she delivered Lanny and Laurel, and they made her happy by assuring her that they loved her and would be really truly friends from that time on.

"Well, there you are," said Lanny when they were alone. "There's Hansi's fate if he wants it."

"Oh," exclaimed the wife, "I came near to fainting when I heard you begin to tell the secret."

"What could I do? She had recognized him, and if we hadn't hushed her up she would have called Genie as soon as she got home, and the story would have been all over town in an hour. The reporters would come, and a lot of people would decide that he was a fugitive from justice and call the FBI."

"I think she's an honest person," ventured Laurel. "But I'm afraid she's making a mistake throwing herself at Hansi's head."

"I'm not so sure," replied the sapient husband. "There's an old saying, catch him on the rebound."

"Yes, but not before the rebound," said Laurel.

"We'll see," said Lanny, and this is what they saw. Next morning they called the office of Hansi's motel and asked for him. The clerk reported that he had left a message; he had gone for a drive. They went about their business of looking up several friends. In the evening the Armbrusters were having a party—which was their business. On the way to the party the Budds stopped off to see Hansi, and the report was that he hadn't got back, or if he had he had gone out again.

"He's telling her his whole story," said Lanny, "and it's a long one."

"God help us if she talks about it," said the wife.

"She talks an awful lot," added the husband.

"That's because she's nervous. She thinks he's the most wonderful man in the world, and she's trying to impress him. If she gets him she'll settle down and write a book about him."

XIII

The Budds went to the party and met a number of Hollywood celebrities, some of whom they had met on their previous visit. You were used to seeing these people enormously enlarged upon the magic screen; to meet them in a drawing room, walking around and chatting, was, as Rose had said, like "being introduced to Beethoven." Lanny and Laurel stayed late, and on the way home they drove by Hansi's motel and found his cabin dark. They had no way of knowing whether he was there or not; they did not knock.

Next morning they telephoned again and got the same reply: Mr. Zinsenheimer had left a message that he had gone for a drive. They were about to set out on their own affairs when Rose's car came into the court and stopped in front of their cabin. The couple came in, and after everybody had said "Hello" and "How are you?" Hansi, looking very solemn, announced, "I have asked Rose to marry me." Promptly Rose put in, "That's a fib—I asked him."

"Anyhow," persisted Hansi—it looked as if he were blushing a little— "we want to go and get married."

"Oh, fine!" said Lanny.

"Congratulations!" said Laurel; and then, always the first to face unpleasant realities, she added, "But you can't get married, Hansi, until you have divorced Bess."

"I know that. We're going to Reno. I have to establish residence there, and then I have to wait six weeks."

"We asked a lawyer about it," added Rose.

Lanny said, "Sit down." They had all been standing up. There were two chairs and a couch in the little living room, or whatever it was called. The engaged couple sat in the chairs and the already married couple on the couch. It seemed quite formal.

"Now listen, children," said Lanny. "You've consulted a lawyer. Did he tell you about the Mann Act?"

"No, what's that?" inquired Rose.

"It's something that all runaway couples have to know about. Don't blame me for it, because I didn't pass it—I think it was passed before I was born. Anyhow, it provides that any person who transports a woman across a state border for immoral purposes is committing a felony and is liable to ten or twenty years, I forget which, in a federal prison."

"Good God in heaven!" exclaimed the author of *The Rabbit Race*.

"It was intended to put an end to what was called white slavery, the transportation of women for work in brothels. Then presently it was discovered that the law was so worded that it could be applied to any extra-legal affairs. It became a device by which wives could get

revenge upon runaway husbands; also blackmailers discovered that it
could be used to force guilty husbands to pungle up a lot of money.
For that reason the law has been discredited, and I haven't read about
its being dug up for a long time. But you never can tell, it might be.
Tell me, how are you planning to get to Reno?"

"I am going to drive him," replied Rose.

"Well, you see, when you cross the border into Nevada, that is
interstate commerce, and brings you under the federal law. If you're
living together in Reno it might be perfectly possible for Bess to dig
up the evidence, and if she could prove an act of transportation she
could take it to the federal district attorney and could practically
force him to prosecute you. The law is the law, and it doesn't leave
him any discretion."

"This man act, does it apply only to a man?"

"It is called the Mann Act because that was the name of the congress-
man who proposed it. I never saw the text, but I suppose it reads 'any
person.' There are plenty of women procuresses."

"Yes, but it says transporting a woman, doesn't it? Can you transport
a man for immoral purposes?"

They couldn't help laughing over that; but it was a serious matter,
and Rose continued her cross-questioning. "I am driving my own car,
and Hansi doesn't know how to drive, so they certainly couldn't say
he was transporting me."

"I remember reading about cases in the newspapers," said Lanny.
"It was a long time ago, but I believe the evidence depended upon
money put up for the transportation."

"Money?" said Rose. "We can fix that. Hansi, how much money
have you got?"

It was evident who was going to manage this new family, at least
where the practical affairs of life were concerned. Hansi took out his
little coin purse. "Put it on the table there," commanded the wife-
to-be. "And have you got a billfold or something?" Hansi took out his
billfold. "Is that all the money you've got with you?"

"That's all."

"Leave them on the table. Now, in the presence of witnesses, he has
no money; he won't have a penny on this trip. If he wants a newspaper I'll buy it for him. I'll feed him, I'll rent the apartment for him—"

"He'll have to rent the apartment," said Lanny; "as a matter of legal
evidence the receipt will have to be in his name."

"All right then. I'll cash a check for him in Reno, and he can rent
the apartment. He's allowed to have money there, when there isn't

any interstate commerce, I suppose. The point is he's got no money on the way, and we can prove it. He's just a helpless piece of merchandise being transported. How's that?"

"It sounds all right," answered Lanny, "but you'd better consult that lawyer again before you start."

Hansi said very humbly, "Laurel, I hope you won't feel that I'm running out on you."

"Good heavens, no," she exclaimed. "We are happy for both of you." And she said to Rose, "Not every great man is a good man, but you have got both in one package." There is a jingle that runs, "She kissed her and made her a sister"; and so it was.

XIV

Somehow the fun had gone out of the journey for the Budds. They had been intending to go up and see the big redwoods, the coast sequoias; but now suddenly Laurel began to think about the bundle of letters she had received from home and the problems they had brought up. It was hard to get satisfactory speakers in summertime because so many went on vacation and didn't want to bother to come back; she and Lanny had to fill out. And there were the children; every day she was away from them they seemed more wonderful in her mind. Suddenly she exclaimed, "Lanny, let's go to Reno!"

"Oh, good!" cried the other couple; and it was no sooner proposed than they began to arrange it. Hansi and Rose already had their belongings in the car, ready for the trip. Now Hansi would go out to a telephone pay station and consult the lawyer and make sure that he could be transported as a bundle of merchandise. Laurel would telephone Genie and say good-by, and Lanny would load up their car.

They could travel by the interior route, east of the Sierras, but it was desert country and hot; to travel northward by the coast would be longer, but it was a delightful trip over a new highway. It wound along the sides of mountains and had taken a long time to build—not only because of the mountains but because the owners of great estates had fought the project with all the power they possessed. One of these owners was William Randolph Hearst, and Laurel and Lanny had visited his combination of palace, playground, and zoological park. Lanny asked, "Would you like to see him again?"

"That old reprobate!" Laurel said. "No!" She was a censorious lady; and oddly enough Hansi had got the same sort.

They bade farewell to Hollywood and its glamour and drove amid scenery that reminded Lanny of those Corniche roads familiar to him since his childhood. He led the way, and Rose followed. They had agreed to take their time and put safety first. For a hundred miles or so they drove along the sands of the Pacific and presently were on the shelves high up above it. All that time there were cool breezes blowing on them. When they came into the interior it was hot, and the peaches and prunes were ripening.

They did not go to San Francisco but around by the east shore of the bay to Oakland, and from there took the great highway up the valley of the Sacramento River and into the High Sierras, the gold country, made famous to all the world by Bret Harte and Mark Twain.

The road climbed through gutted pine forests, and presently they were over the ridge and rolling down through the Donner Pass. Here was a little mountain lake which had been the scene of a dreadful tragedy a century ago; an emigrant train of covered wagons had been caught by premature snows and blocked through the winter; half of the people had died of starvation, and the living had eaten the dead. Now it was nothing but a legend, and tourists rolling along on a ribbon of smooth concrete mentioned it casually as they passed.

They came to the Nevada line, and no one stopped them to ask if they were bent on any immoral purposes. Nevada was mountains and deserts, some of it irrigated. Soon they came to the place that was proud of being the wickedest little city in America, but they had no interest in its gambling palaces. They spent the night in an auto camp on the outskirts.

In the morning they parted. Laurel restored to Hansi his coin purse and billfold, so he could buy a newspaper once again. He had got the name of a lawyer who could be counted upon to charge him a liberal fee for getting him a divorce. Then he was going to find a furnished apartment—and he wouldn't be asked a word about his purposes. Half the persons who came here for six weeks brought along their future new partners, and it was good for the business of lawyers, landlords, and owners of restaurants and gambling palaces. How pleasant it is to have money, heigh-ho, how pleasant it is to have money!

BOOK SEVEN

Bright and Yellow, Hard and Cold

19

Root of All Evil

I

LANNY and Laurel continued rolling eastward over the ribbon of smooth concrete, through a land of red and yellow mountains and valleys shining with tame water in ditches. In that high western country when it gets hot it is really hot, but you do not mind because it is dry. The sun was dazzling, and dark glasses were a comfort. They drove fast on roads whose curves were easy and gradual, and presently they were in Wyoming, with vast high plains where cattle grazed, and you could see ten or twenty miles of the road ahead of you. It came down from the Rocky Mountains, and presently the state was Nebraska, where the descent was even more gradual. These were the plains over which the buffalo had roamed in vast herds—some of them stretching fifty miles in one direction and twenty-five in the other. Huge shaggy brutes they had been, the bulls weighing close to a ton, and so powerful that they were known to catch a horse on one horn and carry him for a hundred yards. Now they were all gone, and even the bones had been gathered up and taken to market.

The descent continued, but more slowly, and presently they were on the farmlands which had once been prairie. These extended for a thousand miles, and the highway ran through them with only a few turns. They could look at a thousand miles of farms, all pretty much alike but smaller as you came east. There were always a red barn and a silo and a white house with trees in front of it. It was the corn and hog country, and the corn was three or four feet high already, and when the weather was hot it would grow a foot in a night. There were villages and small towns with tree-shaded streets and white-painted houses. Many of them had a sign informing you that they had a spare bedroom for tourists. You paid your two or three dollars in advance and slept comfortably, and in the morning you could have breakfast if you wanted it, or you could just put your bags in the car and depart without a word.

It was the Middle West, one of the world's breadbaskets. Its perfect roads made a checkerboard pattern, and the rivers all had steel bridges over them. The farmers had their prices guaranteed and they liked that and voted the Democratic ticket, to the dismay of Republican newspapers and politicians. They had fed a world at war and now were feeding the nations that had lost as well as those that had won. It was a new and unexpected development in civilization: you had to feed them or they would go Communist. The Communists of both Europe and Asia were clamoring for power, and the free world was in a state of bewilderment.

A comfortable land, but monotonous. You wanted to get through it so you drove as fast as you could, but you had to slow up at crossings. The towns grew bigger, and presently there were cities with the usual traffic problems. Millions of new cars were being poured out from the assembly lines, and where were you going to park them, and how were you going to get by them? Speedways were being built to get people out of the cities, but they only made it easier for people to come in. Lanny and Laurel wanted to get home, but they wanted to get there alive, so they took two days to pass through the Middle West. They drove by day on the Pennsylvania Turnpike and got into New Jersey in the evening, reaching Edgemere so late that the children and the servants were asleep.

But what a time they had in the morning!- -early, of course, because the little ones wake up. They had to see the baby and marvel how she had grown and how many words she had learned. Junior had a perfect Niagara of them, and they had to tell him of their adventures, and hear his laments because he hadn't been taken along, and promise to take him next time. And then there was the mail, stacks of important letters to be read; there was the office and all the people to be greeted. There had to be conferences in which the state of the enterprise was reviewed and new plans were made. It was at least two days and two nights before they were back in harness again and everything was going as always. They hadn't told a soul they were taking Hansi Robin along, so now they didn't have to tell why they had left him behind or what had happened to him. Let the newspapers tell when they found out!

II

Among the letters was one from RIAS, thanking Lanny for the material he had sent and telling him about the new developments. "We

wish you could pay us another visit," they said. "You would be
pleased to see how fast we are growing, and we could use your help."
But Lanny had said no in his mind. He had all the work he could do
here, and he knew his work was worth while.

Then one day he was called to the telephone; it was Bernhardt
Monck in Berlin. The frugal German had never done that before, and
Lanny could be sure he was not doing it at his own expense. His voice,
sounding as clear as if he were in the room, said, "A very serious
situation has arisen in connection with old Ferdinand. You might be
able to handle it. I doubt if anyone else could. It is really urgent. Can
you possibly come?"

Lanny had never said no to Monck in his life. They had been
through so much together, and Lanny trusted him more than any other
man he knew—at any rate in secret affairs. He said, "I'll come if you
really need me."

"I wouldn't be calling otherwise," Monck said. "I will arrange Army
transportation for you."

"How soon?" Lanny asked.

"As soon as possible; tomorrow morning perhaps."

Lanny said, "I'll be ready." And that was that.

He went and told Laurel about it, and she clutched her heart and sat
down suddenly. "Oh, Lanny, how terrible! I hoped I was through with
these emergencies."

"We are in another war, dear," he said. "We can't go on advising
other people to face it and not be ready to face it ourselves. I'll take
good care of myself, and I don't think there is any danger."

"Danger?" she echoed. "I never draw a free breath while you are up
in the air."

He smiled and kissed her. "You oughtn't to tell me," he said. "You
have to do your share of keeping up morale." He told of the Spartan
matron who told her son to come back with his shield or on it.

"Old Ferdinand" of course meant Kurt Meissner; nobody else. Lanny
hadn't asked what the trouble was; he knew that if it had been something that could be said over the telephone Monck would have said it.
All Lanny could do was to turn his imagination loose on the Völkischerbund, and on *Treasure Island,* and on young Ferdinand and the
Soviets in East Germany. Or would it be the counterfeiting outfit
which had been moved to Hungary? They could hardly be expecting
Lanny to go there. What he looked forward to was another pleasant
trip to the Tegernsee in early summer weather.

III

He packed his bags; he signed a lot of letters and dictated some more and gave instructions to this person and that. Laurel put a smile upon her face and stored up her tears until after he had got into his car. Somebody in Washington must have got busy indeed, for late in the afternoon came a telephone call from a Pentagon official. "Mr. Budd, can you be at Idlewild Airport at nine tomorrow morning?" Lanny said he could, and the voice said, "Your tickets will be there. Be on time." Lanny promised.

He allowed himself plenty of time; a flat tire was always a possibility. Freddi Robin drove him, and on the way he talked about his Uncle Hansi, and how terrible it was, and what had become of him? Lanny, of course, could give no hint that he knew. He said that Uncle Hansi's communism might not last; it was Bess who had prodded him on, and most decent people who got into the Communist party got out again after a year or two. He said that the case would probably drag along for a considerable time; if the accused were convicted they would appeal and use all the legal tricks. If they were sent to prison they would be treated well, especially Hansi; federal prisons weren't so bad nowadays, and they probably would let him give concerts for the inmates.

When they reached the airport Lanny sent his young friend home and sat and read the morning paper. He had been at a hundred airports and the sights were familiar to him; he was more interested in reading about the mounting tension in Berlin. The Reds apparently were trying to make the Allies so uncomfortable that they would vacate the city. It was a policy of pinpricks, and it seemed rather childish, for the Kremlin should have known that the Allies would never get out without a war. The blow to the prestige of all three would have been unendurable.

Lanny would say that in his own mind—it was unendurable to him. But then he would begin to wonder, Would it be unendurable to the State Department and to a half-isolationist Senate? Lanny thought of all those farmers back in the corn and hog country through which he had just driven. What did it mean to them, the "prestige" of holding Berlin? They wanted their sons back on the farm; and all those "moms" who rented the bedrooms to tourists, they wanted their boys to mow the lawns in the summer and rake up the leaves in the fall.

The flight was the routine one, by way of Gander and Prestwick.

It was pleasant in mid-June. This was the land of the midnight sun—only most of it was sea. The plane was carrying Army personnel and stopped in Scotland only to refuel and then went on to Berlin. Lanny, who had been an assimilated colonel, first having to do with art works and then with atomic scientists, talked with interest to military men who were now seeing service in West Germany and in Greece and Turkey and Iran. Different indeed was their outlook from that of the corn and hog farmers and the "moms" of Nebraska and Iowa!

I V

This time Lanny was put up at one of the hotels the military had taken over. Monck came to his room. There was no chance of dictaphones or spies in this place, so they did not have to go for a walk.

The intelligence man reported, "There has been no word from either Fritz or Anna. The reason I have called on you has to do with Kurt Meissner. He made you a pledge that he would give up all anti-American activities. He has been breaking that pledge right along. The fact that he made it gives us a hold over him, and we mean to come down on him and come down hard."

"You're really sure he's been breaking it, Monck?"

"We know it positively. We have a man who has got into the Bund. Of course you mustn't say a word about that to anyone. The group is active, and they are men who will stop at nothing. It amounts to a conspiracy, and we cannot permit it to go on spreading."

"The passing of counterfeit is still going on?"

"The outfit has been moved to Hungary, and we have no certainty that Kurt is still connected with it. He has taken up a better-paying line of activity—treasure hunting."

"I guessed as much from your letter; I had read *Treasure Island* as a boy."

"I assumed that you would have. There is quite an extraordinary situation in the Alpine Redoubt, as the Nazis called it—one that will provide material for the writers of adventure stories for the rest of time, I imagine. You know how diligent the Nazis were in accumulating treasure. They confiscated everything the Jews had and everything their political opponents had, and when the Allied armies were advancing they loaded it into trucks, and whole treasure trains came up into the southeastern mountains. They buried it in caves and in salt mines—you were in the salt mines at Alt Aussee and saw it."

"I was more interested in the art works," Lanny said. "That was my business. But I looked into a few chests full of gold vessels and jewels. I remember one chest full of teeth that had gold fillings—you don't forget a sight like that."

"They knocked the gold teeth from the mouths of millions of Jews," said this man who had been working as a secret agent against the Nazis all through the war and before it. "They took off the finger rings and tore the earrings from the corpses before they threw them into the crematories. And when they saw that we were coming toward their Alpine Redoubt and realized they couldn't defend it, they took the chests full of treasure and sunk them in the lakes; they buried them in the crypts of churches, and in the forests, and even under the paving in public plazas. No one can state the amount, but I would wager there must be fifty million dollars' worth of treasure of one sort or another hidden in the Bavarian and Austrian Alps."

"Make it twice that," said Lanny. "Fifty million might go for Göring alone. He carried a whole trainload that we caught near Berchtesgaden."

"Well, now they are digging it up, a little here and a little there, and a lot of the top people and their wives are living in luxury on it. Kurt Meissner is in on it."

"I had the idea he would think it was a matter of honor not to use such wealth for his personal needs."

"You're mistaken. The way they figure it, they have to live, and if they're working for the cause they are entitled to a living. They dig it up and take it away, hidden in trucks; they get it to the ports and carry it to Spain or the Argentine, and invest it in great estates and business enterprises—there's been a lot of scandal about it and squabbling among the top people. They have accused some of their former chiefs as grafters, but the answer is, What is the use of letting the wealth lie idle? Why not put it to work and make money for the cause? They send back part of the income, and it's being used to print and circulate propaganda—the kind of stuff that Kurt Meissner is writing, and that they believe is inspired."

"I've heard we are getting a lot of the treasure ourselves," said Lanny, and his friend replied, "We get tips and send a party and find the stuff, or sometimes we find we are too late. There will be shots up in the hills at night, and we go and find a hole dug in the ground, and the digging tools lying about, and a lot of blood. They carry off the wounded and the dead, but they leave the tools because it wouldn't do to be caught with them. I suppose they tie weights to the bodies and dump them into the lakes."

"A nice line of activity you've picked out for me," said Lanny with a smile, not altogether of amusement. "No doubt the government can use the money, but I'd rather pay my share in the form of taxes."

"It's not just a question of the money," said Monck. "It's a question of the use the Nazis are putting it to. We'll have to get out of this country sooner or later and leave them behind; they have their plans to win over the new generation and prepare for a comeback. You know what the Germans are saying already, 'We had it better under Hitler.' "

"Yes," Lanny had to admit, "and they did, before he went to war."

"All the old gang are in on this thing, the wives and the families of the worst war criminals, those we hanged or have in prison now. The families of these men are enjoying themselves in Bavaria. When the income-tax collectors come along they have no explanation of the sources of their fortunes—just a smile and perhaps a bribe. The Strelitz family—you know that wholesale killer—is running an electrical business in Austria with branches all over. When we go to arrest such criminals we find they have been spirited away to Egypt or Morocco or Brazil or wherever, and we know that the money for the trip came from the sale of gold bars on the black market. There are regular operators who travel to Salzburg or Bregenz and buy up the stuff and smuggle it out by way of Italy. Sometimes we catch them with gold vases or pieces of jewelry which we can identify from photographs provided for us by the Rothschild family in Paris."

V

"Tell me about Kurt," said Lanny, and his friend went on with the strange tale of an episode that had occurred at Grundl Lake near Bad Aussee several months earlier. A convoy of trucks and cars had arrived there. The men hired boats and went out on the lake and began surveying operations. When they found the right spot they anchored the boats. They went down to the bottom of the lake in diving outfits and attached ropes and began hauling up heavy chests. When the local police asked about it they said they were engineers from the French headquarters in Innsbruck, and of course the local police, being Austrians and a conquered people, couldn't interfere with what French engineers were doing. They pulled up twelve large chests and loaded them on the trucks and went away.

"Investigation proved that there were no French engineers. It was a crowd of these Neo-Nazis, and we succeeded in tracing the trucks to the town of Tegernsee. We have an exact description of the man who was in charge of the expedition, and we believe that he was Heinrich Brinkmann, who was Kurt Meissner's top man. We have reason to believe that this is SS General Dollmann, one of the heads of Hitler's Youth Ideological Training program. We haven't a doubt that Kurt Meissner was in on that scheme, and he doubtless had to do with hiding the treasure. The money will be used for carrying on his propaganda here and abroad, and we are going to stop it if we can."

"You want me to try to get that out of him?"

"We hold over him the fact that his admission to West Germany was conditional, and he has broken his pledge; he knows he has broken it, and we don't have to tell how we know it. It is up to him to tell us where he got the money to build himself a cottage—"

"Oh, he's built a cottage?"

"A six-room stone cottage, fireproof and very comfortable, and he has a studio nearly finished. That money has come from the sale of counterfeit British pounds, or from some of the Nazi treasure. Either Kurt is going to come clean and tell us all he knows about these matters, or he is going back to the East zone of Germany where he came from."

"Will the Soviets take him?"

"We haven't a doubt that they will, and gladly. They have a part of Austria right close to Salzburg, and no doubt there is plenty of treasure buried there, and they'd like to get hold of it. They have ways of getting secrets out of people—ways that we are not allowed to use. You can point that out to him, and add that his wife and children will go along with him. The Soviets will take that brood and put them in their schools and make little Reds out of them instead of little Nazis. Personally, I don't see anything to choose between, but Kurt may, and that is one of the arguments you'll have to use."

"That's a pretty rough job, Monck."

"You don't have to be rough—that's not your line. The reason I'm asking you is because of the prestige you have with him."

"I doubt if I have the least bit left."

"You are mistaken, surely. However angry Kurt may be with you, he must respect you in his heart. He knows that you have a faith and are working for it. You believe in social justice, and so did he when he was young. Those things are never entirely erased from a man's mind. What you have to do is to make him realize that he cannot fool us any longer. He has to make a clean break, and publicly, with the Nazis; he has to come over to us, or he goes back to the Reds."

"He will choose to be a martyr, I'm sure."

"Maybe so; but there is the question of the children, and that may move him. Either they have to be brought up as free democratic Germans, or they will be little Stalinist monsters. Use your eloquence and try to make him realize it. You can put it up to him that we are doing him a favor because of his friendship with you. You can say that you pleaded for it—I think you would have done so if I had told you that we were about to order him and his family turned over to the Soviets."

"I suppose I would," Lanny admitted. "Do I understand that I am free to tell him what we know about his connection with the Völkischerbund?"

"Tell him everything—except, of course, about Fritz. Lay all the cards on the table. You can put it up to him that he has broken his word of honor and hasn't a moral leg to stand on. Knock him down and beat him up."

Lanny smiled a wry smile. "A man with only one good arm?" He knew, of course, that it was to be a moral and intellectual beating, and that can be more painful than a physical one.

VI

The Army flew its onetime assimilated colonel to Munich. When he had last been there it was half in ruins and many of its streets impassable with rubble; but now everything had been cleared away and the Germans were working diligently at rebuilding. The men Lanny met in AMG were nearly all new—those who had fought the war had gone home to their reward, and a new outfit was learning to know Germany and the Germans. "Fraternizing" was now the order of the day, and everybody was letting bygones be bygones—or at any rate pretending to. The genial South Germans were making their good beer again and selling it to the Americans for good marks.

Lanny would have liked to stay and meet some of his old friends. Some of their palaces and villas were intact, and they had got back their paintings—to live and stay rich in Nazi Germany you had had to make a gift of a painting to Hermann Göring's collection every now and then, and to do the same thing for Adolf Wagner, the lame Nazi boss of Bavaria.

The Army provided a car and a tank of gasoline, and Lanny set out on a drive of forty or fifty miles through the beautifully tended farming country, climbing gradually into the fir-clad foothills of the Alps. The road climbed to the Tegernsee, a lake about four miles long, a favorite summer resort with many hotels and villas. Because of the housing shortage throughout Germany people were living here all the year round; in summer they rented their homes and slept in barns and haylofts or put up tents.

Lanny drove first to the humble dwelling of the General Graf Stubendorf. He knew the high regard in which Kurt held this old-time patron, and he had a faint hope of enlisting this patron's aid. He found the old gentleman in plus-fours and a leather jacket, inspecting the early vegetables in his garden. They sat in the summerhouse, which had been constructed since Lanny's last visit, and there the visitor told the sad story of the plight into which a great musical genius had brought himself by his refusal to recognize a defeat in war. Lanny said, "I gather that you yourself have recognized it, and it was my hope that Kurt might be willing to take your advice."

The Graf shook his head. "No, Herr Budd," he answered, "I have made up my mind that the future belongs to the young and not to the old. Kurt Meissner must be close to fifty, and that is old enough for him to know his own mind and be responsible for his own choice."

"As events have shaped themselves," pleaded Lanny, "Kurt has to make a choice between a democratic Germany and a Red dictatorship. Surely there can be no question as to which he should choose."

Said the elderly aristocrat, "I am not at all sure that other choices are excluded. I understand the devotion you Americans feel to your doctrines of democracy, but I am not convinced that you are wise in trying to impose your system upon us Germans. We do not have two great oceans to protect us, nor do we live in a natural fortress like the Swiss; we live out on open plains where through the centuries hordes of wild horsemen have been able to gallop over us; and now come the steel horses, the tanks. Our only defense lies in our technical skill, our diligence, and above all our discipline and solidarity. Twice you Americans have felt it your duty to come and help the British and the French to wear us down and roll over us. Now you have us on your hands, and you have the task of keeping back the Eastern hordes. Before you get through, I believe that you will have a better understanding of our need for solidarity and discipline. Now, apparently, you think that we are as clay which you can mold to whatever shape you please. Your loyalty to your own institutions is perfectly natural and I respect it, but I am not convinced that you can make us over in your image."

"*Lieber Herr Graf,*" replied Lanny, "you pay us too great a compliment when you attribute the discovery and development of democracy to us. It seems to me it is a world-wide movement, an automatic consequence of the spread of education."

"Many believe that, I know. Education was spread in Germany, and the German people got the ballot and attempted to assert themselves. Surely you know that the Hitler movement was a democratic movement, originating in the lower classes of our society. The National Socialists carried an election, but somehow that failed to please you."

Lanny's answer was, "It is not according to our conception of democracy that a man should climb to power and then kick the ladder from under him. We are hoping that all the world has learned a lesson from the fate of the Third Reich and that the German people will establish a government by popular consent and keep their control over it."

"As long as I am permitted to stay here," answered the old man, "I will watch your experiment with interest; but you must not expect me to take part in it. It must suffice if I retire and refrain from doing anything to interfere with your efforts."

So that was that. They chatted a while about common friends and about the art works which the Graf owned and which he had rescued from Stubendorf; he had them in storage—he did not say where, merely that he did not wish to sell any of them. Then he told the visitor how to get to Kurt's place. "It would be a tragedy indeed if you had to take him away," said the Graf mildly. His tone said, "Don't expect me to discommode myself."

VII

They shook hands and Lanny took his departure and drove to the other side of the lake. There was a little valley, and on a slight rise of the land stood a new stone cottage of moderate size. The studio was off to one side in a clump of trees, and Lanny could see at a glance that it also was built of stone and duplicated the one the Graf had provided in Stubendorf for his court musician. Sounds of hammering came from it. Lanny observed that there was a good-sized garden behind the cottage and several children working there. Presumably school had closed, and few indeed were idling or playing in Germany now.

Lanny went to the cottage and knocked on the door, and the mother of the family answered. His reception was different from the last occasion. No doubt Kurt had told her that it was Lanny who had obtained permission for them to come to this place of peace and security; so the prematurely old woman was all smiles and gratitude.

She said that Kurt was at the studio, so Lanny walked over to it and found his old friend superintending a carpenter and two fair-haired lads who were helping. Lanny recognized these as Kurt's second and third sons, and after a brief greeting and a glance around at the work he took Kurt out to his car, where they could be alone and quiet.

It was not a social occasion, and Lanny stopped for no preliminaries. "I have bad news for you, Kurt," he said. "The American Army is going to send you back to East Germany."

"*Herr Gott!*" exclaimed the man. "What does that mean?"

"You know what it means, Kurt. You have been breaking your word to the government, doing it systematically and continually."

"Lanny, you must not say that!"

"Don't waste your breath, Kurt. The Army has been watching you, as it was their obvious duty to do. They know all about the business of selling counterfeit British pound notes that you and your friends have been carrying on. They know the names of your associates. I have been privileged to read some of the writings which you call *das Wort*. They know about your activity with hidden Nazi treasure and that you have been shipping it out to the underground abroad."

"Lanny, I swear to you—"

"Don't swear to falsehoods, Kurt, because it's just possible there may be a God, and He wouldn't like it. I know that you have your faith which you believe justifies what you're doing. I only point out to you how you make it impossible for me to help, and you make it necessary for the American Army to take action against you. You're bent on preserving the Hitler legend, you're helping to establish Nazi centers of propaganda in all the countries abroad. You're doing it after warning and with full knowledge of the consequences. I can only tell you that our Army authorities are not altogether fools and dupes. We've sacrificed a hundred thousand American lives and three or four hundred billion dollars of American treasure to destroy that Hitler dream, and we're not going to sit back quietly and give you shelter while you build it up again."

"Lanny, I can only assure you that I have nothing whatever to do with the Nazi centers abroad."

"Don't say any more, Kurt. I have examined the dossier dealing with your activities and your associates. I came to Berlin this time because RIAS wanted my help in broadcasting. It just happens that I have an intimate friend who is in the Intelligence service, and he told me confidentially of the status of your case. I begged for just time enough to come and see you—if my request hadn't been granted the Military Police would have been here now."

"Lanny, this is monstrous!"

"I think what you've been doing is monstrous, Kurt. You gave me your word of honor that you would do nothing contrary to American interests. I had no right to count upon your friendship, but I thought I had the right to count upon your honor."

There was nothing Kurt could answer to that, and he didn't try. "You can't send us back," he declared. "The Russians wouldn't take us."

"Don't count on that," advised the other. "All the Army need do is to tell them what you know, and the Reds will take you and get it out of you. They use methods we can't use."

"I'll die before I tell them anything, Lanny."

"I know; but you won't die until they're through with you, and they learned a lot of Hitler's own arts. But what you really ought to be thinking about is your children, who will be put in the Red training schools and turned into perfect little robots, worshiping portraits of Stalin as big as a house. You know what that training is, because Hitler took it over."

"What is the point, Lanny? Have you come here to gloat over me?"

"That is the last thing on earth that would cross my mind. I came because I still have in me the memory of our old friendship and the pledges we made to each other. I'm still clinging to the idea that I might be able to touch your deeper self and bring back to life the Kurt I used to know."

"If I have changed, Lanny, it is because I have learned what the world is like—how evil it is, and what harsh measures are necessary to control it."

"There's no use in our arguing about the National-Socialist movement, Kurt. I know what you think, and you know what I think. The point is, so far as your lifetime is concerned, National Socialism is dead. You have to take your choice between Stalin's measures, which are the harshest of all, and American measures, which are comparatively mild and lamblike. Do you want to go over to the Reds, or do you want to come over to the 'Amis'?"

VIII

Such was the proposition. There followed a long silence. Lanny knew that Kurt had a lot to think about and gave him time. It was a last call, and the Neo-Nazi must have realized it. Finally he asked, "Just what is it you propose for me to do?"

"The last time I made you a proposal it was that you would live in Western Germany and do nothing to oppose our effort to establish a democratic government here. Now the terms are harder: you are to go to AMG and tell it everything you know about the counterfeiting industry, the methods of marketing Himmler money, where the stocks are, and the plates and the presses."

"I can tell you right now, Lanny. It has all been moved to Hungary, and there is nothing left in Germany."

"All those quantities of British pound notes? And the paper stock?"

"Every scrap of it."

"And those we now find being circulated here?"

"They must be brought in by people I know nothing about. I have had nothing to do with it for some time."

"And the presses on which your Nazi 'Words' are printed?"

"My friends have carefully kept me from knowing anything about it."

"And the men who are running the enterprise here?"

"You've already told me that you know their names, Lanny. You've told me that you know everything."

"I mean everything in the sense that we know what you have been doing. I don't mean that we know all the names; and it doesn't mean that we know the location of all the Nazi-buried treasure your friends have been handling."

"You are seeking that treasure?"

"Of course we are seeking it. Part of it belongs to private individuals, and where we can identify it we return it to them. We have done it with a couple of hundred thousand works of art of various kinds. The gold and the coins and the jewels that cannot be identified belonged presumably to the Nazi government and are to be divided among the occupying governments. Wouldn't your government have sought such treasures if you had won the war?"

"And wouldn't you have tried to keep them hidden if you had lost the war?"

"Certainly, Kurt. But if you are defending the Nazi government you can go back where you came from—to East Germany. My proposition is that you come over to the American government. If you do that you tell us what you know. What became of those twelve cases that were recovered from the Grundlsee?"

"I assure you I know nothing about them."

"You only poison your chances when you go on telling me falsehoods, Kurt. We know that they were brought here to Tegernsee and that Heinrich Brinkmann had charge of the job. If you don't know where they are you can easily find out, and that is part of the price you have to pay. You have to help us find it, and you have to help us find other stuff that we are looking for."

"If I did that, Lanny, I wouldn't survive a week."

"If that's all that's worrying you, it's a simple proposition; the Army will keep you safe. You can be our prisoner, and we'll take the blame for having wrung it out of you."

IX

Again a long silence, and it was as if Lanny could look into the soul of his boyhood friend and see the duel going on between his pride and his concern for his family.

Lanny resumed, "You know my ideas, Kurt, and I know yours. I believe that Western civilization is superior to Stalin's. We are going to defend Western Germany and try to make it a democratic regime in which the Germans will govern their own country and determine how they want to live. If you consent to help us, really help us, all right; on the other hand, if you want to go over to Stalin you can do it. We won't torture you, and we won't brutalize your family; we'll just let you go where you belong. But, of course, once you've chosen you've settled it; you'll certainly never have another chance. What you must get out of your mind is the idea that you can settle down comfortably in our zone of Germany, build yourself a new home and a studio out of stolen funds, and set up a spy center and propaganda agency to work against us and help Stalin."

"You know I have no idea of helping Stalin," said Kurt in a low, bitter voice.

"You are older than I am and you are a highly educated man—you have one of the best brains I know. Therefore it must be assumed that you are capable of realizing the consequences of your actions. You know just as well as I that the only thing that keeps Stalin out of Western Germany today is the American Army, pitiful though it is. But it's enough to make Stalin realize that he'll have an atom bomb over the Kremlin if he moves against us. That's the basic fact of this hour, and it's because we're civilized people, because we are decent and don't torture prisoners to wring secrets out of them—because of that you're sitting here chatting with me on a basis of friendship instead of hanging by your thumbs in a dungeon. That's the situation, Kurt, and the one question is, Are you willing to help us keep Stalin out of West Germany or are you not? Are you going to reward our decency with lies and treachery, or are you going to give us the loyalty one civilized man has the right to expect from another?"

Lanny waited, and as Kurt did not answer he added, "That's all I have to say. I'm going away to visit a friend and I'll be back some time tomorrow for your answer. And don't think it will do you any good to run away to Italy, because we can certainly find you and arrest you on a criminal charge of profiting from the sale of counterfeit bills. You can't possibly take the remaining six children, so you'll know they're going back to East Germany."

"Don't worry," said the German coldly. "I'll not run away from them."

Lanny experienced one of those waves of feeling which interfered with his sense of duty. "I don't want to be hateful about this, Kurt," he said earnestly. "I came here to appeal to you in the name of friendship. I want you to be a Western man. That is where you belong, and all our old-time memories are calling to you."

"Let's not be sentimental about it," was the reply. "This is a harsh decision I have to make." He got out of the car and said, "I'll have an answer when you come back." Then he stalked away.

20

In Flagrante Delicto

I

LANNY drove to the outlet of the lake and followed the course of the little River Mangfall; he turned eastward, meaning to pay a visit to the Obersalzberg. Hilde von Donnerstein was a good source of gossip, and—who could say?—she might have heard rumors about buried treasure. Also, she had promised to keep a lookout for worthwhile paintings. In return, he had got some groceries from the PX in Munich; he would never eat a meal with Germans without taking something along, for they were all living close to the margin.

He came to her like a breeze blowing from the gardens of Grasse, so she told him; that was where they made the perfumes. He had been visiting the places where she had been happy in the past, Berlin and Paris, London and New York, even Hollywood! He could tell her news of her old friends who had forgotten her and never wrote to her any more. She was living here like a peasant—in the wintertime like an Eskimo, she told him.

But now it was summer, and they could sit in the sunshine, looking out across a valley to the ruins of Hitler's Berghof, where only four years ago he had summoned his counselors and planned the future of his thousand-year Reich. Now he had died and been burned to ashes, leaving only a bad smell behind. But over there a little farther to the east was another set of fanatics and plunderers, the Soviets in their part of Austria, and they showed not the slightest trace of any intention to get out. What did Lanny think? Did they mean war? Were they going to take the rest of Berlin, as everybody said?

Lanny couldn't tell her, alas. He said he didn't think they wanted war, but they wanted a lot of things they surely couldn't get without war, and it was a question of how badly they wanted them. The decision lay with a little group in the Kremlin, and he had no connections there.

But he had been to Bienvenu and could tell about the friends on the Riviera—about Beauty's gray hair with a bluish tinge, and about Marceline's new baby, and the gout of Sophie, Baroness de la Tourette. He could tell about London and Irma's devices for not paying income taxes. He could tell about Paris and the strike he had seen and the Rembrandt he had bought. He could tell about Edgemere and the Peace Program—he was still sending her the little paper. He could tell about Genie and De Lyle and the marvelous fashionable life they were living. All their elegance had been transported to Hollywood. Hilde said, "Poor old Europe is a mortuary."

Lanny brought in his groceries, and they had a feast. Then they listened to the news over Radio Munich. Presently there was a recording of the "Tales of the Vienna Woods," and they became inspired and waltzed in that large, almost bare drawing room, with Hilde's invalid sister looking on and laughing with delight. Lanny didn't ask, but guessed the bareness of the room was due to the fact that they had sold off furniture to get money for food, or perhaps to pay taxes.

II

There were elegant villas scattered on these mountain slopes, and in the morning Lanny went to look at some paintings. He made notes about them and the prices asked; then in the afternoon he set out on his melancholy errand to the Tegernsee.

He parked his car a short distance from the house, and Kurt came out. He was abrupt and businesslike. "I have decided that it is necessary for me to yield to *force majeure*. I will agree to abandon all connections with the Neo-Nazi movement from this day forth, and I will keep the agreement."

"You understand, Kurt, you made that agreement once and broke it. This time you will be on probation. You will have the deportation sentence hanging over you, and if at any time you break the agreement there will be no more parleying and no preliminaries."

"I understand that."

Lanny continued, "You must realize that I have no authority to make an agreement with you; I am not an official of AMG. I am simply a friend who begged permission to come and put the situation before you. I was told the requirements: that you would come over to our side and give the government all the information you possess about the activities of your movement. AMG will be the judge as to whether you have done that in good faith."

"I understand," said Kurt. "I am ready to start talking now and tell you what I'm able to."

Lanny had brought along a notebook, without much hope of using it. Now he took it out and with his fountain pen made notes while Kurt told about the treasures that had been buried in the Alt Aussee district. They had been put under the care of SS Generals Stefan Fröhlich and Arthur Scheidler. Ernst Kaltenbrunner, chief of the SS, who later was convicted at the Nürnberg trials and hanged, had delivered gold bullion, coins, banknotes, and jewels to a value of over ten million dollars. The total amount of the hoards collected and buried amounted to somewhere between forty and fifty million. On the second of May in 1945 the so-called "gold transport Strelitz" had arrived at Alt Aussee, including twenty-two cases of gold teeth collected by the chief of the death camps. There were the cash boxes of Nazi secret agents in several of the Balkan states, and there was a "special action fund" handled by Otto Skorzeny, the man who had been charged with the task of delivering Mussolini from his captors. There were also great quantities of narcotics, worth more than their weight in gold.

What had become of all these treasures? They had been dug up in small lots and transported by Nazis escaping into the Tyrol, and from there into Switzerland, and from Switzerland by air to points in the Middle East. That route had been used by Strelitz, and also by those high Nazi officials who had been in charge of the wholesale killings of Jews. These men were now serving on the staff of the Grand Mufti of Jerusalem, who was living in the Villa Aïda in Cairo.

Other fugitives had gone by the way of the Brenner Pass to Milan; they had had cars with diplomatic license plates, and these the Austrian police could not check. Most of them had joined a group known as the "Black Hunter," which had its headquarters in Madrid. This group was under the control of a countess, the former secretary of the German Embassy in Madrid. Lanny said, "I met her there." Otto Skorzeny was prominent in this group, and a relative of Himmler had belonged to it for a time but had gone to the Argentine and set himself up in business.

This Madrid group was the strongest propaganda agency, and Kurt named a number of its members: a Frenchman, Jean André, who had formerly been a volunteer officer in the Waffen SS; also the Belgian Nazi, Leon Degrelle. It was from there that the great mass of propaganda went out all over Europe and South America.

"I know," said Lanny. "I have seen the leaflet containing the letter that General Alfred Jodl wrote to his wife from the Nürnberg prison before he was hanged."

III

Kurt went on to tell about underground cells that were operating in various parts of Germany and Austria and the code names they used; but he did not name any of those men and said he did not know them. Lanny asked, "Where is Walter Scheider?" When Kurt said he did not know, Lanny said, "He is reported to be hiding somewhere near Munich, and it seems rather likely that you would know."

Kurt replied, "I don't"; and when Lanny asked about Eugen Dollmann, and then about Emil Herzig, Kurt declared that he didn't know about these either. So Lanny declared, "All this is very interesting, and if I were getting up a story for a magazine I might be glad to have it; but when you offer it to our CIC you are just being childish. You name the groups abroad and the men who are in them; all these men are safe from our clutches, and you know it. Our Intelligence people in Madrid and Buenos Aires probably know ten times as much about all this as you do. Even I know that Otto Skorzeny has taken the name of Steinberger and is living in Madrid as a darling of fashionable society. But when it comes to the groups who are operating

right here in Bavaria you don't know *who* they are, and when I name
the head men you don't know *where* they are. And yet you have been
actively directing one of these groups!"

"That is not correct, Lanny. I have been doing some writing for it.
I have been what you might call its intellectual head, but I've had
nothing to do with its practical affairs."

"When you have written what you have to say, what do you do
with it?"

"I used to turn it over to a man named Johann Josef Schultz, but
he took alarm a month or two ago; he departed, and I don't know
where he has gone."

"And you don't know where any of the treasure is buried?"

"I really do not. I am told that it has nearly all been taken out of
the country."

"Including the twelve chests Brinkmann took out of the Grundlsee
and brought here to Tegernsee?"

"If he did that, Lanny, he did it without telling me."

"Kurt, as you know, we had a terrible civil war in America, and
when that war was lost by the South there were many proud South-
erners who wouldn't give up. They called themselves 'unreconstructed
rebels,' and they went on plotting and scheming; but their efforts came
to nothing, and today we have peace in our country; the states that
rebelled are back in the Union, and the old struggle is just an occasion
for reunions and picnics. It will be so in the new democratic Germany,
I hope, and I came here with the idea of making one last effort to get
you to see that and join us in bringing real peace to the country. I
see that I have failed, and there is nothing for me to do but go back
and inform the Army. You have always patronized me, Kurt, and
taken an attitude of superiority; I didn't object because I knew you
were older and I thought you were wiser. But now I don't think so
any more. I think you are very foolish. I am sorry for you but I can't
help you, so I now give up and promise never to trouble you again."

IV

That was a plain enough invitation for Kurt to get out of the car,
but he didn't. He sat there, frowning and silent. Lanny waited.

"I have told you that I really want to quit," said this unreconstructed Nazi. "I said it and I mean it—I have to. I cannot give you
the names of other men because it would cost me my life. That is a

small matter, but it would leave my children disgraced and helpless. Your offer to protect me means nothing, because your people are slack and mine are active and determined."

"Our people are not so slack as to take that proposition from you, Kurt. If you have no more to offer the deal is off."

"One thing more I can offer—that is, money. I gather that is what your AMG wants most."

"My AMG is spending several hundred million dollars to feed the German people. If it were possible for any part of this to be covered by Nazi-stolen treasure I don't think any reasonable person could call us mercenary. Certainly I don't think any Nazi could set up such a claim."

"What amount of money do you suppose AMG would consider a proper ransom for me?"

"Ransom is an offensive word, Kurt. You have not been kidnaped. You came here as a refugee under false pretenses and under conditions you never intended to keep. We're not Nazis and we're not Reds. We're not proposing to imprison you, or torture you, but merely to send you back where you came from."

"All right, Lanny, let us not dispute about words. Have you an idea what amount of money surrendered would cause AMG to continue to let me reside in this home I have built, on the condition that I withdraw from all political affairs and devote myself to my music?"

"You would publicly announce your withdrawal?"

"I would announce it both publicly and privately, and I would agree to let your Army shoot me if I did not keep the agreement."

"I cannot answer the question, Kurt, because I do not know the Army and have no authority to speak for it. I am only a messenger boy. If you care to make an offer I will take it to those who have authority."

"All right, I will make the offer. I'll turn over to your Army something between six and eight million dollars' worth of gold bullion."

"And whose gold is this?"

"It belongs to the Neo-Nazi movement. It is 'outlaw treasure,' as you would call it. It has been turned over to me to keep, and I'm honor-bound to do so. But it appears that there are traitors in our movement and that I have been betrayed by at least one person."

"I don't know all the details, Kurt, but I am quite sure you have been betrayed by several persons."

"Our movement is shot through with betrayal, and I can no longer refuse to recognize the fact. People whom we trusted—whom we *had* to trust—have taken millions of dollars to Spain and Brazil and the Argentine, to Egypt and Morocco and I know not how many other places. They are living lives of luxury and refusing to contribute a single pfennig to the cause that lifted them out of the gutter. I have been ordered to hold this treasure, and sooner or later I will be told to give it up to somebody, and that person may take it abroad and do what the others have done. I have spent the night pacing the floor, asking myself if it is my duty to sacrifice my surviving children in the interest of such persons. I might also think of my art, but I have no assurance that I will ever again be able to compose anything worth while."

He stopped, and Lanny said, "You might give yourself a chance, Kurt. Your present activities must take a great deal of your mental and emotional energy."

"I have been able to think of nothing else for a long time. I have now made up my mind. I will surrender this treasure; but it must be done in such a way that the world will think that the Army has made the discovery by its own cleverness."

"I am sure the Army will not object to that," said Lanny. Under other circumstances he would have said it with a smile, but now he was in no mood for subtleties.

"Your Army will have to come and raid my place. They will have to arrest me for a while and hold me; that will be the only way to save my life. In the end they may release me with a statement that they have no evidence. You yourself, being clever, may provide them with some story as to how they came upon this treasure. It is what came in the chests from the Grundlsee, and since the Army already knows that Brinkmann is the man who brought it they can put the blame on him."

"That sounds easy," said Lanny. He was excited, as much so as when he had read *Treasure Island*. "But it may be the Army knows about it already."

Kurt replied dryly, "If they did they would be here instead of sending you."

V

Kurt opened the door of the car. "Come," he said, and they walked together toward the house. They went to one side where there was a clump of bushes; they stood behind it, attracting no attention. "You see that cottage," said Kurt. "It has six rooms and is well built. It has a good concrete foundation, walls of hollow tile, and a slate roof. It is fireproof—a permanent home for a family. The studio is the same. The property was purchased and the buildings were erected with the proceeds from the sale on the black market of those gold teeth which your propagandists delight to tell about. That might be a pretty good subject for a musical fantasy, a 'Totentanz,' or a 'Danse Macabre,' don't you think, Lanny?"

"Yes," said Lanny, his voice somewhat faint.

"I am not offering the house or the studio to your AMG," said Kurt. He always used the word "your," as if he were holding Lanny responsible for the American Army and all the evil it had done to Europe. "I need the house for my family and the studio for my art. I am showing it to you so that you can make it a part of the bargain with your AMG that they are to take care of the house and not wreck it."

"Why should they wish to wreck it?"

"I ask them to agree to bring along with them several competent masons. We have able ones in Germany, and this should be a simple matter. They will go to work on the foundations of the house and studio without doing injury to the buildings. These foundations are built in a very special way. There are portions made of strong concrete blocks that are necessary to the support of the house. These must not be disturbed. In between these, which you might call the real foundations, are interstices of several feet, and these are not necessary to the foundations and may be taken out. They have been covered with plaster, and this may be chipped off, but you must be careful not to chip the bricks. Also, you should guard them carefully; there are supposed to be twenty-one hundred and forty-seven, but, of course, some may have been stolen. They are all of solid gold, refined in the government mint in Munich. When your General Patton made his noisy approach they were put into metal chests and taken to the Grundlsee and dropped in. A buoy was put over them, and a surveyor made exact measurements of the location; then the buoy was removed. Recently, as you know, the chests were taken up and the gold was brought here. Some associates of mine knew that I was going to build a house and a studio, and they made me the proposition that the buildings should have foundations partly of gold. I have never counted the bricks or weighed them, but I was told they are worth somewhere between six and eight million dollars of your American money. AMG may have them, and I am only asking that they spare my life by keeping the secret."

"That certainly will be done, Kurt," his friend assured him in a properly solemn tone. Even the son of Budd-Erling had never handled a sum of money like that.

"I am a traitor to the Neo-Nazi movement," announced Kurt. "I have been a traitor to the memory of my Führer, to my art, and to my philosophy. I am a defeated and ruined man, and the only reason I consent to go on living is that I have a devoted wife and a brood of children whom it is my duty to care for. I hope to teach them to be wiser than their father."

There was a break in Kurt's voice as he said, "Now, go!" He turned and walked into the house, and the messenger of AMG made his way to the car, got in, and drove down the sloping road toward Munich.

VI

Lanny thought hard as he drove. In the town of Holzkirchen he got out and went hunting for a public telephone. The only one he could find was in a café, and there were a number of people in it. He would speak English, but that wouldn't help much, because most educated Germans understood it and had had plenty of practice during the occupation. Fortunately it was not the first time he had used doubletalk with Monck. He said, "I have been reading the motion-picture script by that fellow named Stevenson—you remember?"

"I remember," Monck said.

"It's a wonderful script. It has to do with a man named Old Ferdinand. He's in the hands of the pirates and he's afraid of them. There's an immense amount involved, and if they find out he's double-crossing them it may be his finish. He might lose his nerve and flee to some foreign country; the pirates are watching him and may have seen him talking to the enemy. It's a regular melodrama, the kind that used to be called 'ten, twenty, thirty' on Broadway—those were the prices of admission. The villains think they have everything in their hands, but the cavalry comes galloping up at the critical moment, waving the stars and stripes. It's the most promising script I've read in a long time."

"I get you," said Monck, who had been to New York.

"I'm taking it in to Munich. It ought to go into production without delay. Tell me the man I should take it to."

"Colonel Armstrong of CIC," said Monck. He wasn't in a café and there wasn't anyone listening at his end.

"Okay," replied Lanny. "Will you telephone him and tell him I'm coming? Tell him I'm a first-rate judge of motion-picture scripts."

"I'll tell him," said Monck. "Congratulations."

VII

Lanny hung up and walked out, leaving the café patrons to make what they could of that one-sided conversation. It wouldn't be the first time that Hollywood had come to Germany, but it was probably the first time for the little town of Holzkirchen.

It took only about half an hour to drive into the city, and it didn't take many minutes for Lanny to find the headquarters of Colonel Armstrong. While he was parking his car he was pleased to see two jeeploads of GIs with battle equipment draw up in front of the place and settle down to wait.

So Lanny went in and told the colonel his story. It wasn't as strange to an Intelligence officer as it had seemed to an art expert; the colonel said it wasn't the first time the Neo-Nazis had had the bright idea of using gold bricks in the foundations of buildings. Gold being unaffected by the weather, it would always be there—unless someone gave the secret away, as in this case.

"Are you sure it isn't a hoax?" asked the officer, and Lanny said he was fairly sure; he knew Kurt Meissner and didn't believe he would make a successful actor.

The point was that Kurt had important secrets he might be induced to part with if properly handled. He was really a great man and must be treated with courtesy; it was to be a "protective arrest," but it must be made to look like a real one to the outside world—otherwise Kurt wouldn't live long enough to get to the border of Italy or Switzerland. The GIs must stay and guard those two buildings overnight and be sure that members of the Völkischerbund didn't come with crowbars and pickaxes. Next day, presumably, the good German masons could be sent up and the digging out of the treasure could proceed. "Don't let them do any harm to the houses," said Lanny. "Kurt would never forgive that."

The sergeant who was to head the expedition was called in and given his orders. Then Lanny put in a call for Monck, meaning to tell him the full story from this safe telephone; he learned that Monck had already left the office for the Tempelhoferfeld to take a plane to Munich.

Many planes were flying between the two cities, and the flight took only an hour or so. By the time Lanny had gone out and got something to eat Monck had arrived, and there was a conference of half-a-dozen officers, in the course of which Lanny told them all he knew about Kurt Meissner. He was a proud citizen of a proud land and both had been humbled. He was to be treated as a distinguished guest, a great artist. "Call him 'maestro,' " said Lanny. "That is the honorable title for a musician in Europe."

VIII

The sergeant had been ordered to send the distinguished guest out at once; the trip was only an hour or two each way, so here he came. Lanny introduced the officers, and they shook hands with Kurt and offered him a cigarette. The Intelligence chief explained that they were grateful for his help and wished to make everything as agreeable to him as possible. Did he have any choice as to where he should be kept?

Kurt answered that it made no difference to him. If the Völkischer-bund got the idea that he had been responsible for the discovery of the gold they would find him sooner or later, and more probably sooner. Colonel Armstrong said AMG would take him to a villa near the city that had been taken over by the Army. It was set in a large garden; they would watch him, but the watch would be with its back turned, to keep his former friends away from him. The Army would make the announcement of the affair as realistic as possible. They would not press him with any more questions at present but give him time to make up his mind how far he was willing to go with them. He would write a note to his wife, assuring her that he was being well treated and that she was not to worry. Lanny undertook to send him some books and music scores he asked for. If there was anything else that Maestro Meissner wanted he would only have to mention it to his guard.

Lanny had something to say to Kurt privately. There was his brother Emil, the general. Lanny had seen him a year or so ago, and Emil was unhappy because of the attitude Kurt had taken toward him. Would it not be possible for Kurt to see him now? The prisoner thought it over and said, "All right." Lanny realized that it was the first step which had cost him so much, and the others would be easier.

Lanny explained the situation to Colonel Armstrong and said he would like to be flown to Nürnberg to bring the general back. If

Lanny had asked to be flown to the North Pole and back as a reward
for the coup he had pulled off the officer would no doubt have granted
the favor.

There were always planes flying to Nürnberg, and Lanny was taken
before dark that evening and spent the night at a hotel the Army had
taken over. The next morning he told Emil the story, in confidence
of course. Over the retired general's small radio set they listened to the
first account of the sensational episode that had occurred at the Tegernsee. The distinguished German pianist and composer had been
arrested at his home by the American military, charged with conspiracy to smuggle Nazi-owned gold out of the country. Nothing was
said about where the gold was—presumably that would come after the
good masons had done their work.

Emil said he would gladly see Kurt and do everything in his power
to keep him on the American side. Emil would get excused from his
school duties, and they would fly to Munich the next morning. Lanny
didn't offer to be present at the family reunion; he considered that his
work was done. He told Monck the story and left him to take matters
up with Kurt after Emil had got through with him. Lanny was flown
back to Berlin to keep his promises to RIAS.

IX

The new building of RIAS had just been opened, on the Kufstein-
erstrasse in the Schöneberg district of Berlin. The street made a wide
turn there, and the building followed it, so that it looked somewhat
like the entrance to a stadium. It was five stories high and had the
four letters R I A S mounted conspicuously on the front. It had been
a chemical factory and was all newly repaired and seemed magnificent
to a staff that had been operating from three small badly damaged
buildings. It was a symbol of the fact that the American people had
at last made up their mind to talk back to the rude makers of the cold
war.

Lanny Budd, alias Herr Fröhlich, was by now an experienced radio
man. He told his German audience that the American people were
ardently desirous of peace and had proved the fact by the disbanding
of their armies. But they would never give up their determination to
see a free, united, democratic Germany—and they meant the word
democratic in its true sense, not in the sense of elections with only
one ticket prescribed by a party dictatorship. America was proving
its good faith by taking steps to give democratic self-government to

West Germany; the Communists were proving their bad faith by proceeding to make East Germany into one more Red satellite.

Lanny was speaking at a critical time, when the people of West Germany, and particularly of Berlin, needed all the reassurance he could give them. Little by little, upon one pretext or another, the Soviets had been cutting off the roads leading through their zone to Berlin. They would suddenly decree that trucks needed a different kind of permit and would cause blockades extending back for miles and delaying traffic for days. Obviously they were trying to make the situation as uncomfortable for the Allies as possible, in the hope of wearing them out.

The agreement for the division of Berlin into four sectors had been made at the Potsdam Conference by the heads of the Big Four governments. It was the result of a compromise, and as usual both sides thought they had granted too much. The critics of President Truman at home used the Potsdam Agreement as a stick with which to beat him, overlooking the fact that the resultant difficulties were caused by the Soviets breaking the agreement—and how could President Truman have foreseen that? Was he supposed to assume that an ally to whom we had given eleven billion dollars' worth of aid was going to turn into our enemy the very day the war was won? How could he guess that the Politburo had already resolved upon that policy even before the winning?

Stalin had no critics in Russia, at least none who was ever heard or heard of. But his military people who had to administer the Potsdam Agreement found it highly inconvenient to have the American, French, and British occupation forces stationed in the middle of their new East German satellite and having access to it by highways, railroads, and canals. The agreement had provided for free access of all residents of Berlin to all portions of the city, and that meant continual misunderstanding and clashes. It meant that the people of East Berlin had the opportunity to see how much better the people of West Berlin were being treated. It meant that freedom and slavery were allowed to mix—something which they never in history have been able to do.

X

Now, at the end of June 1948, the Reds had apparently made up their minds to put an end to this annoying situation; they suddenly announced a land and water blockade of Berlin. The last railroad freight line, that by way of Helmstedt, was closed down—they said on account of technical difficulties, an entirely fraudulent statement. If the Soviets couldn't keep a railroad marshaling yard in order the Americans would have been glad to do it for them—but they were not asked.

Lanny Budd talked with officials, both military and civilian, about the curious Soviet practice of telling the most barefaced and obvious lies and maintaining them in spite of any facts offered in rebuttal. Was it an assertion of their ego, that truth was whatever they chose to make it? Was it a consequence of their denial of the existence of any moral law? Or was it just an expression of their contempt for their opponents? They would tell you a lie and then laugh in your face—not because they thought you believed it but because you were foolish enough not to understand that they were superior to both the truth and you. Because you were foolish enough to believe that there was actually any such thing as truth in the world! Because you were inferiors, doomed to early extinction, and it didn't matter in the least what you believed about anything! That was really the way they felt, and lying to you was part of the process of your extermination. They, the new master class, the future possessors and rulers of the world, yielded to nothing—not even the truth!

So now there were "technical difficulties," and freight trains couldn't be brought into Berlin. The two million people of the city would be slowly starved. They couldn't grow potatoes on their concrete pavements, nor on lots from which the rubble of bombed buildings had not yet been cleared away. A modern city has to have electric light and power, and in Berlin this was made with coal; in the days before the war this coal had been brought from Silesia and recently it was being brought from Belgium and the Ruhr, from England and even from America. Now there would be no more of it, and the factories of Berlin would stop working and the people of Berlin would sit in darkness at night. This would make the "Amis" unpopular with all West Germans, and soon the Allies would have to give up and get out.

There was much discussion among the "Amis" as to how to meet this problem. There were military men who were for accepting the gage thrown down; they would supply armed forces to convoy the trucks and freight trains, and announce to the Reds that these convoys were going through at any cost. In all probability the Reds would back down, as they had many times before when force was shown. But they might not back down, and that would mean war. If war came there could be no question but that the Allied troops in Berlin could be surrounded, cut off, and forced to surrender. They would put up a fight, and the city would be wrecked all over again, but in the end they would have to yield. The "moms" had had their way, and the boys had gone home "on points," and AMG could do very little to keep the Russian steamroller from rolling at least as far as the Pyrennees.

To be sure, we had the atom bomb, and we might destroy Moscow and Leningrad and the Soviet oil fields and installations; but in the meantime the Reds would be in Brussels, Amsterdam, Paris, and the other great factory cities and ports of the West—and would we atom-bomb those? No, the Reds would turn them into slave-labor camps; and what would be the process of liberating them?

Such were the questions being asked in the council chambers in Washington where the decision had to be made by the General Staff, the Cabinet, and ultimately the President. Two days after the blockade was begun the C-47s, the two-engine planes of the Army, began hauling supplies to the Tempelhoferfeld. It was announced that this "shuttle service" would be continued and increased. The Communists chuckled, because they were sure the Americans meant to feed and supply themselves and let the Berliners starve.

The Soviet military withdrew from the Allied Kommandatura in Berlin—the last of the Four Power arrangements. Marshal Sokolovsky refused to lift the blockade, and the city administration of Berlin began cutting down the electrical supply to two or three hours a day. Such was the beginning of a battle of industrial and propaganda power that would continue through the summer and the following winter and that for eleven months would be a dominating factor in all Lanny Budd's thinking.

He didn't wait that long. He figured that the events could just as well be watched from his home village in New Jersey, where the mail and the newspapers were delivered twice a day and where over the radio he could get the news once or twice every hour if he was that anxious. He finished his series of talks and then flew home by way of that northern route on which the sun never set at this time of the year.

21

In the Toils of Law

I

AT HOME Lanny found letters from Hansi and his wild Rose. The pair had not taken an apartment in Reno—this on account of the newspaper reporters. On the advice of their high-priced lawyer they had settled in a small mining town in the northern part of the state; it was high there and cool. The lawyer, familiar with the problem of well-to-do clients who wanted a divorce without publicity, gave them the name of a landlady who owned several apartments suitable for occupancy by fastidious persons. They could live there as Mr. and Mrs. Zinsenheimer, and when the six-week period was up Hansi could give this landlady his real name for the first time, and she would make out a receipt for the rent in that name. In this way there could be no publicity until the divorce suit was actually filed.·

So here was a victim, first of Hitlerism and then of Stalinism, starting a new life and really happy for the first time in many years. He loved this wonderful dry climate where the air was so clear that mountains twenty miles away appeared to be within walking distance. It was the wild and woolly West, and he was learning to ride a horse, something which had never in his life occurred to him as a possibility. Hansi played his music, and Rose never tired of listening. They read books and discussed them, they listened to the radio, including the Peace Program, and they had dinner in a little café where no one asked them any questions. They were agreed that they never again wanted to live in a big city, and perhaps not even to enter one.

To Edgemere, New Jersey, late one evening came a telephone call, and a familiar voice said, "This is Moishe." He hadn't expected to get Lanny and was glad to hear that he was safe at home. He said, "The devil has been lifted off my back. I don't have to testify."

"Glory, hallelujah!" exclaimed Lanny, and Hansi went on to explain that the authorities had decided they had a sufficiently good case and feared the possibility that a man testifying against his wife might awaken antagonism in some woman juror. Only in the event that the jury disagreed and a second trial was required would they call upon the husband. The case against him would be dismissed for lack of evidence. Lanny asked, "Is that satisfactory to the rabbit lady?" and her voice broke in, "I'm going to see to it that he breaks no more laws!"

The case was coming up soon; the lawyers for the accused had asked for an extension of time, and it had been granted; but when they asked for another extension the federal judge said no. The date was a week off, and Lanny telephoned Hansi to make sure he was informed. Hansi would have to make an appearance and be discharged before the bonding company could get the bail money back. Lanny warned, "Don't travel together; it's too risky." Hansi replied that they had talked it over and decided; he would come by train and Rose would drive the car.

II

Next morning Lanny received a telephone call from a lawyer in New York who gave his name as Everett and said he was counsel for Mrs. Bess Robin and wished to see her brother. Lanny gave his consent, and the man came to the Edgemere home.

There was a peculiar situation. When Hansi had departed for his runaway vacation he had left a note for Bess, saying that the publicity and excitement had been too much for him; that he was going away to hide and let no one know where he was. He would show up on the day of the trial. Then he had gone to his local post office and left an order that mail for him was to be forwarded to Edgemere. Lanny or his wife had been putting the letters into new envelopes and addressing them to Mr. Moishe Zinsenheimer in Nevada. Post offices are forbidden to give information about anybody's address; but criminal lawyers have a way of getting what they want, and now Mr. Everett came to ask where Lanny's brother-in-law was hiding.

Lanny didn't need anybody to tell him what this state of affairs would mean to the defendants and their attorneys. That Hansi should have gone to a known anti-Communist suggested that he had lost sympathy with the movement and might even be intending to turn state's witness. Lanny said promptly that it had been a regular practice for him to take care of Hansi's mail while Hansi was away. He said that Hansi had told him nothing of his plans except that he would be back for the trial. It was evident that the lawyer had not been informed that the government planned to drop the case against Hansi, and surely it wasn't Lanny's business to tell him.

A criminal lawyer acquires a view of human nature which makes it difficult for him to believe that anyone is telling the truth, and it was apparent that Mr. Everett had doubts as to Lanny's good faith. He said that for a man who stood charged with a grave crime to absent himself and not give his lawyers a chance to talk to him, or even be sure that they were his lawyers, was utterly preposterous. Lanny replied that Hansi was an artist, and artists were frequently preposterous. It was possible that he didn't care if he was convicted or not, that he wanted to be a martyr.

Mr. Everett replied that if he was going to be a martyr he ought to be a good martyr, and he needed a good lawyer to help him. Lanny could only shrug his shoulders and make a little gesture with his hands, after the manner of a man raised in France. He said he had been out of sympathy with Hansi for some time, because he despised the Communists and Hansi knew it. But he couldn't refuse Hansi's request to forward his mail and to keep the address confidential.

III

After the lawyer had gone Lanny talked the matter over with his wife and then called Wilbur Post at the FBI, asking if it would be safe for him to come to the office; presumably it was no longer haunted by newspaper reporters. Post said to come, and Lanny went and told him about Everett's visit. Post naturally was amused to hear about the troubles of "that friend of the oppressed," as he called him. It seldom happens that a man who is engaged in pursuing criminals has admiration for one who is engaged in protecting them.

Lanny said, "I have an idea. It seems to me a bright one, but of course it may not be."

"Shoot!" said the other, and Lanny went on, "You found it convenient to have a man among the Reds to tell you their plans. Has it occurred to you that it might be possible to have a man among the defense to tell you what their plans are? Everett is ready and eager to take Hansi into camp and give him a course of training, and it's possible he might tell him to say some things that aren't true."

"More than possible—probable!" declared the FBI man and added, "We certainly should give them the chance. I'll get hold of Frank Stuyvesant right away." That was the Assistant U. S. Attorney who was to prosecute the case.

Post said that if the prosecutor approved the program he would phone Hansi Robin to come by the first plane. Lanny thought it the part of wisdom to mention that Hansi was establishing residence in Nevada with the intention of obtaining a divorce and that the lady whom he intended to marry was there also. They would probably both come, and Post said promptly, "For God's sake, see that they travel separately and that the lady stays in a different hotel."

"I can do better than that," Lanny said. "The lady may stay in our home."

The official's reply was, "A friend in need is a friend indeed."

IV

When Hansi arrived he did not go to the FBI office but kept an appointment at a fashionable uptown club where Communists were not looked for. Lanny, who knew Hansi better than anyone else in the world, stepped into his car and drove to the place. Present also were Wilbur Post and Frank Stuyvesant, the latter an ex-basketball player from City College with a mind and a tongue as springy as his feet.

These two brought Hansi up to date on the case and told him what he was to do. He was to go to the office of Mr. Everett and present himself as ready for trial. He was to say that he had had a breakdown and felt he couldn't face the publicity; but he had gone away and lived quietly and got himself together and now was ready for the ordeal. The fact that he had had his mail forwarded by Lanny Budd meant nothing except that Lanny was an old friend and relative who had done the same service in the past.

Hansi would have to see Bess and convince her that he was still a loyal party member. The defense might continue to be suspicious of him and might reveal little to him; they might even tell him to get another lawyer, in which case he would announce that he would defend himself. They wouldn't like that and would try to dissuade him. Sooner or later he would learn something of their plans, and if and when he did he was to report. At that time he must make certain that he had shaken off all pursuers—even if he had to drive around in taxicabs for an hour or two or hurry through a crowded department store and out by another door. He was not to come near either the FBI office or that of the federal attorney; instead he was to go to a secret address which they gave him and telephone from there.

So Hansi went, and played his part carefully, and after some hesitations and difficulties he was taken into the conferences of those able high-priced lawyers, who, of course, were not Communists or even fellow travelers, but who believed ardently in civil liberties and in the right of every accused man to have a fair trial in court. In so believing and so doing they were upholding the high traditions of their honorable profession, and by a happy coincidence they were being paid high fees.

It is a painful but obvious fact that criminal lawyers are sometimes tempted to become criminals. Successful lawbreakers often have a lot of money, and if the lawyers they employ are unwilling to suborn witnesses and frame testimony the criminals will look for some other lawyer who will. So it had come about that in the great metropolis there were men who had the reputation for being willing to do such things and knowing how to do them, and this reputation and knowledge was worth millions of dollars to them. The underworld has a name for such attorneys—they are "mouthpieces."

So after a while Hansi Robin came to the secret address and reported that the Dane, Johanssen, who had been caught redhanded opening the safe, was going to admit his guilt. Bess, on the contrary, was going to deny that she had ever transported any film or documents to be photographed and that she had ever had anything to do with any form of espionage. She was going to explain her visits to the neighborhood of the Jones Electrical Works by saying that she had old friends there and had attended Saturday evening parties, and she was going to produce half-a-dozen witnesses who had been present at those parties; some of them she had picked up on her way and brought back to their homes, and some she had taken to her own home to spend the night.

And Hansi? He was instructed to say that he had driven with his wife on many of these expeditions. They had gone to social gatherings and never anywhere near the Jones Electrical Works for secret meetings with Johanssen, a man he had never heard of. They had been purely social gatherings with a number of friends, some of them comrades and some not. He was to be taken and shown the house where these parties had taken place so that he would be perfectly familiar with it.

The two government men found all this quite according to the rules of the game as it was played; they expected it and would know how to counter it. They told Hansi that he must go back to his home; no matter how repugnant it was, it was absolutely essential to convince Bess that he was standing by her and her cause. He might ex-

plain his absence by a nervous breakdown, a panic, anything he could
make plausible. He could say that he wasn't well enough to resume
their marital relations.

V

Lanny went home and reported to his wife. Rose Pippin had showed
up; she had driven across the continent as fast as the law would permit. Lanny and Laurel explained the strange situation to her, and she
didn't like it a bit, but there was nothing she could do about it. There
were a lot of things in the world that she didn't like, she admitted.
In order to keep her from brooding over the situation they put her
to work on the Peace Program; they introduced her to the staff, gave
her recent copies of the little paper to read, and set her to preparing
a program of her own. It wouldn't be her first radio appearance, because Hollywood had been exploiting her. But this would be the first
time she would be serious, and she meant it to be for keeps. No jokes
about the habits of rabbits!

The announcement appeared in the papers that the government was
intending to ask for the dismissal of the case against Hansi Robin on
the ground of insufficient evidence. Lanny waited to learn what was
going to happen after that, but nothing happened that he heard of.
He was afraid to phone Hansi and didn't want to force himself upon
either of the government officials. If they needed him they knew
where to reach him.

Lanny wasn't attending the trial. As brother of the principal de-
fendant he would attract attention, and the newspaper reporters would
besiege him for comment. He and Laurel would get the news over
the radio and from the newspapers twice a day. Rose was going; so
far as anybody knew she had nothing to do with the case, and there
wasn't any reason why she shouldn't satisfy her curiosity. She had
been to see her publishers, and they, of course, had grabbed her and
were proceeding to use her for publicity purposes. She was to have a
luncheon to which the prominent critics would be invited; she was to
have a literary tea party for the smaller fry. As soon as the publishers
learned that she meant to follow the boilerplate-papers case in court,
they got busy with the newspapers, and Rose found herself signing
a contract to report the case for one of the tabloids at five hundred
dollars a day as long as the trial lasted, or as long as Rose lasted.

So she had a perfect excuse to be present and had a seat right up in
front and a table on which to scribble notes. She could study the faces
of the four defendants: the poor little rich girl who had been born

with a gold spoon in her mouth and had spit it out; the Danish working man who had been embittered by being beaten in a strike; and the
couple who kept a stationery shop and had not been able to make
money as fast as they wanted to.

The time came when she interviewed Hansi Robin, and that was
one of the oddest comedy-dramas that Lanny and Laurel had ever
come upon. Rose wrote seriously, because Hansi was a great artist;
she said she knew because she had both heard him and watched him
in a concert hall in San Diego. She reported him now as repeating the
tricky Commie phrases about peace and brotherhood and civil liberties; but she believed that, unlike most of the Commies, he really
meant them. What had happened to him was that he was being led
by a mistaken sense of loyalty to his wife—and Rose wondered, Would
that loyalty still hold him in the event that the wife was given a long
term in a federal penitentiary? Lanny and Laurel commented upon
one especially amusing aspect of this case: that after the Nevada divorce was granted and Hansi and Rose were married, the readers of
newspapers would take it for granted that the "romance," as they
would call it, had been the consequence of this interview.

VI

The government proceeded to unfold its case, and Lanny's curiosity about it was gradually satisfied. The beginning was peculiar. Of
the two women servants in Bess's home one was a middle-aged woman,
who, while not a party member, sympathized with communism and
had been employed for that reason. She was loyal, but at home she
had a niece, a high-school girl, who disliked the strange people who
came to the aunt's home and talked politics all the time; she disliked
them especially because food had to be prepared for them, and she
had to wash the dishes when she wanted to go to a movie. The girl's
name was Lindy, and she was thinking her own thoughts. When her
aunt fell ill she took up the aunt's duties in the Robin home, and there
she heard arguments going on between husband and wife.

They were prominent, and in her eyes very wealthy people and
objects of intense curiosity. She listened through door cracks and behind curtains and remembered everything. Presently she heard the
husband warning the wife that the things she was doing would get
her into serious trouble with the government. The girl's curiosity was
thoroughly aroused. In her high-school class on current events she had
been assigned to write a paper on the Canadian case in which a prom-

inent atomic physicist had been accused and convicted of furnishing
data to a Soviet spy. The importance of this had been impressed upon
her, and here she found herself in the midst of such a case in actu-
ality. She took to opening Bess's handbag, taking out papers and carrying them off and copying their contents. In that way she got the name
of Dumbrowsky, the Russian, to whom the microfilm was being delivered. She listened to Bess's telephone conversations, all carefully
guarded but containing mysterious hints.

One thing she learned was that Bess was crossing on the ferry to
Long Island and going to a place called Jonesville. Knowing her own
ignorance, Lindy went to the woman librarian of the town and asked
about Jonesville and learned that it was the site of the Jones Electrical Works; that it was a carefully guarded place surrounded by a
high steel fence and reportedly doing secret government work. Little
by little she put things together and made up her mind that Bess was
lying to Hansi and that he didn't realize the seriousness of what she
was doing; she thought the proper thing to do was to warn him.
From the reading of a paper-backed detective story she had learned
how to prepare a communication without handwriting, by cutting
out letters from a newspaper or magazine and pasting them onto a
sheet. So she had composed the message "Bess is courier for Russ spy."
On the envelope she had cleverly written the letter n wrong, to make
it appear the work of a foreigner. She had mailed it in New York for
safety.

She waited several weeks but nothing happened that she knew of,
so she mailed a similar letter to Lanny Budd, whom she had seen in the
home and had heard over the radio. In her testimony in court she did
not mention this second letter; the FBI had taken up from the first.

They had put skilled agents on Bess's trail and also in Jonesville to
hunt up the Communists and watch for spy work going on. Having
permeated the Communist party, they had no trouble in getting the
names of members and sympathizers in the town and also in locating
a Russian Communist named Dumbrowsky in New York. One of the
first things they did was to have the Jones people take away from
their plant all documents concerning the proximity fuse that were
really important and put in their place a mass of others having to do
with their groping and abortive attempts. On this basis they let the
spying go on for a considerable time. They didn't tell this in court
because they wanted the Soviet authorities to go on working from
these false leads. Suffice it that they caught Johanssen in the act of
taking documents from the safe, and they had taken his fingerprints

from the safe on previous occasions; they arrested him in the act of
leaving the photograph studio, having in his possession microfilm of
material which had come from the Jones plant. Also, they investigated
the families and friends of the Hansibess servants and came upon
Lindy and quickly got acquainted with her.

VII

And then there was presented the evidence concerning Bess's automobile. It came out in court that the FBI had got impressions of the
tires of Bess's car; they had also found, by chemical analysis of the
earth in the tire treads, material which they had spread at the place
where Bess was accustomed to keep her rendezvous with Johanssen.
They had taken photographs and impressions of the markings in the
earth after Bess's car had left, so they didn't have to depend upon the
testimony of agents who had observed her car at the place.

More important yet was the fact that in their search of the car they
had found a single piece of microfilm, not much bigger than a postage
stamp, which had slipped down into the crevice between the seat and
the back. This material had not come from the Jones Electrical Works.
The government produced a leading physicist who testified that it was
a formula concerning the production of plutonium; and the FBI agents
testified that Bess had refused to say a word about how it had got
into her car. She just said it was a frame-up.

And then the boilerplate papers! That had been easy, because the
gardener was a Finn, and the Soviets had attacked Finland and seized
part of its territory. Another Finnish workingman had shown up in
the neighborhood and made friends with the gardener; he had pointed
out to him the fact that he was in the employ of a notorious Communist and that it might be worth while to keep his eyes open and see
what those people were doing. The gardener promised, and, coming
back from a week-end holiday, he noticed that somebody had been
digging under the seckel pear tree. You can take up sod and put it
back ever so carefully, but you cannot conceal the traces from a gardener. If you leave the earth in the cracks the earth will show, and
if you wash it out the hollows will show. The gardener had only to
take hold of the grass with his two hands and lift out the squares of sod.
He was sure that something had been buried there—possibly a dis-
membered human body. He had told his friend, and that was the news
which had brought the half-dozen FBI agents with court warrants to
search the house and grounds.

The government produced a list of the papers that had been found in that capacious washboiler. They were membership records of the Communist party, accounts of its receipts and expenditures. The government introduced samples of the papers as evidence, but it did not claim that any of the papers had anything to do with the spying. It was just evidence that Bess was a trusted party member.

VIII

Such was the government's case, and the public in general agreed that it was a good one. Nobody could imagine what the defense would be; but one of the highly paid mouthpieces told them at the next session of the court. This gentleman made a speech to the jury in which he informed them that this whole thing was a dastardly frame-up by the FBI. It was part of an effort to discredit the Communist party, which was a legal party and had the right to exist under our free and glorious American system. It was an effort to intimidate Americans who ventured to defend the rights of that party, and at the same time to awaken prejudice against a friendly foreign power, the Soviet Union, our gallant ally in the recent war against nazism and fascism. This conspiracy of the redbaiters would be exposed to the jury and ultimately to the American public.

The first witness for the defense was the accountant Johanssen. He admitted that he was guilty of stealing, but not of spying. A man whom he had never met before had come to him and said that he wanted the papers for the benefit of a rival corporation. He had offered Johanssen five hundred dollars, and Johanssen had got the papers. Subsequently the man had come again, and Johanssen had attempted to get more papers and had been caught. He said he had never had anything to do with Communists or with Russians in the Consulate; he had never met either Bess or Hansi Robin, had never even heard of them. He stuck to his story through the cross-examination. He couldn't describe the man very well because the man had come to him at night and they had talked while walking in the dark.

And then the two people of the photographing studio testified. That was their business, the way they earned their living, or part of it. It was their practice to do any developing work that was brought to them, and they had no interest whatever in what they handled; they looked at it only to see that it was clear and perfect work. In the case of microfilm, they magnified one page and examined it for flaws; that was all that was necessary, because it was all developed together. They saw that it was some kind of technical material, but it was far over their heads and they didn't try to understand it. They knew that the man who brought it to them and took it away again was a foreigner, but they didn't know he was a Russian, and it didn't make any difference to them. They were not Communists and had no interest in communism. And that was that.

IX

Bessie Budd Robin was saved until the last, she being a person of prestige, both musical and social. Her lawyers brought out the facts about her family, her upbringing, her education, her musical career; about her husband and where she had met and married him. They asked about her political ideas, her belief in civil liberties and true democracy, in social justice, in peace. She was there to make political speeches, as many as she was allowed to, and they were all upon this noble and exalted plane. The judge stopped her many times, but she went on trying. Above all things it must be got over to the jury that she was an idealist, a person who had sacrificed a great deal and was ready to sacrifice more for a cause in which she ardently believed. Was she a member of the Communist party? Yes, and proud of it, because peace and democracy were the things for which the party stood.

Then they got down to business. Had she ever done any spying for the Communist party? Absolutely never. Had she ever carried any stolen documents? Absolutely never. Had she ever engaged in any secret work? Never! Everything that she had done had been open and aboveboard; she had studied and thought and expressed her opinions about the course on which the country was being led, a course of aggression and ultimate war. So there came another Communist speech.

Had she ever handled any documents belonging to the Jones Electrical Works? She insisted that she had not. She said that her trips to Jonesville had been on party business and also on social pleasure. She had friends among the workers there, and they had had friendly gatherings on Saturday evenings and she had attended them. Had she ever got any documents of any sort in Jonesville? She had not. Had she ever driven on Second Street? She said she couldn't be sure because she didn't know the names of the streets; she only knew the way to her friend's house. She said she had never met Johanssen and never heard of him. She looked at him now and said she had never seen a man in any way resembling him until he had been brought into court with her. She gave the names of the friends she had visited and of several persons she had met there.

Then she was asked about the boilerplate papers. She said of course she had consented to their being buried in her garden. The Communist party was a legal political party and had a perfect right to have membership lists and records and accounts. The party was being slandered and persecuted, and it had a right to protect these papers from being seized and misused. That started Bess off on another speech and then another. It was rather hard to stop her—she was so much in earnest and so firmly convinced of her own rightness. She was dignified and ladylike about it, and no one could find any fault with her manner of speaking. She was looking at the jury all the time and trying to convince them of the fact that this was her form of religion—not the same as theirs but held with the same conviction.

And through the cross-examination she kept the same firm and serene manner. Mr. Stuyvesant didn't ask anything about her political ideas; he asked about that bit of microfilm that had been found in her car, and she answered that she hadn't even known what microfilm was and had never seen a bit of it in her life. Obviously if it had been found in her car it had been planted there by someone trying to get her into trouble. She said the same thing about the trace of chemicals which had been found on the tires of her car; it would obviously be very easy for her enemy to have fixed that up. She was not in the habit of making chemical analyses of the dirt in the streets over which she drove. As to the government agents who had traced her from these excursions and had seen her receive packages and carry them to New York, she said they were simply not telling the truth. She had driven from Jonesville to New York on party business; she often met friends of her cause in the city late at night.

She was questioned in great detail about the parties and the social affairs she had attended in Jonesville. She described the house and everything in it, the members of the Berger family who had entertained her and the guests who had been there. She said she had been there on a number of Saturday evenings because they were old friends and she enjoyed their company. Her husband did not go because he preferred to practice his art, at which he worked tirelessly.

Then came the witnesses to her story. The persons she had named told about their old-time friendship and their pride in knowing a great musical artist like Bessie Budd Robin. They described the entertainments they had given for her and the guests who had been present;

they were ready with the details, even of the conversations they remembered and the food they had eaten. Yes, they were Communists,
they all said, and were proud of it; it was no crime to be a Communist;
it meant that you believed in peace, social justice, and freedom of
speech—they all got in their little free speeches.

One by one these persons were cross-examined, and they stuck to
their stories. They told what they remembered, and when they were
asked if they remembered other things they usually said they didn't.
When they were asked if they had compared their stories they all said
they had been tremendously interested in the case and naturally had
talked about it among themselves. They were quite sure that Mrs.
Robin was innocent because they knew her so well and knew she was
a great idealist and teacher and no spy or secret agent.

X

So then it was time for rebuttal. About ten days had passed since
Post and Stuyvesant had got the tip as to what the defense was to be.
They had gone right to work on the proposition and they now produced the neighbors who lived on each side of the Berger family and
across the street. They testified that the Bergers were people who
went out frequently but very seldom had company at home and then
not more than two or three persons at a time. No such parties were
held as had been described; it was impossible that such a number of
cars could have been parked, or such a lot of piano playing done, or
such a number of persons assembled in the house without attracting
the attention and curiosity of the neighborhood. One such Saturday
evening party might have been forgotten, but a series of parties every
week end would certainly have changed everybody's ideas about the
Bergers, who were known to be Communists and distrusted by their
neighbors. One woman said, "If I had seen such parties I would have
reported them to the police." Such gatherings had taken place during
the last few days and it had been assumed that they had to do with the
coming trial.

Then came a government witness, a youngish woman who gave her
name as Mary Huggins, and the moment she stepped to the stand you
could see dismay in the faces of the Communist witnesses, and whisper-
ing went on among them and their lawyers. Mary Huggins testified
that she had been a Communist party member for three years and had
been in the service of the FBI all that time. She had been sent by the
party to interview Communists and sympathizers in Jonesville and to

put to them very tactfully and carefully the idea of their appearing and testifying to the effect that they had attended parties and met Bessie Budd at the Bergers'. She named those who had just testified as persons who had agreed to do so and who had been assembled at the Bergers and been taught from a written list of statements exactly what they were to say. They had all spent an hour or two together rehearsing these statements. Furthermore she named two persons whom she had approached and who had refused her request. When she was through the government put these two persons on the stand, and they testified how they had been approached by Mary Huggins and had turned down the request.

The defense lawyers tried their best to break down those three witnesses and to imply that they had been trained as part of the frame-up. All the Jonesville residents who had testified for the defense took the stand and denied that they had ever been approached by Mary Huggins or had ever seen her or heard of her. So it was a square issue of veracity, and great indeed was the excitement among the newspaper reporters—including Rose Pippin. All over town and indeed all over the country the issue was debated, and sums of money were wagered on the outcome. After twenty-four hours of discussion and after twice coming back and asking questions of the judge, the twelve good men and true women brought in a verdict of guilty against all four of the accused.

XI

Lanny got that news over the radio; he was in the room alone, and he sat motionless and let the tears run down his cheeks without any effort to wipe them away. It was one of the saddest moments of his life. His imagination swept back over the years; he was in his father's home in Newcastle, a smaller home then, meeting Bess for the first time. He was seventeen and she was nine. He seemed wonderful to her because he had lived in Europe and had seen so many sights and met with adventures thrilling to a child. She had been tall for her age, with thin features like her mother's, but differing from her mother in being eager and demonstrative. Lanny had no other sister at that time and the relationship was new and delightful to him. She asked questions about everything he had seen and experienced; she listened to him play the piano, and he was the cause of her own eager determination to learn to play well. He had taken her with him upon a visit to their great-uncle Eli Budd, a Congregational minister who went back to Emerson and Bronson Alcott, and who played a part in Lanny's future development by willing him his library.

It was perfectly true, as Robbie had said, that Lanny was in good part responsible for the development of Bess's thought. They had been utopian idealists, all three of them, dreaming about a world of equality and justice, and never for a moment imagining the violence and terror which would turn that dream into a nightmare. They had come to a fork in their ideological road, and those two roads would never meet again; it would not be belaboring a metaphor to say that they might curve gradually and meet head on—upon a battlefield.

Lanny got up and went to Laurel and told her what had happened. She was firmly prepared for it in her own mind and thought only of him. He had wiped his tears away, but she knew there were more inside. She put her arms around him and told him there was nothing he could do about it, and there was no emotion in the world more wasteful than grief. Bess had chosen a bed of martyrdom, and in her own Puritan way she would enjoy lying in it; her fanatical pride would sustain her. Anyhow, it would be a long time before she had to go to jail; those shrewd lawyers would use all the delaying tactics and would carry the case right up to the United States Supreme Court. It was all good propaganda, and the Communists had plenty of money for that. Meantime Bess would go on working for her cause; she would appear on public platforms, wearing her martyr's crown of thorns. Laurel had never known the young Bess as Lanny had, so she could not be blamed if there was a touch of acid in her comments.

They put their minds upon the problem of Hansi. His difficult task was done; he would no longer have to take orders from the FBI or from the United States Attorney for the New York district. But it put him in a rather awkward position regarding his wife. He had espoused her doctrines and had publicly painted himself a bright red. And now that she was a convicted felon was he going to desert her? Of course he could say that he had been an informer, and no doubt the FBI would back him up; but many people would find it hard to forgive him for having denounced his wife.

Lanny said he hoped that Hansi wouldn't take to brooding over that problem; and Laurel said, "Rubbish! He's been miserable with Bess for years, and now he's got a woman he can love. My guess is she'll take charge."

XII

Lanny considered it his duty to drive out at once to Newcastle and see his father and stepmother. He did not take Laurel along, because this was a family matter. They were proud people and would not wish to discuss their disgrace in the presence of an in-law.

Poor old Robbie! He would not say it now, but Lanny knew he had not given up his idea that his oldest son was responsible for this calamity; it was the son who had taught strange notions to the young Bess, notions the father had fought with all the energy he possessed. The distinction between revolutionary communism and truly democratic socialism was entirely metaphysical in Robbie's eyes; to him both doctrines threatened the American way of life—which meant his control of Budd-Erling Aircraft. He suspected that Socialists were merely Communists who thought it bad tactics to announce their true aims; if ever they got a chance they would revolt and seize the great plant and turn it over to the control of the labor union, which Robbie now had in his place and had to deal with politely but which in his secret heart he both hated and feared.

This much concession he would make; he would say, "I am old and tired and the future belongs to the young." There were his other two sons, Robert, Jr., and Percy, who had learned to run the plant, and he was gradually turning over authority to them. He observed that they got along amiably with the labor leaders, took them for granted, and didn't seem to be afraid of them. Robbie would shrug his heavy shoulders and say, "All right, all right, maybe there can be such a thing as industrial democracy; maybe they can work it out, even if it means squabbling and corruption. I judge by the politicians I have known."

Lanny would grin and say, "Yes, Robbie; you used to buy politicians, but now the price is getting too high."

They had been having arguments like that for just about thirty years. Lanny would point out that the workingman's sons had been to high school and the politician's sons had been to college and there was a new generation with different ideas; they couldn't all be boss and they couldn't be held down, but they could be reasoned with and programs could be worked out. Percy once told Lanny that one of the young labor men had said, "If only we could keep the old man out of it!" Lanny mentioned the fact that over in England he had met one of the young Tories who had spoken the very same words—meaning Winston Churchill.

They did not talk about such matters now. They talked about Bess, and the chances of an appeal, and would the Communists be able to raise the money. Lanny said, "Sure thing—and let them!" They talked about the sentence she was likely to get and could she stand it. Lanny said she wouldn't mind it too much; she was too certain of her own rightness. She would be conscious of her role and sure that she would be more useful in jail than out. "She has learned to find her happiness in hatred," he said—a hard saying to her parents.

Seeking to comfort his stepmother, Lanny pointed out that Bess was just one more of the stern old Puritans, clinging stubbornly to what her conscience told her and lacking only in sound judgment. How many, many Puritans had been like that! But driving home and thinking the matter over, he was more strict with himself. He told himself that he was being sentimental about his sister and that he had to put sympathy out of his mind. She had her own world. Sooner or later she would find some man who agreed with her ideas and so her personal problem would be solved. If she had to go to jail she would busy herself making converts among her fellow prisoners and changing them from individual to collective crime. Instead of breaking into houses they would break into nations; instead of stealing purses and jewelry they would steal a world.

XIII

Back in Edgemere the telephone rang, and Lanny heard a familiar voice, this time not disguised. "This is Moishe Zinsenheimer. We want to see you."

Lanny replied, "I am glad to hear the word 'we.' Will you drive out here?"

"Yes, but we don't want to come to the house. We'll meet you in front of the post office at Shepherdstown at six o'clock, and we'll go somewhere for dinner."

"Fine," said Lanny and repeated the message to Laurel.

"I told you that Rose would see to it," said she, who was so often right. "My guess is they're on their way to Nevada."

When the Budds reached the spot the Zinsenheimers were already there, and a single glance at their car told the story; the back seat was piled with belongings, and doubtless there were more in the trunk.

The runaway couple got into the Budd car and told their story. Hansi had been at home, waiting for the verdict, and Rose had phoned it to him. He had a note for Bess already written, telling her that he had tried his best to adjust himself to her way of life and had failed. He was going away and would not return. He had put that on her dressing table, together with a check for a thousand dollars. She had money, but he thought it proper for him to pay a share of the cost of closing up their domestic affairs.

He had packed his suitcases, piled his clothes and his music scores and other papers into boxes. He had called a taxicab and been driven into New York to meet Rose. She had dictated her last article to a stenographer, collected her fat check, which she said was now burning a hole in her handbag, and made certain that no newspaper reporters were trailing her.

Here they were, she said, footloose and fancy free as any pair of wild rabbits. They were setting out that night for Nevada, delaying only long enough to dine with their two best friends on earth. Rose said that Hansi had promised to wipe his memory free of everything in the past except musical notes. She added, "I have told him if I catch him brooding I'll break his fiddle over his noodle."

That was the robust way of looking at it, and Laurel hastened to back it up. She spoke first because she did not trust Lanny to be sufficiently emphatic. She said that Hansi had done everything in the world a man could do to restrain Bess from a course which was a peril to the entire free world. Laurel could testify to that, because she had been present at their arguments and had taken part in them. All three, Laurel, Lanny, and Hansi, had pleaded with Bess and used every argument they knew. Long before they had any idea of espionage they had tried to make it clear that Stalinism was a betrayal of socialism; really it was fascism using a more clever camouflage.

The deal that Stalin had made with Hitler in the late summer of 1939 had proved it, and Bess had almost been convinced. But of course when Hitler attacked Russia the face of the problem had changed and Russia had perforce become an ally; millions of Socialists and other liberals all over the world had decided that this ally must be trusted. Three years of cold war should have been enough to open their eyes; yet many of them chose to shut their eyes to the evidence, and surely they had no right to expect their friends to walk into the trap with them.

Lanny backed this up, and not merely because he knew that otherwise Laurel would have broken a fiddle over *his* noodle. He did it because his reason told him it was right, and it was Hansi's only chance at happiness. He was lucky to have such a chance; the breaking up of a marriage has wrecked the lives of many a man less sensitive than a musical genius.

XIV

They drove to a town where nobody knew them and had dinner, talking in the meantime in low tones about the extraordinary trial and the efficiency with which the government had gathered the evidence and presented it. Too bad they couldn't have started earlier, and before the atom-bomb secrets had been stolen. But during the war everybody from Franklin Roosevelt down had been deluded by Stalin's cunning— and that had included Lanny and Laurel as well as Hansi and Bess.

Rose explained that Hansi had telephoned the lawyer in Reno, instructing him to airmail a letter that had been prepared in advance, notifying Bess of Hansi's intention to file suit for divorce and to claim the custody of the two children. Her conviction for a felony had destroyed any claim she might have had. Hansi wasn't going to mention the conviction in his complaint, but of course the judge would know about it. It would suffice to allege that Bess was a member of the Communist party and that her activities were a source of humiliation and distress to her husband. Almost any grounds would do in Reno, for the prosperity of the town depended upon its reputation, and to have refused a divorce to a prominent person might have caused the loss of hundreds of other customers. If people wanted their freedom enough to be willing to travel two or three thousand miles to get it, they ought to get it with certainty and without delay.

For a fortnight more there would be Mr. and Mrs. Zinsenheimer in retirement; then there would be the Hansiroses instead of the Hansibesses. This humor was in Rose's style, and she proceeded to joke about the Laurelbudds and marvel that nobody had thought of that before. They all had another laugh when she stated that she had already ordered Hansi to shell out the contents of his coin purse and billfold; for it had been interstate commerce when she had brought him into New Jersey. Once more he wouldn't be able to buy a newspaper until they got into the state of Nevada. She was serious about it—she had been getting lessons on the subject of legal evidence, and she wanted two witnesses to the fact that she was transporting Hansi and paying the bills. She could afford to do it, having received eleven thousand dollars for her services during the twenty-two working days of the trial. "Easy come, easy go," she said but vowed it wasn't going to be that way much longer. She was going to buy a real ranch and put Hansi on it and put a fence around it to keep out both the Reds and the rabbits!

XV

The talk came back more than once to the problem of Bess. Both Hansi and Lanny were inclined to be sentimental about her, while the two women were firmly in opposition. They insisted that Bess had chosen her bed, and if it proved to be a bed of spikes that was her hard luck. Laurel said that her means had become the end and the means were evil; so she had become an evil woman, and they all had to harden their hearts in dealing with her.

Most important, of course, was the problem of those two boys. Laurel said to Hansi, "You have to make up your mind to just one thing: Do you want them to grow up into Communist conspirators? If you don't, you have to take a firm stand; you have to separate them from Bess. You'll have to tell them the truth about her, no matter how much it may hurt their feelings, or yours." And Rose supported this, though more tactfully. Of course she didn't want to have to raise two Communist stepsons or to have her life involved in such a problem. Hansi had promised that this was not to be.

And then there was question of the property settlement. Hansi had always been generous with Bess, and as a result she had money. They had gone on concert tours together and she had been his piano accompanist. There could be no question that he had been the drawing card, and from the business point of view she was entitled to only a small share of the proceeds. But since it had been a matter of love he had gone fifty-fifty with her.

Now he had the idea of giving her the house, and both Lanny and Laurel said this was preposterous. "What you have to ask yourself," declared Laurel, "is whether you want to contribute fifty thousand dollars to the Communist party's war chest. She will put the house on the market, and that is where the money will go. From her point of view that's inevitable; from the point of view of a fellow traveler it's very noble. If you feel under compulsion to be noble, give the house to the Peace Program, and let us sell it and use the money to expose the fraudulent nature of Communist peace talk."

They had a laugh over that, and then Hansi, the sentimental one, expressed the idea that Bess might not want either the house or alimony; she would spurn the idea of taking a renegade's money. Laurel replied, "Would she spurn it if the party ordered her to take it?" When Hansi said he hadn't thought of that, Laurel went on, "I have met some of their top intellectuals, and I assure you they don't lead ascetic lives. They live in penthouses and enjoy luxuries which in the old days in Russia were reserved for the grand dukes."

Lanny's sharp-tongued lady added one thing more. "Take my advice and keep Rose hidden until after the divorce has been granted. If there's one thing that would provoke her to fight, Rose would be it."

Lanny took little part in this discussion. He sat listening, and every sentence they spoke increased the ache in his heart. It was his sister they were talking about; and while Hansi had found another wife, Lanny could never have another sister to take the place of Bess. There was Marceline, but she lived a long way off and hadn't the intellectual qualities to bring her as close as Bess had been. It was part of himself he had to cut away and bury in the cold ground. He had to do it, because he had no answer to his wife's arguments.

BOOK EIGHT

Whom the Truth Makes Free

22

And Back Resounded, Death

I

IN JUNE and July the two major political parties held their presidential nominating conventions. To each of these quadrennial jamborees came more than two thousand delegates and alternates from places all over the country and as far away as Hawaii and Alaska. Twice as many newspaper reporters and photographers and radio men came, and so many spectators that the vast auditorium could hold but a small part of them. Standards bearing the names of states were set up on the floor, and the delegates were seated around them. Nominating orators invoked the American eagle and ego and the spirits of Washington and Lincoln; thunderous cheering echoed through the hall, bands crashed, and the heads of delegations seized the standards and began marching through the aisles. The popularity of a candidate was based upon whether the marching and the cheering continued for three minutes or thirty. The proceedings continued day and night, and during that time a million hotdogs would be eaten and several million soda-pop bottles emptied.

In this year of 1948 both conventions were held in Philadelphia. The Republicans met first and nominated Governor Dewey of New York; all the political fortunetellers were certain that he was destined to become the next President of the United States. The Republicans were in a glow of exultation, for Franklin Roosevelt was dead and his elegance and charm were a devastating memory—devastating to the Democrats, who had learned to live upon them and couldn't live without them.

What they had got in place of the Squire of Krum Elbow was a man who seemed small by comparison, and who looked like anybody you knew in any town of the Middle West. He didn't know how to stick a cigarette in a long holder and cock it in his mouth at a jaunty angle; he had no golden voice over the radio, but on the contrary a

Missouri twang with a slight rasp. He didn't know how to emphasize his points but had a tendency to finish every sentence in a sudden gallop. In short, he was just plain Harry Truman, an everyday American, and people who were kindhearted were sorry for him and people who were malicious found him a shining mark.

Two years ago the country had given him a reactionary Congress, and he had been fighting it with tongue and pen. The Eightieth Congress it was, and he said it was the worst of the lot. He was standing for the New Deal, inherited from his great predecessor, and this Congress had turned down one New Deal measure after another, and on several occasions had passed reactionary measures over the presidential veto. The American government was designed as a government of checks and balances, but the Founding Fathers could hardly have contemplated the cat-and-dog fight it was being turned into by all the agencies of publicity in the land. Now the Republicans were going to take over, and there was going to be harmony at last and the end to what they called the "drift into socialism."

The Democrats met, and they had to nominate Truman; they had nobody else, and it had been a long time since a President had been unable to force his own renomination. The machine politicians had so little enthusiasm for Harry that when he went out to Los Angeles to make a speech they couldn't find a hall for him—or maybe they didn't try very hard. When he was nominated the convention was so busy with its routine affairs that it kept him waiting for several hours before hearing his acceptance speech. He had to sit outside with three friends on a fire escape, waiting for a summons which did not come until two o'clock in the morning.

Everybody was bored and exhausted by then, but he gave them the surprise of their lives. He was full of fury against the combination of Republicans and reactionary Democrats from the South, and he leaped into them after the fashion of a wildcat. He made a fighting speech that took the convention by storm; everybody woke up, and there was a new birth of hope. The delegates went out with new determination, and later in the morning when the people read that speech the excitement spread throughout the land.

Such was the beginning of a political campaign that lasted for three months and a half, through hot summer and cool and pleasant autumn. Lanny and Laurel and their staff read about it and heard about it continually; they tried hard not to take part in it, at least not over the air or in the paper. Their program had to be nonpartisan; they had to confine themselves to one problem, which seemed enough for one small group—keeping peace in a world where an irresistible force called communism was meeting an immovable body called capitalism.

II

There came an airmail letter from Rose, telling them that Mr. and Mrs. Zinsenheimer were no more. The lawyer had insisted that they must live apart until the divorce was actually granted. It was a question of protecting the future of the two boys, for it was quite possible that Bess might hire detectives to watch Hansi. So they had rented separate apartments, quite expensive. Rose sat in hers all day and worked on her book about the movie industry; Hansi sat in his and fiddled and worked on a composition. The extent of their immorality was to have dinner together and go to a show. But it wasn't to be long; the six-week period would be up in a few days.

Lanny had no communication with Bess or her lawyers; he followed the case in the newspapers. The lawyers made their customary demand for a new trial, and the judge turned it down. The prisoners were brought up for sentence, and the judge read them a severe lecture, pointing out the gravity of the crime they had committed. He gave the accountant and the photographers eight years. He said that Bess's case was even more serious, because she was an educated person and had had an upbringing which should have saved her from going astray; on this account he gave her ten years and hoped it would be a lesson to other Communist "intellectuals"; if it had been wartime he could have sentenced them all to death.

The lawyers, of course, appealed the case, and the prisoners came out on bail—this time fifty thousand dollars. The lawyers pleaded that the sum was excessive, but the judge said no, for convicted Communists had established a reputation for disappearing. The lawyers appealed again, and the various front organizations of the Communist party proceeded to get out eloquent circulars denouncing the frame-up and requesting funds to carry on the expensive legal case. The money they would raise would be several times as much as needed, and the rest would go to party work.

In an afternoon paper Lanny read the news that Hansi Robin, violin concert artist, had filed suit in Reno for divorce from his wife, Bessie Budd Robin, recently convicted of espionage on behalf of Russia. After the fashion of newspapers, the details of the case were repeated, and would be repeated again every time either of the persons was named. When Lanny got home he learned that Rose had telephoned, saying that Bess had consented to the divorce and to be represented by the lawyer whom Hansi's lawyer had suggested. She consented to his receiving the custody of the children and would ask for no money.

So once more the conscientious Lanny had to revise his judgments and realize that he hadn't been accurate when he identified a Communist with a criminal. Bessie Remsen Budd was in truth what he had been calling her since long ago, a granddaughter of the Puritans. She was acting from what to her appeared to be the highest motives; she had convinced herself that the way to end poverty and war forever was for all the peoples of the earth to submit themselves to the dictatorship of the Politburo in the Kremlin. In exactly the same way Torquemada, chief of the Spanish Inquisition, had convinced himself that the way to save millions of souls from burning in the eternal fires of hell was to seize all teachers of heresy and torture them until they confessed and named their fellows, and then to hand all the lot over to the "secular arm," to be burned at the stake with a fire that was soon over.

III

The Reno divorce mill grinds promptly. Those who can afford to travel across a continent to get free from a marriage are important people accustomed to having their own way. Lanny and Laurel listened frequently to the radio these days, because they never knew but that a world war might be starting in Berlin; instead of that they learned that Hansi Robin had got his divorce. Later in the newspapers they read how the judge had questioned the violinist on the subject of the custody of his children. The judge was hesitant to grant such custody to a Communist; but Hansi explained that he had been persuaded by his wife that communism was an American movement, democratic and constitutional; when he had discovered that the party was engaged in espionage on behalf of a foreign government he had broken with her.

Already there had come a second call from the Hansiroses, both laughing and both trying to talk over the telephone at the same time. They had stepped around the corner to a justice of the peace and been married. The fee was five dollars, but Hansi had given the JP a twenty-dollar bill and told him to keep the change. Hansi was allowed to have money now and to transport Rose across state borders. They were heading for California and planning to spend the rest of the summer driving around, looking for the most beautiful ranch in the whole state. They said in chorus, "We are so happy!" Then, "Thank you, thank you!" to Lanny and Laurel, listening at the same telephone receiver.

Next morning all the papers had the story; and of course they didn't fail to put two and two together and surmise that the romance had started in the New York courtroom where Rose Pippin, author of *The Rabbit Race*, had reported the conviction of the former Mrs. Hansi Robin for espionage. "Romance" was the polite term the newspapers used for what Rose had called "the habits of rabbits." But Rose said she didn't care what they called it, or what they called her: she had the man she wanted and she had the certificate of ownership in the glove compartment of her car. They were going to stay away from New York for a while and let the excitement die down. Hansi wasn't going to undertake another tour until the public had had time to forget that he had been a member of the Communist party.

That same evening Lanny heard the voice of his half-sister on the telephone. "Lanny, I want to see you."

He had rather expected it and couldn't say no. He couldn't think of anything to do that would soften the series of blows which had rained down upon her; but if it would help her to talk about them, all right. "Where shall it be?" he asked.

"Will you come to New York?"

He answered, "If it's easier for you I can just as well come to your house as to drive down into the city traffic."

"It is no longer my house," she countered and could not keep the bitterness out of her tone. "I am getting out. But if you will come here I'll wait." She added, "I wish you would come alone."

He knew what that meant; Laurel was the enemy. He said, "I'll come alone."

He told Laurel about it, and she cautioned him, "Don't let her worm anything out of you about Rose; and don't waste your time getting emotional. Remember, you are part of the world she is trying to destroy."

"I can't help being sad about her," he replied. "I doubt if talking to her will make me any more so."

He drove the roundabout route, across the great bridge and over to the Connecticut shore of the Sound. He turned into the familiar garden, which forever after would be known to the neighborhood as the site of the boilerplate papers; he stopped in front of the villa which had been the scene of so many happy hours. Bess's car stood in front of the door, and he could see that it was loaded up with her belongings.

IV

She was waiting for him, and there were no tears; if she had shed any she had wiped away the traces. He noticed that she kept her hands tightly clenched while she talked to him, and several times he thought she was near to losing her self-control, but she didn't. She said, "I have been ordered out, and you can see I'm getting out. I'm in no position to contest it."

"Better so," he said quietly. "There has been publicity enough. Where are you going?"

"I have rented an apartment in the city." She gave him the street address and the telephone number and then went on, "I was stunned by Hansi's change of heart, and I don't know what to make of it."

She waited for him to answer, but he had nothing to say; he had thought it over and decided that he would say as little as he could. Arguing for years had got them nowhere.

"You have won, Lanny," she said, "and I'm sure you enjoy your victory."

"You are mistaken, Bess. Hansi is a grown man. He knows his own mind and makes his own decisions."

"And I'm supposed to be satisfied with that? When you have loved a man as I have loved Hansi, you can take yourself out of his house but you can't take him out of your mind so easily. Tell me what has happened to *his* mind?"

"You must know what has happened, Bess. It has happened to tens of thousands of people who have joined the Communist party. They find that it isn't what they hoped, they decide that they don't like it, and they get out. I doubt if there is any other organization in the country with so large a casualty rate."

"I was prepared to have all my non-party friends desert me when this hateful frame-up was successful, but I surely didn't think Hansi would. Tell me, who is this woman who has got hold of him?"

"She is the author of a book, and you can find out about her by reading it. The important thing is that she agrees with his ideas, Bess, and so he will not have to spend his time arguing."

"And that means you don't want to tell me about her. You don't have to worry, because I know I am helpless, and anyway I am much too proud to want a man who casts me off. I certainly don't want a cent of his money, and I have no desire to punish him. But I am tormented by the thought that he may have been one of those who betrayed me."

Lanny knew that the more quickly he passed over that question the better it would be for all of them. "You have heard the old saying, Bess, that a man convinced against his will is of the same opinion still. That is the way it was with Hansi. I listened to you arguing and I knew what tremendous pressure you were putting on him. He is a sensitive man, as every artist must be, and such a man is at the mercy of the woman with whom he lives; she can destroy that serenity which is necessary to his work. She can bring him to a state of frenzy where he says, 'Anything for peace! Anything to be let alone!' He says, 'Oh, all right, have it your way!' He says with Matthew Arnold, 'Let the long contention cease! Geese are swans, and swans are geese!' That's the way it was in Hansi's life. So long as it was a question merely of opinions, he could stand to join the party; but when he discovered that it was a question of espionage and possible destruction of our government, then naturally he couldn't stand it."

"So you believe I'm guilty, Lanny!"

"I understand your position and why you have to talk as you do; but there's no use expecting me to take part in it. I have read the *Communist Manifesto;* I have read one or two books by Lenin and one or two by Stalin. I know that communism is war and that it calls itself peace in order to be more effective. I played a game against Hitler and his National Socialism, and I know that you're doing it against American capitalism. There is no reason for you to be frank with me, and on the other hand there is no reason why you should expect me to be a fool; so let's just leave that out of our conversation."

That was one of the times Bess had to bite her lips and clench her hands until the knuckles showed white. "You are being cruel, Lanny," she said.

"I'm being honest with you, and, of course, under the circumstances honesty means cruelty; but I cannot forgo my convictions, any more than you can forgo yours. I did my best to keep you out of this trouble, and now there is nothing I can do except to tell you that I'm truly grieved and sorry. Any time you're ready to tell me that you are through with a program of force and fraud I'm ready to do my best to help you. I don't suppose that time has come yet."

V

She told him that it surely had not—and that was enough conversation along that line. "I don't suppose you have invited me out here to make me into a Stalinist," he said, "so tell me what I can do for you."

Her answer was, "I want to see my sons. I called up Mama and she wouldn't tell me where they are."

"I will tell you this much: they are in a summer camp and are happy with their companions, living an outdoor life and getting instruction half the day and play the other half. That is the ideal thing for boys; and surely you don't want to go there and blast their happiness by pouring out your troubles."

"No, I don't want that, Lanny. But I think I have the right to see them. Have they been told about my conviction?"

"Of course they have been told, Bess. How could you imagine otherwise? Everyone of their playmates has heard about it in one way or another, and the boys have to know how to face the problem. They have to face it all the rest of their lives; and it's you who have put that burden upon them."

"That means they have been told I'm a wicked woman!"

"I don't think anyone wants to tell them that, for it would make them unhappy. I have talked with both Mama and Johannes about it—with the whole family. I was asked, and I agreed that they should be told that their mother helped the Soviet government because she believed it was a good government; the rest of us believed she was mistaken and that it was an evil and cruel government. Obviously they have to be told that; there is a war going on, and although it is called a cold war it is plenty hot enough to burn up the peace of mind of two sensitive lads. It is a war for the minds and the souls of every human being on this earth, and more especially for the minds of the young. The Communists specialize in that; you know it, and you know that I know it. I can only tell you frankly that if ever Hansi asks my advice I'll tell him that you should not be permitted to see the boys. You can do nothing but destroy their peace of mind and turn them into little bundles of neuroses."

"Even if I promise not to mention the subject to them?"

"What other subject could you mention, Bess? You are an incarnation of the problem. Also, we know that promises mean nothing to a Communist. That is a matter of policy, which Lenin advised and which Stalin has made into a first principle for every Communist in the world. It is a terrible thing, because it destroys all honor between human beings, and it destroys all family life; it makes it impossible for a brother to trust a sister and compels him to tell her so frankly."

"Lanny, you have become absolutely implacable!"

"I am facing an implacable man who has declared implacable war upon me and my country. Three years ago I was sent to call upon him by Franklin Roosevelt, and a year later I was sent by Harry Truman, both hoping to divert him from his implacable course. Both times he was breaking solemn agreements he had made in writing; he was breaking them systematically, whenever he thought it was to his advantage and that he could get away with it. I pointed out that our country wanted nothing but peace and that we had proved it in good faith by disbanding the greater part of our armies and decommissioning our airplanes and war vessels. He heard that news gladly, and renewed his promises blandly, and then went on breaking them, because that is his policy, his creed, his religion. He is a religious fanatic of a new sort. I certainly don't want to fall into his power, and I don't want my country to be enslaved by him."

"Lanny, you're talking nonsense—"

"Yes, old dear, we're back in our old argument. Let me tell you that I met Jan Masaryk shortly before his death; he went back deliberately, a martyr to human freedom if there was ever one in history. So let's not waste time trying to change my mind about Stalinism."

"So you are going to advise the Robin family to keep me from seeing my sons!"

"I won't go that far. I will say that if the Robins ask me—as they have done and are apt to do again—I shall advise them that you should not see your sons until they are mature, until they understand exactly what communism means and what it is doing to the world. Then they may see you and tell you what I'm telling you—that you're a pitiful victim of a set of delusions and that you are sacrificing your happiness and your life to a new form of fascism, subtly camouflaged to deceive all the poor and backward races of the earth."

"Who *keeps* them poor? Who *keeps* them backward?" Bess started from her chair and almost screamed the words; she thrust her finger at Lanny's face so that it seemed almost like a pistol. "You, with your privileges and your comforts, you tell the poor and backward peoples to stay peacefully in the chains of wage slavery! You tell them to go on toiling twelve or sixteen hours a day while the great capitalist powers drain the lifeblood out of their veins! You taught me rebellion! You took me as a child and opened my eyes to the cruelty and oppression that exist all over this earth. You taught me sympathy for the poor and oppressed, both at home and abroad! And now you have turned traitor to your cause, to *their* cause. Now you can't find words bitter enough to denounce the men and women who are devoting their lives to ending capitalist exploitation and war! Now you are working against them—for all I know, you may be one of those who betrayed me to the government!"

"No, Bess," he said quietly, "you have never misunderstood what I taught you. You know perfectly well at this minute that you never heard me advocate force and violence, nor did you ever hear me advocate a program of deception. What I talked about was democratic action, and education for it. The distinction between democratic action and dictatorship is fundamental. When you get something by democratic action you can keep it; but when you get it by dictatorship you have a dynasty. You have one cruel tyrant ousted by a still more cruel tyrant; you have a succession of murders; you have a whole plague of concentration camps for slave laborers whom the tyrants fear. You have horror piled upon horror until the world is sick of it, until the very word communism becomes a stench in the nostrils of thinking people."

The finger was again trembling in front of Lanny's face, and he saw that his sister's face was convulsed with emotion—anger or fear or grief, or all of them mingled. He saw there was no use going on, so he got up. Then he saw that tears had begun to come into her eyes, and she sank into her chair and covered her face and wept hysterically. He waited, because he wasn't sure what was in her mind. In her heart she must know that what he had said about the Stalinist terror was the truth; every Communist, at least in America, must know it and be fighting against a realization too awful to be faced.

But she wasn't going to give up her dream. She got herself together, wiped her tears away, and stood up, facing him. "I am ashamed of myself," she said. "It is weak of me. I have a great cause and it is an agony to hear it abused. There is nothing more for us to talk about, Lanny. I'm sorry."

"I'm sorry too," he said. "The time may come when events will force you to think it over and change your mind. If that happens you may count upon me to help in any way I can."

And so he left.

VI

All this time the strange new kind of aerial war was continuing in Berlin. The Americans had taken up the challenge of the Soviets. They were not going to be driven out of the city, and the people of West Berlin were not going to be starved. If the Reds blocked off the railroads, the canals, and the highways, all right; there remained the air and the cargo planes; there was the great Tempelhoferfeld, and in the American zone a field at Frankfurt and in the British zone one at Hannover and one at Hamburg. America would put its great cargo planes to flying food into Berlin; it would bring new planes from overseas, depleting its own domestic services in order to call the Communist bluff and give the world a demonstration of American might.

At home there had been discovered an ingenious process of preserving war materials for which there was no storage room available but for which there might be future need. The process was popularly known as "putting them in mothballs." Guns, tanks, planes, and even the vital parts of great battleships were covered with a thin transparent plastic impervious to weather; it lasted forever, and the costly objects could stay outdoors without the slightest damage.

And now there was another process—taking them *out* of mothballs. So once more, as in the days of the hot war, the big C-47s and the bigger C-49s would fly from American airfields to Newfoundland and from there to Scotland and on to Berlin. From East Coast ports, from Boston down to New Orleans, the cargo ships brought wheat and other foodstuffs to Antwerp, Bremen, and Hamburg, and from there the stuff came by railroad and canals and trucks to the airports. Coal came from Britain and Belgium and the Ruhr and was put into sacks; oil came from Texas and Venezuela and Arabia and was put into tins.

It was a shuttle service to Berlin, with a plane flying every few minutes. The moment a plane landed at the Tempelhoferfeld it would be run off the field and unloaded into the waiting trucks; then it would be wheeled back to the field and take off for the return trip. At the height of the enterprise each plane was making as many as three trips a day and being serviced while the pilots were getting their meals. On holidays and after working hours the population of Berlin would turn out and watch the sight. All day long through the summer the children of the city would perch on the roofs of buildings and on the fences and the rubble heaps to enjoy that marvelous free show, waving their caps and cheering each plane as it came down with its load of food for them.

Bernhardt Monck wrote about these matters and sent clippings from the *Neue Zeitung*, the newspaper AMG was publishing in both Berlin and Munich. Now and then for comic relief he would send clippings from papers the Reds published in their sector. They were raging furiously against the blockade; they were indignant because the Americans were violating the most elementary rules of air safety—so concerned they were for American safety, and for the safety of Germans who lived in the houses around the Tempelhoferfeld! They were saying that the Americans might keep Berlin fed and provided during the summer but could not possibly do it in the winter, when the ground would be deep with snow and when furious storms would last for days and nights. Then the West Berliners would require not merely electric light and power, but also heat for their houses and factories, which took immense quantities of coal. But Monck said the Americans were making their plans to do it and were accumulating stocks. He said that West Berlin had become a symbol to the whole of Europe; it was like a flag flying over a fortress, proclaiming the fact that it was still holding out. The free world was surely not meaning to capitulate!

VII

Now and then Monck would put in a sentence or two about secret matters. He would say, "No word from Ferdinand or the deaf girl"; he would say, "Old Ferdinand is going straight this time; he is useful." Once Monck enclosed a clipping from a Munich newspaper, telling how the German government of Bavaria had arrested Heinrich Brinkmann on a charge of attempting to transport state-owned treasure out of the country. At the top of this item Monck had put in red pencil the initials "O.F.," which of course meant that the information had been given by Old Ferdinand.

Lanny didn't show such things to Laurel, but he did tell her of the statement that Kurt was "going straight this time." She knew about the treasure, because the story had been published in the American press while Lanny was still in Germany. Lanny hadn't been mentioned —which was the way he wanted it—but Laurel had had no trouble in guessing that this was the important errand which had taken him overseas. She had never met Kurt Meissner but had been hearing about him for many years, so he was vivid in her mind; and now Monck's letter caused her to talk about him again and to think about him. That, no doubt, was the cause of the strange event which now took place, one of a series of events which she and her husband had experienced together and about which they speculated in vain.

All our thoughts and impressions sink down into that underground repository we call memory. Millions of facts and thoughts and impressions, names and places and dates, are there, and there is some kind of mysterious elevator; we press a button and a messenger goes down and picks out from the million of shelves and compartments a single detail we have called for—the name of a man we met fifty years ago, a line of poetry we read, a fish we caught, a bird we saw flying—and brings it up to the surface and delivers it to our consciousness. Sometimes the messenger cannot find it; but it is always there, the psychologists tell us. Perhaps under hypnosis we can get it; or if we just wait and repeat the order now and then, suddenly it comes popping to the surface, like a bubble of gas in a stagnant pond. How these things happen the most learned psychologist in the world cannot tell us. But they do happen, we know, and we take them for granted.

What goes on in the bottom of that stagnant pond when we send no messengers down and give no conscious thought to it? Do the memories just lie there awaiting the summons, or do they by any possibility have a life or energy of their own? Are there by any chance strange psychic entities that writhe and wriggle about and perhaps get into one another's way? Are there personalities there, other modes of life? Lanny had read more than once a book by a learned psychologist of Boston, Dr. Morton Prince, called *The Dissociation of a Personality*, the case record of a young lady of good family who developed five different personalities in her subconscious mind; these personalities would dispute the possession of her conscious mind, and now and then a different one would come to the surface and be the young lady whom Dr. Prince called Miss Beauchamp. He took the two of those personalities he considered the best and put them together while his patient was hypnotized, and made a new Miss Beauchamp; the other three personalities he psychically murdered, or at any rate put them permanently to sleep; he hypnotized them and told them they would no longer be Miss Beauchamp or have anything to do with her, and they obeyed him.

All through the ages men have been aware of the existence of this mysterious pond or well or mine or whatever metaphor one chooses to use for it; all the metaphors are misleading, because it doesn't exist in space, and it may not exist in time. But we who do exist in space and time have to imagine it that way. We become aware of things going on there, and sometimes we call it God and sometimes we call it the devil; if we are materialists we invent strange names such as the ego and the id. Men have a way of giving a thing a name and then assuming that they know all about it. They will say, "Oh, that's just hypnotism," overlooking the fact that they don't know what hypnotism is or how it works. They will say, "I believe in telepathy," overlooking the fact that if they could really find out what telepathy is and make it work they would completely put an end to the separation of our individual lives and bring about a state of being in which we would either have to love our neighbors or else destroy ourselves.

VIII

The bubbles continue to rise now and then from this stagnant pond, and sometimes there is an explosion of them. Laurel Creston Budd had been hearing about Kurt Meissner; he meant much to her because he meant even more to her husband, who went abroad on dangerous errands, and always when she tried to guess what her husband might be doing Kurt Meissner was one of the personalities of whom she thought. Recently she had learned that her guesses had been right, and that had made Kurt still more active in her consciousness, and presumably had made him active in her subconsciousness as well.

Anyhow, this is what happened. Laurel was lying on her daybed, reading some letters, and Lanny was in the next room. She laid the letters down and spoke to him, and when he came to the door she said, "Lanny, we are forgetting our psychic powers."

"*Your* psychic powers, you mean," he answered with a smile.

She said, "I have a strange feeling. I suppose it is what people call a hunch. Let's try a séance."

"Okay," he replied and made the preparations, which were simple. All that Laurel had to do was to lie back and close her eyes; Lanny pulled down the window shades to diminish the light and then got a pad of paper and a pencil and sat in a chair by the bedside.

Laurel closed her eyes and began to breathe deeply. Two or three times she sighed, and then the room became perfectly still. After a minute or two Lanny asked in a soft voice, "Is anybody here?"

"Is that you, Lanny?" answered a voice; it came from Laurel's lips and yet wasn't entirely like her voice. Lanny didn't believe in spirits —at least he didn't want to believe in spirits, but he had learned that in these séances the entities, whatever they were, took themselves to be living beings and were to be addressed politely, precisely as if they were alive on earth. So Lanny said, "Is that you, Madame? I am glad to see you." He didn't see her, but that was part of the game.

"I have missed you for a long time," replied the voice, speaking quietly and slowly.

"I've been very busy, Madame. Laurel and I are trying to prevent another war, and that calls for a lot of time."

"I am afraid you will not succeed, Lanny. The world has come upon evil days. There is a young man here, the one who was here before, the German. He has suffered terribly."

"What is his name, Madame?"

"He says Ferdinand. He says you know him."

"Yes, I know him. He is with you?"

"He is here. He wants me to tell you that he is happy, he is at peace."

"I know him well. Has he anything else to tell me?"

"He wishes to tell you that his father is here."

"Ferdinand's father?" Lanny's fingers trembled as he wrote his notes. When he looked at them afterward he saw he had given a violent start. "I didn't know that he had come over, Madame."

"He has just come. He is a sad old man; not so old, but he looks old. He knew you well. He quarreled with you. He wishes to say that you were right."

"What happened to him, Madame?"

"He says it was the—he uses a word I do not know—the Vehm—Vehmgericht."

"I know that word."

"They tried him and hanged him by the neck. It was a terrible thing. It frightens me, but he says not to worry. He talks about his family; he wants you to advise them."

"Tell him I will help them, Madame."

"There are other men here. They are all in uniform. They are Germans. There is a fat man who laughs all the time. He wears a lot of medals. There is a lady with him. He calls her Karin. He says you sold him paintings, and now you can have them all. There is a pale young man here; he is talking. They are both talking at the same time. He was an officer; he was killed in battle. He says you know his mother. Her name is Hilde. You are to tell her that he is happy—they are all talking and it disturbs me. They are all Germans, and you know I never liked Germans, they destroyed my country. I will talk to you some other time, Lanny. The power is failing now."

IX

So the voice faded away and there was silence in the room for a minute or two. Lanny said again, "Is there anyone present?" but there was no reply. Laurel began to sigh and then to moan as if in distress. Then her eyes opened. She always appeared perplexed for a few moments, as if not quite sure where she was. Then she asked, "What happened?"

Lanny said, "Madame came, and she said that Kurt is there."

"Oh *no!*" exclaimed Laurel. She sat up. "What happened to him?"

"She says he has been hanged. I suppose by his associates. She quotes him as saying it was the Vehmgericht."

"What is that?"

"It is a name they have taken over from the Middle Ages in Germany; a secret court, a sort of lynch-law affair. Kurt himself told me that if it became known that he went over to the Americans he would not be allowed to live for a week."

"Oh, Lanny, how awful!" exclaimed the wife. "Do you suppose it is really true?"

"We can only try to find out," he replied. "It may be only an expression of your anxieties."

He described the rest of the séance but didn't mention Kurt's son; he just said, "Madame referred to a young German who had appeared previously." But so far as Kurt was concerned the facts were no longer "classified." A leading Nazi propagandist had come out on the Allied side, and if he had been murdered it was obviously because he had been giving information to the Americans.

Lanny said he would telephone Monck and find out. It was then the small hours in the morning in Germany, and he waited until early next morning. Then he put in a call for Monck's office and had the good fortune to find him. Lanny asked, "Have you any news about Old Ferdinand?" The answer was, "The Army turned him loose at his request. I wrote you about it a few days ago."

"The letter hasn't come," Lanny said. "Is he all right?"

"So far as I know. Why do you ask?"

Lanny said, "Laurel had a message in a séance to the effect that he had been hanged."

He knew this wouldn't make much of a hit with his old friend. German Social Democracy is Marxist and bases its theories upon old-fashioned German materialism. The universe and everything in it consists of little round solid lumps called atoms, and the behavior of these atoms is fixed in a chain of causations that nothing can ever break. The Germans knew that, because a philosopher named Ludwig Büchner had proved it a century ago in a book called *Kraft und Stoff*, and Karl Marx had read it. So now a German named Bernhardt Monck tolerated with patronizing kindness the fact that an old friend believed in "spooks." It seemed to him a characteristically American thing that a wealthy playboy should spend ten dollars or so on a telephone call because one spook had given his wife some messages from another spook.

The ex-sailor said politely, "I'll inquire and let you know." Then he added, "The airlift is flying. You should come and see it, Lanny. It's the finest piece of propaganda ever devised. All Europe is watching it."

X

Lanny went about his business for the day and did not let himself worry about Kurt Meissner. The report might not be true. He had received many psychic communications, and some had been veridical, and many more had had no relationship to reality. Those which were true produced a deep impression, while those which were not were apt to be forgotten quickly.

In the evening he was listening to a radio program, as they always did; it was a world in which cold war might change to hot at any moment, and if it did there might be an A-bomb over your head. So it came about that Lanny and Laurel, sitting on their front porch with Rick and Nina and listening through an open window, heard the following words: "A dispatch from Munich reports that Kurt Meissner, well-known German musician and onetime intimate of Hitler, was found hanged in a forest near his home on Lake Tegern. It is believed that he was murdered by Nazi fellow conspirators because he had given information to the American authorities concerning the treasure concealed in the foundations of his home."

So there it was, first a murder and then a miracle, for most people would call it that. Rick and Nina were witnesses, for Lanny had called them on the previous evening and told them about Laurel's message. Rick, like most moderns, was inclined to materialism but wasn't dogmatic about it; he couldn't doubt the reality of psychic experiences, because Lanny's first, at the age of seventeen, had had to do with Rick's flying accident.

It was a perfect demonstration of a mysterious power that lies hidden in the human psyche. There were thousands of such cases recorded in the books; Lanny had read many cases and had witnessed a few and had told other people about them, but without much result. The average person was interested, as he would have been interested in an account of a visit to the moon or to Mars; but he didn't know what to make of the phenomena and let them slip from his mind.

Lanny was prepared for the airmail letter he received from Monck a few days later. "It is really an extraordinary thing," he said, "and I don't know how to explain it; but if I believed what you believe about it, I would have to change my whole way of thinking. That is too much to expect of a man nearing sixty." So, go on believing Büchner and Marx, and leave the facts lying unread in the libraries!

What Lanny had to do was one concrete thing, to send off a letter to Elsa Meissner expressing his sympathy and asking what resources Kurt had left and what help she would need from Lanny. Kurt Meissner had become in fact, if not in name, an American secret agent, and his family might have a proper claim to a pension; but that would have meant cutting a lot of red tape and persuading a whole row of bureaucrats, and Lanny decided that it would be better to devote the same amount of time to selling another painting.

23

The Nations' Airy Navies

I

ALL through these weeks the Berlin airlift was constantly in Lanny's thoughts. There came a letter from Boris Shub, saying, "This is the crucial struggle. It is a question of holding the people of Berlin to our side. They will stick it out, but only if they are sure we are standing by them. You ought to come over here, Lanny, and help. This is RIAS's great hour; this is what we exist for. Can't you help make Washington understand the importance of winning the German mind?

We are willing to spend billions for guns but only a few tens of thousands for ideas."

Then came a letter from Monck, saying much the same thing but from his special point of view. "The Russians are coming over to us," he said; "more of them every day, risking their lives. And still more of the East Germans—they have extraordinary stories, and you ought to be here to listen and put them on your radio. We all have such a feeling of impotence; the American people do not understand our problem, they do not understand the importance of education. In America, yes, but not here; they do not realize that this is a world struggle and that your country cannot win it alone."

Also, there was Lanny's private business, which he could not neglect entirely; he expected to live for some years yet and he wanted to earn what he was spending. There would come a letter from one of his clients, and he would have to set aside his concern about saving the world and devote himself to thinking where he could find a good Renoir, or an Ingres, or whatever. He had to keep his files up to date, and his information about prices, which varied like waves on the ocean; some painter would rise to the top, and then before you realized it he would be on his way down again. For a while you wouldn't buy his work because the prices were too high, and presently you wouldn't buy his work because nobody wanted him any more. To keep in touch with these things Lanny would go into town and meet his friend Zoltan Kertezsi; they would go wandering on East Fifty-seventh Street, strolling into the dealers' galleries, looking at what they had and listening to the gossip which dealers dispense as freely as housewives over the back fence.

One of Lanny's most important clients was old Mr. Harlan Winstead, who lived in once-fashionable and rich Tuxedo Park. He had been disappointed in his family life and was distrustful of nearly everybody; most of his old friends were dead, and he was afraid to make new ones. The darling of his affections was his art collection, to which Lanny had contributed scores of items. That collection would never betray him, never deceive him; its charms would never fade nor its financial values diminish. It was his intention to set it up in an absolutely fireproof building that would bear his name through the centuries. Lovers of beauty would come from all over the land to wander through the Winstead Museum, and at least a few of them would read in the catalogue the full name and career of its founder.

Old Mr. Winstead read a great deal, especially about art. He would read about new painters and new appraisals of old painters. He would wander through his rooms and look at his collection and decide that the French Impressionists were not completely represented, or perhaps the Florentine School, or the English portraitists. He would call Lanny up and invite him to lunch, and Lanny never failed to go. The old gentleman liked him and trusted him and would follow his advice.

From that luncheon Lanny would go back to Edgemere and consult his card file in which were listed all the paintings he had ever dealt in, or inspected and priced, or even heard rumors about. He had been collecting it for a quarter of a century, and it was precious indeed; there was a duplicate in a vault of the First National Bank of Newcastle. It had increased immediately after the war, when he had served in the operation known as "Monuments," engaged in recovering a couple of hundred thousand works of art which had been stolen by the Nazis and were to be returned to their proper owners. Lanny had made notes on many of these and knew where to find the records of others; so when Mr. Winstead took up a notion to expand his collection in this line or that Lanny would say, "I will find out for you."

That meant that he had to visit Washington, or send someone, and write to dealers and private parties in Europe. He had to get photographs and prices and send or take them to his client. And when the client said, "I want this one," Lanny would go and inspect it and make sure it was genuine and worth the price. If he could save a little money by scaring the other fellow, all right, but the important thing was to get Mr. Winstead what he wanted before the owner found another customer. Lanny's clients seldom talked about their incomes, but from watching through the years he could figure that Mr. Winstead had about half a million dollars a year to spend on paintings. Like Irma, Lady Wickthorpe, he had turned his money over to a foundation so as to avoid ruinous income taxes. Being a conscientious New England gentleman, he would never spend this money for anything but art, the foundation's duly established purpose.

II

So it came about that Lanny was required to take another trip to Germany, to inspect some fragments of that Hermann Göring collection which was to have astounded posterity through the thousand years of the Hitler Reich. Laurel didn't want him to go, and before she gave her consent she extracted from him a pledge that he would not visit Munich or that deadly Alpine Redoubt over which the Vehmgericht kept guard. He telephoned Monck that he would come and speak for RIAS and do whatever else he could for the cause of free Europe. Monck, a trusted man in the Counter-Intelligence Corps, could arrange for things like passports without delay.

So for the second time Lanny got his seat in an Army plane. He stopped off in London, and after telephoning Laurel to let her know that he was safe he called Wickthorpe castle and learned that Irma and Ceddy were in Scotland for the salmon fishing. He wrote them a note explaining that Frances and Scrubbie had postponed a visit to England until Lanny's return. Then he called up Alfred Pomeroy-Nielson, M. P., and spent an evening with him. Paper was scarce in Britain, and news from across the Atlantic was meager. Alfy wanted to hear the whole story of Bess, and how the Pater and Mater were, and all that they were doing. In return he gave an inside view of the British Labour government, which was having a hard time because money was so scarce. Next morning, on the plane flying to Nürnberg, Lanny made this into a little article, which he airmailed to Edgemere.

The *Kunstsachverständiger* attended first to his business affairs. In a mansion far outside the bombed city he found an excellent collection of French Impressionist paintings. At the beginning of the century the Germans had taken much interest in this movement, and several of its own painters had become imitators. So here were Menzels and Liebermanns, and also works by Monet, Degas, and Renoir. They were what Lanny's client wanted and their prices seemed reasonable, so he bought half a dozen examples and saw to their careful packing and shipment.

Then he was free to think about his personal friends, and he had the sad duty of calling upon Emil Meissner. The onetime Wehrmacht general said that Kurt had definitely gone over to the Allied cause and had definitely expected to pay for it with his life. So far as Emil had heard, neither the American Army nor the Bavarian government had been able to find any of the conspirators; they had just faded away and quite possibly had escaped abroad. He said that the Vehmgericht was an effort to carry Germany back to the Middle Ages. "You can read a picture of its activities in Goethe's *Goetz von Berlichingen*. They hold a formal trial in the forest at night and pass the sentence and execute it on the spot." Then Kurt's older brother added, "You do not have to trouble your conscience about it. I would far rather he died opposing nazism than have him live supporting it. There is a new Germany being born, and I believe it will survive—that is, if the Reds do not roll over us."

Lanny asked about Elsa. Emil had been to see the family and had given them advice. The older boys had agreed to heed their uncle's warning and keep away from the Nazi intriguers. Elsa had enough money to get along—Kurt had been able to save some. Lanny divined that Emil didn't know anything about the counterfeiting activities; possibly Elsa didn't know about them either. Emil agreed that it would be wiser for him to keep away from that part of the country. He said that Lanny's part in the discovering of the hidden gold was known and that the Neo-Nazi fanatics were really dangerous. The ex-general himself was a marked man, a traitor to Hitler. He never went out at night if he could avoid it; he slept with his Luger under his pillow and kept it in the drawer of his desk while he worked.

III

They talked for a while about the airlift, which Emil said was the most prominent subject in the mind of every German. A strange turn of the wheel of fortune that the Germans now rejoiced to see that they were remaining "occupied." Emil said that Stalin, an Asiatic, set great store by what was called "face," and now he was losing it rapidly.

Lanny mentioned the paintings he had bought and found that his old friend knew the owner and had visited the house. When Lanny mentioned that he had a similar commission to carry out in Frankfurt the other said, "You may do me a favor there if you will." He explained, "There is a young Luftwaffe officer, son of an old friend of mine, a classmate from my cadet days. The family belongs to the old nobility—this officer is a great-grandson of Prince Bismarck. He made a flying record in the war, shooting down thirty-five Russian fliers, and then he himself was shot down over Stalingrad and captured. You know how the Communists try to make converts of everybody, and I'm told they succeeded with many of our officers. Now this young fellow is in jail in Frankfurt. It appears that the American Army thinks he is a Soviet spy. It doesn't seem likely, but I can't say because I haven't seen him for seven years. I imagine that a large percentage of those who come in from East Germany have been told to spy, whether they do it or not. Anyhow, I can't imagine that Heinrich would be working very hard at it, his family connections being what they are."

"It may have been just an excuse to get loose," Lanny suggested.

"Quite so; but again it may be that a young idealist has been won over to the Soviet point of view. You know how it is, they say they are for peace and democracy, and it is possible to believe their words until you see their actions. It occurs to me that you might visit him and explain the American point of view. One of the last things Kurt said to me was, 'Lanny is a powerful persuader.' "

"I am glad to hear that," Lanny said. "I laid myself out to persuade him, because I esteemed him."

"I think you will like Heinrich," said the other. "Heinrich Graf Einsiedel is his name. When I knew him he was a charming and genial lad. He was taken into the Luftwaffe at the age of eighteen, and he was only twenty-one when he was shot down, so you can see that he probably doesn't know very much about world affairs. The Russians have had him ever since Stalingrad, which means six years. You Americans have had him only three or four months, and I doubt if you are anywhere near as active propagandists as the Reds."

"Alas, no!" agreed Lanny.

IV

The art expert had himself flown to Frankfurt-am-Main, a city of West Germany which had been his headquarters at the war's end, when he was helping to capture German atomic secrets; it had now become the headquarters of AMG. In the home of a well-to-do wine merchant, a villa on the Bockenheimer Landstrasse in the hills behind the city, he found a couple of Manets, which he knew well because they had been in Göring's hunting lodge at Karinhall. Now they had been restored to their former owner, and Lanny bought them at a reasonable price and sent off a cablegram announcing them.

Then he inquired concerning the Luftwaffe officer, Count Einsiedel, and learned that he was in the investigation prison in Frankfurt. Lanny then telephoned to Berlin, asking Monck to fix it up so that he could have a confidential interview with this great-grandson of Prinz von Bismarck. Monck said okay. No doubt he reminded the authorities that Lanny had been responsible for the finding of the Nazi gold, and that made him a VIP. Anyhow, they didn't take him to the cell, but seated him in a comfortable room and brought the young Graf to him and left them alone. Of course there might have been a dictaphone, but Lanny wouldn't have minded; he had nothing to conceal—quite otherwise.

Heinrich Graf Einsiedel proved to be a tallish, slender young man, pale from his confinement. He was, as the general had said, a cheerful, even a gay person, in spite of his troubles. He said he wasn't angry with the Americans; he was inclined to take the whole affair as a joke. They had been decent to him, except that they had kept him two or three months in solitary confinement without an explanation; he was sure they didn't have any evidence against him and were just holding him while they tried to get some. He said he had declared a hunger strike by way of protest, but nobody had paid any attention to that, so after eighteen days he had decided to give up. He said he had come into West Germany to see his mother and some old friends; he had been visiting his mother in Wiesbaden when a couple of Army agents had picked him up. They said there was something wrong with his pass, but it was a perfectly good pass, signed by the proper authority in the American sector of Berlin.

"They say you are a spy," remarked Lanny. "I have been one myself, so I know all about it. Tell me."

Heinrich grinned. "You know how it is, Herr Budd. Any time anybody plans to come from the Russian zone into the Western zones he is interviewed by the MVD for his pass and ordered—not invited but ordered—to send in information or to bring it. I was ordered and I said to myself with a smile, 'I will write you a few inconsequentialities'—*einige Belangslosigkeiten*. It is silly so far as I am concerned, because I don't know anything that they don't know already. I am an editor—perhaps you don't know, I am one of the editors of the *Tägliche Rundschau*, the newspaper in East Berlin."

"General Meissner didn't tell me that," Lanny said. "Perhaps he didn't know it."

"Being an editor in the East sector is very different from in the West. Perhaps you can't imagine it. You do not print the news; you follow policy, and all the news has to be made over to fit the policy. You are told that the party is monolithic, and so is the policy; it is a most impressive word, but, alas, when you come to watch the proceedings you discover that what exists is one clique fighting another clique for power. Whichever side is out is watching eagerly to catch the other in some action or some phraseology that isn't 'monolithic.' It is hard for me because I am naturally an outspoken person, and I have never belonged to any clique."

"Why don't you come over to the West and stay?" inquired Lanny.

"I don't know whether they would have me; and anyhow it's rather hard for me to make up my mind. I have a great many friends among the officer corps—the German officers who have gone over to the Soviets. You must understand, I am deputy president of the Bund Deutscher Offiziere, and we think we are important, and I hate to hurt their feelings. It is a strange life that I've lived. I was brought up as a German officer and was taught that my first duty was to defend the

Fatherland. I despised democracy precisely because I had seen the German people vote Hitler into power; that was why it was possible for me to go over to the Soviets. If I should change again I wouldn't know quite what to make of myself; it would be too much for anybody to believe. You must realize, I have lived six years among the Russians, and they have taught me most of what I know—or think I know."

"I can understand easily," Lanny said.

V

He didn't want to put pressure on the man or to seem to, so he chatted for a while about old times. He told of buying paintings that had once been in Karinhall. "Did you ever meet Hermann Göring?" he asked.

"Never, thank God!" exclaimed Einsiedel. He called his air commander "a vain, overstuffed peacock" and added, "He knew as much about air strategy as an ox knows about skiing."

"I visited his Luftwaffe headquarters once," Lanny said. "I helped him with his art collection—not those paintings he stole but some he bought."

"I have been through the Tretyakov Museum in Moscow, and that is all I know about painting. You must understand that for a good part of those six years I was a prisoner of war. They gave me their propaganda to study, and I studied it, and when they saw that I was a diligent student they sent me to an *antifaschule*—you know how they make up words—that is, an anti-Fascist school. There they trained German officers to be Communists, and I learned the whole ritual and bible. It seemed to me quite wonderful, you know; they are going to end poverty and war, the proletariat has arisen and is going to build a new state, and when it is all done the state will wither away and every man will be free. I took it all just as I had taken the Bible from my mother and *Mein Kampf* from Hitler. Each time there was a complete program of salvation and a ritual that you had to go through if you wanted to be saved."

"I know all about it," Lanny said. "I never was a Communist myself, but some of my friends were, including a sister. What you have to learn is that revolutions may degenerate. The state doesn't wither away; on the contrary, it becomes the prey of power-loving men, and they hold on to it and proceed to murder everybody who might by any possibility disagree with them and try to get rid of them. The utopian state turns into a police state, and differences of opinion become the occasion for secret arrests, tortures, and other horrors. The basis of American social thinking is the right of the individual to life, liberty, and the pursuit of happiness; but in the Soviet Union the individual is nothing and the regime is everything."

"The theory, Herr Budd, is that the regime is delivering the individual from exploitation."

"It is a plausible theory and has seduced many minds. But after watching it for thirty years I have concluded that the regime is a small group of individuals protecting their own power and exploiting everybody else. To me the Stalinist regime is as evil and treacherous as those of ancient Rome in the days of its decline and fall. Did you by any chance see the picture that Sergei Eisenstein made about the life of Ivan the Terrible?"

The other had seen it, and Lanny went on, "Ivan was a perfect monster of cruelty, syphilitic and a veritable maniac, yet he represents success to the Soviets. He survived, he put down his enemies and expanded his empire, so they glorified him, they spent millions of rubles, even in the midst of their poverty, and set their creative genius to making a magnificent film about him. I can assure you that such a thing would be inconceivable in America. In the first place we have no such figures in our history. Our folk heroes are men like Columbus, who sailed out in three little ships and discovered a new world; Daniel Boone, who went out into the wilderness and survived so many hardships; Paul Revere, who rode out to rouse the farmers of the countryside when the British soldiers were coming; Thomas Jefferson, who wrote the Declaration of Independence; John Brown, who tried to awaken the slaves; and Abraham Lincoln, who actually did emancipate them. Someday we shall add Franklin Roosevelt, a crippled man in the White House who broke the power of Wall Street and forced it to come to Washington for its orders. From such things you can know the soul of our people; and you will see how different it is from a land of blood and terror, building up military might by the labor of millions of starvelings in concentration camps."

"I am very ignorant, Herr Budd," said the great-grandson of Prinz von Bismarck. "I have never even heard many of these names you mention."

VI

So Lanny set to work to complete the education of this young Prussian aristocrat, whom he liked because he had a keen intelligence and a genial smile. He had been buffeted by fate but had taken it in a mood of gaiety. The Americans had locked him up, but they had no way of knowing about him, so he couldn't blame them very much. Speaking as an aviator, he said that when you were up in the air and the winds pushed you this way and that you didn't blame them, you learned to ride them.

Lanny tried again that eloquence which he had wasted upon his sister during the years since she had come back from the Soviet Union. He answered those arguments Einsiedel had been taught in the *antifaschule*. Yes, there had been lynchings of Negroes in America; there might still be as many as one in the course of a year. But the millions of Negroes who had been slaves a century ago were getting education, they were earning money and putting it by, they were gaining their rights in one court decision after another. They were on their way up in America, and for that reason the Communists were not able to make much headway among them.

And again, yes, there had been oppression of labor. Unions had been fought and sometimes broken up, and workingmen had been beaten and shot in riots during strikes. Such conditions had been portrayed in books—books written thirty or forty years ago and now circulated in Stalinist Russia with nothing said about the dates. The Russian masses were being taught that these conditions prevailed in America today; but that was not so. In America today there were some twenty million workers organized into unions that were wealthy and powerful and that were accustomed to negotiate with bosses upon equal terms; they were free to strike and did so—something they would never dare to do in Stalin's empire. During the past sixteen years of the New Deal these unions had had their full say in the affairs of government and had helped to bring about numerous social reforms. In England this was called Fabian socialism and in America its enemies called it "creeping socialism"; but bad words hadn't stopped it. It had all been brought about by the democratic process; very few persons had been killed, very few had been sent to jail, and while many lies had been told, the lovers of truth had been left free to refute them.

VII

In short, Lanny conducted an anti-Commie school, all in one session. The pupil was apt and attentive, and at the end of the session Lanny waited to hear him say that he would stay in the American sector if permitted. But no, he said he couldn't do that; in the first place it would look cowardly; the Americans would think he had done it in order to get out of jail, and they would never really respect him or trust him. He would wait until they turned him out, which they would surely have to do, because they could prove nothing against him. Then he wished to go back to his job on the *Tägliche*. He had his friends to whom he owed loyalty, and he wanted to tell them what new thoughts he had got into his head.

Lanny warned him that this was a dangerous thing to do. "You do not look to me as if you'd be a very successful intriguer. What you're thinking shows in your face."

Said he, "I believe I have a few friends I can trust, Herr Budd."

Lanny warned him, "It is difficult to have friends in a police state. The moment you change your mind fear begins, and suspicion. You wonder who will be the Judas to betray you with a kiss. It is to every man's advantage to betray you and to no man's advantage to keep your secret. You will never have a moment's peace of mind, for you have to remember that the slightest suspicion is enough to bring about your ruin. In the free world we would rather let a hundred guilty men go free than kill one innocent man; but in Stalin's realm it is just the other way: he would rather kill a hundred innocent men than have one guilty man survive—because that guilty one might bring about the end of Stalin. That is the way with despotism; it automatically breeds fear and suspicion; it thrives upon it and cannot survive without it. In the free world a human being is a soul and his rights are sacred; but in Stalin's realm human beings are beetles and bugs; if they bite, or even look as if they might bite, they are exterminated."

The young Prussian chuckled. "Tell your friends who have got this beetle in a box that if they turn him loose he will not bite, and he will not tell any lies about them. He will go back and tell his friends what he is thinking. Perhaps he will have another change of mind; but he is making no promises and giving no pledges. He is very much confused in his mind and troubled in his conscience just now."

Lanny went out and made that report to the anxious officers of CIC in Frankfurt. Evidently they had arrested Einsiedel because they suspected he was a spy and hoped to get the evidence; apparently they hadn't been able to. Lanny said he didn't think the man was a spy, but of course he couldn't guarantee it. He took the man to be a proof of the cunning and efficiency of Stalin's propaganda machine. They had taken a young German prisoner, miseducated by Hitler and very naïve about the world. Always they had the advantage that so long as he didn't agree with them he remained a prisoner, but when he did agree with them he became a favored pupil and then an honored collaborator. Naturally Lanny couldn't undertake to counteract the work of six years in a couple of hours' conversation; but he felt sure that Einsiedel was thinking new thoughts, and it was to his credit that he wasn't willing to change his mind suddenly in order to get out of jail.

"Why don't you give him books to read?" demanded Lanny, and it turned out that the officers didn't know what books to give him. They didn't know anything about propaganda; it hadn't been taught in West Point or in the Army training camps. It was a new idea to Americans, and uncomfortable, because up to then propaganda had been left to newspapers and magazines and radio—in short, to private enterprise. The average American officer didn't very well understand the difference between communism and socialism—if he had been reading the Hearst newspapers he was quite sure they were the same. Lanny had to admit that it was confusing, because Hitler had called himself a National Socialist, with the idea of fooling the Germans and taking over the Socialist vote; now in the same way Stalin announced that he was building socialism, when in fact he was expanding the old-style Tsarist empire and making it more efficient and deadly. The Americans were building socialism actually, but they didn't want it and wouldn't admit it; they insisted upon walking into the future backwards and not knowing where they were going. The Democrats called it the New Deal and the Fair Deal, and only the Republicans had discovered what it really was!

VIII

Lanny got himself flown to Berlin. In these days you were lucky to get a ride at all; high-ranking officers sat on bucket seats, and others spread a newspaper on a sack of coal or a tin of gasoline. The coal had to be wetted down, in order to avoid spontaneous combustion, so you trod carefully in black slime. Every plane was loaded to capacity; there were rings in the wall, and ropes were passed through these to bind the cargo tight; when the air was bumpy this was important and was done with care. There came to Lanny's mind a scene by Victor Hugo which he had read in his youth, describing the behavior of a cannon on board a warship; it broke loose during a storm and went hurtling from one end of the deck to the other, smashing everything in its path. Nothing of that sort happened during the Berlin airlift.

Here at the Frankfurt airfield was a sight to be remembered. Along one side of the field was a row of the C-47s, cargo planes, many of them war-worn and far from elegant, but they could carry two-and-a-half tons a trip. Beside each plane was a truck, and the cargo was being shifted into the planes by a swarm of German workers with wheelbarrows and dollies. The moment a plane was ready and the cargo made fast, the engines were started slowly, and the plane proceeded under its own power across the field; it was a great bird that rolled instead of hopped to its place at the end of the runway. The signals were given from the radio tower, so you heard nothing; suddenly the pilot gunned his engine, the propellers began to roar, and a cloud of dust shot out from behind the plane; it began to roll faster and faster down the runway. When it got near the end you were worried for fear it was overloaded and wouldn't rise in time; but the men who were handling this operation knew just how much weight the plane could carry and how many feet of runway were required. It always rose at exactly the right instant and passed over the trees and the houses and away.

Lanny was free to stand and watch the sight as long as he pleased, and to ask questions. He was told that there were a few more than a hundred planes on this run, and they were kept working day and night. Some of the big fellows were coming, the C-54s, which could carry ten tons; they were flying from Hawaii and Alaska. When his curiosity was satisfied Lanny entered one of the planes and took his uncomfortable seat. The distance was less than two hundred miles and the flight took less than an hour. He couldn't see outside, and had no one to talk to, because the plane carried no crew and no superfluous weight. He had only his thoughts for company, and his thoughts were that every flight of these planes was ringing an alarm bell in the Kremlin, telling the men of the Politburo that the free world was not going to give up without a fight.

IX

Lanny had telephoned Monck and a hotel room had been engaged for him. They soon got together and had much to talk about. First, the tragic fate of Kurt. Monck said he was fairly sure who had committed the murder, but he had no evidence. The men had disappeared. Perhaps they were hiding in the forest, which was pleasant enough in the summertime; or perhaps they had changed their names and got away to a foreign land. The Bavarian government was conducting a search, but Monck said it was hard to be sure how genuine their efforts would be. It was impossible to keep any German government from being infiltrated by Nazis; frequently you had to employ ex-Nazis because you could find no one else who was competent. Men of violence who had held power and glory for a dozen years were not going to give up, and Monck was of the opinion that the American occupation would have to continue for a long time.

"But is Stalin going to give us a long time?" asked Lanny, and Monck said, "*Ach, leider!*"

This Marxist friend did not bring up the subject of Laurel's extraordinary psychic experience. Lanny understood that he wasn't going to "change his thinking of a lifetime." He was a man full of purpose and courage, but he had no theory as to how these qualities had come into existence, or why they seemed so important. So he and his American friend would go on dealing with the world of material things, which included both nazism and communism, the two extremes on the social scale. Now the extremes were meeting.

The American expressed the opinion that young Einsiedel was an exceptional man and was seriously thinking of coming over to the Allied side. Monck said that was possible. Great numbers of Germans and Russians were becoming aware of the chasm that had opened between Communist theory and practice. He said, "Stalin tries to make converts among them but he has treated them too badly. Nearly half a million German soldiers and officers have died in Russia of exhaustion and hunger-typhus."

Monck said that no information had come about Fritz Meissner or Anna Surden, and he doubted if he would hear from either of them again. Lanny told about General Meissner, and Monck said that sturdy old gentleman ought to be brought to Berlin to be heard over RIAS; he would have influence with the Germans. For the first time since the war had ended Monck was really hopeful of winning the minds of his own people. He said the airlift was producing a tremendous impression; for the first time the Germans realized that the "Amis" meant business. It was a blow to Soviet prestige, and the refugees all agreed that the Reds were in a state of vexation.

Lanny went to see Boris Shub, who had become the political adviser of RIAS. That genial gentleman welcomed him with outstretched hands. He was in a state of exaltation because a poll just completed showed that RIAS now had eighty per cent of the Berlin listeners, whereas the far more powerful Red station had only fifteen per cent. Such had been the effect of the airlift! America was waking up, and the Reds were being told in language they could understand that they were not going to have the world for the taking.

Shub sat right down with Lanny to decide what he was to say over the air. He was pleased with Lanny's suggestions and had only one thing to urge: that when the visitor had any fault to find it should not be with the Russians or the Russian people. They were exactly what the Germans had been under Hitler, the helpless victims of despotism; the worst that could be said of them was that they were dupes. We were trying to open the eyes of the Russians and win them to our cause, and we should always distinguish between them and their masters.

Lanny agreed. "But I don't like to say the Soviets either," he added, "because there are no more Soviets; they have become a farce."

"Say the Stalinists or the Communists or the Reds," replied Shub. "There are perhaps five million of these in Russia, and there are a hundred and seventy-five million of the common people. Say that we are the friends of those common people and are trying to help them. Nothing frightens the Reds so much or makes them so angry; they are sitting on a volcano, and they know it."

Very certainly they were not winning the Germans; the free world was winning them! They came day and night from the East sector to visit RIAS and thank its staff; they telephoned or wrote—a hundred letters a day. Out of that came a spy service which could not have been equaled for a million dollars. People would tell what was going on in the departments of which they had knowledge. They would expose the plans of the self-appointed cold-war enemy; and so the gleeful announcers of RIAS would be able to warn their public in advance, "Be careful if you are traveling on the express from Dresden. The trains are being thoroughly searched, and all passengers must have the proper papers." Or they would say, "There are three spies working for the Communists in the Brehn Chemical Works. We will give their names, listen carefully now," and they would give the names. This had become a regular department, known as the Spitzeldienst, the spy service.

X

So Herr Fröhlich gave his first broadcast along that line. He said that he was speaking for the American people to the people of Germany and to those of Russia as well. He had been traveling back and forth among these people and those of France and England all his life, and he could testify that none of them wanted war, and few of them ever had, even while being forced to live through and fight the two most terrible wars of history. He told of his visits to Germany as a boy, how he had danced in the Dalcroze School at Hellerau, and had visited in a castle in Upper Silesia, and had met kind people, happy people, who wanted only peace.

To be sure, the German workers had wanted social changes, but they were prepared to bring these about by democratic means, and they were on the verge of winning an election and carrying out their program in an orderly way. But the Kaiser, the War Lord, had not been willing for these changes to come, and it was he who had sounded the war drums and led Germany into an attack upon her neighbors. Always it was the dictators, the men of violence, the men who could not let other people be free but were determined to force them to live their way, to take their orders, to give up their territories and their freedoms—these were the people who made the wars.

And then had come Hitler, the man of fanatical nationalism, who had taught a whole generation of German youth to hate and fear other peoples and to find their glory in forcing other peoples to submit to his will. First he had seized a part of Czechoslovakia, and then he had made a deal with Stalin to divide up Poland, and so had come another world war. And before that had been going on very long Hitler had turned upon his ally and proceeded to conquer and seize the Russian land.

"Did the German people want to conquer the Russian people?" asked Herr Fröhlich. "Or did the Russian people want to conquer the Germans? Of course not; they were bewildered by the events, they were as helpless as people caught in a whirlwind. These dictators led them, they told them lies about the other peoples and filled them with fear. In a few months the Japanese had attacked the United States at Pearl Harbor, and so the Americans were in the war. I can testify because I was there: the American people do not want war and did not want to be in that war; they were forced into it because they were attacked. Hitler had made some kind of deal with Japan, and so when Japan attacked us he declared war upon us also.

"It happened that during that war I was flown into Russia and spent some time in Kuibyshev and Moscow. I had a chance to meet and know hundreds of Russians. They became my friends. They were warmhearted people, generous and kind. They did not hate me, they did not fear me. We were Allies and we were friends—spontaneous, natural friends. But now six years have passed, and see what has happened! A dictator has changed his mind again. He got eleven billion dollars' worth of help from America and together we put down Hit-

ler. We were still willing to give him help; we offered him Marshall
Plan aid, we offered it to Czechoslovakia and the other conquered
states which he holds; but the dictator says no, we are enemies now,
and he shuts down the iron curtain between us and declares cold war
upon us."

Herr Fröhlich went on to discuss this strange modern invention.
The Kremlin master ordered all his propaganda machinery to tell lies
about the Americans, to make the Russian people hate them. Here in
the British sector he had the great Radio Berlin, and from it, day and
night, he poured out a stream of falsehoods about Americans and what
they were doing at home and here in Germany.

"It seems like a tale out of a madhouse, but it is a true tale. We
have had to set up our own radio station to tell both the German people and the Russian people that we are not lackeys of Wall Street and
warmongers, but believers in democracy and defenders of the right
of all the peoples of the earth to have their own ideas and their own
way of life, to be free to think their own thoughts and teach their
own ideas, political, economic, and religious, and govern themselves
according to the will of the majority, and not to be invaded—so long
as they do not invade their neighbors but help to keep the peace of
the world.

"The free peoples of the world have set up the United Nations and
pledged themselves to come to it and settle their problems democrati-
cally and cooperatively. The big nations and the little nations, the rich
nations and the poor nations, all are equal in the sight of the law. But
the Soviets come to the meetings of the United Nations only to make
their false propaganda and to obstruct the proceedings. By the power
of the veto they are able to forbid anything the other nations want
to do, and so far they have used that veto some twenty-five times.
We Americans would like nothing better than to see a united and
democratic Germany a member of that international parliament and
forum; but you who hear me know that the Soviets will never permit
that, for they are determined to make a slave Germany under their
system of dictatorship, and if they cannot make a completely united
Germany of that sort, then they will make a half-Germany of that
sort, and will proceed to blockade and starve the other half into sub-
mission if they can."

Such was the substance of Lanny's talk, and when he finished a male
quartet sang "Lili Marlene," the favorite song of the German troops
in the recent war. It was a song of love and longing, and the British
had taken it up; before the war was over it had become the favorite

of all the armies. It meant to them all that they were tired of war and wanted to get back home to their girls.

XI

Two evenings later the Soviet station, Radio Berlin, presented an answer, by none other than the great propagandist of the Soviet Union, Ilya Ehrenburg. For years he had fought Hitler with fury, and now he was fighting Truman and all Truman's agents.

"Who is this crocodile?" he demanded. "This crocodile who pours his tears over the German people and spits his venom in the direction of our Soviet Fatherland! I will tell you exactly who he is. His name is Lanny Budd, and he is the son of one of the greatest merchants of death in capitalistic America. Before and during the First World War this Robert Budd was the European representative of Budd Gunmakers, and he sold tens of millions and perhaps hundreds of millions of dollars' worth of guns and cannons to Germany and Britain and France, all with perfect impartiality. During the Second World War he was the president of Budd-Erling Aircraft, and he made and sold I know not how many billions of dollars' worth of murderous airplanes to the American government. Before the war he sold them to the German and the Japanese governments. His hands are stained impartially with the blood of Europeans and Asiatics. To this international slaughterer all human cattle look alike.

"And now comes the son of this capitalistic exploiter, this Wall Street cannibal. The son was born with a gold spoon in his mouth and the taste of blood. During the war he came to Russia, and he admits that he was received with hospitality. He came posing as a friend and an ally—and how does he treat his host? A rich American woman left him a million dollars to be spent in the cause of establishing and maintaining world peace. He has set up a radio station near New York, and by cunning dissimulation, by pretense of genuine love of humanity, he wins a large audience—and then what does he do to that audience? He does the same thing that he is doing to the German and the Russian people. He is the Judas goat who leads the helpless sheep into the slaughter pen. He reveals himself as the true son of his father, doing everything in his power to bring on a third world war in order that his father may be able to gather in more millions of filthy dollars. He comes here to Berlin, and the bloodthirsty warmongers of RIAS spread his insolent provocations over all Germany."

So it was that the cold war was waged. It made Lanny sad, and he thought it over and learned several things from it. One was the futility of calling names; he decided that when he came to answer Comrade Ehrenburg he would be calm and would deal with facts. The Germans had had the very foundation of their thinking blasted from under them; they didn't know what had been going on in the world during the years of Hitlerism and war, and they had a hard time finding out . what was going on now. Lanny went to the Information office of AMG and got the figures as to the number of troops the American Army had had in Germany at the close of the war and the number they had sent home when it ended. That showed whether or not America wanted another war in Europe. Would Mr. Ehrenburg give the same figures with regard to the disbandment of Russian armies? Of course Mr. Ehrenburg couldn't and wouldn't; he would have been shot if he had tried.

And then those twenty-five vetoes in the Security Council of the United Nations. They had all been vetoes of proposals made or approved by the government of the United States. And what were the proposals? They were for real disarmament, guaranteed by international inspection; they were for free elections and the democratic process in one small nation after another; and in each case Mr. Gromyko or Mr. Malik or Mr. Molotov or Mr. Vishinsky had ridiculed and refused the proposal. With the Reds it was rule or ruin—everywhere, all over the world.

That was the way to answer the Red propagandists—with facts, facts, facts!

24

Man's Unconquerable Mind

I

WHILE Lanny was busy with these matters there came the Kasenkina case in New York. Oksana Kasenkina was a teacher in the school maintained for the children of officials in the Soviet Consulate-General. This school was housed in a brownstone mansion in one of the fashionable residential districts. The teacher couldn't very well be kept indoors all the time, so she went out and walked on the streets and observed the sights of a great capitalist city. She discovered that she could buy for a few dollars a pair of shoes which would have taken a Russian worker a month's labor to earn. She saw many things that pleased her, but she could not come back to the Consulate and chat about them with anybody—that is, unless she said the opposite of what she thought.

The school was a miniature Soviet—which is to say, it was a petty despotism ruled by a dictator, with frightened people spying upon one another and full of malice and suspicion. Oksana had lost track of her husband and her son and was a pitiful neurotic person. Outside the school she met an elderly, white-haired Russian named Zenzinov, who had been one of the old-time fighters against Tsardom. He had belonged to the Social Revolutionary party and had been exiled three times to Siberia; three times he had escaped, once by way of Japan.

Each time he came back to his native land, and he was one of those who made the revolution. They made Russia free—but only for a few months. The Bolsheviks seized power, put down the revolution, made themselves the masters—and Russia was in servitude again. Zenzinov fled once more and wandered first over Europe and then over America. He was one of those men to whom revolution had become a basic instinct; he lived in one furnished room in New York, and whenever he could earn enough money he printed a few copies of a little paper which he called *For Freedom*.

This old man explained to the teacher in the Soviet Consulate how the revolution had been betrayed and destroyed. But she had to hide this secret in her heart and go on telling the children that their country was free and that Stalin was the great hero and emancipator. Soon she could not endure it any more, and she accepted Zenzinov's suggestion to seek refuge on a farm up the Hudson River near Nyack, which belonged to a daughter of the great Leo Tolstoy and sheltered a group called the Tolstoy Foundation. Alexandra Tolstoy had been the count's favorite daughter; she had stood by him through all his tribulations and now was trying to preserve and promote his Christian-pacifist ideas.

The news of this flight to freedom was at once cabled to Moscow, and Foreign Minister Molotov, that iron-faced man who apparently never had an emotion, suddenly lost his head and handed to the American ambassador for transmission to Washington a note in which he charged that Kasenkina had been "kidnaped by the White Guard

Zenzinov and taken to a farm which belongs to a White Guard gang-ster organization masquerading under the name of the Tolstoy Foun-dation." The gangsters on this farm had "attempted by force to prevent Kasenkina from leaving." Molotov went on to demand her immediate return to the Consulate-General in New York, "as well as the punishment of all persons who have taken part in the kidnaping of Soviet citizens."

Kasenkina, alas, wasn't happy in the new home. A hundred refu-gees, lonely and idle, were not the best of company, and she was tormented by the idea that her husband and son might still be living and would be punished for her desertion. She wrote to the Consulate, begging forgiveness, and the consul drove up in haste; he promised her forgiveness for the mistake she had made. Finally she yielded and let him take her back to the Consulate.

Once there, of course, she found that she was a prisoner and was going to be sent back to Russia. It would mean torture; she would be forced to reveal the names of everyone she had met and who had in-fluenced her, and after that they would shoot her in the back of the neck or send her to a worse fate in a slave-labor camp. In her frenzy the woman threw herself out of a third-story window of the Consulate and crashed upon the concrete area in front of the building. The case had become known to the newspapers, and court proceedings had been started to set the woman free; so there was a crowd in front of the Consulate. When the area gate was opened and servants started to drag the woman inside, the crowd interfered, police and an ambulance were summoned, and the badly injured Oksana was carried to a hos-pital.

That, of course, made a tremendous sensation. Most Americans realized by now that the Communists used torture and that people do not throw themselves from third-story windows for fun. Certainly all newspaper reporters realized it, and the story took the front pages. The consul gave out the statement that the woman was deranged, and he rushed to the hospital to try to interview her, but the hospital au-thorities would not let him in.

II

So here was an international scandal, and it made the front page of important newspapers all over the world. Needless to say, it took the front page of the *Neue Zeitung*, which AMG was publishing in West Germany, and RIAS took it up. As it happened, Boris Shub knew Zenzinov, and in West Berlin there were Russian refugees who knew him even better. Molotov called him a "White Guard gangster" —the term White Guard being the name for those Army officers who had fought in various parts of Russia against the revolution and on behalf of Tsardom. The Bolsheviks had taken it up as a term of abuse for anyone who opposed them, and so it became as meaningless as when they called Robbie Budd a "crocodile" and Lanny a "cannibal."

"Molotov is seeing ghosts!" exclaimed one of the refugee Russians. A group of them went to work and overnight produced a dramatic dialogue in which four "Voices" discussed the case and brought out its significant points. So the Germans, and many Russians also, listened to a "thriller" that happened to be exactly true. One of these voices asked the question, "When a Soviet citizen in Moscow or anywhere else falls or jumps out of a window, do you suppose that the whole machinery of state from the smallest vice-consul to the protesting Foreign Minister is immediately set in motion?"

"I cannot believe it," replied the second voice. "They are cool materialists with a precise scientific method, deciding everything through clear objective laws."

Third voice: "And all of a sudden the Kremlin hums like a beehive. What can have impelled the cold Molotov to act so differently? You all know too little of the Russian Revolution. There was once a time when every man in Russia could speak and think as he pleased. The Soviet wasn't in Bolshevik hands then—that was still in the springtime of the revolution, when every simple worker or sailor could talk to his fellow man. Students, officers, workers, women, stream through the streets of Petrograd, singing the 'Marseillaise' in Russian. The headquarters of the Tsarist secret police is in flames! The prison doors spring open, people like Zenzinov and Molotov breathe the air of the Petrograd spring. In these days, Zenzinov and Molotov are elected to the Executive Committee of the Petrograd Soviet. Both of them sit there, one a Socialist, the other a Bolshevik, together with other revolutionists."

Fourth voice: "And where are these men today?"

Third voice: "Yes, where are these men today? With the exception of Molotov and Zenzinov, probably all dead. Molotov lives in the Kremlin, Zenzinov in a small room in New York, and behind them lies a past which to this day conceals the martyrdom of honest Socialists who will one day be resurrected—Socialists of the spring of 1917, the only time the Russian people experienced the intoxication of liberation and freedom. All the goals for which revolutions are made seemed to be attained. In those days Lenin himself wrote, 'Russia is now the freest country in the world.' Yes, that was the time, from March to November 1917. And the men in Soviet Russia who remain silent about it are as little able to forget that time as the few abroad who fight that it shall not be forgotten."

Fourth voice: "Now I begin to feel what must have taken place when Kasenkina suddenly decided to jump out of the window. At last I understand why they are so agitated in the Kremlin."

Third voice: "Yes, my friend, now everything becomes as clear as the history of peoples and rulers in general. Limitless power breeds limitless fear of one's own people, the fear of the jailer. And history knows no cure for this fear. It is easier to deal with fugitive party functionaries and MVD men by trying to make them ridiculous in the eyes of the people; but the little Russian teacher, she spoke to Zenzinov, to Tolstoy's beloved daughter. She retraced the road and became more dangerous. And there are millions of Kasenkinas, for millions would come to understand just as she did, if they had the opportunity to see, to speak. You see, all this still lives in the Russian people, and as long as it lives there is fear among the men in power and hope for all mankind."

III

Through all these events the airlift was going on, with no sign of ending. Berlin, which had called itself "the magnificent city" and now had its magnificence blasted, was the epicenter of a hurricane, the coldest spot in a cold war or the hottest in a hot war—whichever simile you preferred. Berlin's freedom, its very existence, depended upon this struggle; and what were the plain people making of it? Lanny wanted to know, and he went to call upon the family of Johann Seidl, in the Moabit district. They were Socialists and would talk to him frankly and would pass him on to others, as many as he wished. They had once saved his life, and he would make return by taking some of those American foods which were otherwise not to be thought of by them.

The tenement in which they lived had been only partially repaired, and now there was little hope of more work on it because there were no materials; the airlift was bringing only absolute necessities, food and coal and oil, medicines and a little clothing. The Seidls were more crowded than ever, having had to curtain off a part of their kitchen to make a sleeping place for a nephew of Johann, with his wife and child. This young man, Karl, was a refugee from the East sector; he was haggard, undernourished, and obviously honest. Lanny was interested in hearing his story and then asked him questions while the family and some of the neighbors who had been summoned stood around and listened. The curtain had been drawn aside, and several of the people sat on the single bed. Lanny had one of the two chairs which the family possessed; they would have been uncomfortable if he had not sat on it.

Karl Seidl had been a worker in a tin shop in that dreary industrial part of the "magnificent city." The shop had been half wrecked by artillery shells, and anyhow there was no more tin. For weeks he had hunted a job and had almost perished; then at one of the Russian barracks he was taken on as what was called a "fireman" but really was a handyman and slavey. He cleaned up the filth, he carried the heavy burdens, he did whatever anybody told him to do. In return he got a few marks and was able to buy bread to keep his family alive from day to day.

Karl had been a Socialist since childhood, and when the Soviets formed what they called the Socialist Unity party, SED, he had thought it was the proper thing for him to join. He explained that the Reds seldom used the word "Communist," at least not in East Germany; he had hardly ever heard it. They were planning socialism, they were building socialism, they were organizing socialism. There had been only a few Communists in Berlin; the Social Democrats had been the majority party, and now they were taken into the Unity party—the Socialistische Einheitspartei Deutschlands. The party bosses told the members what to do, and they did it, just as Karl did at the barracks.

For a while everything went all right, but then he made the mistake of attracting attention to himself by being too conscientious and diligent. One of the party bosses came to him and told him that part of his duty was to keep watch and make sure there were no traitors in the organization. He must listen to what his comrades said and report on them. Karl said he had never done anything like that and didn't know how to do it; but it was carefully explained to him: he would express "diversionist" sentiments, "Social-Fascist" sentiments, see what the others replied, and report if anyone agreed with him.

This had worried Karl terribly. It meant being a *Spitzel,* and that was a word of shame. He found every possible excuse to avoid this

duty; he became sick and couldn't work. But the party leader kept
after him and began to use threats, saying that he was under suspicion
of being a Social Democrat himself, and he would get into serious
trouble if he refused to carry out his party duties.

While he was in this state of terror Karl visited the home of a friend
who had a little radio set, and they sat listening to RIAS turned low.
They heard what RIAS called the "Spitzeldienst." The radio speaker
named spies who were known in this factory and that and warned the
hearers to avoid these vile persons. "More names will be given at this
hour every evening. Listen and make note of them and beware." So
there was the last straw on poor Karl's moral back; he decided that
he would never have his name called on that dreadful list; he would
make his escape to the Western sector.

IV

It was just a matter of walking across the street, but it wasn't as
simple as it sounded. The little family had a few belongings which
they knew they could never replace, and if you were carrying a large
bundle that opened you to suspicion. Moreover, Karl was already under suspicion, and some spy might be following him. So they waited
for a stormy night, and then in rain and darkness they crossed. They
did not make the mistake, which some refugees in their helpless ignorance had made, of going to one of the various offices the Reds still
had in the West sector—for example, Radio Berlin, which many got
confused with RIAS. There were sad stories of people who had gone
there and naïvely told their purpose, and had been kept until night
and then whisked back and turned over to the SSD, the Eastern secret
police. The end of it was conviction for treason and sentence to ten
or fifteen years in a slave-labor camp. Karl had come to his uncle's
home, and in the morning when his clothes had been dried out he had
gone to what was called "Refugee Row" in the Kuno-Fischer-Strasse.

Here the fugitives were screened. If they could convince the investigators that they had come in peril of life and limb, they were granted
the status of "political refugees"; they were entitled to shelter and an
allowance of sixty marks a month, which would buy just about half
the quantity of food it took to keep them alive. If they were not able
to convince the investigators they were advised to go back; but of
course if they went most of them would pay with their lives, for they
were now considered traitors. So they couldn't be forced to go; they
just stayed on, in the condition of stateless persons having no papers

and exposed to many dangers. They went about begging for work and beating down wages, so they were not popular in the labor market.

Lanny gave Karl a little money to keep him and his family alive and promised to plead his case with the authorities. So the art expert paid a visit to that drab and depressing building on Kuno-Fischer-Strasse, once a trade-union hall, bombed and then repaired. Inside were many rooms, and against the wall in each were rows of chairs occupied by sad, depressed-appearing humans, old and young. They sat patiently; for wars are great developers of patience in the poor. There were a dozen teams of three Germans, each doing the interviewing and then consulting with regard to each case. They had to do their best to sort out the worthy from the deadbeats, and also from the well-trained spies whom the Reds were continually sending over.

Lanny traced down the team which had the Karl Seidl case in its care, and they heard his story and made notes and promised to expedite the decision. Incidentally, they gave him some idea of the problems which had fallen upon their shoulders. The refugees were pouring in, not merely from East Germany but from all the border states; the military barracks on the outskirts of the city were jammed, and new shelters were being built. "But how can we get materials now? And what will happen, Herr Budd, if we have to leave Berlin?"

V

Many people had asked this question of Lanny, and he knew that many more would ask it at home; so he went to call upon General Lucius Clay, the military governor who had the problem in his hands. In the days when Lanny had first begun to observe his country's government and to think about it, the power had rested in a few aggressive men of big business like his father, who had subsidized both political parties and given their orders through a "boss." But in the days of Franklin Roosevelt the power had begun to shift, and the process was continuing under Truman; in spite of all cries of protest, the bureaucrats were taking over the power in the name of the public interest. And here was one of these bureaucrats—the fact that he wore an Army uniform with four stars on each shoulder did not keep him from being a member of that new caste. His entire career had been in the Army, but he had never fought a battle; he had been an engineer and instructor of engineering, he had built great dams and airfields, and had been General Eisenhower's deputy in charge of supplying the material needed in the greatest military campaign of history. Now he was in charge of a campaign to take nearly fifty million conquered Germans and make them over into a democratic community. The Soviets had taken seventeen million to be made into Reds, and the three free nations were in process of putting the rest under one government with General Clay in charge.

He came from Georgia and had an accent an American would notice but probably a German wouldn't. He was moderately tall, slender, with a thin face and prominent nose. He gazed at his visitor intently with dark eyes, which heavy eyebrows made to appear cavernous. He was completely absorbed in his tremendous job and eager to have it reported correctly to the American people. AMG was trying to do something new in history, to teach conquered peoples the idea of governing themselves. Lanny said that everybody asked him if we were going to "stick," and General Clay answered, "I will show you what I said on the subject over the telecon."

That was shortening of the words "telephone conversation"; it was a recently perfected device by which officials in Berlin, London, Paris, and Washington could carry on a conversation among themselves. The words spoken were taken down as if on a teletype; the machine automatically put them into code and transmitted them by wireless; they were received by another machine in each of the other cities and there decoded and typed on wide sheets of paper. Now General Clay pushed one of these sheets toward Lanny. "This is what I said to the Department of the Army when the blockade began."

And Lanny read, "When Berlin falls, Western Europe will be next. If we mean to hold Europe against communism we must not budge. We can take humiliation and pressure short of war without losing face. If we withdraw, our position in Europe is threatened. If America does not understand this now, does not know that the issue is cast, then it never will, and communism will run rampant. I believe the future of democracy requires us to stay. This is not heroic pose, because there will be nothing heroic in having to take humiliation without retaliation."

"That was approved," said the General, "and there has been no change. I'm quite sure there will be none."

"Would it be proper for me to quote that?" Lanny asked, and the answer was, "It would be helpful."

VI

From that office Lanny went to call upon Ernst Reuter, Oberbürger-meister of Berlin. Lanny had met him in the old days when he had frequented the labor college which Freddi Robin had helped to establish in the city. After the ending of World War I, Reuter had left the Social-Democratic party and become general secretary of the Communist party; but he had quickly come to realize the dishonesty of that organization and had returned to his first love. That made him a renegade in the eyes of the Reds, and when he was duly elected mayor of Berlin they refused to let him serve. Now, during the blockade, the three Allied sectors were being merged and Reuter was on the point of taking his office.

Lanny was embraced by a big, shaggy bear of a man, voluble and explosive. Nobody would have any doubt what Ernst Reuter thought or what he intended to do. Yes, the Americans were going to stick, he said, and the Germans were going to stick with them. Of course the Reds could take them at any time, but the Reds knew it would mean a general war, and they didn't want that, because their own social structure was too shaky. All you had to do was to call their bluff, and they would back down every time. The Oberbürgermeister of West Berlin became poetical and declared, "We have gazed into the face of the Red Medusa and we have not been turned to stone!"

He had only one fault to find with the Allies and with his own countrymen: they did not fight back at the enemy hard enough, they did not spread enough propaganda. Reuter, as elected mayor, was doing all he could, but the Bonn government of Germany was confused and split up among political parties and perhaps afraid that, if war came, the Americans would fall back of the Rhine before they tried to make a stand. "But we must have the courage of our convictions," declared Reuter. "We have the truth on our side, and we must speak it boldly and keep speaking it day and night. Everybody in Germany wants a united country and everybody must be made to realize that it is the Reds who have seized a part of Germany and are holding it as a satellite. We can have a united Germany any time the Reds are willing to let us have it on democratic terms. Let the German people decide what kind of united Germany it is to be."

Reuter had listened to Herr Fröhlich over the radio but hadn't known the speaker's real name. He had never heard the Peace Program from New Jersey and was enthusiastic when he learned about it; he wanted to send Lanny forth as an evangelist to tell the world that the German people had got their freedom back and were going to keep it this time and not surrender it to any sort of dictator.

VII

Lanny Budd went on the air again. RIAS gave him a spot early in the evening when the workers of East Berlin would be in their homes, crouching by their cheap radio sets and keeping them turned low. He addressed the East Germans especially, though of course those in the West would be listening in too. He spoke as one who had loved Germany from boyhood; the genial and warmhearted and enlightened Germany, the Germany of Goethe and Schiller, of Beethoven and Heine. Those great masters had been world citizens, men of the free world. They could never have worked and taught, they could never have survived, in a police state, a land full of spies and torturers and concentration camps.

Herr Fröhlich said he had been talking with Germans who had escaped into the Western world and told him their stories. He set forth the differences between democracy and dictatorship, not in abstractions but in the concrete experiences of one man after another, men of all classes—workers, students, college professors, Army officers—who had been through the Russian anti-Fascist schools and could perceive the difference between the ideals the Communists taught and the horrors they practiced. He closed with a plea to the Germans to come back to the Western world—not physically, for their services were needed in the places where they were. They were needed to teach others and help to save the mind of East Germany. He wanted them to come to the Western world in their minds and hearts, in their way of thinking and feeling about the struggle between the two great world forces which had torn Germany into halves.

A few seconds after he finished he was called to the telephone; it happened in Berlin, just as in Edgemere, New Jersey. A voice said, "*Guten Tag, Herr Fröhlich.* No names, please. That was an excellent talk and a pleasure to hear."

The voice sounded familiar, but Lanny couldn't place it. "You must give me a clue," he said, and promptly the voice replied, "*Das Untersuchungsgefängnis,*" and again, "No names, please."

That overlong German word, which means investigation jail, brought back to Lanny's mind in a flash his visit to Frankfurt. "*Um Himmels Willen!*" he exclaimed. "Where are you?"

"I'm only a few blocks from you, at a friend's house."

"How did you get here?"

"That is something not to be explained over the telephone. Can you have dinner with me?"

Lanny countered, "Can you afford it?"

"Oh yes, I have some of the new Westmarks which I must spend before I go back where I came from."

"I wasn't thinking only of the marks; I mean can you afford the risk?"

"Tell me some quiet place where we can sit and talk," said Einsiedel; and Lanny named a place where he had occasionally gone with Monck.

VIII

The pair met, and after they had ordered the meal and the waiter had gone away the ex-flier reported that he had been released immediately after Lanny's visit to him. "I'm deeply grateful to you, Herr Budd," he said, "and I would not fail to thank you personally."

"But really," protested Lanny, "I didn't do anything."

"You mean they didn't ask you about me?"

"They asked me, of course; but all I could say was I didn't think you were a spy."

"Well, they must have had respect for your thinking. So I am in your debt, and I hope that someday I may be able to return the favor."

Said Lanny, "I hope that you will not find me in an *Untersuchungsgefängnis*."

"Be careful," said the young Graf, "it can happen, you know." So they joked, having no psychic powers and being unable to foresee even a few days into the future.

Lanny asked, "How did you get here?" And the answer was that he had taken a train to Leipzig and from there to East Berlin. He added, "I am still editor of the *Tägliche* so I'm in a position to do you a favor. I will not allow the paper to mention the talks of Herr Fröhlich. If we did so we would have to denounce him as a lackey of Wall Street and hireling of neo-fascism."

"You are very kind," replied the radio man, "but you are making a mistake. It would be much better to give me a scolding, because that is the way we become known and get our ideas across to the Germans on your side."

They joked for a while about this, amusing themselves by assembling a collection of Soviet clichés and abusive formulas. Lanny would be a Wall Street flunkey and a Truman bootlick, a capitalistic para-site, a diversionary mad dog and a counterrevolutionary wrecker. By the time the waiter brought their wienerschnitzel the American had become a cannibal, and they examined the meat with such concern that the waiter inquired if there was anything wrong. Fortunately other customers appeared and he had to go away and leave them.

Einsiedel remarked, "I noticed that at the end of your broadcast you advised East Germans not to come over but to stay where they were and work for the cause of the free world. But that is not the advice you gave me."

The answer was, "It is easy to give that advice in the abstract, to people you do not know. It is not so easy when the person is a friend and you are in his presence. I have done it in more than one case and I have them on my conscience."

"You must not have me there," replied the other. "I am an inde-pendent person, and I shall do what my own conscience directs. I want you to know, Herr Budd, I am not really so naïve as I must seem to you. My trouble is, I find it so hard to share your faith in democ-racy. You Americans may have the good luck to choose fit leaders; but for us in old Europe the tyranny of the majority can assume fright-ful forms."

Lanny, having watched the rise of Hitler, found it hard to answer that. He said, "Tell me, how have you been getting along with your friends since your return?"

"They expected me to be more bitter against the Americans. They say, 'You have changed. You are not so sharp as you used to be.'"

"Ah, there you have it!" exclaimed Lanny. "There begins suspicion, and out of that grows fear. *Hab' Acht, mein lieber Graf!*"

IX

Immediately after this came an interesting development; one of the examiners at the refugee clearing station called Lanny on the telephone at his hotel. He reported that half-a-dozen students from Berlin Uni-versity had shown up at the station, saying that they were sick of the propaganda fed to them at that institution, which was in the East sec-tor. Might it not be possible for the Americans to set up some kind of embryo college in which truth could be taught instead of propa-ganda?

Lanny hurried over to Kuno-Fischer-Strasse, and there he met a group of Germans in their early twenties, each of whom had a tale to

tell of the boredom and futility of Soviet education. For technical subjects it was all right, they were factual and efficient. But when it came
to cultural subjects, to literature, history, philosophy, it was "the
bunk"—the young Germans had learned this term. It was all dogma;
independent opinion was absolutely excluded, and one was bored to
extinction. There ought to be in the American sector a "Free University," to which students from all the sectors could come. Lanny
took fire at the idea; he telephoned Lasky, and Lasky took fire; he
telephoned Shub, and Shub took fire and said that Lanny should come
at once and they would give him a spot on the radio to talk about it.

These young Germans groping their way caused the visiting art
expert to think of Fritz Meissner; he asked if any of them had known
him, but none had. Somehow he felt that the Free University would
be a memorial to Fritz—a secret memorial, in Lanny's heart. It would
be a way of winning absolution for what he had done to Kurt's eld-
est son. It would be what the son himself would want, or would have
wanted had he been alive. It was a real idea, and Lanny could tell by
the fury it aroused in the Communists that it was one which would
grow and spread.

He went to see General Clay about it, and that officer agreed. There
would be the problem of getting a building, but he would find one.
He would set aside funds and get some teachers and some books.
Wouldn't Mr. Budd like to become one of the teachers? Lanny was
immensely amused by the idea of becoming a university professor—
he, with only two years at St. Thomas's Academy by way of formal
education. But he told the general that he had a family at home, also
a Peace Program. He would go home and tell the American public
about the embryo Free University of Berlin. Radio listeners would
send books, and teachers would volunteer; also, some of the foundations might help; many people who didn't want to pay income taxes
might be willing to have their money used to set up a rival to the great
Berlin University which had fallen prey to the Reds. Lanny counted
that a good day's work; he would have been still happier if he had
been able to look forward and realize that within three years the Free
University of Berlin would have a couple of hundred teachers and
five or six thousand students.

BOOK NINE

No Fiend in Hell Can Match

25

Into the Jaws of Death

I

LANNY went to RIAS and gave what he intended to be his last talk. His subject was the embryo Free University. He explained carefully the difference between the teaching of dogma and the free inquiry into truth. He referred to some of the absurdities that were taught as dogma in various parts of the world, not failing to include East Berlin and Moscow. He told of some of the persecutions for efforts at free inquiry, beginning with Socrates being made to drink the cup of hemlock juice, because he taught that the Hellenic gods did not really exist; and then Galileo, who had been shut up in a dungeon for teaching that the earth moved around the sun.

He said that all we called progress in the modern world depended upon the sacred right of free inquiry; the right of every individual to take part in the free competition of ideas, not merely the search for them but the propagation of them. He stated that a university dedicated to this cause was to be started at once, and that his hearers were to talk about it and spread the good news; and very soon they would be informed where qualified students might report for enrollment. Students from East Berlin and East Germany would be welcome, and it was hoped that they would assert their right to attend a university of their own choice.

Then Lanny shook hands with his friends and set out to walk to his hotel. It was a pleasant warm evening at the end of August. He watched the crowds and reflected upon the courage and endurance of civilized people in the midst of the worst adversities. He turned into a side street on the way to his hotel, and at the corner he stopped and waited for a car to pass before he stepped down from the curb; but the car swerved and bumped over the curb, and as he leaped back it struck him a glancing blow on the shoulder, knocking him off his feet.

The car sped on; but another car that was not far behind it stopped with a grinding of brakes. Lanny was a bit dazed and did not realize exactly what was happening; some men ran toward him and helped him to his feet, expressing concern and asking if he was badly hurt. He said no, he didn't think so, and one of them said he ought to be taken to a hospital. "No, wait," Lanny said. "I think I'm all right." But the man insisted, "You should not take a chance, you should go to a hospital." He started to push Lanny toward the car, and the American realized that there were three Germans and that they had him surrounded and were leading him to their car.

Suddenly a stab of fear smote him; they were trying to take him by force, and quickly. There flashed into his mind the words that Monck had spoken to him so solemnly, "Don't be afraid to make a noise! Don't think about the proprieties, scream! Scream as loud as you can!"

And Lanny screamed. He was amazed at the sound of his own voice when he really turned it loose. "*Ich bin Lanny Budd! Mein Name ist Lanny Budd!*" Monck had said there was no use calling for help, because the kidnapers would be armed; the only thing to cry was your name. Your one chance was that some passer-by might hear it and might be moved to telephone AMG or the German police.

The man who had demanded that Lanny come to the hospital clapped his hand over Lanny's mouth. Lanny bit with all the power of his jaw, and the man jerked his hand loose and struck Lanny a blow on the side of his head which made his head ring and deafened him. But he went on struggling madly and yelling at the top of his lungs, "*Mein Name ist Lanny Budd!*" But then he felt something soft and wet clamped over his face. He smelled a strong, sweetish smell and tried his best not to breathe it in. He fought with all his might, but these two things are incompatible; when you make exertions you have to breathe, and when you are breathing chloroform you do not fight. The three men had him in their grip, and the cloth was clamped tightly against his face, and in a few seconds he had passed out and knew no more.

II

His consciousness came back in a wavy blur. He realized that he was alive, but he wasn't sure where or how, or what it meant to be alive, or what had happened to him. Mostly his sensations were of pain, a headache, a ringing in his ears, an aching in his shoulder. He began to move his hands feebly, in the effort to make sure that he was alive, or whether perhaps this was some state of consciousness in the next world. He opened his eyes and saw nothing; he couldn't be sure about that,

and thought that maybe he was blind. Only gradually did he realize
that he was in total darkness. There were sounds, and it took time to
realize that they were in his own head; only gradually did he become
sure that outside was utter and complete stillness, the like of which
he had never imagined before. He began to feel himself; yes, he was
all here. He moved his shoulder; apparently it was not broken, it was
just a bad bruise. One elbow hurt; he had struck it when he fell. He
tested it and it seemed to work all right. He tried his voice; he could
hear it, so presumably he wasn't deaf. Or could a deaf man hear from
inside? He wasn't sure.

He felt beneath him; there was something hard and cold and smooth,
and he realized that he was lying on a concrete floor. He began to
recall what had happened to him. It was hard to think; the effort hurt,
and he shrank from the pain; but the instinct of life drove him to keep
at it. Yes, he had been struck by an automobile, and then he was to be
taken to a hospital. Could this be a hospital, or was it a tomb? Had
he been buried alive? Or was it the future life? Would he meet Madame Zyszynski and presently be talking to Laurel in a trance?

He had lost the sense of time and didn't know how long it took,
but in the end his consciousness cleared and he said to himself, I have
been kidnaped. I am in the hands of the Reds. This must be a dungeon,
and what are they going to do to me?

He remembered what Monck had said, "If they get you without
witnesses you are gone for good. Your only chance is, if somebody
has reported your name." Lanny tried to think. Had there been other
people on the street? Yes, he was almost sure there had been several.
Some would have seen the accident; they would have stopped and
might have approached out of curiosity. But when they realized that
it was a kidnaping they would have moved away. They were helpless
civilians and knew that the kidnapers were desperate men and to interfere might mean death. But after the kidnapers were gone, to run
to a telephone and call the police would involve no risk.

Lanny remembered that he had screamed his name half-a-dozen
times. Somebody must surely have heard it. They wouldn't know that
it was the man they had listened to on the radio, but they would guess
it was an American name, and they would know that the kidnapers
would be from the East. There was at least a good chance that the
incident had been reported. And in any case he would be missed, and
his friends would guess. RIAS would make a fuss; but would the Reds
care?

There had been two cars; one had deliberately struck him, and the other had picked him up and carried him away. No doubt he had been followed from the radio station. The Reds of course had known who he was; they knew everything, it was their business. Probably they had spies in RIAS; they had them everywhere among the Germans in American employ, among the servants in every department of government and in the homes of officials. So Ilya Ehrenburg had got the information and had broadcast it.

All this thinking took time and caused headache. He was in the hands of the enemy—the cold-war enemy. He had been in danger before and always had managed to escape, but this time he could be sure there would be no escaping. They had him, and they would give him the works, they would put him through the mill. He had talked with many persons who had been through that mill; he had read about scores of others. His first impulse was to panic at the thought, but he checked himself. No, that wouldn't do any good; he must use his wits, he must be better than they were, better in mind and in spirit.

They would torture him; and what would it be for? What would they want? Would they do it for revenge or for the sheer pleasure of making him suffer pain? No—for they were not savages, they were scientists. They were scientists of Marxist materialism; they were practical men, and what they did was for a purpose, for their own clear advantage. What would they want from the son of Budd-Erling, from the cannibal, the son of a crocodile? They would want information; they would want the names of the people who were helping him, his fellow conspirators. They would know a lot about him already; they would have a card file on him, a large dossier. Lanny had studied many such, including one the Nazis had accumulated on him. The Reds would have an even better one; for where the Nazis had had only a dozen years the Reds had had thirty, and they had taken over all the Nazi techniques.

III

He felt around him cautiously; the smooth, hard concrete floor. Leaning over to one side, he found that he could touch a concrete wall. Leaning over to the other side, he found that he could touch another. He made certain that he was in a box a little more than six feet square. He wanted to know how high it was, so, very cautiously, he tried to get to his feet, leaning against one of the walls. He found that he couldn't stand and had to sit again and wait to get firmer control of himself.

Finally he was able to get up, and he found that by raising his hands he could touch the ceiling; the room, or box, was about seven feet high. Then he groped his way around it and discovered that there was a door, solid, smooth, and hard; it was steel. The idea flashed over him: Was he put in here to be suffocated? Was that the reason for the ringing in his ears and the dizziness? But by feeling every inch of the wall, one side after another, he discovered there was an opening of about four inches square high up in one wall, and that down near the floor on the same wall was another opening of the same size. Obviously these were ventilation ducts. He felt the air coming in, and it was cool. He knew there was no cool air in Berlin on the hot day he had been experiencing, and suddenly a horrible realization flashed over him; they had put him in one of their temperature chambers.

They had a name for it, but he had forgotten it. First, they subjected you to cold. They brought you to a precise point, scientifically determined, where you did not quite freeze; you did not die but your faculties were paralyzed. The Nazis had determined all that by experiment, and the Soviets had taken over both the experimenters and their data. When they had all but frozen you for exactly the right time they warmed you. They turned the heat up to the precise scientifically determined point where you could endure that for a certain length of time without perishing. So, without damaging you permanently, without bruising you or making any marks, they could paralyze your will and break your spirit, bring you to the point where you would tell them anything they wanted to know and confess to anything, true or false. It was something they could do without waste of time or bother; it was something that worked while they slept.

Yes, the air coming in near the floor was getting colder, and Lanny realized that he would have to think fast. What would they want from him? What were the things he could tell them, and what were the things he couldn't tell them? He must make up his muddled mind, and he must manage to hold on to the ideas regardless of whatever might be done to him. Would they ask him about RIAS? But what could they expect to get? They undoubtedly had spies there and knew everything. Would they ask about his talk with General Clay? But there was nothing confidential about that, the General had authorized him to quote what he said. Would they ask about Bernhardt Monck? But Monck was an old-timer—they no doubt had people who had been his colleagues away back after World War I. They knew he was a lifelong Social Democrat, an ex-sailor, ex-labor leader, an American agent who had worked against Hitler and now was working against the Reds. His present position was known, his place of residence, his family, all such matters. Monck himself had told Lanny they would know all that; and Lanny knew no more.

Then, Fritz Meissner; undoubtedly they had caught Fritz and had put him through the mill. How much had he told? Lanny could never feel sure that any psychic message was valid; Fritz might still be alive, and if so Lanny could do him great harm by talking about him. No, he would not take that chance.

But then, thinking more about it, he began to wonder if he should say he had set Fritz to trying to catch the men who were circulating Himmler money. He had assumed that it was Neo-Nazis who were doing it, and they were doing harm to the Soviets just as much as to the Americans. Surely it had never crossed his mind that any Soviet officials would be engaged in promoting anything so low, so obviously criminal! But then, if they were doing it, they would take that for an insult; and above all he must say nothing to affront them and their wonderful, their holy Soviet system. Lanny, who had done some interrogation for General Patton's army, remembered how different his attitude had been toward prisoners who had answered freely and cheerfully and those who were surly and insulting. He made up his mind that he would be polite and obliging; his life might depend upon it. The official who questioned him would be a Communist fanatic, but he would be doing his duty as he saw it, and there would be no use in adding personal antagonism to his professional severity.

Then, of course, the Kurt Meissner story, the treasure of the Tegernsee. They would be sure to know about that and they would be anxious for hints as to the location of other treasure. Unfortunately Lanny had already told all that he knew; but how could he get them to believe this? It was quite possible that he might be tortured for weeks and months for the purpose of forcing him to reveal facts about treasure of which he had no knowledge whatever. Yes, he had assumed a grave risk when he had mixed himself up in the uncovering of six or eight million dollars! He wished that he had taken his wife's advice and stayed away not merely from Munich but from the whole of Germany.

IV

He began to think about America. What was there in America they might want to question him about? Would they want to ask about Robbie? Hardly; they would know about him, all there was to know; but they might think there was more! Would they want Lanny to report that Robbie was one of the principal financial supporters, the

power behind the throne, of the fascistic Truman government? Would
they want to know how much money he put up, and who carried his
orders to Washington? Or would they by chance want to ask about
the case of Bess? They would know all about that, or would think they
knew. Would they want Lanny to confess that he was the one who had
betrayed his sister to the FBI? They would be coming uncomfortably
close to the truth in that, and if they were to put a lie detector on him
the consequences might be embarrassing. Would they have any reason
to suspect Hansi, and would they try to get Lanny to admit that Hansi
had been the betrayer?

In the course of his talks with refugees from East Germany, Lanny
had heard over and over again the statement that the MVD cared nothing about the truth but required their victims to confess to anything
the MVD desired to prove. Lanny tried to imagine what they might
desire to prove about him; he would have to decide whether he would
be willing to admit this or that. Which way would he be apt to fare
the worse, to anger them by refusing to give them what they wanted or
by obliging them and making himself guilty? Which would mean more
to them, having their own way or protecting their Soviet regime?

He tried to think steadily in spite of his aching body and brain. He
might have only a short time to make up his mind; he must choose the
best course of action and stick to it resolutely through whatever ordeal
might be coming. He must fix in his mind certain things that he would
be willing to say, and certain others that he would refuse to say under
any circumstances. He would refuse to implicate any innocent person.
That seemed elementary; but then he bethought himself, What harm
could it do to implicate anybody unless it was someone who was in the
power of the Reds? So far as he knew, there were only three persons
of his acquaintance who were in that power, or might be: Fritz Meissner, Anna Surden, and Graf Einsiedel.

Suppose they had heard about his having lunch with Einsiedel in
the West Berlin restaurant. All he could say was that he had helped to
get Einsiedel out of an American jail and Einsiedel had come to thank
him. But suppose they wanted him to say that Einsiedel was a traitor,
a fascist spy, a Trotskyist diversionist, a left-wing deviationist, a Bukharinist counterrevolutionary—would he say that? Of course he wouldn't!

V

Lanny had learned that these ordeals were usually protracted; time
was a commodity of which the Soviet Union had an abundant supply.

Lanny had talked with a man at RIAS who had been through the mill, had been exiled to Siberia and escaped from there. He had been put in the Butyrka Prison in Moscow, in a huge cell so crowded with a horde of other prisoners that frequently it was impossible to find a space in which to lie down. In that place and under those conditions he had been held for eight months before he had his first examination. Lanny had talked with another man who had been an official concerned with the production of tanks. He had fallen under suspicion and had been held in Lubyanka Prison; he had been questioned off and on for three years before a compromise confession had been worked out, and then they had turned him loose. He said there were eight great jails in Moscow alone, and all of them crowded. In Lubyanka there had been thirty thousand prisoners. It was a kind of delirium, an epidemic of suspicion and fear; it spread by what the mathematicians call an arithmetical progression. One person was browbeaten into implicating half-a-dozen others, then these half-dozen were arrested, and each in turn implicated another half-dozen.

Lanny could guess that his case might be different, first, because he was a foreigner, and second, because he was well known. He had met General Clay, he had many friends in RIAS and in Monck's CIC. All these persons would be active in his behalf; there would be something of an uproar when he was discovered missing. Even if his kidnaping had not been reported, the truth would be surmised. The Reds who had dragged Lanny into a car and sped away with him to East Berlin would have no means of knowing whether any of the spectators had taken the trouble to report the kidnaping; but if RIAS went into action the Reds would know it. Lanny could guess that these facts explained his present situation; they were figuring that they might not be able to hold him for long, so they were going to work on him without delay.

He realized that the cell in which he was confined was becoming chilly. He reached over to the vent near the floor and found that colder air was coming in; not a blast of it, just a gentle, quiet flow. He moved to the opposite corner, but that was not far away, and it took the colder air only a few seconds to reach him. He found that he was beginning to shiver, and he could not control it; he had a tendency to nausea as a result of the chloroform, and he was thirsty. His head ached, and his shoulder and elbow; all that combined to frighten him and weaken him, which was the way they planned it.

He did not want them to have their way and got up and moved about to keep warm; but he knew that wouldn't help him for long; he would grow weaker. He must use his will power, his moral force, not to let himself be overcome. No matter what they did to him, he must not say anything that would injure any other person or violate his sense of honor. If he erred in that he would never afterward be able to endure himself.

VI

It seemed to him that he could feel the temperature dropping minute by minute. He did not put his hand to the vent, because that frightened him. It seemed to him that his very bones were freezing, and the time came when he no longer had the strength to stand up; he had to give up and lie still regardless of consequences. Perhaps they were actually going to freeze him to death as a cheap and convenient way to get rid of him. If that was the case there was nothing he could do about it, and he would die an honest man.

He knew about the freezing experiments the Nazis had tried at Dachau; they were called "scientific" experiments, and he had studied the reports of them. The heart beat slowed up, the pulse weakened, the temperature of the body declined. The Nazis had found it most interesting to see how near to death a man could come, and how quickly or slowly he could be revived, and what his condition would be at the end of the ordeal. But there was nobody here to take Lanny's temperature or pulse, and he himself was not a competent observer.

What he thought about was Laurel; he was bidding her good-by and was sharing the anguish of soul he knew she would experience. She would never know the details, but she would guess the worst. She would never cease to blame herself for having let him come. She had a hard problem, loving a man who considered it his duty to go and risk his life every so often. She could suggest that the time had come when he might let younger men take up these duties; but she saw where his heart was, and she dreaded to put obstacles in his path and weaken his will.

It was not so unpleasant a way to fade out; to lie still and contemplate his love for Laurel and remember what their life had been. A strange courtship they had had, on board the yacht *Oriole* on its way across the Pacific to China. Lizbeth Holdenhurst, daughter of the owner, had wanted Lanny very much, and Laurel had decided in her quiet way that her own claims were superior. Later the yacht had gone down somewhere off the harbor of Hong Kong; Lizbeth had gone with it, and of her bones were coral made—if you could believe Shakespeare's song. Laurel had been the busy and protective wife, and she had two children to care for, so she would not let her spirit be broken. Vaguely her spirit floated before him; everything was vague, as if seen through a mist.

In the midst of that dimness, that pleasant fading away into nothingness, he became aware that the door of his cell was opened and a flashlight was turned upon his face. He closed his eyes, because even that small amount of light hurt him. The next thing he was aware of was that his arm was being lifted, that someone was feeling the pulse in his wrist. Then his arm was laid down again, and that was all. The man did not speak a word, and neither did Lanny. The door was closed again.

Evidently there was to be a decision; either he had been frozen enough or not enough; but Lanny's consciousness was too feeble to care. He lay there and only gradually became aware that his consciousness was coming back to him, he was thinking once more; he was wondering what was happening to him and what was going to happen. Again he had the same speculation: Was this life or was it death? Was he coming back to the world of tormented men or was he coming back to that dim world of the spirits, or "psychic entities," a world which appeared to be inhabited by an odd assortment of beings.

He was able to put out his hand and feel the concrete floor, hard, smooth, and still cold; but the air was warm, and he drew delicious breaths of it. His strength returned, and with it curiosity; first he sat up, and then moved a few inches over and stretched out his hand to the vent; yes, warm air was coming in. They had decided that he was near enough to freezing and so they were giving him warmth again; but he knew from what he had been told that this was only temporary. They were going to give him a baking, and that would be still more unpleasant. So his mind told him; but that did not keep his stubborn body from enjoying the moment's respite. Eat, drink, and be merry, for tomorrow we die!

VII

But it didn't take until tomorrow; it took only a few minutes. The delightful warmth changed to unpleasant hotness and then to what seemed unbearable furnace temperature. Lanny's heart began to pound and he gasped for breath. He had been thirsty before, and now the heat drew the moisture out of his body and his thirst became agonizing. It wasn't so pleasant to die this way; Lanny could have told the scientists that it was a fiery anguish.

He searched desperately in his consciousness for some way to bear it, and there came back to him words and ideas that had been taught him, first by his great-uncle Eli Budd in Connecticut, and later by his stepfather, Parsifal Dingle, New Thought advocate out of the Middle West of America.

Thirty years ago his great-uncle, a Congregational minister, had explained the Transcendentalist philosophy, the concept of the immanence of God; He was in us, and we were in Him; as St. Paul had set it forth, disputing with the Epicureans and the Stoics of ancient Athens, "In Him we live, and move, and have our being." We did not have to speak to Him, we only had to think of Him; He knew our thought, He *was* our thought. Lanny had accepted the idea as a likely guess. It seemed to him impossible to believe that this universe was the product of accident, or that mind was simply a momentary product of chemical and electrical activities going on in brain cells. He wanted to believe that mind was basic to the universe; impossible as it was to realize it, there must be a universal Mind of which we were a part.

To Lanny in his day-by-day life it had been enough to repeat the formula of the Benedictine order, "To labor is to pray"; it seemed to him that efforts to end poverty and war upon this earth could not fail to be pleasing to God. But to Lanny's elderly stepfather that did not seem enough. To Parsifal Dingle, God was not a metaphysical theory, a reasonable hypothesis; he insisted that God was in your mind all the time; that God was alive, God was real, and you were a part of Him and could appeal to Him and make use of Him at all times. It was Parsifal's firm conviction that you had only to hold before your mind the idea that God was helping you; and when Lanny said that that sounded to him like autosuggestion, Parsifal had asked quietly, "What is autosuggestion?" When Lanny had to admit, with a smile, that he didn't really know, Parsifal answered, "Maybe autosuggestion is God." He went on to try to analyze the process that goes on in our minds when we apply autosuggestion or any other kind of suggestion. Some suggestions were stronger than others, and maybe God was a stronger suggestion than suggestion.

That had a funny sound, but Parsifal didn't mean it so. He said that the essence of the process was to awaken your spirit, to apply power to it. When you thought of suggestion you thought of something inferior; you said "only" suggestion or "merely" suggestion, or "nothing but" suggestion; but nobody ever said merely God, or only God, or nothing but God. Parsifal said, "We are dealing with the spirit, or the mind, or whatever name you choose to give to your inmost being. It is exactly like the water tap in your bathroom; you have the power to turn it on, but you have that power only if you know you have the power, if you believe it. If you say that you can't turn it on, then you don't get the water, and that's all there is to it."

Parsifal was fond of a saying by Mary Baker Eddy, that "Man's extremity is God's opportunity." And surely, if ever a man was in extremity, Lanny Budd was in it now. He wanted both water of the body and water of the spirit, and he wanted them with desperation. He knew Parsifal's formulas, and because there was nothing else to do he tried them. He began to say to himself, "God will help me." He said it over and over to himself, concentrating what was left of his mind upon it. And whether you called it autosuggestion or whether you called it God, the fact was that it took his mind off his anguish and his fear. Because that was a form of relief he concentrated with more and more intensity; and so he was no longer afraid, and he no longer was aware of his pain, and in the end he passed quite peacefully into unconsciousness.

VIII

When his consciousness began to come back again he was puzzled for the third time; he wondered if he had died and if this time he was in some other state of being. He opened his eyes, and a bright light was shining in them, and that hurt him so he closed them again. It seemed to him that he was beginning to feel coolness again, and it was pleasant. At first it was a sort of coolness in the abstract, a strange thing that he felt without knowing what it was or what it meant; but then he began to recall what had happened to him, and the thought came that they had shut off the heat.

All the way through this experience the word "they" meant the people who had captured him and were torturing him. The light seemed to move, so he wondered if "they" were in the cell, and if the coolness was because "they" had opened the door. "They" were feeling his pulse again. He became acutely aware of burning, agonizing thirst, and he murmured, first, "Water," and then in German, "*Wasser*." He assumed that they would be Russian and he tried to recall the Russian word but couldn't.

Either they understood his words or they knew the effect of this treatment. He felt his head being lifted and tilted forward, and a cup was applied to his lips. He drank the water eagerly; it had a sweetish taste, not tea but some other flavor. It was like an answer to his prayers, and he drank to the last drop. Then his head was laid back, and his consciousness revived with suddenness. He thought, Maybe they are giving me a drug; maybe it is some of that "truth" stuff that will make me answer without knowing what I am saying. If so, he couldn't help it, he had to drink; but he would fight against this as against the other evils.

His memory of Parsifal came back, and he began to concentrate once more upon the thought that God was here and that God would help him. Courage came to him in sudden waves, and he resolved that he would conquer these enemies, he would not give way to them; he would prove that God was superior to them—the God in whom he lived, and moved, and had his being! "They" repudiated God, and surely God would favor the believer over the infidel!

He heard the door closed, and he opened his eyes and discovered that he was again in utter darkness. He had come to like the darkness. The heat had been turned off, and that seemed an answer to his prayer. Anyhow, he would go on with his prayer; he would make that his life from this moment on. Whatever trials might come he would face them; he had no doubt that others were coming, and he would conquer them all. He was going to train himself for that achievement; he would give himself the autosuggestion of God, and it would be God.

Time passed; he did not know how much time, for when you are praying you lose the sense of time; that is one of the purposes of prayer. When you are in the hands of torturers and they have shut you up in a black hole, time does not matter and the world does not matter; nothing exists for you but your own soul and the resources you have in it. If you are alone, then you are helpless; but if you have God in your soul, then you have everything.

So Lanny went on with this inner fight against his physical weakness and also against his own doubts and fears. Moving his hands, he discovered that a plate of bread had been left beside him. It was a slice about an inch thick; he broke off a piece and tasted it and discovered that it was whole-wheat bread; that was what he liked, so he began to nibble it. He wasn't sure he had the strength to digest it, but immediately he repudiated this countersuggestion.

Jesus had said that with God all things were possible; this had been one of Parsifal's formulas, by which he had healed many persons who had incurable diseases. That is, they were what the doctors called incurable; and maybe Parsifal hadn't really healed them, but anyway the persons had got well. Lanny told himself that it was certainly possible for God to cause his digestive juices to flow. After all, what had ever made them flow? What had ever caused them to exist?

What had caused Lanny to exist? Courage came back to him, and with it his strength.

IX

But before he had had more than a few nibbles he heard the door open and the light flashed on him again. It was a flashlight, and painful. He closed his eyes and told himself that these were the torturers and that God would give him strength to withstand them.

For the first time he heard a voice. It spoke in Russian; the word was, "*Poshol*," and Lanny was not sure of its meaning, but he felt a pull at his shoulder and he made an effort and raised himself. Two men supported him, and he stood somewhat waveringly. The light was shining through the doorway, and he was impelled toward it.

One of the things to which he had made up his mind was that he would do exactly as he was told and give no sort of provocation. Whatever evil things were done to him would be without cause so far as he was concerned. So he went with somewhat wobbly steps toward the doorway and was gently helped along. He saw two elderly Russians in military jackets with green epaulets; they wore green caps and were armed. They were doubtless jailers, and Lanny could guess that they had no interest in the procedure other than to do what they were told. Quite possibly they were sorry for their prisoners and what they had to do to them.

They closed the door of the cell and, using the torchlight, led Lanny along a corridor. They came to a stairway, and that was difficult indeed; but apparently the men understood and half carried Lanny step by step up the stairs.

Lanny had a guess as to where he was—the Prenzlauerberg Prison, which was in East Berlin and had been taken over by the Russians. He had seen it from the outside; it covered an entire block, and all the blocks around it were ruins. It was built like a fortress, and he had heard stories about the cruelties that went on inside it. Now he had no recourse but to pray; to give himself the firm suggestion that God would help him to endure whatever was done to him, and that in the end it would fail. Great numbers of modern men have forgotten how to pray, and the idea embarrasses them. They prefer to use the language of psychology which they have learned in college. It is easy for them to believe in suggestion, but hard for them to believe in that antiquated suggestion called God.

Lanny had been told by one of the refugees that the warders and

attendants in Soviet prisons were often kind; they had no heart for
the cruelties. So now he chose to believe that the men who were helping him up the staircase were kind; he knew how to say *"spasiba"*—
"thank you," so he said it. He was helped along a corridor; and far
down it he saw another group approaching, presumably warders
with a prisoner. He heard a strange clucking noise, the sound which
in the old days one used to make when driving a horse and buggy, to
start the horse and to keep him going when he showed signs of flag-
ging. Many years had passed since Lanny had driven a horse and
buggy, but he remembered the sound. He observed that his warders,
the moment they heard it, stopped him, took him by the shoulders,
turned him with his face to the wall and pressed him close. Lanny
could guess the purpose of this: he was not permitted to see the other
prisoner. If he had turned his head he might have been struck a blow
on the side of it; so he stayed patiently with his nose touching the
wall until the others had passed by; then he was again turned and
led on.

He was helped up another staircase and along another corridor.
Three times he heard the clucking noise, and by that time he had
acquired what the Russian scientist Pavlov called a "conditioned
reflex." He put his nose automatically against the concrete wall.

They stopped at a door, and he noticed on it the number 814. The
warders opened the door and led their prisoner into a room about ten
feet square with one steel-barred window. In the center was a medium-
sized desk, and behind it sat an official wearing a blouse; the rest of
him was hidden behind the desk. He might have been a waxworks
figure, so still he was. Directly in front of the desk was a very small
stool, and the warders led Lanny to it and placed him upon it, exactly
as if he too had been a waxworks figure. Then the green-capped pair
turned and without a word left the room and closed the door.

And Lanny knew just what that meant. He had been told about it by
refugees and had read the stories of others. He was about to be started
upon what the Russians called "the Conveyor"; a process, a course of
treatment, devised by scientists both psychological and physiological
and tested by two decades of observation. He was going to be made to
confess to something. What would it be?

26

God's Opportunity

I

LANNY was so exhausted that everything wavered slightly before him; but he made an effort to concentrate his attention and saw that he was looking at a blond Russian, perhaps thirty years of age; that meant he was a child of the revolution and would know nothing else. He would know only what the regime had told him and would speak in formulas and clichés. He might be personally good or bad, but that would make very little difference in his conditioned reflexes.

He pressed a button beside his desk, and what could only be described as a blast of light smote Lanny in the eyes. It came from several electric bulbs set in a curved reflected. To one who had been in darkness so long it was like a blow, and he clapped his two hands over his eyes. No objection was made, and apparently he was free to keep his hands there until they got tired.

Lanny had heard about this light and knew it would be shining in his face during the entire time of the investigation. He knew also that the ordeal might continue day and night with no respite. There would be a series of examiners. He would be exhausted, but they would be fresh.

The robot spoke: the first words were German, *"Ihr Name?"* These two German words told Lanny a good deal. He had been wondering in what language he would be addressed. German words suggested that they had connected him with Herr Fröhlich of RIAS, and the cause of his arrest might well be their displeasure at his broadcasts.

He replied, *"Mein Name ist Lanning Prescott Budd."* And when he was asked his age he said, *"Sieben und vierzig."* Very quickly he observed that the young examiner's knowledge of the language was faulty; presumably he had learned it from textbooks, and sometimes Lanny had difficulty in understanding his pronunciation. It was advisable not to offend him by making him aware of his deficiencies. He knew no English words, and Lanny knew only a few Russian ones, but they would manage to make out.

The man first addressed his prisoner as *"Obvinyaemi Budd"*—Accused Budd. This was according to the Soviet law, which had been prepared in the early idealistic days of the revolution. Lanny had visited Petrograd in those early days and had been told all of those wonderful things about brotherhood and freedom and justice. He had been told about just laws, wonderful laws; and he understood that while the reality had degenerated the forms had been kept. So he would not be addressed as "Conspirator Budd" or "Scoundrel Budd" or "Fascist Budd"; he would merely be "Accused Budd." And he, in turn, would address his tormentor as "Citizen Examiner"—*Grazdanin Isledovatel.*

II

The questioning continued, and he stated that he was a citizen of the United States of America. He took occasion to enter formal protest against any questioning, since he had been brought into Soviet territory by force and against his will. There was a pause after each statement, and Lanny assumed that the official was writing down the reply; but Lanny could not look to see on account of the blazing light.

The question was asked, "What were you doing in West Berlin?" Lanny replied very politely, "Citizen Examiner, I am suffering greatly from this light shining in my face. There is no need of it whatever, because we can both see plainly in this room. I ask that you turn the light off."

"The light is none of your business, Accused Budd."

"The light makes it impossible for me to think or to answer your questions properly. I ask that it be turned off."

"The light will remain."

"Citizen Examiner, let me inform you that I am familiar with the Soviet law, and I know that you are forbidden to abuse or strike accused persons."

"Have I struck you, Budd?"

"You are striking me, Citizen Examiner, when you cause this light to shine in my face. What is the difference if you strike me with your fist or strike me with atomic particles? I do not know what physical theory you hold, Citizen Examiner, regarding the nature of light, but all authorities on physics are agreed that light is force, light is energy, and you might as well be striking me with your fist."

They got into trouble because the examiner apparently did not know the German word *"Faust."* He must have thought that Lanny was talking about a German drama, or perhaps a French opera; and Lanny was afraid to demonstrate the word, because he might seem to be shaking his fist at a Soviet official. He kept insisting that light was force. *"Licht ist Kraft!"*

"The light will remain," declared the official.

"Then, Citizen Examiner, I regret to tell you that I will answer no further questions so long as the light remains."

"You will be *made* to answer the questions," persisted the other.

"Citizen Examiner, I refuse formally to answer the questions until the light is turned off. I am perfectly willing to answer your questions and tell you anything I know. But I will not answer under torture."

"This is unheard of, Accused Budd."

"Citizen Examiner, I have studied Soviet law and I know that I am within my rights."

That was too much for the official, and he raised his voice. *"Ti sobaka!"* he cried. "You Fascist dog!"

"Citizen Examiner, you know that you are not permitted to abuse a prisoner; you are not permitted to use abusive language."

"You counterrevolutionary bandit, I will break every bone in your body!"

"Citizen Examiner," responded Lanny in his very best German, *"Sie müssen korrekt sein."*

These were magic words. "You must be correct!" The Prussian military caste had taken over an English word and given it a special technical meaning. To be *korrekt* was to follow the code. The code might be ever so cruel, but you must follow it with calmness, with dignity and propriety. The Soviet official caste knew both the word and the concept; so when Lanny told his questioner that he was not being *korrekt* he had the man—in vulgar American slang—over a barrel.

The official—Lanny never did learn his name—calmed down. "Accused Budd," he said almost pleadingly, "you must understand my position. I have been ordered to keep the light burning, and what can I do?"

"Citizen Examiner, it is obvious that I cannot keep my hands over my eyes all the time, and the light is hurting me even through my hands. It is obvious that I cannot think or answer questions intelligently so long as I am tortured. I cannot believe that the great Soviet government wishes to make it impossible for me to think clearly and speak the truth."

"Budd, I am in no position to act in this matter. I am obeying orders."

"But, Citizen Examiner, the person who has given you this order is violating Soviet law."

"You claim to know more about Soviet law than my superiors?"

"It happens, Citizen Examiner, that I have paid five visits to the Soviet Union, beginning in the early and glorious days of Lenin. I have read your books and studied your institutions, including your laws."

This was most impressive, and it was not necessary that it should be strictly true. To be sure, Lanny had picked up many items of information in the Soviet Union, but most of his present learning was the result of talking with refugees and with several of the Germans employed in RIAS, who had either been through the Conveyor themselves or had heard about it from others who had been through. Most accused persons were ignorant and terrified and did not know that they had any rights. It might be that you would fall into the hands of some brutal tyrant, who would order you beaten or otherwise physically tortured; but there was always a chance that if you asserted your rights with proper dignity you might make an impression.

III

Deep in Lanny's consciousness he was clinging to the formula, "God is helping me"; and now what God told him was to be kind to this dumb, bemuddled creature. The creature was doing what he was ordered, and very probably his mind had been so distorted that he thought he was doing right. Anyhow, he was terrified to do otherwise; he had to make a success of this interview, he had to get out of his prisoner whatever he had been told to get. To succeed would be triumph, to fail would be ruin; so make allowances for him and be kind!

"Citizen Examiner," said Lanny gently, "I feel to you as one man of culture to another. I know you are a man of culture or you could not speak the German language as well as you do." This was one of the fetishes of the Bolsheviks, *kultura*. All of them wished to be thought cultured persons, and if you yourself were a cultured person and behaved as one, they would have a sneaking respect for you even while they called you a Fascist dog and a Wall-Street bandit, a vile Trotskyite, a bloodthirsty Bukharinist, or just a plain cannibal.

Lanny went on, "I assure you that we will get along better if we are considerate of each other. I assure you that I have no secrets whatever and nothing to hide from you. I appreciate that you are doing your duty, and I am perfectly willing to cooperate with you. I will tell you the truth; but don't you see that I cannot do it if I am so distressed physically that I am unable to think? Why can we not converse like one friend to another, and let me tell you what you want to know?"

The answer was, "Because, Budd, I know that you will not want to tell me what I want to know."

"But don't you see that that is prejudging the case, and prejudging me? Is it not sensible first to give me a chance to tell you what you want to know; then if I refuse to tell you, that will be time enough to subject me to the discomfort of this light? Surely it is common sense to give me a chance to prove my good faith."

The Divine assistance proved efficacious; the official pressed the button and the light went off. A sudden blessed relief: Lanny took his hands from his eyes and opened his eyes and blinked them two or three times. He studied this blond, blue-eyed Russian, who probably had some Scandinavian blood; he was broad-shouldered, heavy set, and had a broad face with high cheekbones and wide mouth. He didn't look very intelligent, but again he did not look unkind; so Lanny took heart. "Thank you, Citizen Examiner," he said with fervor; and to himself he said, "God is helping me. God is helping me."

"Accused Budd," said the official, "you recently took a trip into Poland."

"That is correct," Lanny said.

"You obtained a permit for that trip from the Soviet government."

"I did."

"What was the purpose of that trip?"

"I wished to visit Stubendorf, a town in what used to be Upper Silesia. In the old days I had visited Schloss Stubendorf and had friends there. I was trying to track down some paintings which had been in the castle and which I thought it might be possible to buy."

"And you expect me to believe that you took that long and dangerous journey only to find out about some paintings?"

"Citizen Examiner, to an American it did not seem at all a long journey. I have driven myself by automobile across my own country—about three thousand miles each way. I have done that many times, sometimes just for pleasure. As for the danger, I had no thought of that. I was traveling in the land of a friendly people who had been our staunch allies in a terrible war. I expected no danger and I encountered none."

"And you are so much concerned with paintings!"

"Citizen Examiner, that is the way I make my living. I locate paint-ings and give my opinion of them, and my clients in America purchase them and pay me a ten-per-cent commission; I have been doing that for just twenty-five years. I have been doing it on this present trip to Germany. I bought some paintings in Nürnberg and some in Frank-furt; I can give you the names of the paintings and the client and the prices that were paid and so on, if you wish."

This offer met with a cold reception. "That is not necessary," said the official. "We quite understand that all spies have to have their camouflage. You do not deny that you are a spy, I presume?"

"Citizen Examiner, I deny that I am a spy at the present time. I was a spy against the Nazis and I did my small part to help overthrow them. But I have never been a spy against the Soviet Union, and I have never taken any action against the Soviet Union."

"Yet you come here to Berlin and abuse the Soviet Union over the radio!"

"We must not let ourselves be drawn into a political discussion, Citizen Examiner. I have my opinions and you have yours. It is our practice in America to express our opinions freely, and I have done that over the radio; but surely you realize that expressing opinions over the radio is exactly the opposite of spying. The two things are incompatible. If I wished to spy upon the Soviet Union I would pre-tend to approve of everything it does. When I publicly state that I consider the blockade of Berlin unjustified I make it impossible to pose as approving of your course. Knowing what I believe, would you, for example, take me as a friend and trust me with your confidences regarding the affairs of the Soviet Union?"

"I am not here to answer questions but to ask them," replied the Russian grimly. He was not so dumb after all.

IV

This process was a slow one. Every time that Lanny answered the other wrote. He wrote slowly, and meantime Lanny sat and waited and tried to guess what was coming next and to prepare his answer; then he would repeat to himself Parsifal's formula, "God is helping me." He didn't ask God *to* help him; he told himself that God *was* helping him, and furthermore he told himself that this was not mere autosuggestion but the statement of a fact that was going on in the mysterious deeps of his infinite spirit. Lanny's spirit and God's spirit were mingled and mutually engaged in a creative process. Whether

God was also in the spirit of the broad-faced young Russian and on what terms He was operating there was a question with which Lanny had no time to concern himself.

"Did you have any particular person you expected to see in Stuben-dorf?"

"I had a number of persons, Citizen Examiner. I had visited Stuben-dorf off and on many times. General Graf Stubendorf had been a friend of mine in the old days, and so had his protégé, the pianist and composer Kurt Meissner. I did not know if I would find them there, but I hoped to get track of them."

"And did you succeed?"

"I learned that Graf Stubendorf was living by the Tegernsee, and I learned that Kurt Meissner was in the Harz Mountains. I afterward visited them both."

"That Meissner is the same man who was recently killed in Bavaria?"

"That is the one."

"And you betrayed him to the American Army?"

"No, Citizen Examiner, I did not betray him. Officers of the American Army told me what they knew about Kurt Meissner's activities to revive nazism. Naturally I was opposed to that—I have considered it my duty to oppose nazism everywhere and in every possible way. So I went to Kurt Meissner and told him what the American Army had learned about him and persuaded him to give up his Nazi activities and come over to the American side. He did that, and some of his Nazi colleagues presumably murdered him—at least that is what I was told."

"And he told the American Army where a lot of gold was hidden?"

"That is true."

"And you got a part of that gold—is it not so?"

"No, Citizen Examiner, I did not get any of it, and the idea never crossed my mind. I have told you how I make my living, and it is not by looking for treasure."

"And did Kurt Meissner tell you where other treasure was buried?"

"He did not. If he had done so I would have immediately told the American Army, and they would have got the treasure. In the case of valuable objects which are recovered and which can be identified, it has been the practice of the Army to return them to their rightful owners. In the case of gold bullion which was Nazi state treasure, it is turned over to the Interallied Reparations Agency and distributed to those nations from which the Nazis had looted gold. I have no doubt that the Soviet Union received its proper share."

"You understand, Budd, I am writing down what you are telling me, and you have given your word to tell me the truth. If you tell me what is not true, you will pay a severe penalty."

"Every word that I have told you is the truth, Citizen Examiner. I have been told by persons who are hostile to the Soviet Union in their minds that in these interrogations the examiner does not want to hear the truth, he wants to hear what he himself believes. I am doing you the honor to assume that this is not the case."

"Budd, I thank you," was the reply.

The watchful Lanny decided that what they were after was more treasure, and he prepared himself for a long and hard siege on that subject. If he had had any such information he would have given it in order to save his life; but he did not have it. He felt that his life might be in grave danger on that account.

V

The next question was, "Did you know the family of this Kurt Meissner?"

"I knew them all very well," Lanny said. "I had visited them off and on in their home near Stubendorf. There was Elsa, the mother, and there were eight children; they were well brought-up children, and when I went to see them I always took them presents."

"Did you meet any of Kurt's family on your last trip to Stubendorf?"

"No, they had all left. They were in the Harz Mountains. I went there, but I did not meet them there. Kurt was very antagonistic to me at that meeting."

"Did you meet any of them anywhere else?"

"Yes, I met the oldest son, whose name is Friedrich; we called him Fritz. He was a student in East Berlin, and he came to see me in West Berlin. He revealed to me that he had become dissatisfied with his father's Nazi ideas, and he begged me to do what I could to persuade his father to drop his illegal activities. I promised that I would see Kurt and try to dissuade him, and I did so."

"And what was the result of your efforts?"

"He promised to cease his pro-Nazi activities, but he did not keep that promise."

"He had that large amount of gold in his keeping at this time?"

"No, I think he got it later."

"How did you find out about it?"

"The American military authorities decided that he knew about it, and they were about to arrest him. I asked them to let me talk to him and persuade him to renew his promises and keep them. I went to see him, and then he told me how the gold was hidden."

"You are sure he did not tell you about any gold or other treasure, other than what the American Army found?"

"He did not tell me of any other."

"Did he tell the American Army?"

"That I am not able to answer. I never asked them or discussed the subject again. You see, I live in the United States, and I come to Berlin only occasionally, and always on my business as an art expert."

"You are the man who speaks over RIAS under the name of Herr Fröhlich?"

"That is correct."

"And you are an enemy of the Soviet Union."

"I deny most emphatically that I am an enemy of the Soviet Union or of the Russian people. I am opposed to some of the regime's present policies."

"What are those policies?"

"Citizen Examiner, there would be no advantage in our going into a political discussion. I have no doubt that Radio Berlin has made recordings of my few talks over RIAS. I am an American, and I believe what Americans believe; that is, in democratic government."

"You have denounced the government of the Soviet Union?"

"I have expressed my disapproval of all governments that are dictatorships and are not based upon the will of the people."

"Then you presume to say that the people of the Soviet Union do not approve of their government?"

"I am quite sure that the people of the Soviet Union have never had an opportunity to say whether they approve of their government or not. Therefore I do not know, and I do not think that anyone else knows. But, as I have told you, Citizen Examiner, it is futile for us to discuss this subject. You and I were brought up in different worlds, and we have wholly different views of political and economic affairs. The great Karl Marx understood that men's opinions are determined by their economic environment, and you must not expect me to be superior to the laws of social determinism."

VI

That was a tactful way to put it, and the Citizen Examiner condescended to change the subject. "You have been permitted to visit our great Stalin, I am informed."

"That is correct, Citizen Examiner. I have had that honor twice."

"Will you tell me the circumstances?"

"Gladly. The first occasion was early in nineteen forty-two. I had been in Hong Kong and had fled from the Japanese with my wife. We crossed China and were flown to Moscow. It happened that I was a representative of President Roosevelt, and there was an exchange of cablegrams with Washington. Anyhow, I was received by Marshal Stalin."

"Where were you received?"

"In some building in the Kremlin."

"You had an opportunity to visit Marshal Stalin in his home?"

"Citizen Examiner, I was not told whether it was his home or not. I was driven into the Kremlin at night and I saw nothing. I was taken into a building, and all that I saw was a passageway and then an oval-shaped room, all white with gold trimmings. Marshal Stalin came into the room, and we sat at a large table and talked for an hour or two. He was very friendly and frank; and I think that if you could consult him he would express a wish that you should be the same."

The young subordinate of the great Marshal did not see fit to follow up this lead. "What were the circumstances of the second interview?"

"The second interview was four years later, about a year after the end of the war. This time I came as a representative of President Truman. I was flown from Washington to Moscow, and I was received in the same oval-shaped room. I remember being struck by the fact that everything in the room appeared to be exactly the same. There were several telephones, each a different color, and I assumed that this was in order to distinguish one private line from another. I will describe other details if you wish me to. It may be, of course, that you yourself have been in that room."

"No such honor has been extended to me. What was the character of your second interview?"

"It was courteous and friendly, exactly as in the first case. I got the impression of a man quiet, self-contained, and friendly to meet personally."

"Yet you went back and carried a report to the warmonger Truman that Marshal Stalin was planning an attack upon your capitalistic country."

"I carried no such report, Citizen Examiner, and anyone who has told you that has told you falsely. I reported to the President that Marshal Stalin had stated to me positively and in great detail that he intended to carry out to the full all the agreements that had been made at Yalta and Potsdam."

"But you reported that you did not believe that he would keep those agreements."

"I reported nothing of the sort, Citizen Examiner. I had no basis for any such statement. When I was asked my opinion, I said that, and added that only time would show."

"But you reported that Marshal Stalin had been personally friendly to you."

"He was not only friendly, he was cordial, in a talk that lasted about three hours."

"And yet you came away from that interview and used your knowledge of Marshal Stalin and his place of residence to help conspirators against his life."

If the inquisitor had pulled out a gun and taken a shot at Lanny, he could not have been more greatly shocked. "*Um Gottes Willen!*" he exclaimed. "Where did you get that idea?"

"You intend to deny that you were involved in a conspiracy to take Marshal Stalin's life?"

"I deny it with all the emphasis that is possible. No such idea ever crossed my mind, and I never heard of it until this moment."

"You deny that your trip to Poland was to meet such conspirators and give them information and money?"

"I deny it most emphatically. I met no one in Poland except in Stubendorf, and there I talked with no one except persons who might be able to tell me where Kurt Meissner was living and what had become of the paintings which had been in Schloss Stubendorf."

VII

The investigator wrote with painful slowness, and that gave Lanny plenty of time to think. His mind was in a tumult. So that was what they were going to try to put over on him! He knew that nothing could be of more deadly significance. The preposterousness of the charge had nothing to do with the matter. The preposterousness of

any charge never had anything to do with the making of it by the
Reds. The preposterousness of a charge no more kept them from
making it than it had Adolf Hitler; and Hitler had said that the bigger
the lie the easier it was to get it believed.

What counted with Lanny was the revelation of their intentions
toward himself. They were going to pin that charge on him and make
him confess it to the world; and when he had confessed it there could
come only one ending, which was the ending of his life. For lesser
charges there might be lesser penalties, even pardon; but for plotting
against Stalin's life there could be no forgiveness and only one penalty.

The man continued, "You intend to maintain that attitude in spite
of all the evidence?"

"Citizen Examiner, there can be no evidence as to any such ab-
surdity."

"We have the evidence, Accused Budd, and you will be confronted
with it."

"If you have any evidence, Citizen Examiner, I assure you in advance that it is fraudulent. It is a frame-up."

Lanny used the German word *Erfindung*, and they were delayed
for a time because the official was not familiar with that word. Lanny
had to invent some other way of saying it, and then the examiner had
to figure out a way to put it down in Russian. "Accused Budd, what
will you say when I inform you that Fritz Meissner has confessed fully
to his share of the crime?"

"What I say, Citizen Examiner, is that if Fritz Meissner confessed
any such thing it was because he was tortured beyond endurance."

The inquisitor brought his *Faust* down on the desk with a bang.
"You dare to accuse the government of the Soviet Union of employ-
ing torture?"

It was truly funny, but Lanny knew it was no joke, and he had no
impulse to laugh. On the contrary, he was praying as hard as he could.
At every respite during the writing he was saying to himself over and
over again, "God is helping me. God is helping me." Now he said,
"Citizen Examiner, when I was brought to this place I was put in a
tiny box and frozen almost to death; then the temperature was changed
and I was almost roasted to death; then I was brought into this room
and had a glaring light turned into my eyes. If that is not considered
torture in the Soviet Union you must tell me what it is."

"I will *show* you what it is." The man pushed the button and the
light flamed back into Lanny's eyes.

VIII

Too late Lanny realized that he had got in God's way on this occasion. He had talked too much. And he could think of nothing to do now but to clap his hands over his eyes and say, "Citizen Examiner, I shall answer no more questions until the light is turned off."

"You will find that we have ways of making you talk," announced the other. And he proceeded at once to prove the truth of this. "You deny that you have conspired with Hetman Skoropodsky?"

Lanny realized in a flash that if he sat quietly while such questions were asked he would accumulate a mass of guilt against himself. It would be assumed that every silence was an admission, and at all hazards he must not make any such admissions. "*Herr Gott!* Is he still alive?"

"You know him then?"

"I never knew him. He is merely a name to me. I understood that he was a Ukrainian White Guardist. I have never had anything to do with him."

"Nor with any of his followers?"

"Never so far as I had any idea."

"You don't know a man named Lilivitch?"

"I never heard the name. It doesn't sound like a real name to me."

"You never handed him a large sum of money to be used to bribe a spy inside the Kremlin?"

"I most certainly never did anything of the sort."

"You deny that you gave him five thousand American dollars?"

"I most certainly deny it."

"You will maintain that denial in the face of his written confession?"

"I will most certainly maintain it. I will say that he is lying, possibly under torture."

"You intend to repeat that insult to the Soviet Union?"

"Citizen Examiner, I am being tortured at this moment, and I cannot deny the evidence of my own eyes. If you will come and sit by me, you will have the evidence of *your* eyes. So let us try to be sensible with each other."

"It is not for you to give instructions, Accused Budd."

"Citizen Examiner," said Lanny, "we are men of culture, and we should treat each other with correctness. I do not know how much you have had to do with the accumulating of this evidence. It may be that it has been handed to you and you have been told that it is the truth. If so, then of course I have no right to blame you; all I can do is to assure you in all sincerity that this is the most preposterous piece of fiction I have ever heard. I do not believe in assassination, I have never believed in it, and I have never knowingly had anything to do with any person who believed in it."

"We have the evidence, and you will see in the end that it is futile to deny it. You will fare much better if you make a full and frank statement and give us the names of all persons who were your fellow conspirators in this plot."

"I assure you, Citizen Examiner, that if I knew of such a plot I would consider the men to be evil and I would give you their names. I cannot give you what I have not got, and you are simply wasting your time in asking me questions about this matter."

"What will you say when we confront you with the signed testimony of Fritz Meissner?"

"I will say what I have already put into this record, that if Fritz Meissner made any such statement he must have been forced to make it. It is not true, and under no circumstances will I say otherwise."

IX

There was no way to keep track of time or to estimate it. The questioning went on and on, wandering from one subject to another without apparent order or purpose. Names were brought in, Russian names, Polish names, German names. Lanny would say dully, "I never heard of him"; it became a formula, very irritating to the questioner. He would express his annoyance, and Lanny, anxious to avoid a scolding, would find a different phrase, "I do not know the man," or "I have never met any such person."

All this time the electronic particles, or waves, whichever of these compose light, were being hurled in a tremendous blast at Lanny's eyes. He kept his hands over his eyes as long as he could, and this had the effect of turning the energies of light into those of heat. His hands became hot and then the eyes underneath. When the muscles of his arms became utterly exhausted the hands would drop and the light would smite his eyes. He was not permitted to turn his head away; he would receive a sharp order to look at the inquisitor, and when he protested he could not see anyone, he was told that he was being insolent and that he would make his lot harder if he persisted in that course.

"Citizen Examiner," said Lanny, "I desire to enter a formal protest against being obliged to submit to examination under this light. I request you to notify the Prosecutor of my protest."

"The Prosecutor will pay no attention to your protest."

"Nevertheless I demand that my protest be entered on the record and be presented to him."

"Very well," replied the man; and he wrote—but he might as well not have written, because Lanny never got any result from that petition.

All this time he was sitting on a very small stool. His buttocks were pressed down over its sides and they began to ache. He had to keep his balance in spite of a tendency to sway, and that meant that the muscles of his buttocks were continually pulling this way and that; and they too became exhausted. His back ached, and his injured shoulder and his injured elbow.

There was only one thing he could do: "Other refuge have I none,/ Hangs my helpless soul on Thee!" Lanny kept saying over and over, "God is helping me! God is helping me!" He no longer had the least interest in metaphysical theorizing about it; he did not care whether it was suggestion or autosuggestion. Man's extremity was proving to be God's opportunity, and God was taking advantage of it. Lanny was saying the words, and he was meaning them with all the power of his being. "Out of the depths have I cried unto Thee, O Lord!"

What this meant was that his attention was concentrated upon the idea of help, and his pain receded into the background of his consciousness; when he realized that this was happening he experienced a sense of victory over his tormentors. After all, they were not going to be able to break him down! And with this thought came a new access of determination; he concentrated with yet more intensity upon the idea of help. Jesus had told his disciples: "And nothing shall by any means hurt you." He said, "Be not afraid, only believe." And the saints and martyrs through the ages had proved the soundness of this formula. Modern psychologists will agree with you, provided that you will put it in their language. Not many are able to practice it, but one of the wisest of them, William James, wrote a book on the subject, entitled, with proper scientific aloofness, *The Varieties of Religious Experience.*

Of course Lanny kept all this in his secret soul. Nothing would have exasperated his tormentor more than to know that his victim was praying. Both Engels and Lenin had declared, "Religion is the opium of the people," and that had been graven in huge letters in a public place in Moscow. Lanny could have used some opium right now, and this opium of the spirit was his without price. Apparently the inquisitor realized that something strange was going on, for he would say with exasperation, "Pay attention to what I am saying!" Lanny would answer humbly, "I'm very weak, Citizen Examiner"; and to himself he would repeat the words of St. Paul, oft quoted by Parsifal Dingle, "I will not fear what man shall do to me."

X

Lanny could not give all his thoughts to prayer; he had to think about what he was answering. He knew that this was a fishing expedition, and the man was a skilled and experienced operator. Lanny didn't want to be hooked, and he would have to collect his confused thoughts and realize what he was saying. The man came back again and again to Fritz Meissner. He had the idea that Fritz had taken a trip into Poland and that Lanny had had something to do with it; or was he fishing to find out? Lanny had the problem, Was Fritz Meissner still alive or was he dead? If the latter, Lanny could say anything about him and put any blame upon him. But because he might still be alive Lanny must admit nothing.

What he had to do was to be the art expert, the *Kunstsachverständiger*, and he must insist upon that as his only interest and purpose in visiting Europe. On the subject of his profession he would pour out names, dates, and prices. He knew this would annoy the inquisitor and that he would be called a "profiteer," a "looter," a "money hog." But he could guess that in his secret heart the inquisitor might envy him, not merely his expert knowledge but also the profit he made out of it. This was an apparatchik who doubtless was crowded with his family in one or two rooms in a tenement, and when he had to buy a new pair of shoes the family would have to skimp on their food.

All this tumult of thoughts and feelings went on in Lanny's mind. He fought the good fight until he could fight no longer; his pain was so acute that he could no longer deny it, and he was about to fall off the stool. But then he bethought himself of a new idea. It would hardly be reverent to suggest that it had come as a result of prayer; perhaps it was the devil this time. Anyhow, he suddenly declared, "Citizen Examiner, I have to go to the toilet."

Wonderful, wonderful! The man replied immediately, "Very well, Budd." He pressed a button, and two warders came—never was a prisoner entrusted to one alone. In Stalin's realm there always had to be somebody to watch everybody. When Lanny tried to rise and found he couldn't stand, the men took him by the arms and supported him and led him out of the door and down the corridor. The act of helping a fellow human to walk is an act of kindness, and William James, the psychologist, has told us that when we perform the actions of an emotion we experience the emotion. It seemed to Lanny that the warders were kind; but Lanny was no longer putting his trust in humans and continued diligently with his prayers. He took his time, as much time as he dared; it was a blessed relief to stand, to walk slowly, to let the blood flow back into the muscles that had been pressed out of shape. "*Danke schön*, Citizen Examiner," he said as he tottered back to the torture room; and to himself he said, "God is helping me. God is helping me."

The light continued, and no pleading or arguing caused the inquisitor to press the button. He was becoming more and more irritated; he realized that he was not getting anywhere, that Lanny was not confessing anything, and he began to bluster and threaten. Again Lanny demanded to see the Prosecutor, or to send him a note immediately. The interview turned into a series of arguments about physical theories on the nature of light and about the legal proprieties, the meaning of the Soviet laws which forbade the abuse of prisoners. Was a man who had been brought into Soviet territory against his will subject to Soviet law, or was he under the protection of American law, or was he an outlaw entitled to no protection? The question became metaphysical and might have taxed the intellectual capacities of the International Court of Justice at The Hague. The climax of the discussions came after what must have been a full day's continuous interrogation. Lanny began to waver on his stool, and then everything faded out and he fell off onto his sore shoulder.

27

Man's Extremity

1

WHEN Lanny's wavering consciousness came back again he was lying on an iron cot which had a straw mattress and seemed of heavenly softness. Somebody was lifting him by the shoulders and trying to give him something to drink. Presently he was able to swallow, and that was another blessed relief. Little by little his senses returned, and he realized that he was not back in that concrete box or coffin; so presumably he was not going to be frozen and baked again. He began saying his prayers right away, and this time there was not merely appeal but also thanksgiving. Two men were in the room, and, incredible as it might seem, one of them was feeding him hot cabbage soup with soft bread in it, feeding him with a large spoon and holding up his head and shoulders with one hand and saying politely, "*Kooshai*," to encourage him to swallow it. "O Lord, how great are Thy works! and Thy thoughts are very deep."

Under such stimulus Lanny's strength came back, and he was able to sit up and take the bowl of soup into his lap and feed himself. He was not exactly a devotee of cabbage soup, but he knew that the Russians lived on it and were a sturdy people; at the moment he could have thought of nothing that would please him more. He swallowed the last drop, and when the man told him to lie down he did so. When he heard the iron door clang it did not trouble him, because he wanted nothing in the world so much as to be let alone. He closed his tired eyes and put his mind upon renewing his faith in God, and it wasn't more than half a minute before he was in a dead sleep.

How long he slept he had no means of knowing. It seemed to him that it had been only a few minutes before there was someone shaking him and saying, "*Ispitanie*"—examination. Lanny knew that he wasn't rested, and it was torture to him to be dragged out of that sleep; but he was shaken again and again and finally dragged to a sitting position. The word "*poshol!*" was shouted into his deliberately deaf ears; with the help of much pulling he was gotten to his feet and was led staggering down the corridor and back into that same room 814.

There was a new man now; they were going to work on him in relays. Each new examiner would have had a night's or a day's sleep; he would have had a meal, he would be freshly spruced and shaved. Lanny had not been shaved and must have looked like a bum out of Skid Row. He was seated on the same stool, and before him was the same desk, and on it was the same dossier, from which passages were read to him now and then. But the light was not turned on!

This one was elderly, with gray hair; he was stoutish and a bit slouchy, but he seemed kind and spoke in a gentle voice. He was speaking English without too heavy an accent; that would make matters easier. Lanny guessed that, having found that severity did not work, they were going to try humanity.

The man explained in some detail that the previous procedure had been due to an unfortunate mistake. It was no part of the program to starve a prisoner or to let him be overcome by exhaustion. It had been assumed that Lanny had eaten the piece of bread which had been placed in the box with him. Lanny said that he had been given no time to eat it, and the reply was that it had been the jailers' duty to stay and see him eat it, and that the accused should not have been taken to the examination room until it had been eaten. The jailers had been duly disciplined, and if the mistake was repeated it was the prisoner's right to call attention to it. Lanny said with due humility, "Thank you, Citizen Examiner."

II

"Mr. Budd," began this elderly one, doing his victim special honor, "I am older than you, and I have seen more of this very sad world. I speak to you in a fatherly way, and I beg you to do me the honor to weigh my words carefully."

"Certainly, Citizen Examiner," said Lanny, not to be outdone. To himself he said, "God is helping me."

"You come from a land far overseas which has never been in peril from enemies; but I live in a land surrounded by deadly foes which seek its destruction. Our country has no natural defenses—only the determination of the Soviet people."

Said Lanny, "It happens that only a short time ago the same words were spoken to me by Graf Stubendorf, a German, concerning *his* country."

"It may be true in both cases. It is a burden which nature or fate has placed upon our shoulders, and we are unable to cast it off. Anyhow, our regime is fighting for its existence, and we assert the elemental right of self-defense. This I assume you will concede."

"I do, Citizen Examiner."

"Millions, tens of millions, of deadly enemies seek the destruction of our regime. They are tireless, unsleeping; they work day and night by every kind of subtle device. They work in the dark, they invent clever camouflage to conceal themselves and their purposes. To meet their efforts requires ceaseless vigilance on our part, time and energy which we would gladly give to the building up of our productive powers, but we dare not. You admit that, Mr. Budd?"

"I admit it," Lanny conceded. He was prepared to admit anything but his own guilt. "But may it not possibly be, Citizen Examiner, that you sometimes exaggerate the danger?"

"Sometimes, I grant you. We are only human and we are bound to make mistakes. That is the reason I plead with you. We may be making a mistake in your case. We may be oversuspicious. I personally admit it, but what can I do about it? This case"—the examiner laid his hand upon the large dossier—"this case is handed to me. My superiors say to me, 'These are the facts. You will proceed upon this basis. There will be no respite for this man until he admits the truth and names his confederates.' And what can I do—I, a humble subordinate? Is it for me to judge my superiors? Is it for me to suspect them? Who am I to go to our great Soviet regime with all its wisdom and power and say that with all its resources for collecting facts and interpreting them—who am I to say, 'You are mistaken'? Surely you must see that, Mr. Budd."

"I see it, Citizen Examiner"; and again, "God is helping me."

"Very well then, I am here. This is my duty, this is my livelihood. I have a wife and two children dependent upon my labors."

"I also have a wife and two children, Citizen Examiner."

"Very well, that makes a total of eight different reasons why we should be considerate of each other and come to an agreement. I am told, 'Make this man confess,' and my career depends upon my succeeding; if I fail, I lose my standing. I go down, and some other man comes up—the man who will know how to make you give way. It may even be that suspicion will fall upon me and that I will take your place as a prisoner and be ordered to confess what motives have caused me, a trusted agent of the MGB, our Berlin organization, to turn traitor to my native land. It may be my turn to state who were the conspirators who put this evil idea into my mind."

"I quite understand your point of view," said Lanny, and to himself he said, "Molasses catches more flies than vinegar."

III

The inquisitor put a good deal of feeling into this discussion, and if he was not sincere he was a well-trained actor. Lanny was trying hard to think of some role that would carry on the little drama and keep the light from being turned into his eyes.

"So," continued the man, "I am pleading with you to come to some agreement with me. You are my prisoner. I have not been told how that happened, but here you are. It embarrasses me; I see that you are a gentleman, and I hate to be rude or to cause discomfort. I speak to you as one gentleman to another. I would speak as a friend if you would let me. Why can't we make things easy, each for the other?"

Lanny answered with due humility, "There is only one obstacle in the way, Citizen Examiner. I feel a moral obligation to tell the truth, and it hurts me to tell falsehoods."

"Truth is an abstraction, Mr. Budd. It is a relative thing. What is true for one person is not true for another. What is true at one time may not be true at another. For me the truth is what is in this dossier; let it be the truth for you today, while you are here in this place. Tomorrow when you go out into your own world you may laugh and say, 'It is nonsense, I signed it to fool them.'"

Said Lanny, "Citizen Examiner, it seems to me highly unlikely that a man who confesses to having conspired to bring about the death of Marshal Stalin will ever go out to his own world again."

"If that is all that troubles you, Mr. Budd, accept my assurance that you are mistaken. To you the charge of having tried to take the life of Stalin seems like a monstrous thing; you cannot understand that to us it is one of the commonplaces. I do not exaggerate when I say that we uncover thousands of such attempts every year. A large part of the civilized world is trying to take the life of Stalin; they are devising ever new and more ingenious measures. Lenin was shot, as you know; and then Kirov, who was Stalin's best friend and closest associate. A large percentage of the executions which you have read about in the Soviet Union have been of persons who have made efforts of one sort or another to take the life of our beloved great *vozhd*."

"That is exactly the reason for my fears, Citizen Examiner. I do not wish to be executed."

"Ah, but Mr. Budd, you fail to allow for the difference in the circumstances. For a citizen of the Soviet Union to make such an attempt is the vilest treason; but for a foreigner it is entirely different. For a foreigner, unless he is a party member, it is the most natural thing in the world to desire the death of Stalin. We take it for granted that the whole capitalist world desires that death, and if we catch a foreigner at it we are concerned with only one question: What Soviet citizens or what Communists are involved? When we have that information from him we let him go. We are sure he will not come back, and what he does outside is only what he has always been doing and what all the others are doing. It means nothing to us; we watch our own gates. Ages ago we learned to keep foreigners out, and the few that we let in we watch day and night; we watch everyone who speaks to them. I shall be watched because I have been in a room alone with you and have had hours of conversation."

"Have you thought of the possibility that this room may have some sort of listening device in it?"

The genial inquisitor shrugged his shoulders. "My future depends upon just one thing," he said. "Whether or not I succeed in persuading you to give way."

A lifelong training in urbanity made it possible for Lanny to smile even in the midst of the pain of sitting on a tiny stool. "You have been very persuasive," he remarked. "If you wish, I will give you a certificate to that effect."

"There is only one certificate that would be of any use, Mr. Budd, and that would be for you to sign the list of charges I shall present to you. I am begging you as one man of the world to another to face the facts of the situation and choose the way that is easiest for both of us. I don't want to be disagreeable or to threaten you, but it is my duty to tell you that you cannot possibly succeed in resistance. I assure you that in my years of experience nobody has ever succeeded in that effort; the possibility has been completely excluded. We have employed some of the world's top scientists in many different departments, both of physiology and psychology. We know how the human body works, we know its chemistry. We know how the mind works, we understand the chemistry of the brain, and we do not fool ourselves with any idealistic notions. We know how to bring you to a state where your brain cells will be in utter confusion, every one working against all the others. You will not know right from wrong, you will not know truth from falsehood, you will not know whether you are standing on your head or your feet. What you have had so far is just a foretaste. It will go on day and night for weeks, for months if necessary. We have had persons who have stood out for as long as six weeks, but in the end, without exception, they have confessed and signed their confessions. In many cases they have come into open court and made those confessions. They have done this because we have persuaded them that the good of the party is transcendent to their own good, or to that abstract nothing which they call the truth. The truth for Soviet citizens is what the party needs and requires. For you, a foreigner and a non-party member, we desire no such public appearance; for you we desire only the names of the Russians who are guilty."

"Even if they are innocent, Citizen Examiner?"

"Whether they are innocent or guilty is for the party to decide, Mr. Budd."

"In other words," said Lanny, "there are Russians whom the party intriguers for some reason wish to put out of the way, and they use me as a convenient means of making them appear guilty."

The elderly MGB man looked grieved. "I am sorry you persist in putting it that way, Mr. Budd. I am trying to save you a dreadful lot of suffering, and you should be grateful to me."

"I am sorry too," said Lanny. "I have no appetite for suffering, but I am unwilling to sign my name to charges I know are not true."

Said the other, "I will give you time to think this over. Examine your own mind and see whether it is pride, or stubbornness, or the intensity of your hatred of our regime which causes you to give this refusal."

"I assure you, Citizen Examiner, it is none of those things. It is a phenomenon which your expert psychologists may have overlooked. We call it conscience."

"We have not overlooked it, Mr. Budd," was the reply; "but we have subordinated our conscience to the interest of a party which has been formed for the purpose of helping the proletariat to break the chains of wage-slavery throughout the world."

Lanny said, "I am sorry, sir, to disoblige you; but I have not joined that party, and I must obey my conscience. I might as well give my answer now. I cannot do what you ask."

The inquisitor pressed a button, and the two warders came in.

IV

Back in his little cell on the straw mattress Lanny could lie and think about this illuminating interview. He could understand without difficulty the technique that was being employed. A few minutes ago he had been keyed up. His spiritual hands, so to speak, had been clenched; his will was determined to resistance. But now he would lie here in uncertainty, thinking things over and beginning to doubt and to dread. He would know that the torturers were coming for him again, but he wouldn't know when they were coming, and he would be in a continual state of suspense. His will would begin to weaken, and they would choose just the right time; they wouldn't give him enough time to sleep and recover his strength; they would come soon enough, but not too soon.

Lanny knew now how he was going to thwart them. He was going on with his prayers, not excitedly, not with tenseness or agitation that would wear him out, but quietly, calmly, firmly. His mind went back a little more than three years, to the time of the dreadful war's ending. He had driven to the Dachau concentration camp, one of the hellholes of history. Some ten thousand men had been held there under conditions of deliberately contrived torment and degradation. Thousands of them had been picked out and used in the most diabolical experiments ever contrived in the name of science. All kinds of men had been there, rich and poor, old and young, of a score of nations and every variety of religious faith. Two had died every hour, and the supply had been constantly renewed.

Lanny had talked with the American Army officers who were in charge of the newly delivered camp and its inmates. There were medical men among both captives and deliverers, and they were interested in the problem of how human beings managed to endure such torments. All, whether they were religious or not, agreed that those who had stood it best had been the religious. And the reason was obvious; if you believed that your body was all, then the weakening of your body meant the weakening of your whole being; you gave way to despair and went to pieces and soon died. But if you believed that your body was merely the dwelling place of your immortal soul, and that by your suffering you were earning a martyr's crown in eternal life, then you no longer feared your tormentors but devoted yourself to helping others to share your faith.

Lanny wasn't sure if he believed in an eternal life, but he did believe that there was a Power in this world greater than himself, and that it was a Power which worked for righteousness. He believed that he could use that Power, and he had made up his mind that he was going to try. "Lord, I believe, help Thou mine unbelief!" He recalled one after another the stories of martyrs and heroes he had read; he recalled their words of courage and faith. He was going to show these sophisticated and clever disciples of despotism that there was something in this world greater than all their party apparatus and governmental machinery. He would be the first man to overcome them; he would show them that they could not break his spirit.

V

He had only a few minutes' rest before they came for him again. They took him back to the same investigation room; but there was another examiner. Lanny could guess that the last one had been a higher official who had tried a special technique. Now there was to be a change.

This new one was as different as a man could be. He had a long head and a weasel's face; he glared at Lanny, and before he spoke he bared his teeth like an animal. His first words were: "Sit down, *ti sobaka!* You dirty Fascist dog!" He turned on the light at once, and when Lanny put up his hands over his eyes he shouted, "Put your hands down." When Lanny said naïvely, "The light hurts me," he replied, "You will keep your hands down; if you put them up again I will have them handcuffed behind your back."

So it was to be war this time; what William Blake called "mental fight." Lanny braced himself to face that dreadful light; he clenched his hands, he set his teeth, and he started a clamor of petition inside himself. The man sensed what was going on, and it made him furious; he raged and stormed; but Lanny went on with his silent cries, "God is helping me! God is helping me!"

The man went over all the old ground, making fantastic charges and demanding that Lanny admit them. He asked a hundred questions about Fritz Meissner; Fritz, he knew, had been one of Lanny's agents in the plot to take Stalin's life. Where had Fritz Meissner gone, whom had he met, what had he said, what had he done? Lanny had planted firmly in his mind, both the conscious and the unconscious, that he must make no statement whatever about Fritz Meissner, for the lad might still be alive. The only wise thing was to say that Fritz had been trying to locate paintings for Lanny, and nothing else.

That infuriated the man. He seemed to sense that this wasn't true. Or perhaps it was just his technique; he had trained himself to work up these furies; they were his stock-in-trade. He tried his best to frighten Lanny; he threatened him with all kinds of physical torments, with beatings and mutilations; he went into the details about torturing techniques. He became terribly abusive and revealed the fact that his imagination was captured by ideas of filth, of excrements, sexual perversions, and other nastiness. When he didn't know the German words he used the Russian words, and as it happened Lanny didn't know the four-letter words in Russian; he could only observe that they appeared to have many more letters.

The menaces had no effect, because the prisoner had passed beyond the possibility of fear; he no longer cared what they might do to him. His pride had been aroused, or his self-will. He had been like a man clinging to an overturned boat in a raging sea; he had been battered and half smothered, but now the storm had become like something in a dream; he was aloof from it, he could look at it and not fear it. His eyes were like two balls of fire, and every bone in his body ached, but he was above it all, away from it all; he was rapt in a kind of ecstasy, saying to himself that God was here, and God was living, and God was helping him. The more the examiner raged and stormed the greater became Lanny's exaltation. God really was hearing him, God really was helping him! "Through the greatness of thy power shall thine enemies submit themselves unto thee. . . . For lo, thine enemies, O Lord, for, lo, thine enemies shall perish! . . . Yea, the fire of thine enemies shall devour them. . . . And the souls of thine enemies, them shall he sling out, as out of the middle of a sling."

This went on for hours; time did not matter, time no longer existed. It went on until the inquisitor's voice began to crack. He showed signs of exhaustion; it was a violent act that he was putting on. He pressed a button, and an attendant came, and he ordered food—food for both himself and his victim—a singular thing, almost comical. He was threatening to kill his victim, but the victim had to be kept alive in order to hear the threats of killing. He must not be allowed to die—not until he had signed the confession they wanted.

So the attendant brought food; he put it on the end of the desk, in front of Lanny, and stood solemnly and watched him eat every morsel of it. Lanny had known of nothing stranger since the days of the suffragettes in England, when they had not been permitted to die on a hunger strike.

He asked to go to the lavatory, and the attendant took him and then brought him back. He was seated again on the torture stool, and the demon man hit the desk with his fist and started on his routine. He went over all the details of Lanny's dastardly conspiracy. The examiner called him all the foul names he could think of, in German, in Russian, and a few English. He told him what a scoundrel and an assassin he was, and what a harlot his mother had been. He described all of his physical organs and how they would be crushed and destroyed; and through all the screaming and the pounding Lanny lifted himself to the high dwelling place of that Power which had made and which sustained him, giving him that "courage never to submit or yield,/ And what is else not to be overcome?"

VI

Apparently the torturer had no watch. He went on until the warders came and told him his time was up. Lanny was escorted back to his cell and more food was brought; as before, the warders stood and watched him eat it, and stood for some time afterward, apparently having the idea that Lanny might try to get rid of it.

Lanny lay down and got a blessed rest, but he was sure it wouldn't last for long; and so it was. Almost immediately, it seemed, he was reawakened and led back to the torture chamber. It was Number One again, the man who had been alternately polite and angry.

When the examiner turned on the light again he insisted that he had been ordered to do it and had no alternative. He was very sorry indeed that Accused Budd persisted in subjecting himself to this unpleasant experience. It was all so needless, all so futile; all he had to do was to sign the confession which would be prepared; he was going to have to sign it anyway in the end, so why not sooner? The whole reel was played over again, but this time Lanny was weaker, and several times he came near toppling off the stool. A warder had to come and hold him by the shoulders while the questions were asked. This was a fatherly procedure, but Lanny was hardly aware of it; he had lost the awareness of his own body, which was a bundle of pain and had to be left in a place off by itself.

The questioner had gone back to Moscow, to those days when Lanny and Laurel had been flown there from China. To the inquisitor it seemed inconceivable that a man could have talked with Stalin and failed to be completely converted to the Communist cause. That he had gone away and become an enemy of the Soviet regime could mean only that he had been an enemy all the time, that he had had

treachery in his heart, and had been using his opportunity to find out
everything he could about where Stalin lived, what his habits were,
and how it might be possible for a hired assassin to get access to him.
That was the thesis that Lanny was being invited to subscribe to, and
his refusal could mean only that he was the more stubborn, the more
dangerous foe. Hundreds of questions were asked of him, all centered
around that one supreme personality, that substitute God who had
been set up for the Soviet people to worship.

Whom had he met in Moscow? He could guess, of course, that this
question meant trouble and suspicion for any person he named. One
person had been his Red uncle, Jesse Blackless; Jesse was dead—Stalin
had told Lanny that on Lanny's last visit to Moscow. Maybe it wasn't
true, but anyhow the Russians well knew that Jesse was Lanny's uncle,
and Lanny couldn't add to his trouble by naming him. Also, he had
met Hansi and Bess in Moscow and had attended a concert which they
had given there, almost within sound of the guns; but he wasn't going
to name them.

He bethought himself of the various Soviet officials he had met.
To name them might get them into trouble, but he owed them no
particular duty. To have refused to name any of them would have
looked suspicious and made more trouble for himself; and surely he
had enough already. If he made trouble for Soviet officials, why should
he worry? If he helped a little to disorganize their government, that
would be so much to the good. So he came down from his heavenly
dwelling place and named everybody he could think of with whom
he had discussed the political situation in Moscow, everyone with
whom he had so much as shaken hands. He saw that this gave great
satisfaction to the inquisitor—he was getting something after all!
Lanny thought, Let them stew in their own juice. And he went away
again to dwell in the secret recesses of his soul.

That continued until he fainted again and toppled off the stool.
The polite inquisitor was able to catch him, so he did no more harm
to his sore shoulder. The warders were summoned, and the prisoner
was taken back to his cell and fed again—more cabbage soup and
bread. Then he was allowed to drop down on his cot, while the warders stood outside and watched him through the little window in the
steel door. This process of in and out, off and on, continued until the
victim lost all sense of time and everything in his memory became a
blur.

VII

But his subconscious mind continued to be active; and the subconscious mind of a human being, any human being, is a mysterious and wonderful thing, the least studied and perhaps the most significant of all things in the universe. It performs an infinitude of complicated tasks; it keeps the heart beating, fast or slow according to the body's needs; it keeps the chest expanding and the diaphragm pressing down to draw breath into the lungs; it keeps the blood circulating at unbelievable speed through a multitude of tiny channels; it sorts out the needed food elements and supplies them to exactly the right places; it picks out the waste elements and ejects them through the appointed vents. Above all, it cherishes millions of memories and supplies them on request. Who, for example, could count the millions of musical notes that were stored away in the mind of a musician like Hansi Robin, enabling him to stand before an audience with the certainty of producing tens of thousands of them in precisely the right order and at precisely the right fraction of a second?

Two ideas had been planted in the confused mind of Lanny Budd. These ideas had sunk down into his subconscious; they had taken root there, and after the fashion of living things they had begun to grow and develop a life, a pattern, of their own. The first of these ideas was that it could do no harm to name Communists and to cause them confusion; they were causing him all the confusion they could, having a philosophy of bringing confusion to their opponents. In the old and more robust days of England there had been a stanza in the national anthem which proposed trouble for that island's enemies:

> Confound their politics,
> Frustrate their knavish tricks,
> On Thee our hopes we fix,
> God save us all.

That surely described the attitude of the modern Reds, though they had a new Trinity to call upon—Marx, Lenin, and Stalin. And surely it was right for Lanny to turn their techniques against themselves, to hoist them with their own petar! And that applied to all Communists —to every last single one!

The second idea had to do with the Reds in America. The Number Three Examiner, the vile-tempered one whom Lanny had taken to calling "the Weasel," had brought up this subject for the first time. This Weasel had full information about Bess, her activities, her trial and conviction, and he took it as proof of a special malignance on the part of her brother that he had had such an opportunity to understand the Communist movement and yet spurned it. The torturer had demanded Lanny's explanation of the phenomenon and had suggested that Lanny might have been one of those who betrayed Bess to the class enemy. So he had planted a seed in Lanny's mind, and it had dropped to the place where ideas took on a life of their own and began to combine with other ideas and form projects, solutions, hypotheses, inventions—all those phenomena which are sometimes called proofs of genius and sometimes of insanity.

However this may be, when Lanny was aroused from his slumber and led away to his next torment, he found in his mind a project, complete, mature, perfectly formed, like Athena sprung from the head of Zeus. He didn't have to consider it, to debate it with himself, to change it in any way; it was all ready for him, a free gift, a miracle. And who could blame him if he took it as an answer to his prayers?

VIII

He was led to the examination room. It was the turn of Number Two, the elderly man who was so polite and pretended to be fatherly. Lanny had hoped that it might be this one, and it was another answer to prayer. He was seated on the stool, and the warders went out, and the light was turned into his eyes.

"Citizen Examiner," said Lanny promptly, "I have to tell you of a change of mind. I have decided that your advice was good. I am no longer able to go on, and I have a proposition to make to you."

"Ah!" exclaimed the other, beaming. "That is happy news indeed, Mr. Budd. If only you had listened to me earlier!"

"I am sorry, but I had to make the test. I don't know whether you will be willing to accept my proposition. It will take some time to state it, and I would like to ask a favor in the meantime."

"What is that?"

"I should like to be allowed to lie down on the floor. This stool has become a torment to me, and I am really not able to think while sitting on it."

"The proposal is somewhat irregular, Mr. Budd; but since you have a concession to make I suppose I may make one also."

So Lanny let himself down gently on his back and lay flat. The light was turned off, and he began, "Citizen Examiner, I cannot accept your proposition that I plotted to kill Stalin because that is not true, and I cannot bring myself to sign a statement accusing myself of such an infamy. But it has occurred to me what I can do that may have great importance to you: I can tell you what I know about the Communist party in the United States."

"We already know a great deal about that subject, Mr. Budd—"

"I know, but you don't know what I know. I can tell you the names of persons in your movement in New York and elsewhere who are secret agents of the Federal Bureau of Investigation."

Experienced and carefully trained operatives of the MVD or the MGB do not show their emotions easily, but Lanny could recognize a change in the tone of his persecutor as he said, "That might possibly be of interest to us, Mr. Budd."

"My proposition is this: You will drop your story that I know anything about a conspiracy against Stalin's life and will accept instead my information just referred to. I will tell you all that I know and will answer all your questions so far as I can. You will accept that as my ransom and will release me and return me to West Berlin. The information I give you will be confidential and for your own use, and you will not make it publicly known that I have given it."

The inquisitor wrote every word of this on his pad before he answered; so Lanny had time to think and prepare himself for whatever might be coming.

"You must understand, Mr. Budd, you are asking a great deal of us. How are we to know if what you tell us is true?"

"Citizen Examiner, how were you to know whether what I told you about Stalin was true? I am quite sure that you knew all the time that it was not true; and the fact that I preferred to undergo this suffering rather than tell a colossal lie ought to give you some idea of my attitude toward the truth. It will take you a long time to investigate and verify what I tell you, and certainly I am not going to agree to stay in jail all that period. I feel reasonably certain that when you hear what I have to tell you you will realize that it is, and must be, the truth. I assure you that it will be of much more usefulness to you than any statement I might possibly make about Stalin. If I were to sign the statement that you have asked me to, I cannot see how it would be of much use to you—unless you are looking for a pretext to shoot me. Otherwise I would certainly go out and contradict it, and everybody in the world outside the Communist party would know that my repudiation was the truth. We have learned of too many other persons who have been forced to sign statements which were obviously untrue."

"A decision like that is beyond my authority," said the examiner. "I will have to consult my superiors."

So the warders were called; they helped Lanny up from the floor and half led, half carried him back to his cell. There he lay on the cot once more, and he thought: I don't believe they will take my word. I don't believe they will keep their word if they give it. If I tell them the truth they won't believe me. If I tell them falsehoods they won't be sure. They will investigate and still they won't be sure. But they will be in a state of anxiety and will waste a lot of effort. They will acquire distrust for some persons who at present are helpful to them. The usefulness of those persons will be destroyed, and their movement will become that much less efficient—which is what I want. They have used trickery on me, and so I will use trickery on them. They believe in wholesale lying, and I will adopt their code. I will spare none of them—not even the one I love! Not even my own sister!

That was all there was to it. Whatever happened, he had gained a few minutes' respite. He began to tell himself that God would give him sleep, and he fell asleep.

IX

When they routed him out and took him into the interrogation chamber his friendly enemy was again at the desk. "Mr. Budd," he said, "I am authorized to accept your proposition. It must be understood that what you tell us will be something of real importance. Otherwise, no deal."

Said the prisoner, "What I have to tell you is important. If your superiors do not recognize its importance it will be because they do not intend to keep their word."

"My dear Mr. Budd," said the older man with a pained look, "you must not say things like that. Surely you know it is not proper for me to hear them."

The deadly light was not flashed on, and Lanny was not merely permitted to lie on the floor, he was helped into another room in which there was a couch upon which he could lie. A warder unfolded a little table, and the inquisitor placed his writing pad thereon. He had brought several pads, evidently expecting extensive revelations.

Lanny started to talk. He told about one New York Communist after another, saying that he was an anti-Communist and had been recruited into the party under instructions of the FBI. Lanny didn't choose any of the prominent ones; he knew if he told the examiner that William Z. Foster was a federal stooge he might not be believed. He named those earnest party workers who were Bess's friends, who had haunted her home and made Hansi so miserable that he had been accustomed to seek refuge in his own study and his music. For a year or two Hansi had been telling Lanny about them, their party names, their occupations, their personal appearances, their services to the cause.

Lanny had plenty of time to assemble the facts and weigh them in his mind, for the elderly inquisitor wrote slowly and set down every single word. Only after Lanny had named half-a-dozen men and women did the other inquire, "But, Mr. Budd, how does it come about that you know these things?"

Lanny's answer made the man start, in spite of all the poise he had been able to cultivate in twenty years or so. "I know it on the best possible authority," Lanny said. "It is because my sister, Bessie Budd Robin, is herself an FBI agent."

"But, Mr. Budd," protested the other, "how can that be when your sister has been convicted and sent to prison?"

"How could it be otherwise, Citizen Examiner? Ask yourself what would have happened if she had made known a conspiracy to the FBI, and they had arrested all the other conspirators and left her out. Surely your own MGB must have protected its own agents in the same way."

"Yes, Mr. Budd, of course. But to go to such an extreme—to keep her in jail and sentence her to ten years!"

"The longer the sentence the more surely she is protected. As to being in jail, she was only in jail for a few days, and they were all well treated. The rest of the time she was out on bail, and she is out on bail now so far as I know and able to go on with her party work."

"It seems utterly preposterous to us, Mr. Budd."

"Of course, and it seems preposterous to me; but that is the way it is in America, and you can easily verify it. The case has been appealed, and it will be a long time before the Court of Appeals gets to it. Then it will be carried to the next highest court; it will be carried all the way to the United States Supreme Court. I don't know how long this will take, a couple of years perhaps. It may be that some court can be told to grant her a retrial; then before the case comes up again the government will discover that the witnesses have disappeared, and it may quietly drop the case."

"All this sounds fantastic, Mr. Budd. But pray go on. What caused your sister to take up this career?"

"For a long time she was a sincere party member. But she saw so much corruption among the high party leaders; they were living in penthouses and enjoying all the luxuries of the upper bourgeoisie. They spent their time in night clubs, they spent their time chasing women, they made free with the young party girls; they raised money for various causes, for workers' defense, for aid to refugees, and so on, and they put that money into their own pockets and had a good time. She saw that the party comrades were not like the devoted ones she had known in Russia. At the same time she was displeased by the foreign policies of the Soviet Union; she considered that the policies of the Cominform were not truly international but were becoming more and more nationalist. She heard stories about the great number of persons in concentration camps—in short, she began to lose her enthusiasm. Also, there was family pressure. I think what broke her down more than anything else was her discovery that Soviet agents had been getting the secrets of our father's airplane factories. You can understand, I am sure, how that displeased her."

"I can understand very easily, Mr. Budd. It is a great mistake of the American comrades to put their trust in members of the capitalist class. It would never have occurred to me to trust your sister as a party comrade."

"Nor to trust me either," said Lanny. "Both of us have had easy lives, and we cannot share your willingness to make sacrifices. Anyhow, Bess came to me and told me what she had learned about what was going on at the Budd-Erling plant. I told my father about it, and he took it to the FBI. Because Bess had lived in Moscow and been considered a great artist there, the FBI saw this as an opportunity to penetrate the party organization. They persuaded her to go on posing as a party member and to work her way as high up in the organization as possible. This is what she has been doing; she has known practically everybody of importance in the party and has reported their secrets to the American authorities. That is the story, and I am sure you will admit that it is really an important one."

"Yes, Mr. Budd, I admit that. But, tell me, why are you willing to tell me all this when you refused to admit the truth of the other story?"

"The reason is that the other isn't true and this one is. I think my sister has done her share of hard work, and I don't relish having everybody I know think of her as a jailbird. When this story is known, her usefulness to the government will be ended, and they will have to turn her loose. If I too am released, we can both of us lead our normal bourgeois lives again."

That sounded completely plausible to the examiner. He spent several hours questioning Lanny about the smallest details of the persons involved, and when Lanny said he had told all he knew he was ordered back to his cell. More food was brought to him, better food, and after he had eaten it he was allowed to lie down and sleep. This time they promised not to come after him in a few minutes; this time he was to be a privileged guest!

BOOK TEN

Thy Friends Are Exultations

28

Deus ex Machina

I

LANNY had no means of knowing how long he was left undisturbed; he knew only that when he was routed out of his slumber he had the feeling that it had been a very short time. It was a torture to be dragged back into a consciousness full of pain. The warders lifted him, saying again and again the word "examination." They led him out into the passageway and by the familiar route; when the door was opened Lanny saw to his dismay that it was the same old room, and behind the desk sat Number Three, the vile, evil-faced person whom he called the Weasel.

His heart sank; it was the worst moment of the entire ordeal when they seated him on the narrow stool of agony and turned that hideous light into his eyes. The warders went out, and the evil one sat glaring at him. "So you thought you could make fools out of us!" he sneered.

Lanny murmured, "I don't know what you mean." And the other went on to call him a Fascist ape and a counterrevolutionary imbecile and other such conventionalized names. Lanny was genuinely bewildered and asked, "Have you read the statement I made to the last examiner?"

"I have read every word of it," declared the other. "You insult our intelligence when you think that you can palm off on us a lot of old stuff out of your trash basket."

"Old stuff?" echoed Lanny.

"We knew every bit of that—it is all in our records."

Lanny had been prepared to be double-crossed. He had had only half a hope that they would keep a promise. He was prepared to have them say that they didn't believe a word of what he had told them—even while they went on to investigate it and to act upon it. But to have them tell him it was old stuff and they knew it already— that was fantastic, beyond belief. Their subtlety was more subtle than even his imaginings. If he had not been so utterly exhausted he would have burst out laughing. As it was, he could only murmur, "I had no means of knowing what you would know."

That set the man off on a boastful tirade in which he assured his victim how utterly helpless he was before the omniscience and omnipotence of the Union of Socialist Soviet Republics. All the machinations of the bourgeois enemies were in vain, and the prophecy of the Communist hymn was coming true, the "Internationale" would be the human race. The conclusion of the discourse was that Lanny was going to sign the full confession of his vile plot against the life of Stalin; there would be no respite for him until he did so, and the quicker he made up his mind to it the better chance he would have of saving his sanity and his life.

It was a cruel disillusion, and for a while the victim was tempted to despair; his last hope was gone, and he might as well give up. But deep within him was that hard core of stubbornness; he had made up his mind that he would never give up, that he would conquer these people or die in the attempt. He clenched his hands and began to say, "God is helping me. God is helping me." He really went to it this time, for there was nothing else he could do. This was the final conflict, exactly as the Communist hymn proclaimed it. This time there would be no metaphysical speculations, no dialectical ingenuities, no psychologizing about suggestion or autosuggestion. This time it was God, the living God, the God of our fathers, known of old:

> Other refuge have I none;
>   Hangs my helpless soul on Thee;
> Leave, ah! leave me not alone,
>   Still support and comfort me.

So there was a duel of wills, no new thing in the biographies of the martyrs and the saints. The devil as a roaring lion walketh about, and he assails the man of God and threatens him with fire and sword and destruction. The holy one closes his eyes and prays and endures and is justified of his faith. As Heine has written of a very different subject, it is an old story and yet it sounds always new.

This Number Three was well fitted to play the role of the devil as a roaring lion; he was a creature of hate. It might be, of course, that he didn't really feel hate but cultivated the appearance as a technique. If so, he was a good actor; he stormed, he screamed, he shook his fists in Lanny's face, and once he struck him in the face. Lanny closed his eyes and endured. He said that God would give him strength to endure; he implored God to give him strength to endure, and some-how he endured.

The man went over the whole imbecile and sickening story of a plot against Stalin's life. Lanny always answered, because to be silent would be taken as assent. "I know nothing about it, I was not present there, I never paid the money, I never met this man, I never heard that name," and so on, world without end—but there was no amen. Lanny's eyes became two balls of fire, he swayed on the stool, and when he toppled the man who stood over him jerked him straight and held him.

II

The ordeal was suspended, and they brought him food. He didn't want it, but he was ordered to eat it. The devil in the form of a roaring lion threatened to ram it down his throat, and so he ate.

And then the battle was resumed. He was exhausted, dazed, and he didn't know quite what he was doing. He began to murmur aloud, "God is helping me. God is helping me." The man heard him but couldn't make out what he was saying and told him to speak louder. He didn't know what the English words meant, and he pressed a button and sent a warder for another man who knew English. This man came in and sat watching the proceedings. Apparently they had the idea that Lanny was breaking down and was about to give way.

The prisoner was too far gone to realize just what was happening. The questioning went on; he murmured his formula again, and the new man translated it for the examiner. It had the effect of driving him into a new frenzy; he had a new set of epithets to hurl at his victim, a new set of challenges and taunts. "If thou be the Son of God, come down from the cross!"

Poor devil, poor lion!—no doubt he had been reading *Krokodil*, the supposedly comic publication of the Soviet Union, and perhaps the *Godless One*, an earlier weekly paper in which the Reds had poured ridicule upon the opium of their people. It was possible that some-where deep in his soul the man had a sneaking idea that God might possibly exist and was afraid of Him. Anyhow, he had sense enough to realize that it was this idea in Lanny's mind which was giving him the courage, the determination, to hold out against the questioning. After he had got through calling names he endeavored to reason with the victim, to persuade him that it was beneath the dignity of a civilized man of the twentieth century to cling to such childish notions. Lanny did not try to answer; he had no strength left for any superfluous words; he just kept his eyes closed against the light and went on pounding his formulas into his own mind. Lanny's God in this crisis. was a practical God, one to be made use of and not to be argued about. Lanny's God was saving him from feeling pain.

He was a mighty God, and mightier than the holy trinity of Bolshevism: Marx, Lenin, and Stalin. The examiner devil, the roaring lion, roared himself out before he roared Lanny out. The perspiration gathered faster on the man's brow than he could wipe it away—the light was at his back, but the heat was everywhere. His voice began to crack, and finally he gave up. He gave his victim one last assurance that he would be beaten in the end, that a whole relay of examiners would be put to work if necessary. Then he summoned the warders. and ordered the victim back to his cell. The victim was unable to rise from the stool, and the warders had to put strong arms around his waist, hoist him up, and, leaning sideways, carry about two-thirds of his weight along the corridor.

III

This torturing went on for several more times. Lanny lost the power to keep count. Days and nights were all the same, and only pain existed. He had only two thoughts: the first was not to give up; the second, to die, and thus escape. Exhausted, he fell into a deep sleep; and as usual he had no idea whether it was half an hour or several times as long. The two warders dragged him out of that sleep, and it took both of them. They lifted him up and put one of his arms around each of their necks, and walked him down the corridor. They did not say "*ispitanie*"—examination, they just said "*poshol*"—come. They were taking him down a flight of stone stairs, and he wondered if this was to be some new kind of torture or if perchance he was to be mercifully shot in the back of the neck. Presumably they had some quiet place in the cellar where they did that and where they could conveniently wash away the blood. Whatever was coming was bound to be unpleasant, so he would not make the mistake of giving way to hope. He continued saying his prayer and thinking about nothing else. "Other refuge have I none!"

After being helped through several corridors he emerged into a spacious, high-ceilinged place. He saw large double steel gates and an armed guard sitting by them. He saw a large desk or counter; behind it sat a man, and in front of it stood another man in military uniform, a Soviet officer. Lanny was half led, half carried to this counter. To his confused mind came the thought, I'm being taken away! And then the thought, I'm surely going to be shot! He looked at the officer and saw that he was smoothshaven, good-looking, rather amiable; but he knew from experience that officers could look like that and still order shooting when it was called for.

There was some conversation in Russian, which Lanny could not follow. There was a bit of business to be transacted; the officer signed a paper, presumably a receipt for this prisoner. Then he spoke to the warders who were holding the prisoner, and they walked the prisoner to the double gates of barred steel. The guard rose and drew back one of the gates. There was a heavy wooden door beyond it, and he opened that. The officer spoke again, and the warders put their arms around Lanny's waist, half lifted him off the ground, and without a word walked him through the open doorway and down half-a-dozen steps. There was a high wall with heavy gates, and one of these was swung open before them.

It was night and the street was empty, except for a car waiting at the curb. Lanny was shoved in, half falling. The officer followed at once, and the car started up. All around this prison were ruins, but Lanny didn't see them. All he knew was that the officer leaned over to him and whispered quickly, "This is a rescue! I am taking you to West Berlin."

IV

It was a moment before Lanny could take in the meaning of those words. His heart gave a great leap; but at once the skepticism he had learned with so much pain asserted itself. This must be a trick, he told himself. But no—his dizzy mind tried to sort out the thoughts—there could be no need for such a trick, the Soviet Army had plenty of men to transport prisoners, and it would not have such a menial task performed by one officer.

Lanny found sudden strength; he had called for help and he had got it! "Who are you?" he murmured, and the answer was, "I am a friend."

A friend! Lanny guessed that he was not supposed to ask, but he was permitted to think, and the power of thought came back to him. "Has my arrest become known?" he asked. He used the word arrest deliberately; he was talking to a Russian, a stranger, and he thought the word kidnaping might be offensive.

"The papers in the West have been full of it," was the reply. "RIAS has been talking about it day and night."

The car had swung round a corner, and then another, as if to throw off pursuit. A minute or two later it ground to a halt. They could not have gone more than two or three blocks. Lanny was helped out and saw an entrance to the *Untergrundbahn*, the Berlin subway. "Senefelderplatz" read the sign.

He knew that this was the quickest and safest of ways to get into West Berlin. Thousands of workers lived in the East and worked in the West, or vice versa. They came and went for all purposes, and there was as yet no way to inspect them, to sort them out; many might be riding from one station in the East to another station in the East. In the middle of the night there would not be much traffic, but unless the alarm had been given there would be no enemy keeping watch.

They found no enemy; the officer helped Lanny down the stairs, paid the pfennigs of the fare, and they stood on the platform until the train came. The effort and excitement had been too much for Lanny; he found that he was growing dizzy, and his rescuer, who was carrying a suitcase in one hand, had difficulty holding him up. The train came along, the doors were opened, and Lanny was half carried in and let down into a seat. The few passengers in the car showed little interest, and the officer whispered with a smile, "Don't worry; they will think you are drunk." Lanny was willing to have it that way; he leaned his head on the other's shoulder and, incredibly, fell sound asleep.

V

He was used to finding it hard to be aroused from slumber and to suffer pain. His thoughts were in a whirl. Which would it be, Number One, Number Two, or Number Three? It took seconds for him to realize that he was no longer in the hands of the torturers; it would be weeks before he could waken from sleep without a throb of terror. The heaven-sent Russian spoke reassuring words, lifted him from his seat, and half walked, half carried him out of the car, onto the platform, and up the steps. "Cheer up!" he said. "It's all right now. We're in West Berlin—well inside!"

They stood on the sidewalk and breathed the fresh air, the free air—how different it was, how marvelous! They were safe now; it was conceivable that the enemy might send scout cars to look for them in the West sector, but the chances of being found in this vast city were slim indeed.

Lanny couldn't stand, and the nearest place to sit was the curb. The street was unlighted, and there was no one to observe them. The officer opened his suitcase and became suddenly very active; he explained that he was changing his uniform for a civilian suit. "If your military police should see a Soviet officer they would ask for my pass, and they might send me back where I came from."

"Who are you?" Lanny asked. And the answer was, "My name is Tokaev. I'm a regular officer of the Soviet Army with the rank of engineer lieutenant-colonel."

"But why have you helped me?"

"You have a friend. It is better not to ask about him. Suffice it that you are here."

Lanny didn't ask; but he couldn't keep from thinking, and there could be but one answer in his mind: Heinrich Graf Einsiedel! Lanny had helped him, and he had said that if the chance came he would do as much in return. And the chance had come! They had joked about it. The *Untersuchungsgefängnis!*

"But they will arrest you when you go back!" Lanny exclaimed.

"I'm not going back. I had already made up my mind to come across. They suspect me as an enemy of the regime. I have had four warnings from my friends. The government has ordered me to Moscow, and I know what that means. They don't want to arrest me in East Berlin, because I'm too well known." He went on to explain, "I'm a colonel of the Soviet Military Administration; I'm employed as an expert on questions of aviation, rockets and reactive technology, and science. There are hundreds of subordinates and students who know me, and if I were arrested here it would make a scandal. But in Moscow it can be done quietly; I will just disappear. So I decided to come across; and it was suggested that I take you with me."

"You have a family?" Lanny asked.

"I have a wife and a child. They are already across. They went for a stroll yesterday."

Lanny said, "I owe my life to you. I will do what I can to repay you." Then he had to put himself in the young colonel's arms to keep from falling over. "I'm dizzy," he said. "I think I need some food. I have had almost nothing."

They looked around them and saw that the station of the *Untergrundbahn* was close to one of those "villages" which are scattered everywhere in great cities. Once these were actual villages, and then they became suburbs; the city grew around them, and they became shopping centers. The two fugitives saw the lighted sign of a little all-night café, and Lanny was half carried to it and set down at a table. "Don't take too much," cautioned Tokaev, and Lanny assented. He thought that a cup of coffee and a bowl of soup would be about right, and when it came he exclaimed with wonder over its flavor. There was a radio set in the little café. RIAS was playing "The Beautiful Blue Danube," and Lanny's whole being danced with it. Berlin was beautiful too! Beautiful blasted Berlin!

VI

The escapee's strength came back miraculously; he still had pain, but he forgot it and plied his new-found friend with questions. How long had he, Lanny, been in the clutches of the Reds? He had lost all sense of time.

Tokaev said it had been seven days and nights. Lanny replied, "I don't know if I could have held out much longer. I had just about lost my wits."

"What did they want of you?" asked the other.

"They wanted me to confess that I had plotted to kill Stalin."

"They had prescience!" exclaimed Tokaev. "It may happen any day; but it will not do any good. Malenkov will supplant him, and Malenkov will be worse. Stalin is old and cautious; Malenkov is younger and brash. He looks like a scullion."

"You know them?" Lanny asked, thinking it was a polite question; and the reply was, "I know them both well. I must tell you that I am holder of the Red Banner and Order of Lenin lecturer, and former lecturer at the Military Air Academy in Moscow."

Evidently they had taught him English; he spoke formally and precisely, as if out of a book. He continued, "For several years I lived and worked in close contact with the highest representatives of the Soviet Communist party, the Soviet youth movement, the trade unions, and our own military oligarchy. I penetrated the inner sanctum of the Politburo and had frequent meetings with Stalin himself. On many occasions I heard from his own lips and those of his closest collaborators direct and frank pronouncements on internal and world affairs, in unofficial as well as official surroundings."

"My God!" exclaimed Lanny. "You will have things to tell our side!"

"I will tell them all that I know. I have a lot of technical stuff, for I was acting professor of the Moscow Institute of Engineers of Geodesy and Aerophotography, with the diploma of Engineer Mechanic. I was also subprofessor of construction, soundness, design, and aerodynamics of aircraft. I will look to you to put me in touch with the proper authorities and help me in getting permission to stay in the West."

"I will be happy indeed to do that," said Lanny, "and I am sure I'll be able to." Then he added, "Tell me, is our mutual friend determined to stay on?"

"Our friend is a brave man, and he will stay so long as he thinks he can be of service. You must not speak his name to anyone under any circumstances."

"I will not speak it even to you," said Lanny with a smile. He was able to smile again—something he thought he had forgotten. "You were a brave man yourself," he added.

The colonel insisted that it was nothing. The group to which he belonged had blanks of various documents, permits, and so on, which had been stolen, and it was a fairly simple matter to imitate the scrawled signature of the Marshal of the Soviet Union, Comrade Vasili Danilovich Sokolovsky. "Poor Vasili Danilovich, he will feel very much hurt when he finds out about me, because it will give him a black mark that will never be erased from his record. But he has known for some time that I do not approve of his regime; he knows that he himself is no longer a soldier of the people but an executor of the will of tyrants. Mr. Budd, I do not have to ask about your experience in that Prenzlauerberg prison. I have been on the Conveyor myself, and I bear on my body the many scars which the NKVD inflicted. No one in the Soviet Union is safe against their intrigues. If you develop any form of ability and get any position of responsibility there are persons who envy you and spy upon you and tell lies about you. You are not safe if you are inside, because you have rivals in the organization as well as the enemies you have made outside, and sooner or later you will be pulled down and destroyed. We are both of us out of it, and we can count it a good night's work."

VII

They sat chatting while Lanny let his food digest and its energy be distributed throughout his organism. Presently the music stopped and RIAS began giving the news—of course in the German language. Tokaev understood it, and both of them listened attentively. Presently Lanny heard in the quiet, routine voice of the broadcaster a statement that gave him a start.

"Mrs. Lanning Prescott Budd, wife of the kidnaped American

broadcaster, today paid a visit to Marshal Sokolovsky in East Berlin, accompanied by Colonel Slocum of General Clay's staff. She went by appointment, and the marshal received her courteously and gave her the assurance that he knew nothing whatever about the whereabouts of her husband. Returning to the American sector, Mrs. Budd stated that she is unable to accept the marshal's assurance. She is certain that her husband has been kidnaped and taken to the Soviet zone, and she cannot believe that the marshal is ignorant of such an action. She stated over RIAS last evening that to make such an assumption would be to accuse the marshal of gross negligence and incompetence."

"My wife!" exclaimed Lanny. Somehow in all the confusion of his mind and in all his thinking about Laurel it had not occurred to him that she would take a plane to Berlin. But of course! She would have flown first to Washington, to appeal to the authorities there and to get her passport; then she would have taken the first plane and would have been laying siege to Monck and to General Clay and to RIAS—to everybody she could get hold of.

Now, of course, his first duty was to get in touch with her and let her know that he was safe. He guessed she would be at his hotel; rooms were scarce, and she would probably have taken his. There was a telephone in the café; it was set on a wall, and he wasn't sure that he could stand up to it. He asked his friend to come and hold him if need be. He called the hotel and asked for Mrs. Budd; there was some delay, and he thought that perhaps she was asleep. But she would want to be disturbed. Then he heard her voice: "Hallo," as they say on the Continent.

"Hello, darling, here I am!"

For the first time in his life he heard her scream. "Lanny! Lanny! Where are you?"

"I'm in West Berlin. I'm all right."

"Oh, Lanny! What have they done to you?"

"I'm all right. Don't worry, I'll be with you soon." There was no reply; he spoke her name, waited, then spoke her name again. Still there was silence, and he could guess that she had fainted; he had never known her to do that, but this was a special occasion. Perhaps she just felt dizzy and had had to settle down on the floor. He had heard no sound of a fall.

He himself had to sit. He told Tokaev, "I'm afraid she has fainted." So the officer called the hotel and explained the situation. They must go to Mrs. Budd's room and find out what had happened.

The pair sat and waited. The Russian said, "You ought to notify

RIAS. There are a great many people who are anxious about you, and they should spread the news."

Lanny replied, "You do it."

It was three o'clock in the morning, but RIAS was running all night now. Tokaev called and asked for the program director or anyone who was in charge. He told the news: "Lanny Budd has escaped from Prenzlauerberg Prison. He is in West Berlin. He had been questioned for seven days and nights and is exhausted, but after a rest he will come to the station."

"Who is this calling?" asked the voice. And Tokaev said, "It is someone who helped him to escape. Nothing is to be said about me now. You will hear Mr. Budd's voice."

So Lanny took the telephone and said, "This is Lanny Budd. I am all right. You may announce it. No, I can't tell how I escaped, but I will tell later."

There was no one in the little café but the proprietor. He had been listening to this conversation and was in a dither; he wanted to shake hands with Lanny Budd. "I have listened to you on the radio," he said. "You are Herr Fröhlich; they have been telling us about you. All the Germans have been listening. They will be so glad to hear the news."

Lanny realized that he had again become famous. The first time was when he had testified against Göring at the Nürnberg trial. He didn't like it a bit; it was a nuisance. He would have to shake hands with a lot of people, he would have to tell the same story over and over and listen to the same comments. It was one more trouble the Reds had made for him. But they had given him more power, he realized. Many more people would listen to RIAS now; he would tell them about the Conveyor, he would make it plain to a mystified world how it could happen that man after man would sign statements confessing to crimes they had never committed. Some men had come into open court and sworn to it; they were men apparently in possession of their faculties, not dazed, not under the influence of drugs. It was an amazing phenomenon, a triumph of perverted science.

VIII

How were they to get to the hotel? There were no taxis in this neighborhood and at this hour. The proprietor said he knew a man just around the corner who had a little truck and would take them. The proprietor would shut up the café, and they would go.

The Russian officer paid the score. Lanny's change and billfold had been taken from him, his watch, his fountain pen, his notebook—everything. The men helped him along for a distance, and the proprietor rang a bell and banged on the door and presently a sleepy man came to a window. When he was told that he would be well paid he put on his clothes and came down and got out his little truck. All three of them rode on the seat, Lanny squeezed between the other two for support. His buttocks still ached, but the man folded a blanket and put it under him.

So they drove through a city which had great gaps in every block, with half walls and girders sticking up in the moonlight. They came to their destination, the driver was paid, they went into the hotel. Lanny had to shake hands with the clerk and the elevator man and receive their congratulations and tell them that he was all right.

And so to the room and to Laurel. She flew into Lanny's arms—or rather she started to, and then she was afraid that he might fall to pieces; she stared at him in fright, he was so awful. He had a week's growth of brown whiskers and he had lost fifteen or twenty pounds; he looked like the ghost of his usually well-kept self.

"Oh, Lanny, Lanny!" She began to weep; she couldn't help herself. She told him she hadn't fainted at the telephone, she had just grown faint and had to sink down suddenly. "Oh, what did they do to you?"

He said he would tell her by and by; he was never going to tell her all, but he didn't say that. He said he had a few bruises but nothing serious; the main thing was that he needed sleep, to lie down and forget the whole world for twenty-four hours.

Then he remembered his rescuer. He told Laurel that this officer had saved his life. So Laurel dried her tears; she was ashamed of herself, she said. She thanked the handsome Russian; she never would be able to thank him enough, but she would keep on trying. She too had had almost no sleep for seven days and nights. She too had lost weight and looked like a ghost of herself.

They must both sleep, the colonel said. He took charge of the situation in military fashion. He would get himself a room. Laurel explained, "You won't be able to, the hotel is packed to the door. I only got this because it was Lanny's." Tokaev said, "Perhaps they will let me sit in a chair in the lobby. I will make out. I am a soldier."

But Laurel wouldn't hear to that; she was a lady, and consideration for others was her deepest instinct. They had only one room and bath, but it was a large room, and there was a couch in it; the officer could sleep on that. They would shut off the telephone and sleep as long as they wanted to.

Lanny was already on the bed. He took off his coat but forgot about his shoes; he was asleep before Laurel got to him. She unlaced his shoes and took them off, but he didn't know it; he was like a log. She went into the bathroom and changed to a dressing gown and then lay down beside her husband. The officer decorously turned off the light and then took off his own coat and shoes and lay down on the couch and went to sleep.

IX

Tokaev was the first to awaken. It was late in the morning, and he saw the others sleeping soundly. He put on his coat and took his shoes in his hand and stole out into the passage. He rode down in the elevator and had a wash and a shave and a shoeshine and then ate breakfast. There was a radio in the lobby; it was turned on in decorous volume, and several people were listening. Tokaev heard the statement that Lanny Budd had escaped from his captors in East Berlin and was now safe in the West sector. Now he was sleeping; the audience of RIAS would hear his voice later. One of the bellboys told the Russian that RIAS had been giving this item of news every half-hour. Everybody in the hotel knew that Lanny Budd was sleeping upstairs, and they were in a state of excitement about it.

Tokaev had left his hat in the room, but he did not go back for it, he was afraid of disturbing the sleepers. He got into a taxicab and gave the address of the place where his wife and child had sought refuge. They had no telephone, so he had not been able to let them know during the night.

Laurel woke up sometime in the afternoon. She was afraid to move for fear of disturbing Lanny, so she just lay still and said her prayers. Lanny had said that God was helping him, and now Laurel repeated all the words of thanksgiving she had learned in her early days. She found it easier to accept the idea of God than Lanny did; the reason was that her psychic experiences had set free her mind. She did not believe that her mind was shut up in a little bone box called a skull; she believed it was part of the universe. Herbert Spencer had said that a man could no more conceive of God than an oyster could conceive of a man.

It was night when Lanny woke up. The room was completely dark, and he had a nightmare moment; but then he felt around him and discovered a soft mattress and a pillow under his head; he remembered, it was all right, he was in his hotel room. He spoke, but no one answered. He could guess that Laurel had gone to get something to eat.

He sat up carefully. He was sore in half-a-dozen places, but he wasn't dizzy. He got to the edge of the bed and put his feet down and ventured to stand up. He could stand; he had had a rest and was all right. He didn't know where the push button was and had to search for it. Then he got the light turned on, and it dazzled his eyes; he discovered that they ached, and it would be some time before he could stand light. There was a lamp with a shade, and he turned it on and turned off the overhead light.

He sat on the bed and took off his clothes and felt himself carefully inch by inch. His shoulder was sore and there was a blue and green bruise, but he could work the shoulder in every direction and he made sure it wasn't broken. Then the same for his elbow; then for his sore behind—there was no way to break that.

He went into the bathroom and looked at himself in the mirror. He was a sight; no wonder Laurel had wept. He was dirty and wanted a bath, but he was afraid to get into the tub alone; he would wait until she came. His razor was here, but he was afraid to use it; he would let one of the hotel barbers come and shave him. They would do anything for him now; he was a celebrity!

The only trouble was they would expect him to talk. He would have to tell his story everywhere he went. It was, of course, his patriotic duty to tell it. Monck would impress that upon him, all the Army would impress it upon him. He would tell it once over RIAS; they could make a recording and then run it as often as they pleased. Yes, that was the solution; he would get a tape recording from RIAS, and he would get one of those little machines, and when anyone wanted to hear his story he would take the person into a separate room, start the machine going, and then go out and shut the door! His sense of humor had come back, so he was not permanently damaged.

X

Laurel came in and took charge. She was going to watch him and make a fuss over him. He was hungry; all right, he could have some food, but only a little at a time. He could have one slice of whole-wheat bread and one glass of milk and one glass of orange juice. He said that would do for a start, and she telephoned for it to be sent up.

hen he had to let her see his bruises. She shed a few more tears over
is emaciated body; she wanted him to go to a hospital and be examined, but he insisted that he was all right and there was nothing a
hospital could do for bruises.

He told her a little of what he had been through, the parts which
would not shock her too much. The bright light, the lack of sleep,
and the insane project of making him confess that he had plotted to
take the life of Stalin. She sat staring at him in dismay. So it really
was true! She had heard these stories about what they did, but she had
been only half able to believe them. They were really a mad people;
it was a mad regime, they were trying to make a mad world! He told
her about Tokaev, the rescue, and what he had told about himself.
He had gone, no doubt, to join his family. He would have to come
back because he had left his hat.

"We must do something for him, Lanny," she said—the conscientious
one. He answered that he would do everything possible. Never so
long as he lived would he forget the sensations of that moment when
he had realized that he was being carried out to freedom.

Laurel helped him to get a bath, keeping watch to make sure that
he did not slip or grow faint. She laid out clean clothes, and he put
them on. She got the barber up, so that he would no longer look a
fright. Then she mentioned that Monck and Shub were waiting in the
lobby. She had promised to let them see Lanny as soon as he was able;
and of course Lanny wanted to see them.

They came, and he stretched out on the bed. Lanny told how the
kidnaping had been accomplished and about the Conveyor—not all of
it, not until Laurel was stronger and more self-contained. He told how
he had been rescued by a Russian officer who had come over to the
West. He didn't name the officer; the Reds would know his name, of
course, but whether Tokaev would be willing for the West to hear it
was a matter for him to decide.

Shub said that the news of the kidnaping had been telephoned to
RIAS immediately, and RIAS had been on the air at intervals for the
last week, talking about the case and making demands of the Soviet
authorities. Monck told of the repeated demands which AMG had
made, and of Laurel's coming, and how he had taken her to see General Clay, and how the general had arranged for her to see Marshal
Sokolovsky. From first to last the Soviet authorities had denied that
they knew anything whatever about Lanny Budd; they hadn't even
admitted it now, when RIAS had been reporting his escape for some
twenty hours.

Shub excused himself; he wanted to hurry back to RIAS and put that story on the air. He said that the whole of Germany was eager for it; it was another Kasenkina case. The reporters of the press associations were clamoring to know where Lanny was, but the secret had been kept. For the first time he learned that the hotel had posted a guard outside his door during all the time he was sleeping; Laurel had ordered it and paid for it.

In one of his suitcases he had a Budd automatic. Laurel had got it out and put it under her pillow—not under his, because he was sleeping too soundly. She was the one who was keeping watch; when he went out on the streets of Berlin she would be with him, and she would have that gun in her handbag. They were back in the days of his Puritan forefathers, who had marched to church with muskets over their shoulders—and had not stacked the muskets at the door.

29

Sweet Land of Liberty

I

COLONEL TOKAEV came to get his hat. They made much of him, seated him in a comfortable armchair, and ordered a cold drink for him; then they listened to an extraordinary story. He took them into a place seldom visited by Americans, the holy place of Bolshevism, the conference room of the Politburo in the Kremlin, with Stalin, Molotov, Malenkov, and the rest of the inner circle discussing their policies and the date of the inevitable war—*la lutte finale!*

Tokaev was the son of a peasant in the province of Vladikavkaz, in the North Caucasus. He was five when World War I broke out and eight when the Bolsheviks seized power, so he had known nothing else. When he was nineteen the local trade union had recommended him to the Leningrad Mining Academy, and thereafter he had received an elaborate technical education under a state grant. For this he said he would always be grateful to the revolution; it was one of the good results which had been shared by millions.

But he had got the idea of freedom firmly fixed in his mind and had been revolted by the cruelties practiced upon the kulaks, of whom his family was one. He didn't like being "collectivized," and when he returned to Moscow he spoke frankly about the ruin it was bringing to the peasants; so he got into trouble with his party groups and was severely reprimanded and later on expelled. Then he got into trouble with the NKVD section in the Military Air Academy. His crime was that he had told a funny story about Stalin; and as the rumor spread it became that he was engaged in a plot against Stalin's life. That was when he was beaten and kicked into insensibility. He said, "My boxer's physique was reduced to a skeleton, sparsely clothed in flesh and bandages."

That had been more than ten years ago, and he had succeeded in having his case reconsidered and his record cleared. He was graduated from the Military Air Academy and taken on in their aerodynamics laboratory. Soon he became its head and a professor of the Academy.

Then came World War II. Stalin and Hitler made a deal and divided Poland; and then, in less than two years, Hitler attacked Stalin. When the Hitler forces approached Moscow the Academy was moved to Sverdlovsk, and from there Tokaev had watched what he called the "fantastic butchery" of the war and Hitler's final defeat by that ancient ally of the Russians, General Winter. At the end of the war the colonel had been sent to Berlin as First Soviet Secretary to the Allied Control Council. He had started work in the Karlshorst mansion, soon to be known as the "Berlin Kremlin."

Then for the first time this Soviet officer had got a glimpse of the outside world. All his life he had been told about the "misery" and "poverty" of that world as compared with the happiness and prosperity enjoyed by Soviet citizens. He was astounded by what he saw. As he told Lanny and Laurel, "The average German working-class home was a palace compared with the hovel provided for the Soviet laborer; it was graced by luxuries, such as a radio, which in Russia could have been afforded only by a party boss or a Stakhanovite."

The Red armies had plundered and raped, and the inhabitants of Berlin fled and hid at the sight of any Russian; this had greatly hurt the feelings of the gentle colonel of aerodynamics. He watched with dismay the contradictory course of his colleagues, who wanted the Germans to love them, even at the time they were being plundered. The Reds had set up a "House of Soviet Culture" in Unter den Linden; they fed the German population on potatoes and propaganda, while at the same time they took away all the machinery from the factories and left it to rust in the rain on the way to Russia. They had formed the Socialist Unity Party to organize the German people for political purposes; and Lanny remembered the glimpses he had got of this party through the eyes of Karl Seidl.

A presidential agent had watched these events from the American and the German points of view; it was fascinating to him now to see them from the point of view of the new enemy. After a little more than a year of these propaganda activities the Reds had felt secure enough to call a general election in Berlin. "They had to give a gloss of democracy to what they were doing," said Tokaev. "They were astounded when they carried less than twenty per cent of the vote, while the despised and persecuted Social Democrats polled nearly fifty per cent. They spent an enormous amount of both labor and money on the campaign, and they got nowhere."

II

Tokaev continued his story: One day while he was in his East Berlin flat the telephone rang and he was instructed to be flown to Moscow immediately. A few minutes later there was a second call; another high officer in Moscow was ordering his immediate flight; and a few minutes later there was a third call. He was told that it was a summons to appear before the Council of Ministers and that he might see Stalin himself. Nothing must be permitted to interfere with his instant coming.

The reason for all the hullabaloo was a thing called the "Sänger Report." Sänger was a famous German scientist who toward the end of the war had presented to Hitler a plan for an enormous piloted rocket plane which would be capable of flying all the way across the Atlantic, dropping a bomb on New York or Washington, and coming back. A copy of this report had fallen into Tokaev's hands, and he had submitted a summary of it to the Council of Ministers. Nothing in the whole world could excite them so much as being able to drop an atomic bomb on New York and another on Washington.

The humble colonel really knew about the subject, and the first thing he knew was its enormous complications. There would have to be a comprehensive research program, involving prolonged work by experts and the construction of many laboratories and workshops. The Soviet Union was far behind other nations in the sphere of reactive and rocket technology. To examine this Sänger project would be invaluable, because of the experience which such research would give to Soviet scientists. There were German scientists in the Soviet Union, and others in Germany who might be persuaded to come. A commission of four was appointed, and Tokaev was one of them. He began making reports, and so before long he was summoned before Stalin and the leading members of the Politburo, in that same oval conference room with which Lanny was familiar.

"This sudden rise to power was very exciting," said the colonel, "but it was the beginning of my ruin. When Stalin asked me direct questions about the people who were working in my field, I had to tell him they were incompetent and that he would never get anything accomplished through them. I had to say these things, even in the presence of the persons, and that, of course, made them my furious enemies. The worst of all was Vasili, Stalin's son, whom he had promoted to general in the Air Force. He is an ignoramus and a fool, a man incredibly vicious and with a temper almost maniacal. He got himself appointed as the fifth member of the commission, and then he would make the most preposterous suggestions and demands; I would have to report them to Stalin, and Stalin would sit down on him, but that would only cause him to hate me more than ever.

"It was our job to locate Sänger and other German scientists and persuade them to come to Moscow to work. We were supposed to make the most elaborate promises, which we had no intention of keeping; but they did not trust us and would not come. Vasili's solution of this problem was simple: he proposed to kidnap them. It made no difference where they were, in Berlin, in Amsterdam, in Vienna or Paris, he would take them to Russia by force and make them work.

"I gave my faithful services for more than a year and saw that I was accomplishing very little. Every day I became more aware of the evil consequences of despotism, and in the end I began to associate myself with a group which was determined to end it. I was surrounded by enemies, but I had a few friends, and these began to warn me of the plots against me. I was ordered to Moscow; and you know how it is, if you are arrested in East Berlin the Germans know about it and there is a scandal, but if you are arrested in Moscow you just disappear and not a word is heard about it. So I didn't go to Moscow; I made one excuse after another. I was ordered three times, and then the MVD began making things impossible for me; they took away my private telephone, they sent spies to invade my home, and my friends gave me a final warning."

"Your story ought to be told," Lanny said, and Tokaev answered,

"I will tell it when I get to England. I can say it in three words, 'Stalin means war!' I am one man in the free world who can say that he has been present at the inside discussions of the Politburo, with the *vozhd*. From first to last the coming of war was taken for granted as you would take for granted an axiom in geometry. The only question was, when would they be ready and sure they could win. I heard one man, Mikoyan, venture to suggest that it might be the wiser policy to improve the condition of the Russian people and spread the ideas of communism by that means. His suggestion was ignored, and I can tell my friend Mikoyan that if he ventures to broach that idea very often he will find himself out of the Politburo and in a slave-labor camp."

III

"How did you know about me?" asked Lanny, and the answer was, "I had heard Herr Fröhlich over the radio, and then I was told about your kidnaping. When I had decided to cross over, one of your friends came to me and said, 'They've got this man in Prenzlauerberg and undoubtedly they are putting him on the Conveyor. Would you be willing to take him out with you?' I said, 'How can I do it?' and the friend said, 'We will provide you with the order for his release, signed by Marshal Sokolovsky. It will not be a genuine signature, of course, but it will be so good that the people at the prison will not be able to tell the difference.'

"So I said, 'All right, I will try it,' and I took the chance. I admit that I was scared; but I am a colonel of the Army and they could not refuse me. They might have telephoned to headquarters and checked, but apparently they didn't, or they were too slow about it. So here we are."

"We have no words to thank you," said Laurel fervently. "We will do whatever we can to repay you."

"What I want," was the reply, "is to go to England. I have friends there and have promised to join them. It is a question of getting admission."

"I think that should be easy," Lanny told him. "I have a close friend who is a Member of Parliament. You will have to go to the British authorities and make application. I will send copies of the documents to my friend by airmail, and he will get busy on the case."

"I shall call you our *deus ex machina*," said Laurel, and she saw the Russian looked puzzled. He knew a lot about the structure of airplane wings and jet pipes, but not so much about Greek classical drama.

She explained that when those ancient playwrights had got their hero into such a mess that they could not think up a way to get him out, they brought a machine onto the stage and from it there stepped a god who set everything straight. Tokaev was amused at himself in the role of a Greek god; but he was a handsome fellow and could have served well enough.

"You were born some twenty-four hundred years too late," said Laurel, and he replied, "Twenty-four hundred years ago I would have been a wild horseman riding the steppes." The learned Lanny added, "A Scythian."

IV

Alone with her husband, Laurel told about her visit to Marshal Sokolovsky. She had laid siege to General Clay, and he had personally phoned the marshal and had sent an aide to accompany her. To obtain the pass they had had to go personally to the Kommandatura in East Berlin, and a Soviet soldier had accompanied them to the HQ in Karlshorst, that huge group of buildings Lanny knew so well.

A woman's eyes had noted everything, even when she was torn with anguish. First there was a reception room, where an adjutant checked the pass. Then came a writing room, with beautiful old furniture out of some castle. Then came the marshal's room, enormous, and at the end of it sat the commander before a table almost as big as a billiard table and covered with the same green baize cloth; he sat in a high-backed Queen Anne chair upholstered in red damask; there were two similar chairs on each side of the table. The great man did not rise but invited the guests to be seated.

He asked the lady to state her case, and she did so, doing her best to keep from sobbing. Then he told her, politely but coldly, that he knew nothing about the kidnaping and did not believe that it had taken place. Such rumors were continually being spread, and they were baseless, mere propaganda. He had caused special inquiry to be made in this case and was quite sure that no one in Soviet Germany would dare to conceal from him the holding of such a prisoner. He said it several times in answer to her protests and her statements about what witnesses had telephoned. "We pay no attention to anonymous reports from malicious persons."

All the time he was talking there stared down at the visitors from the wall a life-size portrait of a broad-shouldered man with a grim face and heavy dark mustache. He wore a military uniform with a coat somewhat too large for him, and his right hand was thrust in between the buttons at his breast, after the style of Napoleon Bonaparte. There were portraits of Marx, Engels, and Lenin, all bearded, but the *vozhd* was the biggest and grimmest. He looked down upon his subordinate, admonishing him not to deviate by a single millimeter from the party line.

"Uncle Joe," the Americans called him in their jovial way; but Laurel saw him otherwise. She found herself brooding over him, and presently she brought her husband a poem—and this time she said it might go into the paper!

Beyond the Iron Curtain

Lonely eagle, on a peak,
  Safe from any rival's hate,
None to argue when you speak,
  Loveless master of ill fate:
Are you happy all the day
  On your icy, wind-swept throne?
Lonely, lonely bird of prey—
  Gangster, with a heart of stone!

V

Lanny's strength came back, and he was taken to RIAS to tell the story of his experience. He rode in a car sent by the studio, and on the front seat beside the driver sat an armed guard, paid by Laurel. She herself had the Budd automatic in her handbag, the one which Lanny had had in his suitcase and should have been wearing at the time of his kidnaping. For one woman the cold war had turned hot, and she was firmly determined that the Reds were not going to get her husband again, not unless they came with their whole army. She had but one thought, to get him out of Berlin and out of Germany as quickly as possible.

Lanny told his story, and it was effective, they assured him. They made a recording of it and repeated it, as they had done with the Kasenkina drama. A copy would be turned over to the Voice of America and it would go all over the world. Everywhere people would be helped to realize that the Reds had become criminals, with a criminal philosophy.

Surely now Lanny's duty was done, argued the wife. There was the Peace Program, there were the children at home, and there were all his relatives and friends waiting for him. Let him go to New York and tell the story, and then return to Edgemere and be quiet for a while. She was going to have an armed guard even there, for enemies of the Soviets had been kidnaped and murdered in America.

But Lanny couldn't bear to tear himself away from Berlin just then; there was too much excitement. The cold war seemed about to turn hot, and no one could be sure what was going to happen in the next hour. In Moscow, Stalin had received American representatives and was carrying on negotiations for ending of the blockade; in the meantime his Red hoodlums, the so-called "action squads," were raiding the City Hall in Berlin and interfering with the newly elected City Council. The City Hall was in the East sector, and these action squads were brought in Soviet Army trucks. Representatives of RIAS were there, reporting the scene, and its announcers were assaulted, the microphone was torn from their hands, and the cable was cut. American newspapermen who tried to defend the announcers were beaten, and a man and a woman reporter were forcibly detained in the building by the Soviet Military Police. The offices of American Military Government in the City Hall were raided by these police, and government documents were taken away. Western policemen endeavoring to protect the councilmen had been jailed by the Soviet Military Police.

Lanny had got himself a small radio set, and he would lie on the bed in his hotel room and listen to these events. Then he would call a taxi, and Laurel would go with him to RIAS, to consult with the people there and give what help he could. Lanny Budd had become a symbol of these events in the eyes of all the Germans, and what he said to them about it would be heeded. He pointed out what long experience had proved, that any concession made to the Soviets was invariably taken as a sign of weakness and was followed by fresh demands, fresh aggressions. The Western powers must stand firm in this crisis, and the people of Berlin must stand with them. "Your legislators need a vote of confidence from you," said Lanny, "and we Allies need it also."

How was that vote to be cast? The Social-Democratic party, which had polled almost half of the votes in the recent city election, was the proper group to take the leadership in this struggle. The chairman of that party appeared on RIAS and called for an assemblage of all Berliners in front of the Reichstag building, to declare their support of the free world and their opposition to Communist violence. The City Council had been driven into the Western sectors and would have to meet there in future; let the whole population of Berlin assemble in front of the Reichstag and declare their support of their duly elected representatives.

RIAS took up this idea. *"Berlin ruft die Welt!"* was the cry. "Berlin calls the world."

"Men and women of Berlin, nothing and nobody can prevent us from calling the world tomorrow afternoon at five o'clock at the Square of the Republic before the Reichstag! Think of Prague, think of Belgrade, think of the Eastern zone! We can still defend ourselves, still speak our minds freely. The eyes of the world are upon us! The oppressed of the world expect all from our stand. Mayor Reuter and other men and women are our speakers. Freedom is the reward, the peace of the world is at stake! Berliners from East and West, from Schöneberg, Wedding, Weissensee, Karlshorst, Charlottenburg, from all over Berlin—to the Reichstag! Tomorrow at five p.m.! Berlin calls the world! Against the blockade, against the Markgraf police, against Communist terror! The decision lies in your hands! Berlin calls the world!"

There was no way to prevent that meeting, for the people were not going to march, they were just going to come. They would come from the Western sectors, and from the Soviet sector as well. They would come by all the streets surrounding that immense square. They would come through the Tiergarten, the great ruined park which had been turned into vegetable plots. They would come by tram and by the underground, pouring out in streams. RIAS told them how to come, not getting off at the nearest station, which was in the Soviet sector, but at a station safely in the West.

A curious circumstance—the Western sectors which were under blockade were lacking in coal and had electricity only four hours a day; West Berlin could listen to RIAS only during those hours, but the Soviet sector, which got its coal from Central Germany, could listen all day and night! To make up for that lack in the West, Army jeeps and police cars traveled the streets day and night, stopping at the important intersections and making announcements through loudspeakers. These cars bore the letters R I A S written large, and everywhere they stopped there were demonstrations. They would telephone back reports to the radio station, and these reports would form material for new broadcasts.

It must have been a wonderful day and night for the Germans in the East sector, which had no free newspapers and no free political meetings. Lanny became so excited over this opportunity that he forgot his lack of sleep; he knew Berlin as well as any German, and he could point out to them that Colonel Markgraf, who commanded the Red police in East Berlin, was the same officer who had been decorated by Adolf Hitler for his exploits at Stalingrad. Thus reaction recognized its friends all over the world. Reaction was international, universal—and let freedom and the love of freedom be the same!

VI

It was a day that made history, in a place full of it. There was that tremendous Brandenburg Gate which the Prussian imperialists had built to celebrate their glory. It stood at the boundary between the Soviet and Western sectors. There was a great square and great avenues leading to it, and the burned-out Reichstag which had never been repaired. Fifteen years ago, when the Social Democrats had been on the verge of taking power in an election, Hitler's thugs had set fire to the building in order to lay the blame upon the Reds and thus have a pretext for seizing power and setting up a dictatorship. Now the place was a symbol of freedom to the Germans, the democratic self-government which they aspired to and meant to win and hold.

Tired as they were from their work and from all the problems of keeping alive under a blockade, they came to the square. They came not marching, just walking; they came until the square was full, and the park beyond it, and all the approaching avenues as far as the eye could see. It was estimated that there were three hundred thousand people at that meeting. Loudspeakers had been scattered all over the place so that everybody could hear what their elected mayor had to say, and the chairman of their party, and the leaders of their trade unions. Until the hour of the meeting these loudspeakers were connected with RIAS, which furnished music, and at two minutes before the hour the vast audience heard these words:

"Here before the burned-out Reichstag stand the people of Berlin. Here before the burned-out Reichstag, at the Square of the Republic, Berlin demonstrates against Communist violence. The citizens of this city have learned a great deal from the past. This city knows only too well that dictatorship, terror, force, and political chicanery ruined us once. Berlin faces the future with toughened courage and purified hearts. Berlin resolutely rejects Communist dictatorship and terror as a political instrument. Berlin fights for its freedom and its future."

And when the elected Mayor Reuter stepped to the platform the loudspeakers spread his words: "Today no diplomats and generals address this meeting, but the people of Berlin raise their voice. . . . The people of Berlin have spoken; we have done our duty and will continue to do our duty. Peoples of the world, give us your help . . . not only by the airlift, but by standing firmly for our common ideals, which alone can secure both our future and yours."

The last speaker was Franz Neumann, chairman of the Social-Democratic party. Said he, "Berliners, do not forget that you not only defend your liberty, you also defend the freedom of those who are longing for it in the Soviet sector and the Soviet zone. We are also fighting for them. . . . We greet the Soviet zone, we greet Germany, we greet all the peoples who love freedom with our clarion call, *Freiheit! Freiheit! Freiheit!*"

That had been the old Socialist battle cry in Germany. It hadn't been heard from such a crowd in many decades. Now it rang through the square, and the meeting was closed by singing an Austrian workers' song, "Brothers to the sun, to freedom." The words were German, but the melody was Russian, and old. It was a heart-stirring revolutionary hymn, which for half a century had summoned the Russian people to the fight against tyranny. It had been written by a rebel poet in his prison cell in St. Petersburg, during a student uprising almost a hundred years ago. It had been adopted by the Peoples' Will Party, and its members had defiantly chanted:

> We may be tortured by fire,
>   Banished, in mines we may slave,
> We may be killed without mercy,
>   Always remember, Be brave!

Russian rebels had sung this song during the Revolution of 1905. It had been sung by all Russians in 1917 when the Tsar was overthrown, and it had been sung in the early days of Soviet rule; but now it was heard no more—it was too revolutionary! But all Russians knew the melody, and its words were being circulated by the anti-Stalinists among the Soviet troops in Germany. Here at this enormous mass meeting sat Russian MVD men and political observers in their staff cars, watching the meeting through their binoculars; inside the British sector were other Soviet staff cars, lining the middle lane of the Charlottenburger Chaussee, which led to the Brandenburg Gate and to Soviet Berlin. They had come to observe whatever might occur and perhaps to pick out spies and traitors in the crowd. They too knew that melody; what they made of it they kept to themselves.

VII

Lanny carried out his promise to Colonel Tokaev. He had already telephoned to Alfy in London, and now he went with the Russian officer to consult the authorities in the British sector. There were affidavits to be made out and signed, and in due course Tokaev would be granted the status of a political refugee in free England. He would be one more friend whom Lanny would look forward to visiting on his trips.

So then it was time to depart. They said good-by to the RIAS staff and to Lasky and his staff at *Der Monat*. Monck came to the hotel; he had been at Laurel's side all through her ordeal, and she could not find words to thank him. She said she was going to mail him a gold watch from London. When she suggested having his name inscribed in it he said he might be using one or more of his aliases. No names, please!

They were to be flown directly to London. Laurel talked over the telephone with the Air Force officer who booked the flight. "You must give him a good pilot," she said, and he answered that all their pilots were good. He knew what was in her mind. If that plane had to come down while crossing the Russian zone Lanny Budd would be in the enemy's hands again! Laurel said, "Don't tell anyone you are booking us." The place was full of spies, and from time to time the Red fighter planes were "buzzing" the planes of the airlift and threatening them. Laurel wouldn't draw a free breath until they had passed the boundary of the Russian zone.

She was packing their belongings. She wouldn't let Lanny do anything but lie down; she was handling him as if he were made of wet tissue paper. The phone rang and she answered; then she said, "Mr. Budd cannot come to the phone. Who is it?" She turned to Lanny. "He says his name—it sounds crazy—is *Untersuchungsgefängnis*."

Lanny started up from the bed like any well man and stepped to the phone. "*Hallo, alter Bursche!*" he exclaimed.

A laughing voice responded in English, "One good turn deserves another. I want you to know that I paid my debt."

"You have paid it a thousand times," said Lanny. "Where are you?"

"I am in your sector, but I cannot come to the hotel. I have not yet come across, but I am planning to come soon."

"The sooner the better," said Lanny.

"There are a few friends to be helped yet, then I will come. I just wanted to let you know that we have a report on your examination, and you did very well. Don't talk about this call. *Glück auf den Weg!*" And he hung up.

Lanny said to Laurel, "I have been asked not to talk about this call. Suffice it that we have an underground in East Berlin, and in Moscow too."

"The Reds have an underground here," replied Laurel; she would not be comforted.

VIII

They boarded the plane, and she was tense while it was rising into the air and for the first half-hour. By that time they had passed out of the Russian zone, and three hours or so later they landed at London. Alfy met them and drove them to The Reaches, the family home on the upper Thames where Lanny had spent so many happy hours from boyhood on.

The M. P. had already talked with the authorities concerning the case of Tokaev and reported that everything could be arranged; so that was one load off Lanny's mind. Alfy had been in prison in Spain, so he knew how it felt; Lanny had got him out, so he would do anything that Lanny asked him to do. Alfy had recently been married to the daughter of a local squire; the father was a staunch Tory, and the daughter a member of the Labour party—something quite common in these times. The young wife was hoping to present Alfy with an heir, and it would be Lanny's pleasure to take back a favorable report upon her to the Pater, who was stuck in New Jersey while Lanny went gallivanting over Europe.

They rested for three days in that peaceful English countryside, which had not been changed either by war or by socialism. They went punting on the river and listened to the young generation singing the old songs and others that would become old in due course. When the time came for them to travel to Prestwick, Alfy proposed that they make a motor tour out of it—three or four hundred miles through eight counties of England and two of Scotland. They would pass through the Lake country that Lanny had read so much about in Wordsworth's poems.

Ordinarily the art expert would have been pleased; but he examined his sitting-down place and decided that being jounced in a car all day would seem too much like the torture chamber in the prison. Sleeping cars were made for sleeping, and that was what he needed still. So

Alfy drove them to the station and they boarded the night express.

In the morning they stepped out into what had been a small fishing village on the wild west coast of Scotland and had been magically transformed in wartime into one of the great landing fields of the world. Here the bombing planes had come by the score every day; the cargo planes, taken out of mothballs for the Berlin airlift, were still coming. Lanny and Laurel were bound the other way, and were never coming back again, so Laurel vowed. But it was a difficult time for prophesying.

IX

The newspaper reporters consult passenger lists. Some had met Lanny at London and more met him at La Guardia Field. He had become the man of the hour, and they plied him with questions. He was glad to answer; it was one more chance to wake up the American public and make them realize what the Soviet peril had become.

Freddi Robin was there to meet them and drive them to Edgemere. Lanny rested a couple of days and regained more of his lost weight. Then came a call from the State Department; they wanted to see him and have a full account of his experience for their files. They were building up an elaborate "*J'accuse*" against the cold-war enemy. Lanny had tape recordings of his RIAS talk, and he turned one over to the Voice of America and took another with him by the night train to Washington. He visited "State" and talked with the men of the Bureau of German Affairs. He dictated a precise and careful account of his kidnaping and torturing; he signed it and swore to it.

He had been asked to notify the President's office when he was in town, and he did so. As a result he was invited on one of those weekend cruises in peaceful Chesapeake Bay. That meant that he had two days and nights in which to put the fear of Stalin into the heart of Harry Truman and the other guests on board the yacht. He told what Monck had to say, and the other men of CIC. He told about Einsiedel and about the refugees, and above all Tokaev. It does not happen often that an American gets a look into the inner circles of the Politburo and listens to Stalin discussing his tactics and policies. Here was a high-ranking officer of Stalin's Army, a highly trained technician in the most abstruse and most dangerous of sciences, and his message was, "Stalin means war."

Tokaev was going to write a book and give it that title, and Lanny set out to pound it into the President's mind. "Stalin means war in the same way that a lion means meat; it is the nature of the creature, it is what he is built for. When Stalin talks peace it means he is not ready for war. When he is ready for war he will wage it. He will wait until he has enough A-bombs to destroy America's war potential and until he has enough planes to fly them over the North Pole. When that time comes, Mr. President, he will make you another peace proposal; and while you have your pen in hand, about to sign, the bombs will fall on you."

Said Harry Truman, "It is hard for an American to believe there are such men in the world."

30

Sit Thee Down, Sorrow

I

LANNY had one other urgent duty; he must talk to Bess. He told Laurel of this, saying that he hoped his experience might have some effect in opening his sister's eyes. He had not told Laurel what he had said about Bess in the East Berlin prison, nor did he intend to tell Bess; he hoped to accomplish his purpose without that.

He called up and made a date and went to her apartment in New York. She would have read about his experience in the papers, of course, and he could guess that her party masters in Moscow would not have failed to take action in the matter of Lanny's accusations. Would they believe them? The best guess was that they wouldn't know what to believe, but would surely be asking questions. Would they have told her who had made the accusations? That would have been contrary to all that Lanny knew of their techniques.

It was a hot September day, and Bess was wearing a light-colored peignoir. She looked tired and worried and was chain-smoking. She guessed that he had come to make her hear his story, and she didn't relish the ordeal. "I read about it in the papers," she said. "There's no need to go into details."

"I think you ought to hear them from my own lips," he persisted.

"I know, you want to harrow me. You think you can weaken my faith in my cause; but you can't."

"I think you ought to hear what happened to me," he said.

"I know that you are fighting the Soviet Union by every means in your power; you have declared war on them, and naturally they were trying to shut you up."

"And you justify the torturing of prisoners, Bess?"

"I don't justify it, I just know that all armies do it."

"You are mistaken, I assure you; the American Army does *not* do it."

"They wouldn't tell you what they were doing."

"As it happens, they told me precisely. For weeks I was interrogating prisoners; first, in General Patch's Seventh Army, then in Patton's Third. I was told exactly what to do, and I was forbidden to use any sort of threats or violence."

"They knew you were a nice fellow, so they gave you the pleasant jobs."

"That is a foolish thing to say, Bess. Other men were briefed with me. Torture was unknown in our Army. Face the facts: your Soviet crowd had me in their power, and they tried to make me confess to a conspiracy to kill Stalin. They knew perfectly well that it was a complete invention, and they tortured me to make me sign a confession. They told me again and again that they meant to keep on torturing me until they broke me down and made me sign it. When I talked to you about such things you called me a redbaiter; you swore it didn't happen. Now I ask you to face the fact that I was there. I went through it and I *know*. I mean that you shall know about it too."

"Don't get melodramatic, Lanny," she said, lighting another cigarette. "There are a great many plots to kill Stalin, and naturally they find out about them. If they become oversuspicious and accuse the wrong person, that is only a human failing. They are not supposed to be superhuman."

"But neither are they supposed to be subhuman. Don't you see that it is the principle of dictatorship that breeds this oversuspiciousness? Force and terror make it impossible for any human being to have a sense of security. It makes for spying and intrigue, it makes all frankness and sincerity impossible."

"I see that. But it is a stage of development through which we have to pass."

"But what becomes of morality in the meantime? What becomes of the common decencies of life if torturers are permitted to compel people to sign their names to a conglomeration of falsehoods? Can a party exist when its members cannot trust one another, when they spy and betray one another to torturers?"

"I know, Lanny, I know," she said. "We don't have gods to deal with, we have only human beings, with all their weaknesses."

II

He saw that she was worried, and he knew that she had plenty of things to worry about. He was deliberately leading her along one path; but he must be tactful about it and not wake her suspicions. "If it hurts you to hear of your brother's being tortured seven days and nights, I won't tell you about it; but at least let me tell you what is going on in East Berlin and East Germany. I have just come from there, and it has been a long time since you've been there."

He began with the story of Karl Seidl, how he had joined the new Socialist Unity Party and had been forced to start spying upon his comrades, and had fled from it—a decent worker who had been driven out of the Communist party and back to the Social Democrats who could speak the truth freely. He told about RIAS and its *Spitzeldienst*—telling the workers in East Berlin who in the factories were spying and reporting on them. He told about the clearing house for refugees which he had visited and about the various persons he had interviewed and what the officials had told about their experiences. He told about Einsiedel—not naming him or saying anything to identify him, since he was still among the enemy. There was a young German who had been carefully trained in the Antifaschule and had been made a Communist editor and now was in revolt against the job of following the party line regardless of all facts.

He saw that he had got her attention. She was no longer fighting against him, she was listening with curiosity and asking questions. It was a fact that he had been there, and she had not; he had been among the scenes which were of the greatest importance to her, and she could not question the stories he was telling. She might resent his interpretations, but she accepted the fact that he had met the persons and heard the words he was repeating.

He came to Tokaev. She couldn't fail to be curious about her brother's rescue and how it had been engineered. He told her the story of the Soviet officer's career, every detail that he could recollect; and certainly there was no Communist in the acquaintance of Bessie Remsen Budd who could take her into the Kremlin and let her sit in on the secret councils of Stalin and his trusted lieutenants. He didn't say "Stalin means war," he just repeated the questions Stalin had asked of Tokaev, and what Molotov had said about the matter, what Malenkov had said, what Mikoyan had said. Every word of this story bore the stamp of truth, and Bess could not doubt that she was there among the high gods of her Olympus.

And this Russian-born and Soviet-trained officer, this highest product of all their techniques, had sickened of them and was now on his way to England to tell the government of that country all the secrets he had learned. He hadn't been bought and he hadn't been accused of any crime, and Bess could find no fault in him; he was a true revolutionary idealist and had suffered moral revulsion and had fled from an odious thing.

"And then Kasenkina," said Lanny. "You read her story, no doubt."

"I read it, Lanny."

"You got it in New York; I got the Berlin angle. I met people there who had known Zenzinov and his record in the Revolution. Do you believe for one moment that Alexandra Tolstoy is what Molotov called her, 'a White-Guard bandit'? The Reds had set up a Communist school in New York, a perfect little Soviet, with intriguers, spies, torturers, everything exactly like home. Everywhere the smell is the same, the smell of moral decay."

III

He had her listening now, and he told her his own story. He spared no details, the freezing and the baking, the glaring light, the deprivation of sleep, the browbeating and threats, the wheedling and pretended sympathy, and, above all, the patent fraudulence. Bess was not the callous person that her creed required, and the recital shook her. He made note of the fact that she no longer got angry. He saw her clenching and unclenching one hand, and with the fingers of the other she was grinding her cigarette absent-mindedly in the tray. He thought that his opportunity was on the way, and he said with tenderness in his voice, "Tell me, Bess, can it be that you have not noticed the low moral tone of the party?"

"I have noticed it, of course," she answered; "but as I told you before, I have to work with human beings, and in spite of their defects."

"You have made heavy sacrifices for them," he said. "Has it never occurred to you that you yourself might someday be betrayed, that you might fall victim to party intrigue and suspicion?"

He saw that she was biting her lip, and he politely looked away so as not to embarrass her. He waited, and finally she said, "Lanny, if I take you into my confidence, will you betray me?"

"How could you think of such a thing, Bess?"

"I mean by talking about what I tell you. I don't want anyone else to know, not even Laurel."

"I understand," he said, "and you know my position. If you tell me anything against the government I cannot promise secrecy; but anything personal I will keep between us, of course."

"Something terrible has happened to me," she blurted out, "and I don't know what to make of it."

He still did not look at her, because he was afraid his eyes might betray him. "You can trust me, Bess."

"Nobody else seems to trust me. The C. I. Rep has heard some rumor about me and is investigating me."

Lanny knew that phrase; it meant Cominform Representative, a man sent by Moscow, who took precedence over all American party members and officials. He was Stalin in America, no less. At Yalta, Stalin had promised Roosevelt to abolish the Communist International. What he had done was to change its name from Comintern to Cominform, and the same officials went on doing the same jobs. That was a *vozhd*'s idea of being subtle.

"That is bad news indeed," said Lanny to his sister; "but you know how it is, old dear, you are a member of the *haute bourgeoisie*. You are the daughter of a crocodile and the sister of a cannibal."

"Don't be cruel, Lanny. The comrades have known all about me, and they have always trusted me."

"And what have you done now?"

"I can't find out; that's the painful part about it. I have had three sessions with the C. I. Rep, nearly four hours each time. He questions me about everything in my life, everything I've said, everybody I've known, every place I've ever been—and he won't tell me what the charges are."

"Did you have a bright light backed by a reflector shining in your eyes all the time?"

"No, I didn't have that."

"Did you have to sit on a stool that was only half as wide as your buttocks?"

"Oh, Lanny, don't be horrid!"

"I assure you the experience is horrid. You can be thankful that you are in America where they can use only words—except in extreme cases."

"What am I to make of it, Lanny? What am I to do?"

"Don't you know that you are prominent in the party and that there are half-a-dozen others who would like to take your place? Have you never pointed out anyone's incompetence? Have you never had to suspect a traitor or to shut up a fool? Every time you have done things like that you have made an enemy, someone to suspect you and watch you and make up tales about you; someone who hopes to take your place."

"What place have I, with a ten-year jail sentence hanging over me?"

"You have a wonderful place. There are plenty of people willing to be martyrs if only they can be talked about, if only they can be important. They see themselves coming out of jail to become rulers of the world. You are in a system which glorifies hatred; they call it 'class hatred, class war.' But class is an abstraction—classes are made up of human beings, and so are parties. People who hate classes hate human beings, and they learn to hate one another. That is what I've been trying to tell you for years, Bess."

"You're just taking the occasion to preach at me."

"You asked me for advice, and I can only tell you what is in my mind. Hate breeds hate, and it brings out all the worst in human beings. Is the C. I. Rep a Russian?"

"Yes, of course."

"Well then, how can you expect him to come over to this country, which he hates, and meet class enemies, whom he hates, and think no evil about them? How can it seem possible to him that you can have the father you have and the environment you have and still be a genuine hater of the bourgeoisie? To him it is a contradiction in terms, it is a denial of the whole Diamat, the whole gospel of Marxist-Leninist-Stalinism. The C. I. Rep has only to take a walk up Fifth Avenue to know that he can never really trust any American. The terms on which a man holds power in Moscow today are that he hates all Americans on principle."

IV

"Lanny," she said, "it is a dreadful thing to give everything you have to a cause and then discover that you have no place in it, that nobody trusts you."

"And the man won't tell you what you are accused of?"

"He tried to make me believe that it is other people who are suspected. Everybody I know is being questioned. He must have several others working on the case."

"And what does he want you to do?"

"He doesn't tell me anything. But he says I may be summoned to Moscow."

That gave Lanny a severe jolt. "Oh, Bess!" he exclaimed. "*Don't* let them do that to you!"

"How could I go, Lanny? I am under bond. I am forbidden to leave the country. It would cost them fifty thousand dollars if I did."

"Well, they might be willing to pay that to get you. Bess, you must promise me—don't let that happen to you! They get you in that place of horrors and you will be lost forever. There is nothing they won't do to you. You must realize it—you mean absolutely nothing to them— your services, your record, your honor, your faith in the cause. Death will be the kindest thing, and you will pray for it."

He had her now where she had to listen. In past times he had talked to her about torturing, about frame-ups and confessions extracted, and she had said it was all nonsense, it was counterrevolutionary propaganda. But now he had been through it himself, and she could not doubt his word. He told her his own feelings under torture; he spared no painful detail. She sat there staring at him, fascinated, shuddering now and then, clenching and unclenching her hands. All that proud resistance, that flaring anger that he had known of old were gone. Her spirit was broken, and he saw it and went to work all the harder.

"Bess," he insisted, "you must listen to me. For God's sake, don't put yourself in that man's power. Don't meet him again! He is a little Stalin; he owns the world, he is destined to rule it; he will be the Commissar of all America. It sounds crazy, I know, but that is what life means to him, that is his destiny. All this hateful prosperity that he sees—he is going to take it over and possess it. He is going to rule and give out wholesale death to everyone who does not obey. He will take over our newspapers and make them into little *Pravdas*. He will take our radio and pour out Stalinist doctrine varied with the 'Internationale.' He will take our children and make them into little robots, little tattletales turning their parents over to the MVD."

"Lanny," she protested, "you don't have to pile it on."

"I'm telling you what I know, Bess. It is not only my own experience, it's all the people I've talked to over there, people who have been through it, people who have fled from it. They are fleeing from it by the hundreds every day. If the gates were opened half of Eastern Europe would flee into the West. If our gates were opened half of Europe would come to America. Europe is in torment, Bess; they have learned what freedom is by being denied it. It is the most awful thing to live under the terror; to have your lips sealed, to be afraid that your very looks may betray you, to know that somebody may whisper a slander about you—your own child may do it if you punish the child! And to be accused is to be guilty. Someone has accused you, Bess. They don't tell you what—maybe because it's so preposterous it would be absurd to speak it! Something as absurd as the charge that I was plotting to take Stalin's life—and paying out five thousand dollars at a time to have it done!"

V

He saw that tears had come into her eyes, and he believed that she was going to break. "What am I to do, Lanny?" she whispered.

"The first thing for you to do is to get out of this apartment. You must not live alone. Don't you know the part that murder plays in Stalin's techniques? Have you never seen the list of his victims? I don't mean in Russia, for there they are counted in tens of millions; I mean in Europe and America—the onetime Stalinists who turned against him and were no longer permitted to live. There was Trotsky, and his son Sedov, and his secretary, whose headless body was found floating in the Seine, and his guard, and several others of his followers. There was José Robles, a professor at Johns Hopkins University; there was Kurt Landau, an Austrian editor, kidnaped and killed. Carlo Tresca was shot down on Fifth Avenue, and Walter Krivitsky, former chief of Soviet Military Intelligence in Europe, was murdered in a hotel room in Washington. I can't remember them all, but there are books about it."

"That's enough, Lanny. I know."

"What I'm trying to make you realize is that you're only about half an hour from Moscow."

"I don't know what you mean by that."

"I mean there are Russian ships here in the harbor; they're always here, and every ship is Moscow and every captain is Stalin. The C. I. Rep comes here to question you, and all he has to do is to bring a couple of the sailors with him. They grab you and clamp a chloroform rag to your nose, as they did to me; they carry you downstairs in the early hours of the morning, put you into a car, and take you to the ship. They put you down in the hold where your cries cannot be heard, and in three or four weeks you are in Moscow, in the Lubianka. They put you on the Conveyor and tell you what to confess; they torture you until you sign it, and then they ship you off to Siberia in a cattle car, and work you in a mine on half rations, and in a year or two you fade away and are buried in an unmarked grave."

"You really believe all that, Lanny?"

"Believe it? I know it! People have escaped, people have managed to live through it, and I have talked to them. I can find some here in New York if that is necessary to your salvation. There are people who have disappeared from New York, people who have got in wrong with the party—I can get you their names if you don't know them."

"Where do you want me to go, Lanny?"

"I want you to get out of this hideous movement which has betrayed the hopes of mankind. I want you to realize that you are finished in it, regardless of what you may do. You have a black mark, and nobody will trust you any more, nobody will dare to. One or two intimate friends may stick by you, but they will do it at the sacrifice of their own party standing. They will be Trotskyites, Browderites, any kind of left or right deviationists. Maybe there will be Buddites."

"You seem to forget that I have to go to prison, Lanny."

"Maybe you do and maybe you don't. Maybe if you would break with the Communists Robbie could wangle you a pardon. I don't know if he can, but I know how quickly he'd go to it."

"Would they take me back, Lanny?"

"Take you back? Oh, my God! If you'd break with the Reds they would be the happiest couple in Connecticut. Your mother is just eating her heart out about you. If you want love instead of hate in your life, that is the place to go. And, incidentally, you would be safe there. Robbie knows how to take care of property and also of persons; there wouldn't be any kidnapers on his grounds. You might take up your piano practice again and recover your skill."

"Imagine people wanting to hear me play the piano after this!"

"You are missing an important point. In a woman's prison they are pretty sure to have music; they have it even in factories nowadays—they find that it works. Another point, also—you might get to see your children."

Bess began to sob. He had never seen her do that before, and she was embarrassed and buried her face in her hands. He decided to strike while the iron was hot; he said, "Listen, old dear, let me go to the phone and call Esther; she will come, I know. You can be as miserable as you please, but it will help some to know that you are making her happier than she has been in many years."

"All right, Lanny," she whispered, and he stepped quickly to the phone.

VI

It took only a minute or so to get the home in Newcastle, and by good fortune Esther was there. He told her, "I am at Bess's apartment in the city, and she wants to see you. Don't delay, take the first train. No, she's not ill, but she's at a crisis in her thinking. Don't ask about it, just come."

He hung up and told Bess, "She's coming." Then he thought he had talked enough. "I have a confession to make, sister dear," he said. "I can't sit in a chair very long without hurting. Also, I get exhausted easily; so let me lie down and sleep for a while."

She had only one bedroom, and she put him in that. Before he lay down he made her promise that if the doorbell rang she would call through the door and ask who it was, and if it was the C. I. Rep she wouldn't let him in. "You may not be afraid of him," he said, "but I am. He wants me even more than he wants you."

So then he slept. A most wonderful thing to sleep—he had never appreciated it until he had come out of the Prenzlauerberg. And always for the rest of his life when he woke up he would have a moment of fear and would think about the Number One, the Number Two, the Number Three.

This time he heard a murmur of voices and knew that Esther had come. When he went into the room he found them sitting on the sofa, and Esther had her child in her arms. Both of them had red eyes, so he knew that everything was all right. Weeping was women's business, and he would leave it to them. He said a few friendly words and took his departure and went back to Edgemere to tell Laurel. It wasn't a secret now.

The only secret was what he had said about Bess in the Prenzlauerberg, and that secret he would keep locked up for a long time. There would be debate in his soul; he would suppress it, but it would bob up now and then and come to life. He had taken the destiny of his sister into his own hands; and had he done her a great wrong, or a great right? It was like the inner duel that Shakespeare tells about: " 'Budge,' says the fiend. 'Budge not,' says my conscience." Lanny's fiend would say, "You violated her autonomy." Lanny's conscience would reply, "I got her out of the Communist party." Fiend would inquire, "Have you adopted the doctrine that the end justifies the means?" Conscience would reply, "Can people who deny truth claim the right to truth? Can people use liberty to destroy liberty?" Fiend would jeer, "You sound much like a Communist to me!" The debate would go on for the rest of Lanny's life.

One thing Lanny made up his mind to and would never waver about—the right of Hansi and Rose to happiness. He talked it over with Laurel, and she agreed that they would not write or say a word about the change of heart of Hansi's ex-wife; he might take up the notion that he had "done her wrong," and if he started brooding, that might mean the end of his new marriage. Wherever the blame for the mix-up might lie, it surely wasn't with Rose Pippin. She had met a man distracted and forlorn, a man whose spouse, convicted of a felony, had given him the right to a divorce in more than half of the forty-eight states. Rose had given him her treasure of affection and trust, and she had a right to expect that her marriage should be permitted to thrive and blossom. Laurel said, "She has the task of raising another woman's children, and that is danger enough for any woman's one life."

VII

So Lanny Budd was home again and promised most solemnly to stay for a while. He had those two lovely children to get acquainted with all over again. It was astonishing how many new things there were to learn about them. Junior hadn't been told the terrible details about his father's experience; Laurel had said only that some bad men had carried his father off and put him in jail. But that had been enough, astonishingly enough; it had set fire to a young imagination. These "bad men" were hiding behind every bush, and any stick would do to fight them. Any stick became a machine gun to be fired with a rattling noise from ambush. The bad men were mowed down, and Lanny was miraculously delivered. All methods of killing were discovered or invented, and Laurel, a pacifist at heart and hoping to raise a pacifist child, was astounded by the murderous impulses that she saw.

Also, she had the theory that a young mind should not be over-stimulated; but Junior had been given a set of alphabet blocks and had taught himself all the letters, and presently he was finding out how to make them into words. He was teaching himself to read—and in the most awful way imaginable, from those funny papers which came on

Sundays. He learned all the names of those multicolored characters and their wild eccentricities. He would spell out the captions, and when he couldn't understand he would go, not to his mother, but to one of the servants for help. The "funnies" became his wonderland, his mythology. Laurel was horrified; but Lanny said that he was exactly at the mental age of the persons for whom these fantasies were created. He would outgrow them and not be hopelessly corrupted.

The little girl was learning to walk and talk, all according to the Gesell schedule. In short, all was well with the family, if only the father would stay at home and let the world run itself for a while. Rick and Nina had been holding the fort for him, and now they could have the vacation which had been promised them; it would be in the cold and wet season, but they would love it, they had been brought up in it. Irma and Ceddy were coming to New York; they couldn't bring money from England, but Irma had an abundance over here, and she had kept her American citizenship in order to be free to use it here. She and Ceddy were planning to spend the winter in Florida, and Scrubbie and Frances would motor down and pay them a visit.

So Lanny and Laurel would have their hands full with the Peace Program. They would go on, "saying, Peace, peace," when there was no peace. It was a real problem, like staying out in no man's land and dodging the shells and the hand grenades from both sides. You knew that the cold-war enemy didn't want peace, and every time he said the word he was getting ready to throw another hand grenade. Yet you must go on talking peace in order to meet his propaganda, in order to answer his unceasing charges that you were a warmonger. You must enter every discussion and attend every conference, make precise and careful propositions, show exactly why your efforts failed and why he rejected your offers.

You could never convert him, you could never make the slightest impression upon him; but always you must have in mind the humble people who suffered under his despotism, who heard only his propaganda, who were fed upon a diet of falsehoods. The dictators meant war and slavery, but the humble people craved peace and freedom. You must find ways to reach them with the truth and help them to understand it. You would be called a warmonger a million times a day, but you must go on talking peace, praising peace, pleading for peace— and making plain who it was that was blocking the road to peace.

VIII

Lanny and Laurel had brought back from Europe the dreadful conviction that we were failing in our propaganda against the Reds. We were failing because we did not understand our enemies and did not appreciate the importance of propaganda. They were pouring out treasure to deceive and indoctrinate the peoples of their captive states and all the impoverished and oppressed peoples of Europe, Asia, Africa, as well as of the Western world. They were spending a billion, maybe two billion dollars every year, while all that the Congress of the United States could be persuaded to appropriate was a few tens of millions. We ought to be meeting them dollar for dollar and voice for voice and page for page of the printed word. We ought to be meeting them with brains and moral force; we ought to be making clear to all the oppressed and impoverished peoples of the earth that America was not a country of landlords and moneylenders, it was the sweet land of liberty. It was the land of Washington and Jefferson, the land of Lincoln, Woodrow Wilson, and Franklin Roosevelt, the land of Tom Paine, Patrick Henry, and Eugene Debs, of Whittier, Whitman, and Emerson.

These were the names which would carry meaning to the young people of the old world, to the opening minds which were going to shape the future. The Stalinists had set deadly traps for their feet and would drag them into servitude. We must show them the true paths to freedom, and it must be not merely political freedom but economic as well.

Said Lanny over the radio, "It is futile to think that the hungry hordes of Asia and Africa can be persuaded to become our debtors and servants. There is no use thinking that we can win either the cold war or the hot war with our organized labor in revolt, or with a great part of our population held in the status of second-class citizens. We have to make our minds flexible and understand that evolution is a process that applies in the field of industry as well as in that of government. We have to study the ideas of other peoples and understand their needs. We have to offer them more than Stalin offers them, and to make plain to them that what we offer is real and not a fraud, as his offers are.

"And we have to act quickly. We have to realize that Stalin is setting the pace. He is watching like a cat at a mousehole for our every move. He knows all our weaknesses and is quick to take advantage of them. A dictatorship has the advantage of secrecy, whereas democracy and freedom of necessity work in the open. That is a weakness if we leave it unexplained, but it is a great strength if we make the world understand it and what it means to them.

"Tom Paine sounded the call to the American Revolution with this statement: 'These are the times that try men's souls.' We have to be equally clear-sighted and bold. It is not too much to say that our civilization with all its intellectual and moral values hangs in the balance today. It will certainly go down if Stalin wins the victory, and it may even go down if he loses. It is necessary for us to prepare to give military resistance, but we must prepare with no less energy to give intellectual and moral resistance. We must give to that duty the same fortitude and determination that our forefathers gave at Valley Forge and Gettysburg.

"We must win the minds of the masses all over the world; we must win them away from the false hopes of Red communism and to the ideas of democracy and freedom, both political and economic. We have the truth on our side, but it will be of use to us only if we use it and defend it. We must live and speak in the spirit of those immortal words which Thomas Jefferson wrote and which fifty-five of our forefathers signed: 'And for the support of this Declaration, with a firm reliance on the protection of Divine Providence, we mutually pledge to each other our lives, our fortunes, and our sacred honor.'"

Printed in the United States
2885